CONFESSIONS OF THE FOX

JORDY ROSENBERG

atlantic·*fiction*

First published in the United States by One World, an imprint of Random House,
a division of Penguin Random House LLC, New York.

First published in hardback and trade paperback in Great Britain in 2018 by
Atlantic Books, an imprint of Atlantic Books Ltd.

10 9 8 7 6 5 4 3 2 1

A CIP catalogue record for this book is available from the British Library.

Hardback ISBN: 978 1 78649 622 5
Trade paperback ISBN: 978 1 78649 623 2
E-book ISBN: 978 1 78649 624 9

Printed in Great Britain by Bell and Bain Ltd, Glasgow

Atlantic Books
An Imprint of Atlantic Books Ltd
Ormond House
26–27 Boswell Street
London
WC1N 3JZ

www.atlantic-books.co.uk

F

CONFESSIONS OF THE FOX

for Victory Matsui

Love's mysteries in souls do grow,
But yet the body is his book.
—JOHN DONNE, "The Ecstasy"

EDITOR'S FOREWORD

SOME TIME AGO—NEVER MIND HOW LONG PRECISELY—I SLIPPED off the map of the world. I took the manuscript with me.

It was night when I left. The hallways were dark, but then they were also dark during the day. Many of the fluorescents were burned out or broken, and since the building had been condemned, Facilities Management had declined to fix them. They'd demolish the whole thing soon enough.

I hadn't been planning to leave, and yet I was becoming—not exactly *anxious* about the manuscript, but overcome. The manuscript was confounding, its authenticity indeterminate. I had known I'd get wrapped up in it.

But I was more than wrapped up. I was lost.

My ex and I once had a game of inventing German compound words for things inexpressible in simple English. Most of this lexicon concerned cuddling, language that was useless to me now. "Outer spoon with arm resting on hip." "Outer spoon with arms wrapped around inner spoon." "Facing spoons: bodies entangled."

There must be a German expression for "self-loss-in-a-project," I thought the night I left, pulling up an online dictionary to concoct a Frankenword for my current—and, I feared, eternal—condition. *Selbst-Verlust-in-Projekt.*

I think it is fair to say that if my ex had diagnosed me I would have been assigned a different Frankenword. Something far less generous. But since we were not speaking, I was free to diagnose myself.

Surely someone has noted that loss (*Verlust*) and desire (*Lust*) share a root. Which brings me both further from and closer to my point.

———◆———

Several months prior to my precipitous departure, as a kind of Welcome Back to School/Fuck You event, the University held a book sale. It seemed that over the summer the Chancellor's office had emptied out the seventeenth to twentieth floors of the library for a big renovation. Deans' offices and a dining atrium for upper-echelon adminstrators.

The book sale took place out in front of the building, right where new-student tours marched past. The University was proud to display its "optimization" of the library. Some fraternity had received community service credit for manning the tables. Tank-top-clad guys hulked over the piles of books doing curls and glaring. Surrounding the tables were huge posterboard mock-ups of the dining-atrium-to-be.

Wandering by one afternoon, riffling through the University's entire collection of philosophy, linguistics, and postcolonial theory, I spotted it.

A mashed and mildewed pile of papers, easily overlooked. And yet, a rare and perplexing find. The lost Sheppard memoir? The scholars in my field had scoured the records, debunked everything they'd found.

"You can just have that," the kid at the table said.

Back in my office, I stared at the hunk of papers exhaling dust on my desk. It mixed with the other particulate matter that sifted down from the ceiling voids and leaked out of the walls. I wheezed a slightly magnified version of my usual office-wheeze and turned the first crumpled page.

The manuscript had not been read in years, or perhaps ever. There was not a single checkout stamp on it. In fact, there was not even a back-cover card *to* stamp. The manuscript had never been catalogued at all. Someone had clearly just stuffed it into the back of a stack, where it sat, hidden from view, for god knows how long.

Until now.

For months, I worked under the narrow yellow bloom of my ancient desk lamp, transcribing the soft, eroded pages of the manuscript, and hoping in a kind of offhand way that I wouldn't dream at night of either *Lust* or *Verlust* (but what were the chances; this was all I dreamed of), while being rained on by the yellow flakes of asbestos or something that drifted through the holes in the ceiling. Occasionally a mouse or rat would make its way down the hallway under flickering half-light, nails clicking on the linoleum.

On the night I left, flipping between pages 252 and 257, a vague suspicion I'd had for some time suddenly crystallized. There was something very wrong with the manuscript.

And furthermore, I needed to disappear with it.

I put the papers and my laptop with its transcriptions and notes into my briefcase, dodged the hallway vermin and walked to my car. Not an insignificant journey: I had pulled a very bad number in the parking lottery. I am not ordinarily sentimental about my workplace, but it was an uncommonly beautiful evening—the last vestiges of fall snagged by the first hard shanks of winter, edges of ice cutting into the blue New England night—and so I didn't mind the walk. I was saying goodbye, after all. I even permitted myself to briefly enjoy the façade of gentility that the campus took on only in the dark. The birds called sharply to each other in the breezes. The great gray-trunked oaks cast shadows on the buckled pavement.

Ivy wrapped the black iron lampposts, helixing fifteen feet up to blown-glass lanterns tremoring with orange light. The University had installed these recently in an attempt to give the crumbling Humanities Quad a distinguished Old World feel. It was another of the landscaping "improvements" they were constantly unleashing in lieu of actually fixing the infrastructure.

But I digress.

You may not know this, but it is possible to hold back a single set of tears for years straight. Many a filmic crescendo concerning masculinity confirms this fact. Quiet shot of car interior. Aging guy. Beard scruff. Hands on wheel. Black night. Cue music.

Predictably, that night—although I am a guy by design, not birth—as I drove away from campus and toward [undisclosed location], I was fucking crying. Or, tearing up, at least. I couldn't stop thinking about this line that had been haunting me—the epigraph I had discovered on the front page of the manuscript.

"Love's mysteries in souls do grow, / But yet the body is his book."

What did Donne mean by this—and all his filthy innuendo, really?

The body is transformed by love.

I recognize I sound uncharacteristically utopian, but this isn't exactly a utopian sentiment. Not a painless one anyway.

Love inscribes the body—and this is a process as excruciating as it sounds. For some of us it is literal, Kafkaesque. A *selbstverlusting* that is both terrifying and pleasurable. The body does not pre-exist love, but is cast in its fires.

If the body is cast in the fires of love, so too—and this is Donne's point—is the book.

All books, really. But the manuscript you hold in your hands in particular.

The manuscript for which I will surely pay an exorbitant price, distributing it "independently" of the Publisher's desires and control. They will be especially displeased that I publish it with all my original footnotes. But it is important for you to know everything.

Like I said, I was crying when I left.

These weren't actually tears of sadness. I never cry when I'm sad; at those times I just pinch down into a miniature version of myself like an ailing turtle trundling off into the forest to die alone. No, I cry when I'm . . . not happy, but when I see a flash, if only briefly, that something other and better than this world already exists *in potentia*. It doesn't have to be profound. I cry the same set of tears when team members throw themselves into each other's arms after winning a game as I do when we lock arms in front of the police.

So I was speeding down Route 17, the tears blurring the endless strip malls into a dazzling silver-gray with hints of purple, white and several phosphorescent shades of green. And I knew then where I'd go. Where I'd be safe. At least long enough to get the manuscript out. The destination was so obvious, so perfect. It was only owing to my amazing capacity for ignoring the obvious that I hadn't realized it earlier.

No matter. It was clear enough now.

The postindustrial landscape had turned prismatic. Everything I looked at shone and sparkled. Wet light poured out of my eyes. When I blinked, light bloomed in corners, streaked by fast, leaving crystal trails.

Is the manuscript the authentic autobiography? the Publishers used to ask. *Is it a fairy tale? Is it a very long and terrible poem? A hoax?* I am ashamed to say that, for a time, I tried to answer them. I hope that history will forgive me for having told them anything at all. You can be assured that I will not share my findings with them anymore.

I took the manuscript because I could not allow the Publishers to gain custody of it once I understood what it was. I took the manuscript because I had come to realize that it contained a science. Well, a kind of science. The Publishers had been asking me if there was a code embedded in the document. There is. But not in the way the Publishers think.

I took the manuscript because I could not help but take it once I realized it was trying to communicate something. Something just for us. And if you are reading this, then you know who I mean.

And you're like: *Don't say too much! What if this publication has fallen into the wrong hands?*

Don't worry.

Even if I were saying—*hypothetically speaking*—that this is a code, they will never be able to read it.

There are some things you can see only through tears.

—*Dr. R. Voth*
June 2018

CONFESSIONS OF THE FOX

PART

I

I.

JACK SHEPPARD, THE GREATEST GAOLBREAKER AND THE MOST DE-
voted, most thorough carouser* of quim† in all of London, is bound
beneath the gallows beam at Tyburn, about to be hanged—

> *If I am to die today, please God let it be with the memory of
> the taste of her on my tongue—*

The two arts (gaolbreaking and quim-carousing) are of a piece.
Jack is a compact mutt with an intuition for all possible points of
entry, opening, and release. Whether of gaols or of women, there
has never been a lock, door, window, or wall that he could not gentle open into an ecstasy of Trespass.‡ Jack is a creature of Liberation. For him, shaking free from the demonic gloom of a
detention-house is not unrelated to the scorch of a woman dissolv-
ing in raptures upon his tongue. The first releases him from the

---

* Deep-drinker
† Pussy
‡ Such lionizing of Jack's prowess is typical of Sheppardiana, and thus signifies neither one way nor the other as to the authenticity of this document. *Viz., The History
of the Remarkable Life of John Sheppard* (1724); *Authentic Memoirs of the Life and
Surprising Adventures of John Sheppard* (1724); *A Narrative of All the Robberies, Escapes, &c. of John Sheppard* (1724); "A Dialogue Between Julius Caesar and Jack
Sheppard" (*British Journal*, December 4, 1725); *The History of the Lives and Actions
of Jonathan Wild, Thief-Taker, Joseph Blake Alias Blueskin, Foot-Pad. And John Sheppard, Housebreaker* (1729).

poisonous grip of the centinels—hateful husks, blights to all of roguedom, miseries of the otherwise miraculous City.

And the second? What to say of the second. Simply that he is never more free than when Bess's quim pulses hot in the cradle of his mouth. In this embrace, his body writhes from an aching carcass of bone and skin to a lick of flame. And it's this Transformation he needs to effect now. Ignite. Melt to soft glass—the way he does when she blist'rs with Pleasure on his red rag[*]—and slip these fetters.

But conjuring Bess won't light him up now. The noose-knot weighs heavy on his neck. For which ecstasy of Trespass has he been doomed today? The first? The second? *Both?*

Never mind—

This artist of Transgression is about to die.

His hands are bound to the front to allow for last-minute prayers, which Jack has no intention of making—not to the Magistrate's God in any case. He is on his knees—his seeping, snapp'd leg hooked out at a dreadful Angle against the side of the execution-cart. A burlap hood cloaks his head, and a noose encircl's the base of his neck—both having been placed there in a dramatic Flourish by the Yeoman of the Halter as he drove the cart through the crowd. The noose hangs in a loose slipknot, the long ends wound 'round Jack's waist.

The wind rises. The horse scuffs its hooves in the sawdust—neighs hollowly, shaking its leviathan head. The cart trembles and sways.

A cannonade of boots stamping 'round the cart. "The hour of reckoning approaches!" shouts the Yeoman as he claps one hand on Jack's shoulder and releases the harbinger pigeon into the sleety late-afternoon Sky.

---

[*] Tongue

The pigeon lifts into the drizzle, shedding mites and Fleas upon the crowds packed at Tyburn, buzzes through the mist over the red-bricked streets towards Holborn Bridge, left at the Smithfield butchers' stalls, and arrives at Newgate to land on the warden's stern uniformed shoulder as he glares out over the Inmates in the Press Yard, abuzz with Rumors.

Sheppard's stowed on a ship bound for the colonies. Sheppard's taken to the roads, headed for the Scottish highlands. Sheppard's been spirited off by the doxies† of Spitalfields, and is now cavorting under covers, drinking plum wine.

"Cease your idiot speculating! The poor Sinner, Jack Sheppard, who escaped the Tower Hold late in the night and embroil'd himself in immoral and illegal acts all morning, has been captured once again, and is now arrived at the gallows to meet his death on this, the sixteenth day of November, 1724," shouts the warden as the bell-ringer clangs the Newgate toll.

Four times for execution-close-to-hand.

The dark Reports reverberate across the prison yard. The pigeon flinches at the Din, and in his struggle to launch for the chestnut trees waving in the low afternoon light outside the gaolhouse walls, crooks a claw into the thick wool of the warden's waistcoast, snagging a stitch. A Mêlée of flapping ensues as the warden attempts to pry the miserable bird loose from his chest, drawing cries of "Floor the pig!" and "Claw the constable!" from the prisoners as they root the pigeon on.

Under his burlap hood, Jack hears Bess calling to him from her chambers high in the eaves of the bat house.‡

The House of the Dead is the common house; the House of the

---

† Sex workers. I settle on this annotation rather than "prostitute" as, in the anti-vagrancy laws of the period, the doxy was condemned specifically (though not exhaustively) as someone who would not go gently into the *good night* of the capitalist workday.

‡ Brothel. I've arrived at this translation by supposition (more on this below; see footnote †† on p. 10).

Dead is the common house. All things held in common across That River. I'll meet you there, in the Eternal Free Waste Lands, my love.

But *is* Bess at the bat house? Is she, indeed, even alive?

The hood smells like the shit-soaked hay at the bottom of a cackler's ken*. The low afternoon Sun blinks dark gold through the fibers. Jack can no longer feel his leg, but for some distant throb that seems not quite to belong to him. He breathes slowly, the bag's muck itching against his lips. He catalogues the things he knows for certain, or near-certain.

He knows the Mob gathered around the cart must be about the largest London has ever seen. The Town is aflame with talk of him.

It had begun when Wild carried him over his shoulder from the Thamesshore to the Magistrate's stables. With his face press'd against Wild's broad back, he heard passers-by congregating, gawking—'S *that Sheppard?? And Wild??*—and then a swirling wind of Whispers, the rumor-mongers flying off to inform the Town.

Wild had taken his time at the stables, ordered the execution-cart festooned and glory-fied with flags and ribbons while Jack hunched within, bound and soaked, a pile of bloody legs and river-water.

Word had had time to spread. When Wild was finally satisfied that the cart looked pompous enough, they set off again. A Thunder had begun to collect over Tyburn—voices upon voices rising as he was brought to the gallows.

He knows they're there to see if he'll effect another escape—his greatest yet. They expect him to slip a file from his sleeve, unlatch his wrist irons in the Bedlam after the cart is yanked from underneath his feet, and be found later that evening quaffing ale at the Pig and Roses in Fleet Street.

---

* Hen roost

A Sob rises—catches—scalds his throat.
Aurie, where are you?

The cart tilts under the weight of the Yeoman leaning on its edge—pulling the long end of the cord free from its loop around Jack's waist. A tug and the end is toss'd up to the beam, where the Yeoman's assistant perches. Smaller tugs as the cord is knotted tight from above.

The thud of boots hitting the ground—the assistant's secured the knot, and scuttles off to the side. More boots walking away—the Yeoman's job is done as well.

The Din deepens. The Mob knows what's coming.

Heavy footfall approaches. The Executioner.

His hand is on his whip, slapping leather against his palm with each nearing step. Jack has seen enough executions to know by the sound that this is the last suspended Moment before he lays into the horse and the cart is yanked out from under him. He'd long entertain'd the possibility of dying by hanging—most rogues had—but in all his Imaginings, he'd never thought he'd be hang'd on his knees. On his knees and quaking uncontrollably. He focuses on the crowd's roar—"Hang the politicians instead!" "Hang the constables!" "Hang the stockjobbers and the banking-men!"—

The Executioner hisses the whip in three long circles through the sawdust surrounding the stage. The Executioner is a showman, letting the crowd build until just before the second that the Spectacle turns into furor and they are uncontainable. At that precise moment, the Executioner will let them have it—he always lets them have it—and he'll pull the cart—

O God of the Streets—God of the Underworld—God of Rogues—God of Women, God of Softness, God of Sex-Shaking, God of

Muff* and Tuzzy-Muzzy† and the Fruitful Vine‡—O God of the Boiling Spot§ please inter me at the foot of her Bed. Please—so I can still see her—still hear her murmuring—still sense her. God of The Monosyllable¶ please let me still smell her and feel the throb of my unnameable Something when I do—

*   O death that comes for me—O God of the Water-Mill**—at least she once took me in her hands and mouth—at least she once spread her legs for me—at least I once dilat'd with her musk in every pore—at least once was I thus Found and Lost—††*

---

* Pussy

† Pussy

‡ Pussy

§ Pussy

¶ Pussy

** Pussy

†† Regarding footnote ‡ on p. 7. In none of my reference books does "bat house" turn up. "Bat," however, is a different story. Cited in one of the more reliable dictionaries of rogue's slang of the period—Bailey's *Canting Dictionary* (1736)—as a "low whore" (not a complimentary term, by any means); I've extrapolated to conclude that "bat house" indicates the abode where bats congregate. I.e., a brothel.

But the point is this: as this precise slur—"bat house"—is not corroborated in any reference materials, I must surmise that it is in fact not meant cruelly here, but is used in a loving and familiar manner, such as would be exercised only by a member of the subculture to which it applies.

But I've gotten ahead of myself. We're only at the beginning yet.

2.

SOME SAY THAT JACK'S ROAD TO THE GALLOWS HAD BEEN PAVED THE day the Plague Ships arrived in the Thames.

At first, it was only the sneaks and scamps who notic'd, bringing word back to the inns and pubs. The East Indiaman *Repulse* was anchored just off the shore of the Tower Wharf, its boards creaking as it bobbed, its massive rigging billowing and slapping in the breezes. The river was achurn with slick gray Rat heads making their way towards the Booty on board. Rats chugged through the water from all directions towards the lower holds. Claw'd their way up the sides—slipped out of view onto the decks.

Within days, other ships joined the *Repulse.* Two more at the Tower Wharf and another lurking in the shallows at Blackfriars dry dock. The Thames was quickly dotted with stalled behemoths, an Archipelago of brigantines kitted out with guns and cannon dangling heads-down at rest.

The Hum at all the pubs was that the ships were being quarantined.

3·

BUT OTHERS SAY IT WENT BACK MUCH FURTHER THAN THAT. THAT THE road to the gallows began before the Plague Ships. Before Bess. Before Aurie. Before Jack became the most notorious Gaol-breaker London had yet known. Back when he stumbl'd through life delirious as a light-bedevil'd Moth.

His mum made clear she'd had enough of Jack the day she brought him to the master carpenter Kneebone's doorstep in October 1713. As she marched him down Regent Street, sweat formed at the edges of her hairline, pinkening her alabaster face paint.

"Be a good girl.* Do what you're told. Behave. Don't act shameful," she said, regarding Jack sourly. They crossed dubious, slough-filled Tyburn and headed towards Cavendish Square. Sparrows nattered on hedges, tumbled in dust baths Underfoot, disregarding the burghers† and high-toned ladies sweeping by.

His mother snapp'd her knuckle into his ribs as they approached the brown oak door.

"And walk like a lady! Try not t' stomp like an animal."

---

* Jack was assigned female at birth? This is a significant departure from the extant Sheppardiana. While nearly all the texts note him as "slight" or otherwise effeminate—his wiriness and compact size frequently cited as integral to his ability to escape tight spaces (e.g., the stage play *Little Jack Sheppard* [Yardley & Stephens, 1885], starring Nellie Farren as Jack)—*this* I've never seen.

† Bourgeoisie

Jack tried to imagine moving his legs more smoothly, like she said. But it didn't feel right to glide like jewel bearings in the guts of a well-oiled Clock. He liked to sprawl through Space, landing hard on the edges of his feet.

His mother glared down, her nose crinkling like he was a piece of spoiled mutton. Then the door opened.

It was Kneebone. Startled. Then angry.

"What's this?" He wav'd his hand at the hard-negotiated outfit that Jack had arrived in. Tweed trousers and rough muslin smish‡ that had belonged to his brother, Thomas, long Gone now on his Indenture to the colonies and probably Dead of Cold. Or Over-work. Or *incorrigible Tendencies.*

"She's a bargain, sir, and you won't have to keep her in any skirts."

Kneebone's eyes widened, narrowed. His upper teeth munch'd at his bottom lip. Then he gestured to Jack with a long-boned hand full of splinters and slits of dried Blood. "Does she work a handsaw and an awl?"

Nodding. "Strangely adept with Tools."

"And her name?"

—Jack's brain turned off in that way he'd perfected when he felt all the muscles of his Body clench up. Which was often.

He knew his mother said something in response—because he saw her Mouth move.

Kneebone took a piece of Balsam from his pocket. Chewed it. Talked and gesticulat'd angrily. Camphor puffed from his mouth with each word. Jack unheard *she*—unheard it into the swarm of the rest of the sounds Kneebone was making— *She's ugly, isn't she— Quite— But a bargain's a bargain— Still, what am I meant t' do with this.*

Jack imagin'd dropping into the Thames on a summer day, the heavy press of Water 'round his Ears muffling the *she*s and the *she*s and

---

‡ Shirt

the *what am I meant t' do with this.* He peered 'round Kneebone's scrawny limbs—now parked on his hips in a belligerent-chicken posture—into the entry room. It was stuffed with woodworking. The Odor of raw timber and oils hung just inside the threshold. The scent calm'd him.

Sounds began to come back as through a muffling Fog.

"She's dexterous—very," he heard his mother saying and nodding, her voice bouncing. "Always gettin' into things at home. There isn't a Doodad that she hasn't undone and redone much the better for 't."*

Looking up at his mother as she turned to leave, Jack felt his usual flicker of unaccountable sympathy. Maybe even Compas-

---

* Not to get ahead of myself, but if authentic, this memoir could compete with *Herculine Barbin: Being the Recently Discovered Memoirs of a Nineteenth-Century French Hermaphrodite* (English translation, with an introduction by Michel Foucault, 1980) for pride of place on quite a few syllabi.

For those unfamiliar with Herculine Barbin (1838–1868), let me say this. From approximately 1985 to 1995, you could not take a gay and lesbian literature, theory, anthropology or history class without being assigned this book. How many times did I feign excited queer identification with Herculine, thinking, at least (and about this I was not wrong) that it might get me laid by some of the (what were at that time called) "bicurious" members of the class. Meanwhile, I found the book repulsive and terrifying. Herculine's desperation and isolation. The fact that time was kept by Herculine not through any objective measure—workday, seasons, school year—but rather through female encounters. When women could be held in Herculine's line of sight; when they were inaccessible. The narrative would frequently drop off until a woman reappeared.

What happened to Herculine in these interstices? It seemed, in fact, that nothing, absolutely nothing, occurred in the absence of women; that Herculine awakened from a kind of cryogenic stasis only when summoned by the scent of women, of their—

—well, *you know what I mean*—

—that particular draft; one to which I myself would soon awaken, and come to love beyond all measure.

Hot flint of a lightning strike, plum, basil . . .

Lemon, salt, tang of cider from a copper mug . . .

Wet forest flowers, dusted with coriander.

sion. The scent of whiskey drifted down. His Heart twist'd in its red socket deep in his chest. He knew it then: he would never see his home again. As bitter as his home was, it was his. Never again to hear the urchins tumbling down Neal Street, the din ricocheting up the close-packed passageway—never again to smell his mother's particular tart scent—the citrusy Anxiety and disappointment that wafted off her Body like a Wind. He was being left here with the merchants and the accountants, the barristers with their busyness and hollow Eyes and looking-away. Even if his mother looked at him with Horror, she looked at him. To these folks he was a scuttling servant—a dog who spake English.

Pinched between these two Torments—a home in which he was a thing of Nightterrors, and a servitude in which he was another moving Part churning product towards profit—there was no course of action but to try to feel Nothing.

His mother bent down and kiss'd Jack's face. She touched his cheek with her hand, and held it there for a moment—she whispered something in his ear.

Then walked away with nary a backward glance.

At dinner that evening, Lady Kneebone presented Jack with a dress to wear while serving. "Our servant has taken ill, so we're in quite a pinch. You'll have to replace her for now."

As the Kneebones stuff'd their bellies with mutton and hot boiled water, Jack stood to the side. He was a Shade haunting the boreal dining room. The yowl of a nasty wet Cough descended through the wide wooden slats of the ceiling—the regular servant making quick progress towards Death.

Jack shiver'd in his duds, his skin shrinking from the touch of the organza and lace—girl textiles that seemed only to make the chill worse. He had imagined that the wealthy would keep their houses toasty. This was very much not so. And why didn't the Kneebones drink cider? Surely they could afford it. Yet they sipp'd spring water bought from a water-cart merchant. Maybe all of them were different than he'd imagined. A dusty, Bland, bitter lot.

"P——" Lady Kneebone—not looking up from her uninspired progress through a wad of meat lying just inches from her nose—called to Jack.* "Make a Gargle of cumin seeds, the mashed root-stock of an iris, and one blistered long pepper."

She said this as if Jack had any idea how to make a Gargle.

"For protection against the croup," furthered Kneebone, swallowing a gulp of hot water and waving Jack back into the kitchen.

When Jack brought it out at last—having assembl'd it as best he could from an array of items that must have been purchas'd earlier in the day by the ailing servant and set on the counter in what would prove this poor soul's last labor, save the labors of dying itself—the Kneebones proceeded to throw their heads back and Shriek bubbles, then hack the mucus-broth into their empty mugs.

Standing in the corner of the dining room, watching these two sour Wraiths spatter and drool, Jack tried to recall his mother's departing words.

—*I love you—despite everything*

—*I smooth'd your dark curls, once—*

—*Remember that afternoon we walked what seemed forever on the riverbank?*

To the latter of which Jack would have recalled without flaw the exact weather that day—their most leisurely, closest day together. It had been early November. That time of year when the whole City gloams by late afternoon, and the effluvium of dried leaves crunched underfoot inflicts the inexorability of the Seasons upon the Senses.

---

* How curious: the excision of what appears to be Jack's given name (P——) is original to the text.

An autumnal Terror had fluttered in Jack's stomach as horsecarts blasted by, thwacking wet wheels on wet leaves. Wake turbulence swirl'd leaf-fragments in small vortices up and down the darkening Riverbank.

His mother had reached down through the dusking Gloom. And held his hand.

Tho' frankly, she may have said—and this is the most likely— —*You're the greatest Shame of my life.*

Better to just imagine Mum dead, he'd shush'd his pounding heart. *Lots of urchins have lost their mothers,* he reasoned. He saw it daily when he batter'd down the streets with the gang on one of their common ruses, knocking into the apothecary carts, spilling Oils and Emollients on the cobblestones "on accident" in order to descend upon the blanched almonds, mint leaves, and barley seeds like a gabbling Flock of pigeons, scraping them up to sell at a cut rate to the next cart 'round the corner.

None of them seemed to have any parents at all.

He'd be just like them, now, he supposed.

Jack consum'd the Kneebones' scraps while he tidied the kitchen. Then Kneebone fetched him and walked him upstairs to his sleeping quarters. A filthy dark garret in the upper reaches of the spindly townhouse. The unmistakable piercing scent of Mice and rot blasted out of the room when Kneebone opened the door.

Jack's body ach'd from standing, serving, and cleaning. His neck was prickled with pain. His fingers were stiff and cold. His extremely circumscribed horizon of hope fix'd entirely on the prospect of sleep. But as they approached the bed—Kneebone almost projecting him towards it with the negative magnetism of his

Nearness—Jack was thrown into wakefulness. An unwelcome, exhausted awakeness. He heard something jangling, and peered behind him. Kneebone held a heavy Lock and Chain in his hand.

"Receiv'd this from a Swedish importer." Kneebone cough'd. "A
gift for an especially profitable exchange—a Polhem Lock," he continued, with what appeared an Erotick excitement concerning Lock
mechanicks. He caressed the curve of iron, his gray skin sparking
to a pinkish gray.

"This Lock," he said, fixing Jack in his weak, watery glare, "is
unpickable."

Jack lay down. He did so without instruction because it was
impossible to keep his Body from trembling and crumpling to the
bed.

Kneebone reached into his torso jerkin pocket and produc'd a
Key, which he slid into the Lock. Four teeth yawned open, and
Kneebone wound the oiled iron Chain around Jack's ankle, then
the bedpost, and threaded the Lock's jaw through. He snapped it
shut.

Every nerve in Jack's body fir'd against his skin— His jaw tensed
and the muscles of his scalp bunched and held themselves, frozen
in aching Huddles— He willed himself not to look at the Lock—to
Unfeel it against his skin—*Unfeel* its weight on his ankle and foot.

"I'm not extraordinarily cruel," Kneebone said, looking down at
Jack. "But I've bought you body and Soul for the period of ten years.
And I mean to keep you to it."

Kneebone backed away with a Perverse and ashamed half-
smile, shutting the door and locking it behind him. "Will return at
dawn," Kneebone hissed through the boards, and clunk'd down the
stairs.

The next morning, Kneebone hurried Jack through the dining
area—dim, chill, and curtained shut against the dawn—towards
the Workroom, a cluttered chamber that bowed out in a bay window at the far end. Jack took in the items Kneebone had produced

for sale. Dressing tables, chests, armoires, windowsills, and a bizarre quantity of little stools with cushioned tops.

"What's this?" Jack ask'd, reaching down to poke a cushion.

"Don't touch anything!" Kneebone shouted as Jack stumbl'd through the mess. "It's all the property of Kneebone, and Kneebone only. Every item in this room is forbidden to you unless it's being actively worked on."

Kneebone sat Jack at the workbench and took a place across, their knees knocking under the table.

"I'll teach you window-glazing, nail-casting, and the art of screwsmanship," he announc'd. "But mostly I will teach you tuffets. Podiums for the small pet Pups of the aristocrats to perch on whilst having their portraitures painted." He pointed at the cushioned stool Jack had pok'd. "That's where the market is best."

The air filled with Kneebone's stale, arid Breath. It wasn't rotted like so many other high-living folks'. But it was bitter, like a tree emitting old Resin from its whorled depths.

Jack reach'd for a chisel. He didn't need demonstration. Just glancing at the tuffets he felt assured he could make something similar. 'Twasn't difficult. Probably he'd just have to—

And then Kneebone was at his side.

With another Polhem Lock in his hand.

All that first day, Jack did his Thames-trick. He had no other choice against the Terror of the chain. He sent himself floating to cool Depths—morph'd his heartbeat into the thrum of deep water. He'd never had to stay under for so long—but his confinement was so relentless, Kneebone's ownership of him so total—not just his Body, but all his Capacities, all his Potentialities, too—that going Deep was his only option.

This trick, as it turned out, was help'd immensely by working with the wood. For Jack was an ace craftsman with an uncanny understanding of the natural properties of architecture and mate-

rials. The way a sill rests inside the groove of a Wall was something magnetizing and soothing to his Attention. As was how to
sculpt around a particularly recalcitrant knot in a hunk of oak. Or
the cool skin of iron, or how much pressure a walnut board could
take, how much torquing a birch plank would endure.

All this had Jack demonstrat'd through the constant Storm of
Kneebone's droning—a stinking stream on and on, only occasionally about how to craft wood. More largely a cascade of Tangents
and opinions about the horrors of poverty—how it "breeds contagion like an overzealous sow." It seem'd Kneebone considered himself an amateur Doctor. He bragg'd that he'd read a great number
of medical textbooks. Commoners—belching "sweaty winds" and
"stenchy secretions"—were, according to him, prime vectors of
Disorder.

"I've saved you from a diseased life lived amongst the diseased,"
Kneebone said, as he toss'd a moldy bun smeared with rancid butter at Jack for his morning meal when it was nigh on noon. "Saved
you from that Mob"—he gestured with his head towards the window and the street beyond—"that Mob that threatens the Publick's
Health at every turn."

At Nightfall, Kneebone unlocked him from the table and ushered
him into the dining room. Lady Kneebone again instructed Jack to
prepare and dole out the supper. It seemed the other servant had
indeed expir'd.

After the pair had stuffed down their repast, Kneebone escorted
him upstairs.

Bent over him. Latched his ankle to the bedpost—went to the
door and stood there— Why wasn't he leaving?

Kneebone was nailing something to the inside of the door.

"To study on." He gestured at the tacked-up parchment when
he was done. "For learning your letters."

Kneebone read aloud, his finger tracing the words as he
stood there like the pedagogical Father Jack had never had and

frankly never wanted. His threadlike arms waved in the candle-light.

AN ACT FOR THE PREVENTION OF FUGITIVE LABORERS[*]

A Rogue or Vagrant is defined as:

1) all Persons wandering abroad and lodging in barns, outhouses, and deserted and unoccupied buildings, or in carts or wagons, not having any visible means of subsistence, and not giving a good account of themselves;

2) all Common Players of Interludes, Minstrels, Jugglers; all Persons wand'ring in the Habit or Form of counterfeit *Egyptians*, or pretending to have skill in Physiognomy, Palmistry, or like crafty Science, or pretending to tell Fortunes, or using any subtle Craft, or unlawful Games or Plays;

3) all Persons able in Body, who run away, and leave their Wives or Children to the Parish, and not having wherewith otherwise to maintain themselves . . . and refuse to work for the usual and common Wages;

4) and all other idle Persons wand'ring abroad and begging shall be deemed Rogues and Vagabonds and remanded to gaol or returned to their master, with the period of service doubled.

"So you see, when you leave the house, you'll be subject to arrest unless you've got a master's note." Kneebone worked his thin lips back and forth. Turned and clicked the door shut.

Jack's breath shallow'd as he lay bound to the bed.

The one thing his mother would never have done was threaten him with Arrest; she hated the constables. He will'd himself not to think of her, not to wish himself backwards by one day. *'Twas awful there, too—'twas awful there, too.* His mind gritted its teeth against thoughts too terrible to think. The miseries of his mother's household had given way to Torments still worse.

His ribs ached from unsobbed sobs. They stung his chest like a diseased Pulse, and he fell to sleep in pain, a dog of Shame and Sorrows.[†]

---

* Draft of the 1714 Vagrancy Act?
† The usage of plural "Sorrows" is unusual.

4.

BESS KHAN ARRIVED IN LONDON IN DECEMBER OF 1713, ACHING OF foot and sunbak'd from the weeks-long walk across the countryside.

She hadn't been underfed on her journey—not near as starved as back Home. She knew how to tune to Shadows and skitters. Icy air puddled in clouds, ankle high, over the forest floor. Hare were easy prey—curious and frozen, their dove-gray ears poking out of the low Fog. Fish could be plucked through streamside stalking and quick knifework. She flush'd berries from knotty bushes. Nick'd crabapples from trees.

The expedition hadn't scared her. Truth be told, she was too Sorrowful to be afraid. At least the countryside was Quiet—and she could stay clear of strangers. She relish'd the movement, the sun, even the rain for the opportunity to collect water. She didn't fear sleeping in the grasses. She would lie quiet in the cold leaves, listening to the deer skip by in the Night, corncrakes whisking in the Wind currents overheard.

It was towns she found unnerving. Once she'd hit the banks of Black-Wall heading west—and the trees thinned near the rushing Causeway—the sound of hammers crashing on nail and axes slamming through timber had echoed through the Towns. The forest became a parade of weeping Stumps.

The land grew bereft of food. Houses peck'd the banks of the river—nearer and nearer to one another. There was nowhere to hunt, let alone forage and sleep. How did anybody survive here?

Her last leg of walking had been too long of a Day, but she'd been too frightened to rest. Had push'd on past the docks and building yards, the dwellings, churches and shops, all of it accelerating in an unceas'ng Pile towards London.

As she emerged from the relentless outskirts into the heart of the city, the true inhospitality and impossibility of London became a panic coursing through her veins. Her feet throbb'd on the cobblestones, and Bess kept her head down past constables and angry Anglos.

Her father had traveled the opposite route so many years before. Had his Heart fluttered fast in his chest? Had the Anglos glared at him as they did her?

When a street sweeper smiled shyly, halting his broom to let her pass, she gather'd her will to ask where to find Refuge.

"All exiles flock to the Anabaptist Meeting House in Drury Lane," he said softly. "The Anabaptists provide shelter to any soul capable of work."

It was Evening when she arrived.

The bricks of the Meeting House were a dull gingerbread brown. The building was fronted by a lawn—a Murdered forest in miniature: each grass-blade truncated, lopped off, silenced.

At the far end of the lawn, the main doors soared. Bess lost her nerve. *Who will be inside—and what if they don't welcome exiles? What if the street-sweeper was in jest?*

Determining to tiptoe in some back entry without raising an alarm, she wove between the trees at the rear of the building. The walls of the Meeting House were pocked with small glass portals in a bloody tint. Bess stood on her toes, face to glass. She could not see inside.

She duck'd down into the brush that spread along the sides of the building. The shrubbery was a thick mesh of berry-spangled butcher's-broom. It settled as she moved through. A tangle of roots shivered out of the flat gray shale surrounding the foundation of the building, and she tripped in a glut of waxy ferns, stumbling hard into a small wooden door fronted with tarnished steel braces.

The doors gave way—discharging Bess into the low-ceilinged basement chamber of the chapel—then shut hard behind her. The room, alas, was full of congregants, many of whom looked well off, swathed in sumptuous cloaks and emitting that particular dusty effluvia of fine velvet. A sermon was being preach'd. Heads shuffled. Bess shrank into herself, trying for inconspicuousness, nearly turning to leave—but scrambling out now would appear odd and raise suspicion. Besides, her feet Ached badly.

A seat was free towards the back—where the folk appear'd more common. She strove to settle with as little fuss as possible—amidst a nest of whispers from the front of the room. She drew her bones inwards, her hands on her lap. The pews breath'd their humid bark break, hard underneath her.

The pastor, tall and thin with a frizz that reached upwards towards God, stood at the pulpit. His eyes glowed and his narrow chest swelled as he spoke. His voice gonged out of him as he pontificated on Corruption.

"*Individualists,*" he inton'd, as the wind picked up outside and the doors sucked out slightly. A commotion of bird Wings lathered the air, ascending from the brush. "London is a place of *individualists.* No longer busy with simple folk—sheep milling, beer being quaffed, folks picking herbs for sustenance. All gone. Now, a Body be gaoled for perambulating the town without occupation, folks afraid to walk the streets in fear of being arrested for Idleness, and even the open Sewers and the trash piles prohibited—property of the newly formed Nightsoil Concerns, authorized by the Lord Mayor himself.

"Oh, it's a Devilish place!" The pastor's voice rose higher as he preached on, detailing the hazards of City life. Striking a workman-like pose, he crouched down at the level of the congregation, putting his elbows on his knees in a theatrical performance of Ordinariness.

"And yet they say that ev'ry corner holds a new *Opportunity,*" he moan'd. "Dry'd gooseberries for sale from the South Pacific carry'd on Dutch boats and transit'd through innumerable hands. Ornaments and pet pups from the East. Coffee and Sugar from the West. And you might say, *Well isn't this a beneficial thing? An expansion of our Opportunities and our Pleasures?* And the only thing I can say about this, is: No. It is not a good thing— It is a very dangerous thing that holds unknown tribulations. These are terrible times— times in which we see our Enemy for what he truly is, when he reveals his full, horrifying visage."

Bess did not know what "gooseberries" were. But she understood avarice and she could plainly see what the pastor was driving at: London was a place of shopping and Hollowness. It was worse than Bess had imagined. First the murdered forests, the dwindling wildlife and the glaring strangers. And now this entirely new category of bizarre dangers to do with Fruit. She trembled when he blared out, "Truly, Brothers and Sisters, these are times when we encounter, without artifice, the merchanting of our very souls."

And the Merchants at the front of the room lapped this up, humming approvingly and nodding to themselves. Bess saw quickly that what defined this class, above all else, was their ability to recognize the evils of the World and count themselves above it. Their capacity to lie and self-flatter. Merchants, after all, love nothing so much as believing that they alone among their class are in possession of Ethics and Virtue.

And the pastor's advice? Love and peacefulness.

Well, now—this was a problem.

Bess could have overlook'd his popularity with the finer sort. Perhaps he felt he could convert them to his cause. But his belief in peacefulness was unforgivable. Peacefulness would never vanquish unstoppable cruelty.

An image from her past flashed up that Bess did not mean to summon.

· · ·

After several weeks of love and peacefulness—and several weeks, too, of being task'd mercilessly with scrubbing the sanctuary, preparing the Meals, and cleaning the Plates of the well-off congregants— Bess was fatigued in a particular way she'd never before felt: fatigue mix'd with boredom. It was a miserable combination. She had resort'd to napping during the sermons.

On this particular day, Bess could feel sleep zooming up from some warm, far-off Place within her as the pastor roared his usual pap from the pulpit. "All lambs of God must join together in peacefulness, holiness, and love!"

—"Peacefulness!" someone harrumph'd nearby.

Bess peek'd an eye open.

A cloud of Vestments inched its way down the pew towards her. A young being swathed in older-woman clothes. A brocaded silk gown and a prinked-up hat. Boots laced high.

"You don't believe in 't?" Bess ask'd.

The cloud shook its head. "Peace 's useless here." She half-smiled behind her veil.

Finally, a non-hypocritical congregant. Bess caught a whiff of the girl. Gardenia—opulence—the spice of struck matches. A decadent perfume, and yet there was something reassuringly off-kilter about her. She could see, in this young woman, a once coltish girl with an almost-dissolved remnant of awkwardness. Back when other girls were cute sprites, this girl must have been a rangy, nearly ugly thing. But her young adulthood was descending upon her unstoppably, complete with a tangle of chestnut hair, and a beautiful, righteous anger.

"Bene-darkmans," the girl whisper'd.

"Bene-*wha*?" Bess return'd. Bess knew Latin. That was not what the London cleave was speaking.

The girl cocked her head.

"You don't know London cant*?"

Bess ignor'd the pretend-question. She had heard enough of

---

* Rogues' slang

London to guess that this girl was likely an Abbess†—frequenters of revival-houses and meeting halls, scouting for lost young Souls, orphan girls without means.

"You an Abbess?"

"I appear that old?" The girl squinted. Truth be told, she couldn't be much older than Bess herself. *Sixteen perhaps?*

"No, but you seem"—she seem'd, in fact, a strange combination of Composure and a hectic, livid Temperament—"like you know the city."

"Too well. And I do happen to work for an Abbess. One looking for fair-roe-bucks‡ just like yourself."

Bess stiffened. "Just like what in particular?"

Without a second's hesitation: "Full of bosom, lush of hair, but empty of purse."

So she would not mention the lascar§ matter.

Which meant the girl was like any of the London Anglos, the ones who thought not mentioning it meant they were virtuous. And yet something about this girl intrigued her. She had a flash of Bess's mother about her—a certain *persuasiveness.* Some doggedness to join Forces.

"I don't favor the peaceful approach either," Bess said, returning the girl's opening salvo. "Bess Khan." She extended a hand—still a bit wind-chapped from her journey to the city.

"Jenny Diver." The girl took her hand, strok'd the back of it. "And I more than 'don't favor' it." Her indigo eyes turn'd a deep-

---

† Madam

‡ A woman in blooming beauty. Infrequently used.

§ Here is another detail of the manuscript that bears further mention. Bess identifies as "lascar": a term that had broadened from its original usage denoting a South Asian sailor in service to the East India Company (from *lashkar,* or *khalasi,* orig. Persian: "an army"; through the Portuguese, "lasquarin," "lascari"; and then the British, "lascar"; cf. K. N. Chaudhuri, *The English East India Company,* Routledge, reprint 2000).

Not a single Sheppard text describes Bess as South Asian. Not one.

So then, between this characterization and that of Jack's assigned sex, what we have here is either the most or the least authentic Sheppard document in existence.

water black. "These drumbelos* deserve what's coming to 'em." She look'd down at Bess's hand, still in hers. "I have a salve for that. I'll share it if you follow me to the back room."

Bess knew what Jenny was asking. To make a choice. Between sitting and listening to evangelizing that was all too palatable to the merchant classes who liked to pretend disgust with commerce, or catting† these same merchants out of their coin.

And Jenny. How heedless she seemed of the bourgeoisie surrounding them, regarding them with disgust. Perhaps Jenny had attained some of this confidence through Congress with the men of London who held the keys to a map of its Interior. Bess had told herself she was coming to London for a Method, an understanding of the mechanics of the World.

On meeting Jenny, she saw how to get it.

"I'll go to the back with you," she said. "And see."

It hadn't surpris'd Bess that her first job would be the pastor—Ezekiah Smith—himself. He of the agonized declamations on Pacifism.

He look'd upon her in the faint Light of his small back office.

"'Scuse the clutter," Smith said, whizz'ng 'round in excitement, thrusting aside papers and notebooks from an expansive splintery desk. "My scriptural studies, you understand."

Bess *mm-hmmed* vaguely.

But Smith was waiting for something more. Bess realiz'd that she could read men the way she read deer tracks. And she saw at once that Smith's Vanity lay in his belief that he was interesting.

"Tell me more about your studies," she said, unbuttoning her blouse.

Which set Smith on an extensive ramble about the Anabaptist

---

* Dull, well-fed folk
† Prostituting

commitment to the equality of the sexes, all the while conducting a protract'd ogle of Bess's heavers.

"The true believers were such pacifists," he began, leaning his thin haunches against the desk, "that they would never raise a hand, even in self-defense. They permitt'd their own slaughter, running ragged for many days, hunted along the Voderrheim. The German town officers stormed the forests, driving the flocks of Believers down the Gulleys where they'd pitched themselves one after another into the Curnera Reservoir, there to float, frozen and bloated into the Rhine—" Smith caught her gaze with his weepy expression. "Men and women dove into that bright aqua basin together, hand in hand, equal in the eyes of God."

This story was quite a romance to him, Bess could tell. He said *Vonderrheim* like he was masticating a rich cake. And now Smith had some questions.

"Do they have any such fables where you're from?" Smith was unbuttoning his breeches. "What exotick beliefs were you given to learn? I have it on good authority that lascar regions are universally cruel to women. You won't find any such inequalities here."

Smith was naïve and stupid. All his facts were fictions, but what to address first— She open'd her mouth— A Word formed— She caught her tongue—swallow'd the sentence, *I'm from England.*

She could see that in order to begin—and hence conclude— this Transaction, Smith's requirement (as he stood, priapic and Hesitant) was that he appear a Savior. *Helpful and needed.*

Bess lay upon the floor, spread her legs, and muster'd, "What a Mercy is England."

And Smith dove, head-first, and set to work with what Bess would soon realize was the world's worst capacity for such mouth-Touch. Perhaps this was Smith's version of equality: a determination that pleasure be had by both parties. Unfortunately, his technique suffered muchly from an inability to conceptualize female Pleasure.

Smith rotated his rigid tongue like he was churning dough, cut-

ting a horrendous Path around Bess's quim, in which he outlin'd yet
somehow never actually contacted *the Point of Interest*. The episode
transpir'd for many long minutes. Smith was an odd combination of
peacock and mouse—puffing himself and cringing in equal Measure. He was an appalling, dramatically "helpful" sexual actor. Bess
soothed herself with memories of home. The soft, fleshy way the
pages of her book got in the humid air; reading by candlelight in the
cricket-stuffed nights.

Meanwhile, Smith was in a trance, grinding his tongue like an
ancient grandfather Clock thunking its way through relentless seconds, and humming into Bess's madge a muffled Quaker hymn.
When Smith began emotionally spitting the chorus, she sighed and
pulled him up by his armpits.

Consequently his arborvitae[*] now poked dumbly from its collection of wet gray hairs, straight at her. Smith was aiming—and
then achieving—and Bess went numb, as if all of a sudden Smith's
arborvitae and Bess's madge were having a conversation without
her. The edges of her customs-house[†] felt cold and shivery in the
air. Smith made his way in. It hurt a little, but not enough. That is
to say, the hurt felt far away, or split Bess momentarily somehow
from herself. Like she was reading a minor item in a distant rural
broadside about someone who got hurt.

What was there to say? The congress felt entirely unspecific—as
if Bess could be anyone. But men—thought Bess—need *anyone* so
much.

After the disquisition on scripture, the lengthy, chaotic irrigation of
Bess's quim, and numbing Gut-plastering, Smith returned to his
selfish and sentimental monologues.

Bess lay quietly with the pastor sprawl'd across her like a damp
Claw, murmuring inane things into her hair.

---

[*] Penis
[†] Pussy

"If the World could see you as you are right now"—she assumed that meant naked, or clicketed‡—"t'would be Peace everlasting."

And then long contemplative Pauses as he considered the weight of his words.

"Oh, it's Devilish here, all right," he said. "You're welcome to take refuge in my quarters if you need."

Bess had to stifle a laugh.

"I'm due at my Abbess's," she said, her mind flashing to Jenny, waiting—she was relieved to remember—just outside the door.§

---

‡ Copulation (of foxes or persons)

§ We know even less about Bess than we do about Sheppard. Researchers have long been forced to source her "truths" in the Sheppard works, in which she appears regularly, albeit in a variety of shifting forms. (Though, caveat: this profound lacuna in the records cannot be simply filled; it must be encountered head-on as constitutive of the archive as such.)

But to press forward. The two major fictionalizations of Sheppard's life are John Gay's wildly popular 1728 *Beggar's Opera* and Bertolt Brecht's 1928 *Threepenny Opera*. In the first, Sheppard is portrayed as the character "Macheath," Jonathan Wild as "Peachum" and Bess as "Polly"—most likely a hybrid of three historical figures: Edgworth Bess, reputed to be Jack Sheppard's lover, sex worker and partner-in-crime, and the notorious lesbian pirates Anne Bonny and Mary Read. In Brecht's work, Sheppard is "Macheath/Mack the Knife," Wild is "Peachum" and Bess again is this hybrid, "Polly."

So Bess's character has been the location for a particular liberty of speculation. And yet she is consistently, unquestionably portrayed as white—not only in Gay's and Brecht's works, but in the numerous other fictionalizations of Sheppard's life and circle as well (cf. footnote ‡ on p. 5).

Given that London was not by any means a white city in the eighteenth century—and indeed that there were no legal prohibitions on interracial marriages at that time (see Gretchen Gerzina, *Black London: Life Before Emancipation,* Rutgers University Press, 1995)—we have to take the unquestioned nature of Bess's characterization as white as less a reflection of "actual" history than as the occlusion of it.

The departure from this *occluding whiteness*—this whiteness that occludes even the possibility of history itself—in the text at hand thus inclines me to regard this document as potentially more accurate to the period and its personages than either Gay's or Brecht's renderings.

5·

TEN YEARS OF SERVITUDE. NINE YEARS OF POLHEM LOCKS.

Jack lived one life during the days he was sent to the market. More and more the brims* of the streets took him for a boy. (Once, even, a bulky cove† with a ginger-and-black speckled beard, scuffing at some cobblestones in Lamb's Conduit alley, tried to sell him some stolen kerchiefs. *Fancy some fine linens, boy?* he'd whispered. Jack had not realized 'til he'd gotten some way down the street that the man had been speaking to him.) He anticipated traveling to and from the sellers' stalls in Covent Garden, oiling his curls so they would fall just so over his eyes, conditioning his apron with sheep's-fat so it shined. He liked how it sat on his thighs when he bounc'd down the lanes.

At the Kneebones', he lived another life. The life of an ugly, misshapen girl chain'd to workbenches to turn out useless items for aristocratic dogs. There was a constant knot at the back of his neck where his spine met his skull. An Ache that he associated with his vex'd relationship to breathing. It was as if he had been born with a spike between his vertebrae, and, with each failed attempt'd full breath, some Demon hanging just over his shoulder nailed it deeper, deeper. Anyone else looking through his eyes would have known immediately how to remove this Torment. *Flee the house, and the spike will work itself loose.* Even an animal will seek out relief. But

---

* Lewd women
† Man

Jack mistook his Suffering for subjecthood. And consequently, he *desired* the doubleness to which he had been forc'd to resort as a form of survival.

There had been opportunities for Jack to escape. But he had always come back right away, hadn't he. Wide-eyed and full of longing for the free World. Full of longing, too, for the women he'd begun to notice, the women who began to populate his imagination at night.

But he had always come back.

Because of his Demon. This *Something* that hung over his shoulder. This something that set him apart from other coves. Something that had caus'd him to dress his own chest in taut bandages under his clothes since his twelfth year, pinching at his ribs, throttling his every Breath to a forced shallow bird-sipping of the air.

And this *Something* was the same something that made his mother not look back at him when she walked from Kneebone's door, though Jack watched after her until she turned the corner and was gone. This *Something*—what he thought of as *his something*—made his servitude, while a miserable confinement, a hidey-hole too. His whole life was some hidden, rank place. And so his confinement became the door inside him between his waking life and something still unwoken, something lying close-packed like a bomb at his core, poised to shiver into a coruscated, glinting shower of—of—of what, he knew not. But there was *Something* just beyond the door inside him. Some difference within that he did not yet want to know.

A snapping, muttering billow of voices, badgering and chafing, scudding just underneath his thoughts like a low-lying Thunderhead.

Until 12 March 1724.

En route to the New Exchange, Jack caught the eye of one particularly dark-eyed doxy resting against the side of the Ewe's Nest doorway. She was startlingly fetching. Deep-set eyes with a piercing, Haunted look. His preferred sort. The sort he had begun looking at more regularly—a great deal more regularly, truth be told. None had yet look'd back.

This woman held his gaze.

Something loosen'd inside him, spiraling down from his heart to his torso's nether root. It was a Feeling he had always known—it flashed up at the sight of a wash of hair down the shoulders of a cloak—the blink of kohl on an eyelid—the dusty fume of rose blowing off night-chilled skin—but it made itself much more Urgent now. When his eyes caught hers, the word "thamp" occurred to him. His heart was *thamping* against his chest, some combination of thumping and stamping.

With his heart thamping, he rounded the corner, a tuffet in each hand, his walk a bit stilted against the load. He was reviewing in a fizzly, excited manner the way the doxy's eyes had blinked shut for a flicker that practically stopped his Heart—when a butcher's cart loaded with carcasses, dead legs swinging from the sides, blast'd out of the dark at the end of the alley, plowing towards him, raising a complex squall of clove-scented holly berries crushed under wheels, the stale dank of rodent musk, and the rotted rush of drying Blood—and just at that moment, a vision of underparts slamm'd into his Consciousness.[*]

Naked, bared Muff between wide-spread legs—open for him.

There in the alleyway, as he leapt to the side of the oncoming butcher's cart, this sudden and absolute obsession was imprinted upon him. He wip'd his face in the crook of his elbow. Shook his head, blinking. His nethers were pounding. Several years of the

---

[*] Seduction isn't seduction unless it carries a whiff of the perilous—of death, frankly—right?

Be grateful for my dime-store psychoanalysis; at least I'm not quoting Roland Barthes at you.

(Though, for a more considered account of sex and the death-drive—S&M as "embodied subversion"—see Amber Jamilla Musser, *Sensational Flesh: Race, Power and Masochism*, New York University Press, 2014.)

incessant hounding of his waking and dream lives with thoughts of women cohered its chaos into a simple thought. He wanted this— He wanted women not as objects of fascination, dream-images, figments— He wanted them body and soul like he wanted food, drink, air, sleep. He wanted them all over—and he wanted them very especially at their Boiling Spot. But what did he want to do with it? He couldn't make this vision *of nethers* go away, but he couldn't quite understand what he was supposed to do about it either.

As he stagger'd a bit in the street, the breath knocked out of him, he re-heard what the doxy had uttered as he'd passed: *Handsome Boy,* she'd said. She'd called him *Handsome.* He adjusted his smish into his trousers, and found himself smiling for the remainder of the walk to New Exchange. The din and clamor of the sellers' stalls didn't bother him near as much as they did usually. He let the world wash over him.

Because he'd heard *Boy, handsome Boy*—her throat caressing the words as they slid out of her mouth—and the whoop and clatter of commerce cottoned softer, fading into the background.

Later that evening, Jack sat under the windowsill plucking through a news broadside on the Protestant émigrés, the French Prophets stockaded at Smithfield and pelted for days with rotten fruits, accused of *false Visions* and *inciting Panicks in the Queen's Publick.*

As he shift'd, Jack felt the heft of a steel file thump his leg. He'd forgotten to return the tool to Kneebone before lock-in. And Kneebone—distract'd by some escalated fear of an ague, as he'd heard a vagrant cough outside the window earlier that day—had forgotten to check his tool inventory as they vacated the workroom in the evening.

Jack palmed the file. He thought of Kneebone's warning: "This lock can't be picked."

He heard it, now, in a new way.

Jack bent over his ankle, considering the mechanism. Then he inserted the file into the Slot and jiggl'd four times in a rattling downward motion. The teeth slipped free. The Polhem Lock was even easier to pick than the standard British padlocks he affix'd to the hasps of the chests he built. Jack stared at the open jaw of the contraption in his hand. He almost felt sorry for Kneebone for being so mistaken about the lock. Then felt sorrier for himself for not having thought—not once in nine years—that Kneebone had not been *so mistaken.*

He had been lying.*

---

* They take everything from you. Even your imagination. Then and now.

Which calls to mind an extremely regrettable exchange I've just had with Dean of Surveillance Andrews.

I knew something was amiss when, instead of receiving his comments on my annual review by email, I got a call from his office manager during my office hours to set up an appointment to discuss it. She suggested I come in immediately.

I hastened to the meeting midway through my lunch.

Things did not have a collegial tone.

Sit down, Dean of Surveillance Andrews blared as I entered. He was standing, gesturing in a very threatening manner—not even a parent scolding a child, more like a dog owner pointing out shit to the creature who made it; I will add that it was not clear whether I was the dog or the shit—to the ergonomic chair opposite his desk.

I sat.

It was my first view of his new office on the seventeenth floor of the library. They really had done a spectacular job renovating in the style of a high-end Marriott.

I still had my half-eaten turkey sub hanging from my right fist. *Should I finish this sub while he fires me?* I thought. This seemed a step too defiant. But then I couldn't let it just hang there, stinking up the office with its warm turkey scent. I considered tossing it in the trash, but of course the deli odor would intensify and bloom from the bin. Honestly, only a psychopath throws away a half-eaten turkey sub in someone else's office trash bin. *If he definitely is firing me,* I promised myself, *then I'll throw this sub in his garbage can and walk out.*

I opened my briefcase and stuffed the sub, spilling from its mustard-spattered bouquet of butcher paper, in between my University-owned crappy laptop and the "attendance book" I always mean to utilize in class, but then I'm both too scattered and too Marxist to actually police my students that way.

I snapped the briefcase closed.

Dean of Surveillance Andrews really had a nice office. I mused silently about how much thought had gone into appareling this room to make it seem like you were being pampered while being fired. I wondered how many people had sat in this strangely buoyant chair while being canned.

Dean of Surveillance Andrews had been talking the entire time, of course. When I tuned back in, it seemed to have something to do with the language of my contract.

It is the right of the University to requisition "improperly utilized" leisure hours if that period of improperly utilized leisure takes place on the premises.

What "improperly utilized" leisure are you talking about? I managed. I tried to distract him with a metaphysical query. _How can you improperly utilize leisure?_ I lobbed.

This he ignored.

There have been reports of you playing phone-Scrabble during your office hours.

Phone-Scrabble? I sort of shrieked.

Phone-Scrabble. He nodded at me really seriously. He made a sad frowny mouth to reinforce his point, as if maybe I had murdered someone while playing Scrabble instead of just consistently and spectacularly lost at the game.

Office hours are basically for _phone-Scrabble,_ I tried to explain. _No one really wants to talk about the eighteenth century more than they already have to. My office hours aren't exactly well attended._

I realized, too late, that this was not the best approach for self-defense. But also I was thinking: _Reports? What reports? Which one of my senior colleagues went out of their way to tattle?_

Then I remembered the newly installed video cameras in the classrooms, and that's when I realized there must be one in my office as well.

And while I'm realizing this, he's giving me the whole official rundown of how, _Actually no, office hours are meant for meeting with students and—failing that—office hours are meant for resting the brain and your other capacities for more productive work following the office hours._ And that playing phone-Scrabble takes away from that necessary rest. Drying the eyes, preoccupying the mind, etc.

I'm just gaping at him—gaping because this is the issue and also gaping at how seriously he is taking this issue. Nothing is making sense, and then he says, _Why don't you go to Mindfulness Lunch on the ninth floor of the library like everybody else? As a courtesy, the University has emptied out the ninth floor of its entire collection of psychology and anthropology books to create a "retreat" for all faculty. A kind of self-help spa._

And I'm, like, _Right, well I mean, it's "self-help." So, technically, not mandatory._

It's not mandatory, he says with that frowny mouth again, _but it's an invitation the University is extending, and it's strongly suggested that you accept this invitation._ And then he spins his desktop monitor towards me. It's a split screen. On one side, a spreadsheet shows how much phone-Scrabble I've played in the past six months, and on the other, a video playback, generated from the University's in-house cloud-networked surveillance cameras, shows me in clip after clip sutured together by some jerky editing algorithm, my head bent, stuffing sandwiches down my gullet with one hand while moving letters around with the thumb of my other. It was, admittedly, a lot of phone-Scrabble.

You owe your workplace eighty hours of labor restitution, he says. _Next semester you'll teach an extra seminar._

And he means, gratis. Just give the University an extra, free, uncompensated class.

And then the coup de grâce.

•　•　•

Now that he was Free, Jack's mind turn'd to the doxy from the afternoon. Who would—he hoped fervently—be where all the best rogues went after nightfall: the Black Lion Inn.

A quick dash into the street? He wouldn't be missed. He knew the Kneebones' routine as well as his own. After locking Jack inside his attic room, Kneebone would descend to the plain chambers he shared with Lady Kneebone and—as it was a Sunday—calculate that week's Accounts, read together briefly from their Bible, then blow out the Lantern (Jack catching the reflection of the flicker puffing out in the glazes across the way) and fall to sleep. This was Jack's best surmising of the Kneebones' nightly affairs, as he never had heard any sort of Screwing from the room below, nor indeed any suggestive creaking of the floorboards.

There are moments that do not arise as the result of Conscious determination or thought. Such moments—far more than the

---

And you're being put on unpaid leave for the rest of this semester. You will still have access to your office, but we've already reassigned your class.

Access to my office? Oh joy. My shitty office in an OSHA-condemned building. My office that would probably constitute a liability to house anyone who hasn't signed the *no-fault office-accidental-death clause* recently instituted by the person we refer to as "Neoliberal Provost."

See how they fuck you. Do you see how they fuck you?

I was shaking so hard when I left Andrew's office that I didn't even have the wherewithal to fling my turkey sub in his wastebasket.

I took the half-eaten sub out of my briefcase and set about finishing it—*Unpaid leave,* I chewed sourly to myself—as I began the endless cross-campus trek to my car.

By the time I got to the parking lot, the molecular weather system in my brain had shifted in that way it always does: devising a method to pour my misery at something else. I had reinvested myself in a project.

Well, fuck them, I thought with that unnerving optimism of the hopeless. *This is good, actually. Now I can immerse myself in the text. Solve the mystery of the origins and authorship of this manuscript. Once my colleagues at better institutions get wind of my work and invite me to keynote the annual meeting in Reno, won't Dean of Surveillance Andrews be sorry.*

plann'd ones—are those that shape the course of a Life to come. Such moments alter a being in ways that plotting, synthesizing, and future-izing can never do. That is to say, a reaction to Chance is the only method for developing character. This much Jack had gleaned from the novels Kneebone had supply'd him, the pirate romance *Captain Singleton* being an excellent case in point.

And so, unwilled and unbidden, Jack found himself seizing on his Liberation. It was only a matter of jiggling the file into the frail little window hasps 'til it click'd, and popping the nails out of the hinges with the backside of the file. His teachings had given him a powerful sense of exactly how far down the tips of the nails should rest, so it was an easy one-two-pop, one-two-pop. And lo and behold, the glazes swung open to the high nasty air of a March twilight, cramm'd down to the last particle with tanning salts, animal excrement, and the gas puffing from the coal piles upon the decks of the Newcastle boats as they plowed up the Thames.

The stench was an Ambrosia to Jack. Ordinarily he was admitted out only on Tuesdays to the butchers' stalls to pick up the slightly off meats Lady Kneebone reserved at a fraction of the cost of fresh, or to quickly deliver tuffets to market, or to watch the executions at Tyburn with the rest of the rabble. (*This here's a precautionary tale.* Kneebone would nod at the nooses swinging in the wind, flicking his eyebrows meaningfully at Jack.) Now—truly Free—he rampag'd across the roofs—sliding down a gutter at Drury Lane—and into the crowds streaming towards the Black Lion. The haunt—as he was soon to learn—of Bess Khan, moll* extraordinaire.

---

* Sex worker. (For a more recent account of sex work as a category of labor more broadly, see Svati Shah, *Street Corner Secrets: Sex, Work, and Migration in the City of Mumbai*, Duke University Press, 2014.)

6.

THE BLACK LION GLORIED IN A GREATER LACK OF LIGHT AND AIR than most London pubs.

Due to an insufficiency of scrubbing, the bar was an unnaturally dark oak, with the entire chamber smelling like the inside of a cask left to rot. An assortment of tables and low stools faced the bar across a narrow passageway, and if one braved the row of close-packed Bodies, one might fight one's way to the back garden—rather, a Piss-yard—or down the narrow, dubious stairs to the cellar, where everyone knew the mollies* made Love.

To Bess, it was the anti-Anabaptist Meeting House. A loud hot warren of honest Truths and honest Stenches.

On this particular evening, the pub was ship-like in the gray ocean light of Rain, water sheeting down the thick pane at the front. Bess was tired, wishing the bats had spent the night in the foyer of the bat house, as they often did. But Lily Budge—one of the newer and peachier ones—was in hopes of meeting up with a suitor at the Black Lion—some Rogue lately released from debtors' prison at

---

* A broad term that would have covered a range of (what might anachronistically and unsatisfactorily be described as) queer boys and transfemmes. Their houses of love and congress—molly houses—were routinely raided. It is likely that the seventeen recorded molly-house raids between 1726 and 1737 are a huge understatement. (Cf. Randolph Trumbach, *Sex and the Gender Revolution, Vol. 1: Heterosexuality and the Third Gender in Enlightenment London,* University of Chicago Press, 1998.)

the Marshalsea whom she'd encounter'd through the bars on her regular strolls down Borough High Street. The Rogue had profess'd to marry her.

The entire group was in a Tumult, peering about—*is that 'im'*ing and *what'd ye say he looked like again'*ing.

"'S'good we're here. What if the rogue is not in earnest?" Jenny gestur'd with her ale. Golden froth ran over her fingers. "You'd be here, sitting by yourself."

"Or," said Bess, "what if he *is* in earnest, and intends to *marry* you right away here in the Black Lion basement, without pay."

Jenny was laughing—they all were laughing—when the door open'd.

It was the boy Bess was startled to realize she thought of as *her boy*—the boy she'd seen earlier from the Ewe's Nest doorway. The one she'd whispered to without forethought. The one who'd caus'd a rush of warmth and fizz, and a boldness that wasn't usual for her.

He blew in on a puff of freezing filthy air, black curls bouncing over his eyes. And that odd outfit—an extraordinarily shiny apron and a tattered, too-large Smicket that bagged around his forearms.

Some coves enter a pub with the frantic glance of one who must be understood to be meeting a waiting friend—or they quickly take on the impatient head-craning of waiting on one themselves. But this boy moved through the pub as if he had never waited on a friend or been waited on. He scann'd the room once, took a table opposite the bar and sat, pulling an apple from his pocket. He had some bites, chewing thoughtfully as Bess continued to chug her ale with the other bats in a loud cluster in front of the window.

The rain cleared. Ice crusted the pane, sunset tindering red behind the frost.

He's seen me. He must have. But he's just sitting there. Chewing.

Bess cross'd the room—at which, finally, Jack looked up—stood and hustled in her direction, affecting a casual stance.

"Good evening." He lean'd into the bar, striving for Gentility— and stabbed his elbow into a cold puddle of ale.

"Bene-darkmans," Bess said, feigning not to notice the ring of ale darkening his elbow. Smiled briefly and continued to walk, her neck tucked into an upturned ruffled collar. She'd said more than enough earlier. *Let him rise to the Occasion.*

"B-bene-darkmans, rum-dutchess*," Jack projected quickly to the side of her retreating face.

Now this was interesting. She's figur'd him for more of a naïf. Bess paus'd, turning. Adjust'd her collar, pinched it closed where it plunged low at the front. "D'you jaw the bear garden?"†

"I do flash‡." Jack paid excellent attention to the sounds of the streets—had come to memorize its languages.

She look'd at his hands, his thumbs hooked into his breeches' pockets.

"You're grinning like a hell-born."

"Who here's heaven born?" He nodded with his chin towards the room.

She rais'd her hand for him to take.

"I—I—" His damn stutter. He wiped his hand on his trousers. Cleared his throat. "My paw's chilled. From the outdoors." *Or Nerves.* "I'll make your acquaintance—formally speaking—later. When I've warmed some."

A truly absurd proclamation. *But what if this is my only chance to touch her.*

Better not to touch her at all than repel her forever with a clammy paw.

She cocked her head. Squinted. What an odd bird he was. But then Bess's taste ran towards the Odd. "I'm not afraid of chill." She pursed her lips. "But if you'd rather make that sort of acquaintance later, then . . ."

---

* Beautiful
† Speak in underworld tongues/speak cant
‡ Cant

The sun contract'd into its last vermilion clot before setting. The room flickered, illuminating and bedimming at once. A darker Red was briefly thrown across her face, and Jack's Heart fled out of his body for the doxy with the transfixingly Contradictory visage—an arched aristocratic nose paired with surprisingly doe-soft brown eyes, a tumult of dusk-drenched hair brushing her exposed shoulders.

"Bess Khan."

His mouth formed a *P*—then he paus'd—brought his lips back against his teeth—his tongue to the roof of his mouth. He'd said his name so many times to himself. In bed, throughout the workday, walking the streets, swinging his market bag of Lady Kneebone's off-meats and mouse-bitten grains. It sooth'd and excited him.

For the first time, though, he heard himself say to another person, "Jack."

He'd imagin'd this would be easy—*this saying himself into being*—but now it didn't feel entirely right or True. He became loosed from his Body, floating up to the splintered-beam ceiling of the pub. He look'd down quizzically at himself saying "Jack," and it seemed so ridiculous to have thought he could ever be *Jack*—and now she look'd at him quizzically too—and he wanted to slip through the ceiling-planks and fly out of the pub in Shame.

Then Bess said, "I told you *my* surname. And what—you don't have one?"

"Oh," he breathed out. "Shepp—epp—ard."

"Jack Sheppard," she said.

And when he heard his name in her mouth something happened.

The apparition-Jack zoomed down from his watching-spot on the ceiling and sank firmly—and with a heretofore unknown warm *Pleasure*—into his Body.

"Jack Sheppard, surely you meant to tip me a jack§?" Kohl arc'd from the corners of her bottom lids. He breathed in, catching an

---

§ Engage me for intercourse

edge of the scents that belonged to her. Powdered amber. Juniper. Warm smoke.

Was she breathing him in too? He knew his smish wasn't at all clean. The body-salt of his workdays leak'd out, particularly in closed spaces. But she was glittering her eyes half-closed. Inhaling.

"I was hoping for a bit of dry-bob*." Jack had not even begun to recover from her face, her scent, her Nearness, and most of all: her saying his name.

"Even a Dry-Bob costs too much for a cadger†."

Jack's Spirits typhoon'd into a roiling Jubilance. He had always felt that the lexicon of the streets was Music, but it wasn't until Bess intoned it that he truly heard it sung.

"Cadger? Certain I'm a screwsman‡." This last bit of banter came out clean and strong. Jack grinned. "A cracksman§." He cut into his apple with a jackknife, ran his thumb along the Gash. "My dear, I draw latches¶."

The moment of his breaking out of Kneebones was metamorphosing into a chain of events, causing a sea change in Jack. Whatever Blur he'd lived in for every year and every moment up to this one, was lifting and sparkling into Nothingness like fog in the sun. All of Jack's molecules were scrambled and rearranged, and something new was taking shape. Some*one* new.

He was becoming Jack Sheppard. He was entering History.

Something scuttled across the bar.

Something fast. And hideous. Something with a long frond of legs waving out its back end, a front prow of more waving legs, and long sides of many many legs, like a bristl'd boot brush. An armor of frizzy tentacles—it was a blur of non-color—an odd translucent tan—whizz'ng across the puddle-pocked mahogany surface.

Jack didn't relish killing bugs, but this one sped towards Bess.

---

* Copulation without emission
† Beggar
‡ A thief expert in unscrewing hinges
§ A thief expert in breaking windows
¶ Pick locks

Cringing at the imminent squish, but determin'd to reap the rewards of Heroism, he pulled his hand back. Closed his eyes.

He heard something hit the bar with a soft thud.

Bess had her hands cupped in a dome. She smiled.

And now she un-cupped her hands. The creature had gone docile in the shadow of her palms. She petted its strange tan body. *You,* she coaxed, smiling when the creature rose up on its back fronds. *How did you get here?*

"You're staring," she said after a beat. It was true. Jack could have watched her coddle this mysterious insect all night with that open, undefended Smile across her face.

"Sorry." He swallow'd a gulp of his ale, sucking down confidence and a blissful forgetting. *She doesn't outshine and outclass you in every possible way*—(this last he repeated to himself without believing)— *You're just another dry boots at the Black Lion Inn talking sweet with a beautiful doxy— You're not a—*

But he put the thought out of his mind. His ribs ached against the tightly wrapped bandages. No need to dwell on questions without answers—he wasn't anything but another clinker** fox†† tonight.

"Not seen one of those before." He strove to return to casual banter.

"Must've traveled in a satchel from the countryside. Haven't seen one like this in some time."

"Where in the countryside?"

"Do you *know* anything about the countryside?" She assessed

** Clever

†† Man. Although eighteenth-century usage of "fox" indicated a man, now, of course, "fox" broadly denotes a fetching individual of whatever gender. Perhaps "fox" has transited through underworld patois? After all, one of the first things lost in translation is the apparent fixity of gender. As Hobson-Jobson note in their—supremely orientalizing and fucked up—*A Glossary of Colloquial Anglo-Indian Words and Phrases,* a translation results in an androgynization of language wherein "all traces of gender are lost."

This seems a marvelous loss. Perhaps "fox" has emerged, ungendered, from the embrace of early modern rogues to signify simply an object of desire. An endearment. Rather: an *enfoxment.*

that the answer was most certainly *no*. *Londoners*—she sigh'd inwardly. *Why are city folk possess'd of the insupportable and yet unshakable belief that their knowledge extends far beyond the bounds of their experience?* "To return to my point," she continued. "Screwsman, Cracksman and Latch-Drawer are nice, Jack"—Bess focus'd her gaze on his strong-jointed fingers—"but you should be *King* of the Screwsmen. Now you'll excuse me while I let this centipede into the yard."

Just like that, she planted a seed. And she meant to let it grow.

7.

THE NEXT NIGHT, JACK JUMP'D HIS CONFINEMENT AGAIN.
Descended from his garret—
Powered down the lantern-lit streets—

At Cresswell's Seraglio, a splendid house of prostitution in a fine brick building that lorded over the low structures of Oxford Street, the door blasted open and the scent of lime and bluebell—the season's fashion—pour'd out, along with two doxies. The heat of the interior blew across Jack's face. There was the crashing din of laughter, light drunken debating, and the flicking sound of cards being shuffled. He caught the eye of the Lady Abbess, sitting high on a stool just at the threshold's interior sporting a powdered cloud of a wig. She extended her hand, palm cupped expectantly open.

"Ten p."

Jack hiccupp'd at the sum and darted backwards, leaning out of sight as the door closed.

Near midnight and still waiting—

The Evening was spectacular. Deep dark washed with the pale metallic Cloud of constellations slash'd across the upper Vault. Jack was kicking at broken chips of cobblestone when Bess tumbl'd up noisily behind.

She leaned on his shoulder.

"Jack."

Her breath was a warm Dense weather he wanted to inhabit.

"Let's on with it," grumbled a cove lurking behind her—a real burgher-type, with a bright cravat—his dark hair sprouted in a damp crown and his navy topcoat hung loosely off his shoulders. Jack envy'd even his thinning hair and the Hollows under his eyes. The cove looked so . . . *cove-like.* Dogged, persistent, sufferingly intent on his Desire.

"Thought you'd have found your way in, King Screwsman," Bess said as she was towed towards the door, which opened to the shaft of red and gold interior, then shut, and the street was returned to Silence and Dark once again.

Jack stepp'd back, taking care to vault over the Sewers trickling down the sides of the street, crawling with vermin and slimed with Refuse.

He watched the windows.

All with curtains shut but one. High on the third floor. A dark Room that now lit up with the arrival of a lantern, then the shadow of a Body crossing, and a hand holding the cloth. *Bess's?* Then the curtains slid shut.

Jack rounded the back of the seraglio. The verso face was a hectic Assemblage. Bricks unlaced from their mortar moorings, windowsills tonguing out over the alley.

He would skip the bricks that poked out most. These were the bricks jutting up against the wooden Studs, and likely loose. Instead, he pinch'd his fingers around the bricks flush to the face of the building. The effort of the ascent sent sharp twinges under his arms where the bandages abraded his skin. Jack stopped once or twice to gasp against the hard Wrap before achieving the roof— a landscape of crumbling brick that was soft underfoot. He looked over the city. Long parks to the north surrounded by bright mansions ringed 'round with Lanterns. Chaotic huts piled one on top of another to the south. A glob of sea-coal Smoke hung over the outer reaches and the poorer areas, striating to a fine gray mist over White-chapel and Marylebone.

He perch'd at the high ridge of the parapet above the front fa-çade. Waited.

Bess's high-pitched calls mixed with the grunts of the customer. There was a strange incongruity, Jack thought, between her low tone at the Black Lion and these lilting emanations. Then came a very regular series of Weepings-out that seemed to provoke and escalate the grunting on the part of the balding burgher, which concluded in a soprano Squeak that was somewhere between defeat and surprise—not a way Jack thought a man could sound— But perhaps this was how men resonated when taken over, however briefly, by a Woman.

Soon after, the clatter of boots and the pop of a door closing. A light project'd across the alley as the curtains just below were opened. Bess's voice—low again—*Come'n.*

Jack peer'd down. The hang to the window was considerable. But with strong joints, a set of fingers could grab hold of the nails poking from the parapet just enough to flip one's legs into a waiting, open window.

Mid-flight, a flash of Disaster—considering the Consequences if Bess had not thought to press the window fully open— He flinch'd, bracing for impact—and plung'd forward through the wide-open frame.

He half-sailed, half-tumbled, landing just a hair past a daybed that rested under the window. The room was sweet with the ammonia of male emission and amber with Candlelight. A dresser, an armoire, a well-turned mahogany bed with fine linens, an upholstered daybed in crimson damask—enough furniture for a parlor room in a fine townhouse. Bess was standing at an ivory basin in the far corner, patting her neck with a handkerchief. She did not turn, but regarded him out of the corner of her eye—from nerves or disinterest, 'twas difficult to say.

Jack shook out his hands—red and cramped from the recent effort, veins bloated like an animal furrowing under the Skin.

"What did you mean about King Screwsman?" An unfortunate opening salvo. He sounded anxious.

"Only that you seem more than your current station."

Until two nights ago he'd been squirrel'd away at Kneebone's, unaware of anything other than the endless reach of days and nights of his servitude. Now that there was a Horizon, he saw just how far off it was. And if it was unreachable? There was something about the banter, the exclusiveness of her chambers. Bess was accomplished— accomplished and musky and sharply wry.

His stomach lurched. *I can't be this—this* Jack. He turned towards the window to leave, craning his head at the roof, which now appear'd farther off than when he had come in. *Well, it's Manageable,* he assess'd, perhaps wrongly.

"I meant, for one thing"—her voice was close behind him. When he turn'd, she was pushing her hair behind an ear—"that you seem different than the coves that come through here—the ones who see only a harlot or a desperate jilt scouring for a husband."

"You're not hunting for a h-husband?" The stutter again.

He felt the trace of her breath on his face when she said, "Not quite."

Total silence between them.

Then: "Are you hungry?"

Well, yes.

Though he hadn't realized it until she ask'd. He wanted to eat and swallow and—there was no other way to put it but that he wanted to *have a Body* in her presence—*a Body*— Now here was another Horizon come swinging up, this one bury'd so deep inside him it was a Thing unfamiliar.

"Very. But—"

Ordinarily at this hour Jack would be asleep, exhaustion overcoming hunger and empty pockets.

"I'll take you." She handed him a topcoat. "Nicked it from a cove too soused to notice."

The coat was a deep maroon with velvet trimmings. Jack slipp'd his arm into the heavy satin sleeve. It was both too long and too wide. He glimpsed himself in the mirror. He looked surprisingly buckish*. Maybe a touch too deft† for his own liking—he'd like to look a bull-beef‡. But he looked buckish enough, and this pleased him, despite the flash he got of his mother's face hardening in Horror.§

---

* Masculine

† Pretty

‡ Thick

§ Thank god for the women who rescue us from the medusan horror of our mothers' gazes; for the women who see us as . . . *us*.

Relatedly, a couple of weeks ago I stopped into the Rite Aid on my way to work. An ordinary day, my regular stop-by. I could have called in the prescription, sure, but I like the routine and the personal touch. My single-mom neighbor, Ursula, is the head pharmacist there.

Ursula wasn't single when she moved across the street from me. Had a red-haired, thick, rough-looking guy who worked for the Department of Public Works. Always heading out on an ATV at dawn during snowstorms and shit. One night there's a raging fight conducted half inside, half outside on their porch. The next day a trailer appears in their yard. By that evening you can tell he's living in it. A couple of weeks later the trailer and the guy are gone and now it's just her and her kid.

P.S. Ursula is pretty hot. Short, well endowed, and funny. That combination that absolutely destroys me. I enjoy looking at her precisely slipping pills into vials and taping on labels, standing behind the counter at the pharmacy. Her hair all dark and glossy against her white lab coat. Her focused look. I've always thought Hot Pharmacist (also: Hot Vet) would be a good idea for a sitcom. But then again my bar for sitcoms is very low.

I sometimes bring Ursula a macchiato from the artisanal coffee shop next door— the one that specializes in humane-egg challah and Italian coffee—and we chat for a bit if it isn't busy. She has that kind of skeptical squint I tend to fall for.

So I go in with my little gifts. Ursula's back behind the counter, and I hand her the macchiato, which she always laughs at. *You know you can bring me Dunkin' Donuts, right?* she says. I shrug. I like to make it seem that I would only bring her the best Italian macchiato, but also Dunkin' Donuts is out of the way, and the macchiato-and-humane-egg-challah place is next door. Ultimately I can be a little spendy and lazy in my present-giving. I wasn't the one who pointed that out to me.

So I hand her the macchiato and we get to chatting—I ask her about her daughter and how "pharmacisting" is going—and then, I don't know why, but I tell her about the manuscript. I hadn't told anyone else. I mean, I hadn't spoken to anyone *to* tell. But, still, I hadn't told anyone.

She starts asking encouraging and really, actually, specific and interested ques-

• • •

At the late hour, the George on Borough High Street was sparse
with gentry. The wood floors were swept clean, there was a Fire
going, and the tables were set farther apart than at the Black Lion.
Bess led Jack towards a corner in the back. He whizz'd around to
pull out her chair, which she squinted at, then accepted.

Once they were seated, a well-fed pale woman in a complex
many-tiered outfit of blue petticoats approach'd the table.

"I'm the wife of the owner. Barmaid's taken to bed."

Jack look'd down. He had never eaten at a pub before.

Bess ordered two teapots for them and lamb and mint peas

---

tions. What "trans" meant in the period. Whether anyone else had found documents
like this before. And weirdly she has some speculations of her own about early modern
endocrinology. Says they'd learned in pharmacist classes something about nineteenth-
century experiments on French roosters. She really seems to have an interest in the
whole thing. Needless to say, this is opening me up and shit, and once I start talking, it
all comes out. I even forget about my unpaid-leave woes for a bit.

Your project sounds so interesting, she keeps saying. *From everything you're telling
me.* Yeah, I'm really babbling on. But then, the manuscript is the main—only?—thing
in my life since my ex left. Or I left. Or whatever fucking thing happened.

Ursula's being sweet. So sweet, in fact, that what I'm beginning to realize is: this
woman has an appetite for trans, and thank fuck for that.

But also now I'm panicking. Would I even know how to get it on at this point,
given the opportunity? I used to be so—how to put this—*confident. Very confident.*
But god it's been so long. I mean, so very long that now I'm trying to mentally track
through the house, to remember where I even last saw my cock. Under the bed? In
the cheapo cardboard set of drawers I've stuffed in my closet? I have no idea what my
face looks like as I'm running through these thoughts. Likely I'm grinding my teeth in
that way I do when I'm trying to emulate Tom Cruise's jaw-muscle flicker in *Top Gun,*
and ending up looking like a serial killer. A friend once said all white people look like
serial killers, which seems about right. So I try to adjust my face to look less serial
killery but now inevitably look disturbing in a different way.

I focus on regaining composure. I determine I must return her possible flirting
with some gesture—*anything*—of my own. To my horror, this gesture ends up taking
the form of a pseudo-gallant virtual hat-tipping move and a dumb little bow I do at
her on my way out.

I really feel mortified by the time I get to my car—have already cued up Metallica
to channel my embarrassment into pathetic drumming on the steering wheel—when
she texts me.

Do you want to come to dinner Thursday?

for Jack. Neither she nor the pub owner's wife met each other's eye.

"Did you want to take that off? It's warm in here."

Jack hunch'd more resolutely inside the husk of the coat. He liked how it *biggened* him.

The pub owner's wife return'd with Jack's tea and the peas and Lamb.

"Last helping of the night. Was going to have it myself, but since we've got a hungry cove amongst us . . ." She poured the tea into a mug.

Jack grunted an approximation of thanks, then address'd the food. He sat, elbows on his knees, alternately scooping at mint peas and sipping at his boiling Tea.

Bess watched him. "You're bound in Service."

"Who said." This came out *who shayd,* due to the quantity of peas in his mouth.

"What else would you be. You've thus far appeared only at night. You've one set of clothes—as far as I can see. You quite enjoy oiling that apron." She smiled. "And you've strong hands."

Jack made a note not to oil his apron so much. "Carpentry. At Kneebone's."

"That's skilled labor."

He shrugged. "It's mostly a lot of tuffets."

"How long've you been at it?"

"Nine years."

Bess nodded. "Been in London about that long, myself."

The pub owner's wife arriv'd with the tea for Bess. Set the pot and an empty mug down with a clank and left them there. Under her breath, she muttered a cruel slur.*

Jack study'd Bess's face. It was very still.

---

* By 1814, the so-called "philanthropic" organization, Society for the Protection of Asiatic Sailors, had proposed removing lascars from "public view" and remanding them to a barracks at the East End docks. *Of course* it was the East India Company that sponsored these detention centers. The Company had long been a testing ground for naturalizing new brutalities.

He was up from his seat before he even meant to be.

She put her hand on his arm.

"Sit down."

"*She's* the b——*.*"

"Please"—her voice was urgent—"you're creating a scene."

He sat. Reach'd across the table to pour her tea for her.

Now Bess's face flick'd through a series of Expressions too fast to discern.

"Don't call Attention to what you don't understand," she said. She placed her hand on the kettle, pushing it gently down and away from her cup. Her voice was measured. "I can handle my own slights."

A stupid rush of Heroism. Jack placed his hands in his lap.

Bess poured her tea and wrapped her palms around the mug. "Anyway you could have shared yours." She lowered her head over the trickle of Steam.

"You're good at getting in places," she said, after some time. She nodded at the veins and knuckles in his hand. "Must be the tuffet-caning." Her gaze on the back of his hand caused his entire system to Boil.

"Tuffets are not very interesting." He picked up his Fork again, impaling peas on the tines. "It's just an S-caning technique and a pillow top that we get from the quilter." He ate a forkful, then mimicked the caning technique, weaving his hands in the air.

Through the fog of tea-Mist that lifted from her cup. "What do you intend to do after your service with Kneebone is complete?"

"Join Kneebone as a colleague?"

Bess arch'd an eyebrow.

Well, the Company and the ordinary racists of London, as with the pub-keeper's wife, above.

(For more on which, see Humberto Garcia, "The Transports of Lascar Specters: Dispossessed Indian Sailors in Women's Romantic Poetry," in Jordana Rosenberg and Chi-ming Yang, eds., "The Dispossessed Eighteenth Century" [special issue], *The Eighteenth Century: Theory and Interpretation* 55, nos. 2–3 [2014].)

* Language redacted in original.

"Has Kneebone mentioned joining him as a colleague?"

"No."

"Is Kneebone the promoting sort of man?"

He wanted to say: *No, Kneebone's a bitter old husk who chains me to the workbench during the day and to my bedpost at night.* But then Bess would know just how Owned he was—

He swallow'd a pea. "Maybe?"

"I've not heard of a master ever once promoting a servant like that."

"He's not *extraordinarily cruel,*" Jack heard himself echoing Kneebone's self-depiction. "He's just a precise bookkeeper."

"Hm." Bess sipp'd tea. She was a loud sipper. He liked the Sound of it.

"On the off chance that Kneebone doesn't fancy promoting you, but instead has it in mind to work you to Death and then turn you out onto the streets like the starving dog you already halfway are, you might consider turning your capacities for squirreling in places to a different account. A life of nabbing† beats a life of cadging‡, you know. And that's"—she held his gaze—"what I meant when I called you King Screwsman."

---

† Stealing
‡ Begging

8.

THE NEXT MORNING WAS A HARD RETURN TO THE REGULARITY OF Kneebone's. Jack had slept little due to excitement. As Kneebone show'd him a new caning technique at the workbench, Jack's chin dropped to his chest. Kneebone tapped his knuckles with a Rod. "Cane more quickly, girl." In all his years with Kneebone, Jack had labor'd with regularity and precision. This new shift in his demeanor wasn't passing unnoticed.

"I'm docking you the supper portion of peas and oats." Kneebone rapped Jack's knuckles with the rod for the third time that morning. Jack blink'd up at this beady-eyed crow, his master, bustling up pointed feathers, snatching back sustenance with an angry Beak.

At the fourth chin-to-chest drop, Kneebone shook him awake with his spiny hands on his shoulders.

"That's it. Sending you to market." Kneebone bent to unlock Jack's ankle Cuff, then thrust a bunch of tuffets at him. "You're useless today."

Tuffets hung off the crooks of Jack's elbows like overblown, sunsoftened fruit as he tumbl'd down the streets, weaving in and out of the thick mobs at Cheapside market, then down Gin Lane. He hummed happily, thinking of Bess, and the way she'd caressed his hands.

He'd deliver'd the goods at various merchants and was rounding the intersection of Charing Cross and Tottenham Court roads, free of Encumbrances and somewhat bouncy, when a sudden and unusual sound jolt'd him. He halt'd in front of a Watch shop, looking for the source. Inside, the proprietor turn'd over a large rusted clock, peering at its underside—

There came some Squawking from the interior . . . *Every-Day-Same-Day-Same-Time-Different-Day. Can't-Stop*—

Jack squinted through the glaze.

Just then the owner knocked his tool with a distract'd elbow and bent under the bench to retrieve it.

More squawking. Jack's eyes fix'd on a rose-gold Pocketwatch. The proprietor's head was still under the workbench, fussing.

From behind him, the sudden rush of a tattered cloak, the scent of cigar rising from dirty wool, and a red-haired, rail-thin blackguard* had appear'd over his shoulder, noticing what Jack was noticing: the watchmaker unalert, the rose-gold Pocketwatch lying unguarded. The blackguard hurl'd himself at the windowpane, punching in the Glaze with his elbow and nabbing the watch from the sill.

The watchmaker shouted out for the constables. "I've been robbed!"

It was a clumsy, impulsive job—immensely stupid, in fact.

But then the blackguard did something unexpected and canny.

"*I've* been robbed," he shriek'd, drowning out the sound of the watchmaker. His eyes bulged in pretended Horror as he patted his pockets.

In sheer panic at the Mêlée, Jack began to run.

Weatherwax church was spilling out from afternoon mass. The cries of "Stop, Thief!" had a Magnetic effect on the popish lot. They coagulated instantly into a wall, blockading Court Road. Jack spun and headed back towards Charing Cross just as he saw a constable huffing towards him, a musket bouncing off his hip—Jack assessed

---

* Rogue; also: boot cleaner

that he would achieve the intersection before the sentry did. The shops and houses blurred into an ochre wash as he ran, and his estimations were wrong because the next thing he knew, a second constable's musket hit him square in the back—and he flipp'd onto his ass in the street with the catholicks clucking about him like a bunch of fuddled Hens.

Then the constable's hand was on him, rifling through his pockets, tearing at his already-torn woolens.

"I didn't steal anything!" Jack cried.

The Pig issued a rough laugh. A gin-soaked blast of air, and the laugh accelerat'd into a cough that instantly became a seizure of hacking.

The constable's Hands were all over him—feeling 'round his ankles—patting his thighs—pausing over his Chest. A look of confusion cross'd the constable's face.

Jack's heart was racing. "Dueling injury." He waved his hand at his chest. "Bandaged up."

The constable tore Jack's shirt up to his chin—saw the bandages— Jack's throat had become a nest of Birds.

The constable emitt'd a walrusy "humph," and stood.

"Perchance you swallowed the watch Fob," he grous'd, in an effort to save face.

"I can shite for you if you like," Jack said, banking on this being a suggestion too odious.

"Be on yer way—*away* from the pockets of the finer Sort."

Jack righted himself and stumbl'd down the lane in the opposite direction, willing himself not to look back.

After several blocks, his breath returned to him. He was puzzling over why he'd panicked, when—at the intersection of Tottenham— Jack spy'd the blackguard again. Trotting casually down the lane ahead.

And whether it was anger, or righteousness, or simply the leftover Energy in Jack's veins making him dance forward quicker and quicker down the lane—or maybe he was hearing Bess's words, *You should be King Screwsman,* playing through his head—before he knew it, Jack was picking his way quietly up behind the blackguard.

The blackguard puff'd happily on a cigar as he trudged along. Jack walked in rhythm. Inhaling deeply and holding his Breath, he dipped his hand into the blackguard's pocket, mimicking the gentle swoop he used to cane tuffets.

And then the watch was in his Hand.

Perhaps Bess had been right.

Jack turned backwards and rounded the corner of Fleet Street towards Kneebone's.

He had done it—his first—however unspectacular—Jilt.*

---

* The specifics of this interaction with the constable afford details that are not given in any of the other records. I will provisionally regard it as something of an exclusive inside report.

9.

JONATHAN WILD—THIEF-CATCHER GENERAL, MR. THINGSTABLE*, Namer-of-Names, Satanic Cunt-stable† of London—celebrat'd at his desk, alone, the ten-year anniversary of his release from the Wood Street Compter.‡

The Office for the Recovery of Lost and Stolen Property—dug into one unusually thick hollowed-out post—sat twenty-five feet beneath the Tower Wharf. Wild watch'd through green scratched glazes the sewers emptying into the Thames. He catalogued the waft of Dreck, calibrated the waste with the limp map of the City curling off his walls. An accountant of Offal, he notated which carcasses came from which butcher shops and were thrown into which sewers—which tanneries had excess lime to dump in the Channels—which grocers were tossing out soft Turnips.

A single candle burned. A single snifter of fine French Brandy balanc'd in his hand.

.   .   .

---

* Eighteenth-century slang dictionaries offer a delicate way to avoid uttering the first syllable of this word—"constable"—which, in British English, sounds like a very particular indecent *other* word. Though, frankly "constable," when you think about it, is a much more indecent word than "cunt." For there are certain cases where the latter, at least, is used (*verrrry*) lovingly and consensually. The former, never.
† Ahem. Thingstable.
‡ Debtors' prison

The winch chair—Wild's apparatus for entering and exiting the piling—clang'd to an office-level halt. At a timid knock on the door, Wild cleared his throat. "Come in," he said, elongating the "eee" of "in"—an oily snake escaping his lips.

A lady entered. Like all newly monied, this one was fond of flaunting her Wealth. Her shirt was speckled in mica grains, and opal and ruby Pins dotted her complex hairpiece.

Wild strode around the desk to pull out the large leather chair.

"I've come to talk to you about a robbery."

Wild nodded. The gray hairs of his brows cast thick shadows across the surface of his broad forehead, and his hand strok'd the infamous pair of iron manacles he kept jangling from his belthook.

The Newly Monied glanced anxiously about the Office.

Wild's way with the manacles was legend. Though a dense, heavy man, with manacles he was a jaguar, a slip in the night. The speed of his Approach, his perfect aim, were legendary. As was the way he silenced the jangly metal in his beet-red fist as he walked up behind you. Wild's right hand stay'd hot with sweat and bloomed the tang of iron Residues.

His crisp-pressed smish hissed with starch as his shoulders rose and fell with breath. It hardly matter'd what this woman said. Wild had known why she was there the moment she stepped in.

He handed her a dram of brandy and feign'd interest.

"My husband maintains a watch shop in Charing Cross. Yesterday it was thiev'd and a rose-gold watch fob taken." Her sparrowhand shook the glass of Brandy into a small Storm.

"A *warming draught* eases such *traumatic recountings, Madam,*" Wild soothed. "Tell me everything that happened to your *precious personal goods.* But not before"—he raised a finger, coughed—"my finder's fee—'tis but a guinea." He slid a ceramic dish towards her. "Let us get the *nasty particulars* of payment out of the way."

Dragging the dish back across the desk and pocketing the Coin, Wild placed his chin onto his clasped hands. "Now, to return to this *heinous crime* and your *unique and irreplaceable* personal Items."

She began a long recounting.

Wild quickly ceased listening. For he knew very well who had nabbed her jingle-brained husband's Watchfob. He had known the moment she walked through the door. It was in fact he who had dispatched Hell-and-Fury to Charing Cross the previous After-noon, anticipating at that point charging ten guineas for the return of the property, plus his finder's fee. Considering her fine apparel, he now determined on twelve.

Not twenty minutes after the Newly Monied had left—and Wild had boxed the Jesuit[*] into a Chamber pot under the desk—the winch chair descended again.

A soft tap on the door and in tripp'd Tom Sykes—or Hell-and-Fury, as they called him—the most hapless, ham-fingered, cringing Crook in town—as manipulable as a soft Doll lacking innards.

A steam rose off his chalky skin. Hell-and-Fury was a jittery underfed mole—his narrow, bloody eyes squint'd frantically. His thin red hair was parted wetly down the middle of his pointed Skull. He smooth'd his filthy jerkin.

"D'you have the fob," Wild said, wiping the corners of his lips with a pocket square. He was anticipating dining on roast duck at the Iris Inn.

Hell-and-Fury's hands went to his right cloak pocket. The left. Then the interior. And his breeches pockets. His narrow eyes squint'd narrower. He even reach'd down to check the bands at the bottom of his stockings. Repeated the entire check again.

He blinked in terror at Wild. "It's gone."

"Get out," Wild clipped, "before I do something horrible to you."

Hell-and-Fury scuttl'd to the winch chair.

Wild put his head in his hands. *Why do I have to tolerate the dumb fops of this town? Not a canny thief among 'em—not the ones that work for me, anyway.* He curled up, then bit down on his

---

[*] Had congress with himself

tongue—an old affectation from childhood—briefly despised himself for retaining his childish affectations—uncurled his tongue—breathed out. *God, you bastard, bring me Success in a bigger scheme. Immortalize me in this town and across the Oceans, too.*

The winch chair clatter'd down the post again. When the doors opened, Wild, head down, said, "Leave or I'll take you to the gallows tonight and don't think I won't do it."

"I don't appreciate being spoken to in that way." Wild raised his head. Not Hell-and-Fury.

James Evans—a pyramidal man with a wide base, a bushy white wig and a long thin face scorched with a constant Blush—totter'd in the threshold. "I've come to discuss our—my—well, now *our* experiments."

"Yes, Evans," Wild exhal'd, clasping his hands under his chin and staring Evans down. "Please, *please* tell me you've made progress."

"I've drafted a—what could we call it?—a *recipe* of sorts. It's not quite ready. Actually, not ready in the slightest. I'm perfecting it."

Wild's gaze hardened. "You've been perfecting it for some time."

"It's immensely difficult." Evans flutter'd his hands while he talked in the unnerving way that he did.

"If you can hurry up the Experiment, we'll both be rich and you'll never have to worry about the Royal College of Physicians snubbing you again. Nor will I have to worry about managing the dumb clunches that come through this office. We'll be Legends.

—"Perhaps not beloved Legends," he clarified. "But Legends nonetheless."†

---

† Every record of Sheppard features his pursuit by Wild. Not one of them, however, mentions an "Evans."

10.

THE WATCH PULS'D WARM IN JACK'S TROUSER POCKET. A SMALL ANI-
mal radiating heat and possibility—driving him towards Bess, hailing him into a Future where he would be no longer a freezing
chained girl, mustering tuffet after tuffet at Kneebone's command.
A future where he would be with her, and he would be *Jack*.

And so, although it was pouring and very cold, Jack reached into
his pocket for the file—slipped it into the ankle-lock, and freed himself from the warmth of his bed into the swirling wet Wind.

By the time he reached Cresswell's his fingers were gnarled
with cold. He ascended with some measure of pain the rain-
drenched bricks to the parapet. Waited 'til Bess finished with what
sounded like an out-at-the-heels* duke, who climax'd in a tortured
Squeal.

After the exit of the cove, Jack sent down a branch he'd collected from the alley, tapping at the window. It opened to the upper
casing with a thump.

Drop. Swing. Tumble in.

Bess wore a tight black Chemise with a low neck, and black jodh-
purs. She was tying her hair back with a ribbon. The sawdust-and-
Rose scent of her permeated the room—went straight to Jack's
groin.

_____
* Old

He cleared his throat. "I nabbed a watch." He removed the fob from his pocket and laid it before her.

Bess peer'd down. "A nice one"—looked up—"Pull a rum stall?"†

"More just a . . ." It was the blackguard who had pulled off the rum stall, in fact. Jack didn't know the canting term for "unplanned pickpocketing." "Jus' a simple jilt, really."

"You can pawn this, dear rogue."

"Not much of a rogue." He bit the inside of his cheek.

"Are now." She smiled, dangling the watch from her pinky. "Most of the thieves in this city are owned by Wild. Not you."

"What's 'wild'?" Jack sat on the Daybed.

"My gods, you've been squirrel'd away." She joined him on the Daybed. "Wild's a craven scoundrel. A businessman of thieving. Runs the largest gang of blackguards in the city. Controls them through what you might call an 'informal indenture.' Do you know what fencing is?"

"Naturally," he huff'd. "Selling stolen goods." His mother had once described him as "fencing" the barley seeds he filched off the apothecary carts. She hadn't been entirely opposed to it either, as he always gave her most of his Coin.

"Wild was London's most acclaimed fencer until the magistrates got onto him. Imprisoned him at Wood Street Compter for many years; he survived by turning Trustee‡. While at Wood Street, Wild made the acquaintance of every whip-jack§, blackguard and elbow-shaker¶ captured off the streets. He knew everyone by name. And he knew exactly who to put one over on at any given occasion. They called him the *Thieves' Oracle*. Wild was the one to see if you needed an ounce of gin, a Law-book, or a high bunk to escape the rat-frequented damp of the common Hold.

"And Wild was also the gent the Keepers solicit'd for Informa-

---

† Creating pressure in a crowd to pull off a heist
‡ Errand-runner for the guards; snitch
§ Counterfeit Mariners; pretended survivors of shipwrecks. Forgers of calamity.
¶ Cheater

tion on who had pinched an ounce of gin, or who had managed to gain extra pence that day begging through the prison bars. He made Cozy with the Keepers. He was their King-snitch for the term of his Confinement. And now snitching and cozy-keeping have become Wild's very Profession."

In the course of these declamations, Bess had leaned into Jack, her shoulder pressing against his. The watch was ticking forward—he could hear it in her hand. But the time Jack was inhabiting had come disjoin'd from the Watch.

"Once he was discharged from Wood Street, Wild created a new category of urban Blight, christening himself *Thief-Catcher General*. He runs the heists, and he runs the snitches and he snitches out the heisters, too. He's intimate with the Magistrate."

Bess leaned back against the window casings. The warm Impress where her shoulder had been cool'd in the open air.

"Wild's the worst kind of thief. He's as bad as the stockjobbers at the Royal Exchange. No, worse." She touched his forearm. "I think you could be a freelance rogue. You're different."

Would being a freelance rogue mean more of *this*? More touching and talking and—

"Come to the docks tomorrow, 'round noon. I can introduce you to some other Unowned."

Jack flinch'd. "I'm permitted to market generally only on Tuesdays and the occasional Sunday. I can sneak out at night, but during the day—"

"Do you make all your decisions based on the threat of Punishment?"

In fact, more or less he did.

"They don't enforce the Vagrant Act the way you think they do."

"The Act is very clear 'bout what you can and can't do." Sadly, Jack had memoriz'd every threatening word of the Act.

"Has a centinel ever stopped you on your way to market?"

"No. But I've always had a master's Note."

"How do *they* know you have a master's Note? You wear it pinned to your sleeve?"

Jack winced.

"And how do you walk when you have your note?"

"Easy."

"And how do you feel?"

"Easy."

"So"—she shrugg'd—"walk that way without one."

"Bess, that's—"

"Don't you know that all the laws are enforced *selectively*? Now, if you were a lascar marooned in London by the East India Company refusing to pay return passage, then I'd say—"*

"Well, of course!"

She ignored Jack's frantic display of understanding.

"As I was saying, if you were a marooned lascar sailor, then your options would be slenderer. And I'm not saying they're not slender now. But choosing when and how they enforce the law on you is not something you can do. And not a reason to confine yourself before you begin."

The catastrophe of being caught without a master's Note rose up like a clot of Smoke in his mind. "Even if I could, there's Kneebone and the workday—"

"Do you want to be Kneebone's servant all your life?"

This stung.

"Of course not." His words were sticking together in a dry mouth.

"Well, if you find a way."

This was delivered as if there *were* a Way to find.

"Could you wait until Tuesday? On my way to market?"

"Tomorrow's when we meet up. Regular thing." And then Bess

---

* Impossible not to wonder what Bess might have said if not interrupted. Would either she or Jack have reflected on themselves as racialized? (*Viz.*, Gerzina, "The English only began to see themselves as 'white' when they discovered 'black' people," *Black London*, p. 5.)

Yet another constitutive lacuna through which we peer, deriving racialization's crystallization not in the content, but in the formal features of the text. Perspective. Who interrupts whom. Where the narrative breaks off, etc.—

leaned in. Her hand was on his Chest. On the wrappings. "You're not breathing," she said, her breath heating his Neck.

Time went out of joint again because she press'd her lips to his neck, and said, "Did you want to make that Acquaintance with me now?"

Jack had never made any woman's Acquaintance. So he did what he could only imagine a cove would do in such a situation. He put his fingers under Bess's Chin, raising it gently. He kept his fingers there for the duration of which he leaned down and kiss'd her—three seconds that bloomed and bloomed. His heart had turned ocean, was throwing waves onto a shore.

"Nice," Bess said, nodding. "Nice."

Then she put her hand around the back of his head and pull'd him down more firmly to her Lips. "Now do it not quite so nice."

She open'd her mouth wide and they were kissing again—with their Velvets down each other's throats and him groaning and holding her fast against him at the small of her back.

When they surfac'd, he put his head into her neck, breathing deep the scent where her hair met Skin.

"Or," she said. "You don't have to go back to Kneebone at all. I have a place you can stay."

She meant *her rooms*—her rooms with her in them— *Oh God.*

How he wanted this—to be plung'd into her world—to stay with her.

But Jack didn't know how to do this—*to stay.* More properly, to stay Seen—to be seen all day and have it continue into the Night— and how—and what next? Show himself to her—as what?

He must retreat to the aloneness of Kneebone's—the wretched unseenness to which he'd become accustom'd.

"I have to go," he said, already at the window, knowing full well how unsatisfying and yet how unstoppable his release back into anonymity would be.

· · ·

Then he was thundering over the roofs alone, the wind coursing through his lungs—a specter evaporating back into the City— This, he felt, was all he was and all he would ever be—a Shard of metropolis.*

He ran over the roofs to Kneebone's. Unhinged the windows. Slipp'd into bed, his knickers and thin smish filling with the chill that'd collected under the coverlet. And then he fell into sleep Unseen. As he did every night. Every single night, like a Pebble falling silently to the bottom of a dark Pond. Alone. Alone. Always alone.

Jack woke just before Dawn, the sky streak'd pink and blue over the tiled roofs. Why couldn't his own Ceiling change color, deepen, shoot through with sun? Why was he the terrified, careful idiot who had to wait until Tuesday? Always calculating Punishments to come. Would the black-capped horizon of his Imagination never prism into color?

—Oh, how he long'd for her.

For Bess had given him something he had never known. Some confecktion—still just a Concept yet—the flicker of a life lived in tandem. Something to truly want.

And this just about undid him.

The hasps at his door rattled— Jack's heart leapt—he'd forgotten to slip the Polhem Lock back onto his ankle to mask his evening Escape.

And now the Door was opening.

---

* Note to self: This particular relation between the queer/trans body and the city is strangely resonant with a contemporary sensibility; i.e., it's hard not to relate.

We, the emotionally starved; we, who have been thrown from the void, who have turned to the city when there was nowhere else. Well, maybe not all of us, but I know I have so many times felt the city itself was my mother, and I her asphalt nursling.

. . .

Jack could not have guessed that old, rickety Kneebone could move so quickly and with such Force. For his gray eyes had landed on Jack's ankle, lying outside the coverlet. Lockless.

Jack tried to sit up, to say something, fashion some excuse— But before he could speak, Kneebone struck him in the temple, slamming his head back against the wall— In the ensuing on-slaught, Jack was too stunn'd to resist— Kneebone wheezed with the force of his effort as he knocked Jack's head again and again at the same spot. Jack heard high-pitched squeals— He was shattered to realize that the squeals were coming from his own throat. He heard himself calling for help— His own voice rang out, unrecognizable.

When it was over, Kneebone walked calmly to the door. "Your labor is the property of Kneebone. Your rest restores you to labor for Knee-bone, and thus is your Rest my Property as well."

Then he walked through, closed and lock'd the door.

Jack curled on his side, panting. In the sudden silence of the room, he was possessed of a strange Clarity. A sentence ran through his mind. He had never been given to Vengeance before, but what was there now was there without dispute. *You'll be sorry,* he thought, over and over again. *You and all your kind will be sorry.*

Jack snatch'd his cloak and threw the rose-gold watch fob into his pocket. Slipp'd open the window and leapt out. He raced from Kneebone's powered by the Terror—the Certainty—that his master was just behind him.

II.

AT THE CORNER OF STONEY AND CLINK, JACK NEARLY TUMBL'D DOWN the side of a butcher shop onto the street. He was faint with Fatigue. The buildings of the city tilt'd in his vision like unmoored docks in a Storm.

In the fog at the Pool of London, the ships appear'd yet taller than their vast heights, topmasts lost in dense Vapor. It was the muddled purple of very early morning, air thick with Dark. The port was busy. A ground cover of fallen leaves turned to fume in the alchemy of Boots as sellers stormed up ramps to haggle with captains and ships' bursars. The soundscape was stuffed with cooing woodpigeons and yapping Sparrows; cant in a variety of languages, and the din of Prices shouted back and forth. Riggings creaked and wind-beaten Vessels ached against anchors driven deep into the riverbed.

There was Bess. Standing with another doxy, heads bent, reading a broadside together. Somewhat intimately.

He trotted up. He'd done it after all. He'd come.

The doxy looked up first. Chestnut hair, navy blue eyes unblinking.

"I'm Jack," he managed. "Bess's—" He didn't know how to describe the rest.

"I know who you are"—held out her hand—"Jenny Diver."* If

* In John Gay, "Jenny Diver" is likely based on the eighteenth-century pickpocket Mary Young; in Brecht, this character becomes "Pirate Jenny/Low Dive Jenny."

he'd had to imagine a friend and colleague of Bess, he would have conjured a temperament similar to hers—studious and haunted—for the world was already becoming Bess-copies to him. But Jenny was something else entirely. There was an entitl'd Wildness about her. She stood at the docks in full doxy regalia—skirts blooming, tight corset, full face paint—and an air of brazen unconcern.

"Oi, Bess! Jenny!" A cloud of Perfume preceded a slender tall man approaching in a turquoise topcoat, his mustache knitted tightly into an upcurl, accompanied by an equally tall dame togg'd out in a tight-bodiced crimson dress. Her fingers were fawnied*. The man embraced Bess. *"Pa ni mèt ankô,"*† he said, against her ear. Released her. The dame and Bess kissed cheeks in the French fash-ion.

"Jack," she said, touching his shoulder, by way of introduction. He liked very much how his name sounded in her Mouth. "Meet Franny and Laurent."

"Still at Cresswell's?" said Laurent to Bess.

Nodding. "And where have you been?" teas'd Bess. "Come by soon."

"Friday night games and gin?"

"Always!" said Jenny.

"Please." Bess put her hand on Franny's arm. "We've missed you."

"We will! We will!" she said, and the two stroll'd off, arm in arm, leaving the cloud of scents lingering behind.

"Who're they?" Jack ask'd.

"Didn't Bess tell you not to ask questions?" Jenny laughed at him. "But since you did—those are mollies!"

Jack flushed. He'd heard Kneebone disparage the mollies as espe-cial "vectors of Contagion." He hadn't known they'd be so beautiful.

"More like *friends of the House*," Bess explained.

---

* Covered in rings

† Now this is an unusual piece of cant for which I can find no translation whatsoever in any of my dictionaries or any ngram search. I'll have to consult a colleague and return to this passage later.

"'Til later," said Jenny, leaning in to kiss Bess's cheek. Bess put her hand to the side of Jenny's head. Held her there. Jack turn'd away.

Jenny threaded through the crowd quickly—something like a vicious, gleeful cat shredding twine. Coves jerk'd to the sides to let her pass. It wasn't how people grumblingly obliged Mrs. Kneebone's path through the streets. Jenny's walk shatter'd the density of Bodies around her into air.

Jack turn'd back to Bess. Before he realized what he was doing, he'd taken her hand—the first time he'd walked hand in hand with a woman, in fact. He choked with Joy. Bess's hand puls'd, small and warm in his Palm.

Just then he smelled something—the mineral tang of sweat perspiring off metal—and before he knew it, a cold snap at his free wrist—handcuffs—and the words "Charing Cross watch-nabber" snarl'd from behind. A thick hand grabbed his breeches, jammed into his pocket, drew out the watch.

The false accusation had, in fact, turn'd true.

"Taking you to Newgate," gruffed the centinel in a blast of sour Breath.

Jack found Bess's gaze with his terrified own. She squeezed his hand— His had turn'd clammy with terror— Hers was warm, dry— *Calm,* she mouth'd.

"Back on your ship, lascar," the centinel directed at her. A crowd was gathering, separating the two of them with a small commotion.

Jack saw Laurent craning through the crowd at the tumult. Franny slid through the cluster. Then she had her hand on Bess's shoulder, and Laurent drew up alongside. The two of them, flanking her, led her quietly away.

The centinel yank'd on the handcuffs, pulling Jack back towards him. Then he was being dragg'd hard towards Clink Street—and tripped, fell, hitting the cobblestones hard on his Knees.

I was almost Free, he thought, as his Body shook with the impact. *Almost.*

12.

IF ONLY IT WAS A POLHEM LOCK THAT THE WARDEN PRODUCED WHEN Jack arrived at the high-ceilinged stone entryroom of Newgate. The trim, well-attired warden laid the Lock—a heavy iron English padlock—and Chain lovingly on his desk.

"Charing Cross Watch-Nabbing," he intoned, scratching details in his book of Accounts. Jack glanced at the spread pages filled with Names. The handwriting was neat in that erotick way of an author who takes pleasure in the minutiae of a Cruel job. Straight lines ran through near half the Names. Jack did not suppose these lines indicated Release.

"Name?" The warden's quill poised over his book.

Jack's mouth hesitated over *P*——. Hesitated next over *Jack*. He heard himself making a glob of Sound that was neither.

"We do need a name, a proper name with alphabetic letters and the like."

"Jack Sheppard." His voice sounded small.

The warden wrote slowly and carefully. Just then a beetle emerged from between the stones in the wall behind the warden. Jack's eyes followed the creature as it scuttled across the wet gray Wall. He thought of Bess—the way she'd petted and soothed the bug at the Black Lion—how she freed it. The warden traced Jack's gaze—turned—and slamm'd his palm against the beetle—wiped his hand with a Kerchief, picked up the Lock and Chain and handed them to the centinel.

He nodded at a door to the rear of the room. "Below the Keeper's house."*

---

* Speaking of bug-murder and desire, I totally bombed my date last night. Dinner at Ursula's.

Ursula and I both live at the end of this pretty scrubby cul-de-sac. Ursula's got the very tidy house across the way. Really, the only nice joint on the entire sac. She had every tree in her yard cut down a couple of years ago. Never had to rake a single leaf since then. Smart woman. Very organized. Probably hates my yard-slacking.

I ring the bell and the door opens to an inside as bereft of living greenery as the outside, but she's compensated in her décor. Bright red fifties Formica dining set with retro placemats shaped like big palm leaves. That newish wallpaper with fake cartoonish landscape stencils. Bare branches against a white background, which gives the impression of a winter forest. It's a bit cute and overdone, but it's also—well, I'm trying to control that *pang* I get—the desire to be in spaces that women make.

"Sit down," she says, gesturing to a puffy red dining chair.

She disappears into the kitchen. Returns with some pasta, sits with me and immediately—like before her fork even hits her food—launches into this story in that single-mom, thank-god-there's-an-adult-to-talk-to kind of way.

As it turns out, it's a story about how her daughter has just started—you know—*pleasuring herself.*

It's a good story, and Ursula's got this irreverent way of telling it, just throwing it out there about the kid's masturbation habits. Real *not-precious.* I like it.

So apparently this turn to self-pleasuring started the same week that the kid had her first meltdown about death. She says her kid "accidentally" killed a spider trying to put it outside. I raise my eyebrow right there, because what kid kills a spider *accidentally?* Anyway, clearly the kid kinda sorta killed it on purpose, and I almost want to point this out, but she's recounting the course of events really animatedly and it's also strangely racy, and I'm rather starved for both entertainment and sex, so I don't point anything out, and in fact I'm anxiously trying to eat this pile of slippery cheesy noodle tubes in some way that isn't conspicuous, although the possibility of slurping, or dropping a tube on the floor—or making one of the zitis "poop" its tomato sauce onto my lap through the downward pressure of biting—threatens at every turn.

So the kid "accidentally" kills this spider and spends the afternoon dissolved in tears basically far beyond the point of any reassurance. Ursula tends all day to this despondent and hysterical child. Then night falls and the kid finally goes to bed limp and sodden and exhausted from sobbing. Ursula's in her bedroom, getting into the latest reality TV, when she hears this *moaning* coming from the kid's room. Low, guttural, frankly alarming sounds. She races in to check on the kid, ready to call 911, and—big surprise—the kid's fine, standing at the edge of her bed, in fact *giving it* to her shark stuffie. And, shit, when it gets to this point Ursula just—she's freestyling this story, okay, and it's getting hotter and hotter and weirder. Because every possible description of fucking a shark stuffie is coming out of this woman's mouth. *Frottaging, screwing, humping, deep-dicking,* what have you. The kid is just—she's *turning out this stuffie*. And I couldn't breathe from how hard I was laughing. And also, and inevitably, I'm also wondering: just how pent up *is* Ursula? She sure has a lot of ways of describing how *done* this shark got, and I'm considering that maybe she wants to get done too.

Actually, it's unmistakable that she wants to get done because next she's like: *Hey, you know that manuscript you said you're working on. Have you figured out yet if it's authentic?*

And I'm, like, *Well, everything from that period is some weird mishmash.* I deliberately don't get into it at length. Because I don't think she's really asking me a question. She's trying to say something, signal something to me.

You said it's really queer though—or trans, or whatever, she furthers. *And is that, like—*bites her lip—*authentic?*

See. This is what I mean about signaling. Let me just say now that if you're butch, queer, trans, etc., and you're alone in a room with someone and they ask you a question about queerness or transness or the history of queerness or transness, it's not because they want you to answer it. It's because they want you to understand that *they're* kind of queer. And they're inviting you to do something about it.

And—well—maybe I should have done something about it. I know that, technically speaking, I look like I could do someone pretty good. I'm aware that I have this sleazy but not creepy (*says I!*) demeanor. It's sort of cultivated but it's also just there— this wiry, wolfish aspect. You look at me and you just know you wouldn't have to be embarrassed by any shit you wanted to do or get done to you because I'm already giving this kind of shameless, gross vibe. And clearly Ursula already knows everything about me, since she's my pharmacist for crissake. So that's a green light right there.

(Not that that surprised me, actually. A lot of women are relieved not to have to deal with bio-cock, and to be honest, what I have going on—it—it intrigues them. It intrigues them *libidinally,* let's say. And I feel compelled to reflect here on the fact that what I have going on was outsized even before the T, so now it's just—well, I hope you don't think I'm an asshole for mentioning it. Or, you know what, *think* I'm an asshole, I don't care. You didn't spend your early sexual life trying to explain your very—hmm—*showy* junk to confused young women [or maybe you did? If so: Hi!]. Back then it threw people off. *What* is *this?* they'd ask. *Are you a hermaphrodite?* Reader: They didn't ask this with appetite.

But that's in the past. Because now that we're all grown up and everyone's seen a thing or two of the world and of bodies, it turns out there's an entire population of women who really hunger for some mythic genital sublime shit. I mean, you would be surprised how many women like getting fucked by an unclassifiable monster. [Relax: I'm reclaiming the term. I *like* it. I mean, when uttered in certain contexts out of certain mouths. Must I justify everything?] Anyway, who could deny me glorying in this turn of events just a little bit? *Didn't I pay the price for this?*)

But it's been so goddamn long since I did *anyone* that I'm just looking at the innuendos she's dropping, kind of hanging in the air between us like I'm some kind of neutered benevolent alien who's landed amongst humans and is hearing someone speak in vaguely translatable language about something called "sex."

So yeah, I ignore—or just stare uselessly at—the flirting and also, really, the story itself was the highlight of the week for me and I don't really want it to end. It doesn't make me proud to admit that this was my one and only social occasion in quite a while, and I'm drinking it in because the truth is Ursula's got me laughing for the first time in I can't remember how long—and laughing, by the way, is the thing you miss worse than sex.

At this point I've completely forgotten about pointing out to her that her kid is channeling some repressed aggression with the whole spider-murder thing. Cuz, really, I'm too busy giggling away, caught up in this story, and for just one second I find myself in the strange position of loving life. Just for one split second. Like: death-sex-repression, right? *Whaddya gonna do.* And now I'm seeing this kid's whole adult trajectory—emotions, compulsive fucking, etc. And I'm feeling very together in that moment with my hot neighbor, together with her randy little kid and the sex shark. Like we're all just these . . . *beings* who let desire fill us and pilot us like bloated corpses through our lives.

But in a way it's beautiful. And I kind of want to tell her this. To say something that encapsulates our beautiful entrapment-by-desire. Without being all theoretical and shmucky. I just want to convey our togetherness in this predicament. It doesn't need to be smart. But it does need to be hot.

Unusually, however, nothing's coming to me.

Worse still, I change the topic.

To the worst topic possible at this moment. Honestly, an exegesis on Roland Barthes would have been better than this.

I start talking about being put on unpaid leave.

Why—*god why*—did I do this. I guess I was thinking maybe we were going to fuck, and if we were going to fuck, I suppose I wanted to be up front about everything.

But this was—*oof.*

Just to recap, she's all, like, *But is it authentic* (biting her lip, etc.)—leaving a per-fectly good opening for me to amplify the flirting—and then, in some impossible feat of ham-handedness, I go, *Oh hey, did I tell you that I got put on unpaid leave at work?*

WHY!!! Why did I do this?

And it doesn't stop there. I keep going. *Extrapolating* the situation.

It's not like I was laid off, I clarify. *More like aside. Laid aside.*

It's not a good joke, but Ursula laughs anyway. She's trying to keep the momentum going, trying to build me back up, I can see, because now she's asking me about whether I can get a grant, work on the manuscript and get paid for it while I'm on leave.

Maybe something will come through, she says.

Which launches me into a hurricane of self-pity. I tell her about all the times I've applied and gotten nothing. How my colleagues are forever being, like, *All the hu-manities funding has dried up,* on their way out the door to their latest grant-funded trip to Italy. I've given up on applying. I never get anything anyway.

I'm sure something will work out, she says, with sort of a dropping-off tiredness in her voice.

It was clear that was the end of the evening. I came home and jerked off.

. . .

Jack was forc'd through the doorway and down the narrow Stairwell.

"The Dungeon!" the centinel said with obvious excitement when they reached the bottom of the stairs. He push'd Jack down the hall, past cells full of glum inmates.

"Debt-skippers, stingers, area sneaks*, bit-fakers†, blue pigeon-flyers‡, and Body-snatchers§," listed the centinel, proud of the quantity and variety of the Condemned. They reached the end of the hall and turned into a still-narrower, mold-lined stone passage-way to a row of near pitch-black cells—these were empty but for grimy pallets.

He led Jack through the gate of the furthest cell—this one had a chair in it, facing out towards the hallway, as well as a chamber pot—and unlock'd Jack's wrists from the handcuffs. Without warn-ing, he ripped Jack's cloak off, then roughly undid the Button to his trousers and pull'd them down. *How far will this Stripping go?* Jack's legs quivered. He felt himself release a bit of Urine down his thigh.

"Piss!" The centinel jumped back as Jack sank down into the chair with fright.

Tho' at least—faced with the stream of urine—the centinel had halted Jack's undressing. Now he mov'd around to the back of the chair and, holding Jack's wrists fast in one palm, he resecured the handcuffs, then clicked the Padlock through the Chain and wrapp'd the Chain around the chair leg.

And left, taking Jack's cloak and trousers with him.

The Piss grew colder against Jack's thighs.

The sepulchral hallway was choked with dusk. Jack made out a

---

* Robbers of the lower apartments of private houses
† Money-coiners
‡ Lead-metal thieves
§ Corpse-stealers

row of tarnished steel Hooks for keys and a number of scuttering mice and rats. Wind beat across the barred windows at the upper edge of the cell Wall, pouring a cold stream of Gloam into the interior.

He was now wearing only his understocking, thin smish, and Boots. His toes, poking through the sodden brown-topped Marlboroughs, pinkened in the bitter Air. His thighs vibrated with some combination of cold and fear.

As Jack's eyes adjust'd to the Dark he became aware that there was someone in the hold. Not the centinel. Someone else, just beyond the bars of the cell, facing Jack.

Either the man had been there the entire time, or he had enter'd soundlessly. He was sneering. His teeth shone silver-white in the Gloom.

"Nippy."

The man drew closer—handcuffs clanging in his fist—materializing from the patch of shadow. He wore a heavy velvet cloak with leather Boots laced high. A triangle hat was tipped low over a bald skull. He rested a walking stick with a silver Knob against the bars and lit a sulfur stick, holding it apparitionally under his chin. In the quivering light, his eyes shone emerald green. He turned the rose-gold pocketwatch in his hand. Producing a key from his pocket with the other, he clank'd the lock open. Stepped through.

A long pause. The slap of the watch rotating in his large palm.

"In London, commodities transit through many owners. The flow of commerce is a thing of beauty that can have no restriction by law or custom, else it sickens and dies."

Theatrical pause.

"I, Jonathan Wild—otherwise known as the Night Magistrate, Shoulder-Clapper, Arch-Pig, Grunter-Scout, Carrion-Hunter of souls and men—am a *physician* of the economy. I ensure that things"—he glanced down, considered the watch, brought it closer to his face, murmured to it as if it were an infant in his arms—"circulate.

"Now, sometimes elements gum up the wheel of Commerce. Maybe elements that didn't mean to gum it up. But nevertheless they do. And when you gum things up"—he regarded Jack—"there are Consequences. In the spirit of those Consequences, I'm here to let you know that we expect sentencing in the next day. Two at the most."

Jack suck'd his teeth.

"As you must know, property crimes warrant a *capital* punishment."

In fact, Jack *did not* exactly know that.

The weakening sparks of the sulfur stick made it difficult to make out anything beyond a short radius, tho' Jack discern'd that Wild had bent and picked up the chamber pot.

Set it down. Pushed it close to Jack.

"Fill this when you're ready." He waved at Jack's wet stockings. "'Stead of wetting yerself like an infant."

Jack emitted a blur of sound.

"I'm awaiting the arrival," said Wild, sounding aggravated, "of the prison Doctor.* A new concept here but one that is sure to raise the profile of Newgate as the city's preeminent gaol. He is, as usual, late, so I'm conducting his Responsibilities myself."

What do chamber pots—or prisons for that matter—have to do with doctoring? This question—circling Jack's brain—was immaterial in any case because, lacking an arborvitae, Jack would be quite unable to hit the target even if he did consent to giving Wild his Effluvium.

For a watch fob—he inwardly sobb'd, guts burning—*I'm to be so-called* doctored *and then murdered for a watch fob.*

· · ·

---

* Prison Quackery (aka "Correctional Medicine") did not officially begin until the prison reform movement of the later nineteenth century. So says Michel Foucault, in any case. What we have here is thus potentially a fucking miraculous find. A quite unique early document of the biopolitical management/control of populations? If truly authentic, this would set the agenda for Discipline-and-Punish-Studies™ ever after.

Wild placed the sulfur stick on the ground near Jack's feet, where it spat hot Sparks onto his ankles.

"Now, Jack, we're coming up on the hour at which visitors have a peek at the inmates. For a fee, we'll display a mad rogue, cowering in his own feces, a particularly lovely doxy . . . And then, of course, you—"

Quite the profiteer, this chit† in his rum duds.‡

"—a scrawny failed watch-nabber. More a joke than a prized Exhibit—but there we have it. Now, Mr. Sheppard"—Wild peered dramatically—"I can see you're wondering, *How can this mistake be turned to my account?*"

That was not what Jack was thinking.

Because in the spluttering light, he'd twist'd his foot against the floor and spied it. A Nail that had worked itself partway out of his well-worn Boot sole. Enough, perhaps, to—

He rolled his foot back down, hiding the nail's Silhouette from Wild's view.

"Yes, I can see it in your eyes. You're of a generation of abandoned Urchins. Abandoned by your parishes, your parents, by God and Opportunity itself. But I am here to collect all ye Abandoned and give you new life. A new family, too—a confederacy of colleagues—"

Colleagues? Jack thought.

"These *colleagues,*" Wild continued, "are amongst the best and most skillful thieves in London. And our mission is to, shall we say, *doctor and systematize* crime in this town. You're just a chaotic young Lamb, but I believe you can be shap'd— All you've got to do is join in with me— I assure you what I have in mind is far beyond the petty thievery with which you're currently dallying. I'll arrange for your immediate liberation. You'll simply have to come with me, and begin work this very evening."

Jack didn't know terribly many things, but owing to Bess he

---

† Cad
‡ Fancy clothing

knew this: Wild's offer was a sentence of death in terms surer and more profitable to Wild than even his current situation. He would be match'd with a nefarious Turncoat to conduct a job that he'd then himself be fingered for, turn'd back in to the magistrate, and his death sentence expedited.

"I'd appreciate some time to consider your Proposition," Jack said, affecting the language he'd heard many times in the workshop as Kneebone haggled with nail-makers, wood-hewers and other suppliers.

"*Consider it?!*" Wild sneer'd, incredulous. "Yes, do *consider* it. And while you're pondering, there's a group of people who are looking forward to seeing you."*

A din down the hallway. Wild welcom'd it, nuts upon himself† as he opened his arms to the bourgeoisie. "Welcome, welcome! Come gaze upon the deranged and the depraved."

Dressed in brocades and silks, full of leisure and ill will, they emerged from the stairwells, flowing past Jack with a cruel, low-toned Hiss. Wealthy ladies who enjoy'd to spend afternoons gawking at rabble.

"Oh my," call'd the first down the line, adjusting her impossibly inflated citadel of a wig. "You're nothing but a shrimpy thing!"

The retinue crack'd into bleats of laughter, browsing past Sheppard, gaping at him bound in the wolf-gray gloom of his cell, facing death and the magistrate.

A brusque dame clopp'd past on thick heels, whispering, "You're a dead Dog," through the bars. Then toss'd something towards him. A large muslin shawl. "Cover yourself," she hissed.

He hush'd the sound of the constant footfall. The nasty whis-

---

* The entire prison is an enterprise. It is Wild's special, awful "genius" to have recognized this before almost anyone else in British history.
† In love with himself

pers. Did his Thames-dropping trick, imagining Water washing over his head.

And then he heard it. Voices. Something like what he'd heard at the watch shop. Something intimate and close.

He opened his eyes. The awful gentry strolled past, laughing. Closed them again.

First the Red Chapel-over-chimney; there I felt freer and close to God.

Passageway outside was dark, but empty. Breath was there—away from guards and gawkers.

The salt air of the river. Emancipated air.

Jack had heard tell of coves going berserk in gaol. Clearly he was becoming mad as well. But he worried this in a far-off way, for he was very tired, and the murmuring had begun to lull him. He let the voices guide him far away from the clacking gentry, to Sleep.

The next morning, an attendant shoved Papers under the bars. A cloud of Filth fluff'd from the floor. "Death warrant," he said blankly, as if he were dropping a portion of eggs at the back door of an Inn. "You'll hang by Friday. I'll send the Ordinary for your confessions."

"I'll not give them a thing to sell after hanging me," Jack spat. "My tales are for rogues only."‡

---

‡ On the topic of profiteering fuckwads: Today I received a very strange email. The subject line read FUNDING OPPORTUNITY. It came from "P-Quad, Inc."

Yeah, I knew who they were. Canny motherfuckers. See, P-Quad isn't really a publishing company. It would like to think it's a publishing company, but really it's a much-reviled churner-outer of educational testing materials. I know this because last year the administration tried to ram through a similar company as the sole private supplier of standardized tests to the University. Tests that are designed, actually, *to be failed,* in order to legitimate the firing of unionized faculty and indeed decimate the entire faculty union *tout court*. Not to mention the number it did on the students, having to take these tests in the first place.

The faculty used to call urgent meetings to hear themselves loudly complain about private testing, and then not do anything about it. Faculty like to imagine that being upset counts as political activism. Not like I was much better. I went to one meeting just to see if there was anyone cute there. As usual, there wasn't.

Anyway, suffice it to say I knew who P-Quad was.

But how did they know who *I* was?

They had me pegged so perfectly.

Can you imagine: they quoted Derrida in their email to me?

Dear Dr. Voth,

We have heard of your need for research funding for your work with a certain recently discovered manuscript. We have a vested interest in supporting archival work. Indeed, we are establishing an Archival Text Authentication Division that models itself on Derrida's view that "Archival meaning is also and in advance co-determined by the structure that archives."

Our Authentication Division, as just such a structure-in-formation, is prepared to pay you handsomely to work on a freelance basis to establish the meaning of the archive which you've come upon.

I was quite sure that they and I did not have the same understanding of "the structure that archives." I mean, Reader, the violence they did to Derrida in this email was truly unconscionable.

I responded.

Dear P-Quad,

As I am sure you are aware, what Derrida means is that the archive is less a record of what has been said, and more an ongoing problem of what cannot be.

What is forgotten, repressed, disallowed.

The stakes of this become clearer, in fact, through the lens of decolonial theories of the archive. Following Walter Mignolo (The Darker Side of Western Modernity: Global Futures, Decolonial Options), *the "meaning" of the archive is clearly less important than that of the archive's inevitable "epistemic disobedience."*

Not that a private testing corporation would understand.

So let me put this plainly:

I decline your offer.

The email rattled me. I paced my kitchen gnawing the chocolate off the contents of an entire bag of chocolate peanut butter cups and worrying—How did they know about this manuscript if it had never been catalogued by the library? How did they know I had it? Was I being watched?—until I reread the email enough times to realize that they had never mentioned *what* the manuscript actually was. So okay, I concluded, this was likely the kind of spam email that the book-buyback companies sent around. That fake personal "Professor, are you on campus and could use some extra cash?" kind of thing.

13.

WORKING OVER HIS IRONS IN THE DUSKY CELL, DARK CURLS PLASTER'D across his forehead, and inky circles ringing his eyes—Jack's lips strained as he twist'd his feet against the iron chain between his legs.

The voices came back to him.

Red Chapel. Dark passageway. Salt air. Emancipation.

They were, he thought—he hoped—

He worked the nail most of the way from his boot by lever'ng the side against the ground—pressing down hard 'til his ankles bulged and ached. Thence to pressing one handcuff against the nail tip, placing it gingerly into the Slit—holding his breath—feeling for the Voids where the key was meant to catch. On a *click,* Jack wiggled the cuff against his foot until the catch popp'd. Did the same with the other wristcuff until both were sprung free, releasing a layer of fine red Rust.

Crossing the room to the Chimney—Red-chapel-over-chimney— Jack wedg'd himself into the sooty Enclosure and peered up. The egress had been filled with brick. He set to work at the mortar-cracks. Fat gray grubs fell by the squirming dozens, and within moments he had produced a pile of bricks and a Hole not much wider than his shoulders.

Tho' some former craftsman had installed an iron bar across the vault in the event that an inmate should attempt an Exit, Jack thrust the Bootnail between the bar and its casings, loosening it with a shower of dust.

He stood, brushing grubs and soot from his thighs. Hoisted himself into the chimney and up into the dark.

At the floor above, the chimney opened into a Hearth cluttered with Charcoal and wood chips. The room had an unused look, tho' Jack recalled a rumor that the Spitalfields tailors had been once hous'd here for eight days, several of them hanged for the crime of "confederating" for better wages and hours.

There was neither Handle nor Knob on the inside of the far door, adjacent to a window looking over Holborn Street. Flashes of yellow Light from the sputtering oil lamps outside the chapel window threw a menacing air.

With his shoulder press'd hard, Jack tested the door—found it latched tight from the opposite side—and began to break away part of the wall around the hinges. Still wielding the nail from his boot, he scrap'd, all the while fearful of being heard by the wardens, or even the debtors in the common hold directly below, should they raise an alarm.

The wall was thick, and noise considerable—a battery of scraping from the Nail, and plaster rain'd down. Just as Jack's spirits began to fail him, he found he had produc'd a small hole in the wall. He poked the nail through to dislodge the bolt fastened on the other side of the door, slid, then push'd the door open with a small strangled Cry from the hinges.

Now he came to a passageway in full darkness—*Passageway outside is dark, but empty. Breath is there—away from guards and gawkers—* that concluded in a stout door guarded by Bolts, Locks, and Bars. The chimes at St. Sepulchre's rang eight o'clock. Time was short. He attack'd first the nut at the hinge. Tried to discern how much rust was clogging it—tho' it was hard to tell—so, patting up the side of the door 'til he reached its hinge-knob, he caressed its dome, then smelled his fingertips to assess the quantity of tang. *A fair bit.* He attempt'd to dislodge the Nut upwards through the rusted hinge, flapping his elbows like bellows—to gain nut-loosening momentum—alas, Nothing.

In something of a panic, he attack'd the fillet of the door—the ring encircling the nut—straight on with the nail. It cleav'd with a soft silvery Mutter.

Having now gotten through the door and to the next, Jack found it locked from the inside. This he could simply unlatch, and lo, he was on the Roof of Newgate, looking over the street. The lights still lit, people milling in shops. It was a simple jump down the front-Face of the prison wall to the largest overhanging Gargoyle. He could land full on its back, then dangle off the Snout—an eight-foot drop to street level.

But, with the quantity of street traffic, he was sure to raise quite an Alarm.

At this side of the prison wall, the nearest adjoining roof was a private Residence. He might escape that Rooftop way—unseen to the Hagglers and strollers—but this was a much more considerable seven-yard Jump. A bone-breaking, uncertain leap.

A terrible thought occur'd to him— He had to go back—to retrieve the long muslin shawl from the Condemned Hold.

When Jack return'd to his cell, he found the shawl was moved—in fact, dragged off to the puddle of muck just outside his cell but quite beyond reach—and a rat chewing happily at it.

The chimes struck. Shortly the Newgate Ordinary would be by to strive to take his confession once more. He'd broken his cuffs —they were lying scattered across the floor. Bricks everywhere and nowhere to hide them. He would be hanged immediately.

Jack lung'd against the bars, reaching for the shawl. His face ached against the Iron. He tsk'ed desperately at the rat, calling to it like a frisky Pup.

He was roundly ignored. The rat continued chewing, its tail flicking contentedly in the dank shallow water.

There was only one way about it— He would have to use his only item of clothing—his stockings—to climb down.

He would be dangling stockingless above the streets of London.

Back through the dark passageway, the Red Chapel, and then the sooty chimney, returning the same way through the passageway once more 'til, with his Heart thrumming, he burst out the door, sprinting back across the roof like a Housecat broken from its confinement. The salt air of the docks stung his face—*can smell the salt air of the river. Emancipated air.*

The prospect of being caught escaping in *dishabille* press'd upon him. *They'll paint me in the papers. Bess will see it.*

He had a flicker of hesitation—perhaps he ought to return to his cell. Let them kill him in the morning for his escape attempt— Let them kill him before all of the Town—at least let them kill him with his breeches on.

But then— Bess, this thought of Bess, the Horizon of Bess and he-knew-not-what—spurr'd him on. Jack removed his Stockings and tremblingly fixed one end to the wall with the indispensable Nail, and let it fall. There was no turning back.

Jack's mind went blank—he went to his Thames place—and then, half-Naked, clinging to his breeches-rope, he fell for a stomach-jittering length of time—and landed square onto the neighboring house.

His legs held, but just barely. Quaking, he looked about—the garret door was open—he slipped inside and down a stairway.

A woman within gave a cry.

Jack froze—

"What noise is that, John?"

"'Tis nothing but the cat, wife," a man shush'd.

—and unfroze. Descended the stairs to a dressing room where he spy'd a most handsome set of breeches, waistcoat, and topcoat.

Jack paus'd briefly to smile at the quantity of coin in the breeches-pocket— Thence quickly down the next narrow stairway, and Jack was strutting out the door looking quite the proper gentleman.

Jack passed by St. Sepulchre's, tipping his hat. Down Snow Hill, Holborn, the Watch-House by Holborn Hill Bars, then Grey's Inn Lane into the Fields outside the city walls. He achieved a pasture where cows were kept, some of them lying in the wet Night grass. He stretched out amongst their soft snuffles and snapping tails. He dreamt of his Confessions—the ones he would not give to the Newgate Ordinary. The book of his confessions was illustrated in silver filigree. He was leafing through this book of his life, and it was beautiful. There was him and Bess in a forest of pale, silvery leaves. They were making love. He was free and easy, his heart open, unguarded.

In the morning, Jack was awoken by a dull gray rain. The cows had abandon'd the Field for the stables. Not even a field mouse skittered in the cold Dirt and grasses.

Jack struggl'd to his feet, gave his coat strategic tears—to feign a beggar's cloak—tied a kerchief around his head for Disguise, and staggered towards the City thinking of a warm cider and breakfast Steak.

The Olde Eare Inn occupy'd a cellar below the street, and Jack entered to a cloud of warm, thick breath. The room was pack'd with folks; none looked up. He took the only free spot, at a small round table at the edge of the fray, underneath a begrim'd pane of glass looking out at a variety of passing shoes.

The room was abuzz. With news of *him*.

Sheppard broke the lower hold at Newgate—Sheppard—Gaol-breaker General—Son of Eternal Night—Uncatchable Sheppard—Sheppard showed the wardens the face of their hubris—Sheppard made a mockery of the gates and the bars and even the walls—Sheppard'll come liberate us all—free all the Newgate birds—a rogue greater than Wild—more canny than the architects of confinement—geniuser than all the magistrates in London.

They were at ev'ry table discoursing about him, unaware that they were in the presence of this same *Gaolbreaker General*.

Jack grinn'd into his roast meat. Conversation rose all around—white-gray Light illum'd the thick window Glaze. Steam rose from the fry pans fogging the Hearth.

A woman at a neighboring table, making her way through a plate of peas and veal, shouted, "I pray a curse might befall anyone who betrays *Sheppard!*"

The innkeep, passing by with a plate of sugared crackers, retorted, "Overheard the pawnbrokers in Drury Lane conspiring to put together a Watch to catch the thief and claim a reward."

Fear gripp'd Jack's throat.

As the rabble commenced a song in his honor—*Rawhead and Bloody Bones! Now is come London's true rogue!*—he slipp'd out the door.

14.

BESS HELD JACK CLOSE IN BED, EXAMINING THE SCRAPES AND BRUISES from his excarceration.* Jack squint'd morning Sun out of his eyes.

"You're all right," Bess said, patting at his temples with a damp cloth. "You're all right now."

Somehow, he *was* all right—was beginning to be more than all right. A door had closed between him and Kneebone and all the Mousehole of his life and all his timid rules-following. The door had shut fast.

While he was inhaling the warmth off the mug of hot water Bess had given him, she ask'd, "What part of Newgate?"

"Underground."

"Under the Keeper's Chamber?"

Nodded.

Bess put down the cloth. "You were in the condemned hold. No one's ever broken out from there—ever made it out alive."

"*I'm* alive, though," he said, after some quiet. "*I* broke out." Half-smiling, half-shuddering with retrospective Terror.

There are not terribly many things to do in the face of such specters of *What-might-have-been*.

---

* Who is this capable of letting a woman see him when he's broken?

Clearly this is just my problem. I oughtn't universalize it.

So, just me then. Me, the fucking fetishist of my own self-sufficiency.

Yes, I'm stewing.

NB: This stewing is relevant, as I consider the jealousy (nay, *misery*) the text provokes a register of its "authenticity."

In addition to which, Bess was wearing a dark gold Negligee.

Her eyes were bright and dark. She and Jack look'd at each other for some Time. He tried not to become too absorb'd in watching her breasts breathe against the silk— He leaned forward— kissed her. A long one. A not-so-nice one.

Reach'd down—coaxed her legs open—her upper thighs were wet—inhal'd the scent rising— Her hands were in his hair, pulling him down to her. The word "love" presented itself to him, unbidden.

He wrapped his arm around her waist, drawing her to his lap. She took a cozy place across him, in his arms, and from here he was able to drop the Straps of her nightgown down her shoulders—and let his head fall to her breasts.

There he spent an incalculable quantity of time in joy, hunger, lostness.*

The heat of her in his lap caused wave after wave of tumult to crash against Jack's breeches.†

He kiss'd her breasts—her mouth—her Neck—petted between her legs, where she puls'd against his Fingertips.

Periodic'lly he dropped his face to her Armpits—nose-deep—

---

* Of course this is what you get for allowing a woman to see you in your vulnerability. She'll show you hers ten times over. Note to self: could you *please* fucking try to remember that.

† Remarkable that Jack's genitalia are not described in detail. Unlike almost any other sexological or protosexological document from the period (and after), which exfoliate layer after layer of prurient fantasies about the sex organs (e.g., George Arnaud de Ronsil, *A Dissertation on Hermaphrodites* [1750], or, really, just about any colonial "first contact" narrative—as, for example, John Marten, *A Treatise on Venereal Disease* [1711], which is less about treating venereal disease and quite a lot of speculation about genitalia in Guinea. Or the odious Johannus Riolanus's fascination with hermaphrodites, etc.: "[t]he Clitoris grows inordinately long, and counterfeits a penis; it is called a Tail with which women abuse one another" [*A Sure Guide: or, the Best and Nearest Way to Physick and Chyrurgery*, 1651]).

"Best and Nearest Way" my ass.

Look, I'm not saying that I haven't lovingly "abused" a woman or two with my own "tail." But to be compelled to pull it out and wave it around for some so-called scientist . . . ?

sucking hard as if air—*real air*—only lived in the Nooks of her body. He held, toyed with, drenched his fingers in her Quim. His love for her Quim was encyclopedic. How she was ashamed and thrilled at once to show him— How it clenched around him, throbb'd and breath'd— How she gasped and stared at him when he filled her full with his hand, squeezing at her little Sponge inside.

But he loved the Scent, the taste most of all. Sweet marshmallow and warm breath; saltwater threaded with Violet. All these bouquets—and more—and more. He toyed with her between her thighs until she shiver'd magnificently in his arms.

Then Jack reach'd for the handkerchief he'd pinched from the Kneebones. The one he kept in his pocket.

He took it to her and slowly dried her. Lovingly. Quite lovingly, in fact, touching her cheek intermittently, bending down to kiss her lips while he massaged the handkerchief just at the softest place where her upperest Thigh plumped out, then tunneled into the hot tang of groin.

When she was lying limp and easeful in his arms—smiling up at him—"You won't tell the other bats 'bout this, will you?"

"'Bout what?" Bess teas'd.

Jack twist'd and perspired, his mouth searched for Words of tenderness unknown to him.

"'Bout how I'm touching you."

"How are you touching me?"

"Oh, Bess . . ." Frustrated, his fingers gripped tighter the Rag. He couldn't find a term to capture the way her madge called out to him—how he knew how to pet it to make it flutter under his fingers.

"I don't give language to things that are beyond it." Her forehead crunched in concentration. "Things that aren't a matter of free will. I mean, in that Spinoza-sense."

This occasion'd silence.

"D'you know Spinoza?"

He shook his head. Was "Spinoza" a person?

"Dutch philosopher. And lens-grinder. Liked to watch Spiders catch flies in the brown corners of his ivy-riddled cottage. Was the only good thing to ever come out of Amsterdam."

It was Amsterdam, Bess said, that had taught the world *profiteering*. Had sent its surveyors to drain England's fens, to starve the common folk.

"The Dutch've innovat'd every technique of efficient Cruelties," she said. "And *Spinoza*—because he watched it happen—knew something about the World we're now coming to inhabit."

He was still stroking her hair in his lap. It was terrible, what she was saying—but, then—something was also so perfect: *touching and talking at the same time*. One or two Doors inside him were peeking open.

"London will be just like Amsterdam soon—a place of only merchants and commerce. Still, some things are beyond our will—those things that connect us—and that's where we can be free."*

"Isn't free will . . . *freer*?"

"It's better to know we're connected to a vast universe of living things."

When Bess said it, Jack could feel the air stir around his Body. *We're connected,* he thought. *Connected.*

Then, without further ado, Bess's hand was unlacing his Trousers.

Jack push'd her hand away.

"I want to make you feel good." She pulled at the Lacing on his breeches. *"Connected."*

---

* "Spinoza's thought is monstrous," writes Antonio Negri from Rebibbia prison.

What Negri meant was that Spinoza's thought did not exist separately from the monstrous violence of Dutch capitalism. Spinoza-the-lens-grinder peered at the world through a ferocious prism. He saw firsthand "the savage adventure of accumulation"—capitalism's *desire*.

Capitalism desires, said Spinoza, to persist in the cruelness of its being. This desire is neither rational nor bound by law. It cannot be lawyered away or reasoned out of existence. And thus only the desire of the multitude to persist in its being can oppose the desire of capitalism to persist in its horrible own (cf. Antonio Negri, *The Savage Anomaly: The Power of Spinoza's Metaphysics and Politics,* University of Minnesota Press, 1999).

"I *do*." He inched backwards on the bed.

Bess sat up. Brought her knees against her chest. "You're being Odd and stubborn."

Jack didn't want to be Odd and stubborn. He imagin'd other coves—easy, unstubborn coves, losing themselves joyously with her. Not having this conversation.

He lay down, pulling her next to him. *Wasn't it enough how I touched her?*

She laid her head on his smish. He felt her furrowed Brow against his chin. With time, it relaxed and she slid into Slumber. They slept.

Sometime in the night she woke with a Terror.

"Popham's Eau!" she called out, her voice thick with dreaming.

Jack sooth'd her back to sleep. He knew enough of Terrors—and of Secrets—to know not to ask what Popham's Eau was.

15.

IT ISN'T THAT JACK IS SO SPECTACULARLY GOOD, BESS THOUGHT WHILE she dressed for the market.

Jack was still deep in sleep, the edge of his lip curled up, with a crooked tooth peeking through. Bess rustled into clothes, took a Piss. He did not stir.

Though it's charmingly obvious he thinks *he's spectacularly good.* It was in the messy, pleased smile he flashed at her afterwards.

And, she suppos'd, he *was* good, but not in a way that would be impossible to achieve with someone—really, anyone—else.

It was something else. Something to do with his Body's relationship to Retrospection. Or the Lack thereof.

When other coves gave themselves over—at that moment of happy release and Splendor—they were transformed, however briefly, into Children. This phenomenon, Bess thought, was consistent across men. One moment, she was being embraced by a fullgrown man; in the next, a hairy young boy was struggling away inside her, spiraling backwards before her eyes into some gleeful Youth. Some became again the Babes they were when their mums washed their nethers. When they giggled in loving arms with perfect Openness.

How boring, thought Bess, swirling her cloak onto her shoulders, nodding goodbye to Jack's glinting Tooth, and clicking out the door.

How infantile, how easily given to abandon, how secure and pleased with themselves are these sorts of men. Such men have no idea that in that flash of joy they felt—in that flash of what they imagined was so-called *union*—Bess saw them clearly for the nurslings they were. For in that flash, men were lost in a Carnival of the free and simple childishness that lived inside their sugar sticks*; lost to their partner; lost to Togetherness. And while Bess knew other doxies who reveled in producing this spinning backwards in time, who puff'd with power at the moment of male descent into babyhood and happy babbling, Bess found it lonesome.

Throughout her erranding-walk—the mist of dirty dove-feathers, the inescapable Soot, the shouts of cherry-vendors—she mused on this.

Jack, alone amongst the coves she'd ever been with, showed no sign of childishness when he felt pleasure. Not even the slightest hint of infantile Joy.

When he toyed with her and she squirmed in his arms, Jack groaned with pleasure. But it was the groan of an adult. And this— what she could only think of as his relentless and slightly irking masculine Composure; his body's foreclosed relationship to time, to traveling backwards, to becoming a child again in pleasure— impelled her to want something from him. Some cracking-open. *Something*.

Did it exhaust him, this untouchable adulthood? This refusal to lose himself? While the other coves were only too eager to undo themselves for her, to throw themselves back upon the arms of the past and become the boys who haunted their own arborvitae, Jack was the only cove she'd wish to see undone in just this way. Precisely because he was the only cove who refus'd to let himself be so undone.

---

* Penises

16.

Nightfall and Jack was wandering the Shore, recalling the occasions Kneebone had warned him against gleaning. *There's provisions 'gainst that, you know,* he'd said more than once, nodding at vagrants picking garbage from the Sewers and at Thames-side. *Property of the Municipality, that is.**

The black water crawl'd with weeds and dusk-Beetles plinking against the riverskin. Lost in remembrances, he stumbled over a reclining Form in the dirt.

A man sprawled like a toppled statuary. The figure jolted and stirred, striking at the air in front of him. Jack skipp'd to the side, but half-heartedly. Part of him wanted to be pummeled. 'Twould replace the ache of his own "odd stubbornness" with something else, at least. The man grabb'd his ankle, tripping him to the ground.

"You a constable?" He wiped his face with a large palm. Jack realized with a start that it was the speckle-bearded man from

---

* On the Propertization of Offal:

Britain declined to cover its shit until well into the nineteenth century. Canals of garbage, animal carcasses, feces, rotten vegetables, etc., ran in open channels down the streets. You might think the upside of this was that, in a pinch, you could probably glean some sustenance from the sewer. But even by 1670 the sewers and their surround were quite regulated.

Viz., the 1670 Sewer and Paving Act: "The said Mayor Alderman . . . shall . . . have power and authority in order and direct the markeing of any new Vaults Draines and Sewers, or to cut into any Draine or Sewer already made, and for the altering enlargeing amending cleansing and scowring or any old Vaults, Sinks or Common Sewers."

In short, the management of capitalism begins with the management of its waste.

Lamb's Conduit alley. The one who had tried to pawn off nicked goods on him.

"Are you in jest?"

The man barreled over and pinned Jack facedown in the wet shoresilt.

"Why're you out here? Looking for some buggery?"

"I—" Jack panicked.

"Answer in cant, or I'll know you're a constable."

"I *do* cant," Jack rushed.

"Then answer that way."

"You're a molly," Jack said stupidly, his mouth crammed with dirt.

"And you're not?"—small, gruff laugh. "We're on the Thames-shore at dusk, after all."

Fair point. But how to explain that he was not even a—

"I'm not looking for any catting. I'm jus' strolling."

"Jus' strolling!" A puff of laughter. "Where d'you live? Answer in cant or I'll snap yer neck."

"Under the rose†."

"What game d'you go on‡?"

He searched. "I'm music§." He repeated this, shouting over his shoulder, "I'm music."

"Not without a game you're not."

The man pressed down harder. The silt smelled of sewage and Oysters gone to rot.

"I'm Jack Sheppard."

The man lifted slightly, and Jack sat up—rearranged himself opposite—breathing hard. Silt shadowed his cheeks with the false outline of a beard.

"Sheppard that just broke out of Newgate?" Scowling. Head cocked.

---

† Wherever I can get.
‡ What species of thieving do you specialize in?
§ A friend

"No gaol can hold me."

"A bit scrawny for Sheppard." The man squinted. "From what I've heard."

Jack's heart skipped. "I'm not."

"Not Sheppard?"

"Not scrawny." Jack chewed his lip. "Not *overly*."

"Sheppard"—the man's voice gentled—"they say, is come to claim his crown as the Gaolbreaker General of all London." The man was studying Jack's hands. Regarded him up and down slowly. "But I hadn't realized Sheppard"—brushed the dirt off Jack's cheeks, ran his hand over the smooth skin—"was kin."

Jack managed not to flinch.

"If you want to learn knapping I could use a nimble pall*." The man removed his hand.

"You work for Wild?"

"Never."

So there was at least one other unowned rogue.

It was only just beginning to dawn—a rouge Laceration at the horizon.

"Nor I," said Jack.

The man grinned, and the beard covering his jaw, cheeks and neck flex'd like some underwater body rippling an ocean's skin.

"Blueskin Blake," he said. Paused. "Well, that's what they call me in the Newgate Register. I'm Aurelius Blake by birth—descendent of the Aurelian Moors at Abavalla. *Aurie* to rogues."†

---

* Partner in crime

† In none of the records is "Blueskin Blake" ever noted as Afro-Roman. Though I suppose this is entirely likely (for more on which, see David Olusoga, *Black and British: A Forgotten History,* Pan Macmillan, 2016). Furthermore, I believe that *The Complete Newgate Calendar* (aka *Malefactor's Bloody Register,* aka the Ordinary's Reports) suggests, in fact, that Blake may have once been Wild's underling. I'd like to double-check any of these so-called facts, but the University has cut off my access to the online library system. Some fuck-you from Dean of Surveillance Andrews, no doubt. Goes with the unpaid leave.

Let me bookmark this for later. For now I am left to suppose that either the author

. . .

Now Jack and Aurie were catching their breaths against a brightly painted wooden parapet on a roof in Covent Garden. Purple rain clouds blanketed the sky, delaying full Daybreak. The market stalls were empty down below. They had time for the quickest jilt.

Jack bent over the parapet. Lilllihammer's Toy Shop.

"This's a good one to jump," 'splained Aurie. "Crammed with bebobs, but centinels'll overlook toy shops for more profitable Endeavors. It's a good mark—opens late—the children don't tumble in 'til their mums have lounged sufficiently and been dressed for London paradings. Rich little sprats. Their shop deserves to be— *Hey!*"

Jack was swinging off the splintered candy-colored boards and dropping into the Alley alongside the shop. A thud and Aurie landed beside him.

"—robbed," Aurie finished.

Jack was studying the windows.

There was a small Glaze set into the birch with one of the newer Sash-types that had become increasingly popular around town. With older wrought-iron casements, the wood surround would buckle, leaving gaps, easy to pry open. But the newer sashes were set flush with the window box and fastened with thick glazing bars. Unskilled persons would have trouble with these, and resort to kicking in the glazes, which made a most noisy crashing Sound.

Aurie had already balled his fist, ready to break the glaze.

"No." Jack had produc'd Kneebone's file, and in moments the heavy glaze was aching free of the sash with a small but audible Creak.

Setting the glaze against the inner wall, Jack slipp'd through, and Aurie followed. The toy shop was suspended in the deep dark of After-Hours.

---

of this text had personal reason to cloud the truth, or else the author has more knowledge of Blake than the Newgate Ordinary did.

And then the quiet broke. Sound flooded from every corner. Something of the chatter at the watch-maker's—or the Newgate-voices—but this was a still more unleash'd version. A tripling, qua-drupling of sound. Vivid and desperate.

Jack jumped, then spun, trying to fix on the source. He raced along the walls, grabbing at bebobs, sending them scattering.

"Ordinarily we try to be a bit more deliberate in our choos-ing . . ." Aurie muttered, frowning.

But Jack could see where it came from now.

The sounds came from *things.*

A blond-haired doll in the window wailed. A stack of Chessboards emitted muffled groans. A roar emanated from clusters of marbles. All these objects shriek'd out to Jack, begging for something. Beg-ging for release.

Aurie was inspecting baubles, peering carefully at the shelves before selecting an item and placing it into a sack. He seemed un-affected by the Chaos.

Unless.

"Do you not hear all that?" Jack tapped at Aurie's shoulder.

"I hear you pawing at the shelves like a lunatic."

"You don't hear the . . . other sounds?"

Aurie shot him a look. "I hear you wasting precious moments overwrought about phantoms," he grumbled. "We're exiting this shop extremely shortly, so unless you mean to do so empty-handed, I suggest you choose your items now or not at all."

Jack gazed back at the shelves. The Mayhem was unrelenting, but it was resolv'ng into a kind of meaning. It wasn't just sound—it was desire.

Iron jacks squawk'd— *The wilderness of wolves—birthed in the white vapor and the smoke-dark Blue, forest kilns of Killarney— We smelt in the relentless Air, in the furious Hollows.* It was nonsensical, but Jack could hear what he felt sure was a wish. To be tangled, thrown, caress'd.

A row of straw-haired dolls begged to be held.

A pile of wooden Blocks jockey'd to be stacked.

They all wanted something.

They wanted him to take them.

The room filled with righteous yowling—it had turn'd church-like with the sublime thrum of holy truths. Rain rumbled closer up the Thames. The air throbb'd with charge, prickled and heated.

One sound called to Jack louder than the rest. A groaning thump from the center of the store. *Rhimey rhimey rhimey rhimey.* It was a syncopated, repetitive swarm of Sound.

Jack stumbl'd past child's mobiles, sport balls of all kinds, and dollhouses, seeking the source. Once he saw it, he couldn't turn away, even though at that moment he knew for certain how cumbersome the Heist would be. Not dangerous—though surely a tad idiotic.

It was a rocking Horse.

Not even the most beautiful rocking Horse he'd ever seen. Not like what he'd spy'd through the large-paned glazes of the fancier cribs near Marylebone. The gray dappled steeds of the bourgeoisie; Stallions riding high on iron legs affix'd to smooth, oiled planks.

This was a simple thing. A raw, unpainted Horse without legs. 'Twas just a dome of linseed-oiled elm mounted atop a crescent-shaped Base. But it was transfixing. Some kind of legless horse-ship with a glossy Pommel that Jack could feel in his palm before it was even in his palm, and then he was lifting it while it breath'd—he could hear it now—*ride me ride me*—the words getting softer and softer now that he held it.

"What's that for?" Aurie ask'd, grimacing.

The horse-ship was calming in his arms. "I jus' need it."

He blushed.

Aurie nodded. "Say no more."

• • •

Some far-off rustle of the city's Awakening was making itself felt. The accelerating stream of Footfall towards the slaughterhouses and the coalworks—the collective press of the laborers towards labor. The chirruping, hectic racket of burghers discussing quantities, numbers, methods of extraction. Doors clanking open, whooshing shut.

Aurie nodded at him. They jetted out the open sash and clambered back up to the roof. Jack achiev'd this one-handed. Aurie took note.*

---

* What must it have been like to witness the rise of the bourgeoisie and the bureaucrats? The awful weather system of them closing in, raining banality and evil.

On which topic: so today I go into the Rite Aid to pick up my prescription. I'm psyching myself up to be *less weird* than I was at dinner. Maybe I can recapture whatever Ursula was throwing my way that night.

Worth a shot.

So I stroll in. I've got a Dunkin' Donuts this time due to cash-flow issues. When I get there, Ursula's kind of busy. The line is stacked with people picking shit up. Flu season, I guess. Or oxycodone season.

I wander around the store, killing time, needing nothing. Maybe twenty minutes later, when the line has died down, my arms laden with the now-cold Dunkin' Donuts coffee, batteries, a bottle of seltzer, gummy vitamin C, melatonin and antibacterial wipes, I trundle up to the counter.

Sorry, I gesture apologetically at the coffee with its now unappetizing splashes of dried murk on the plastic lid. *It got a bit cold.*

It's all good, Ursula says, kind of abstractly.

She's putting my stuff into a bag when I get a call. I don't answer. It rings again. And again.

She pauses. *Don't you want to answer that?*

I look at my phone. It's the University main number.

No, I definitely don't want to answer that.

Sounds important.

Probably some bureaucratic bullshit.

I've now ignored the phone for three consecutive sets of rings, which just makes embarrassingly apparent to Ursula how desperate I am to chat with her. Not good.

So, I say, grabbing things to help bag, and just making the process awkward. *Do you want to have dinner again?*

Way too long of a pause. And then, *Sure. I'll give you a call.* She puts the gummy C's in the bag and pushes it across the counter toward me.

And I go, *Yes, thank you, I'll look forward to your call*—painfully formal, while try-

---

ing to sound blasé, stumbling backwards out of the Rite Aid, my elbow unseating a row of alcohol pads and nose strips.

Just leave that, she says.

When I get to my car I listen to the message. It's Dean of Surveillance Andrews' office manager. Wanting to make another appointment with me.

17.

Jack near broke the window, knocking against it with the horse's base. *Dammit if she's with someone.* He toss'd the horse in—swung through.

Bess observed this frantic entry from the bed. The horse clattered at length to a stillness against the floor Beams—Jack was panting hard and wet-faced with rain. She looked back down at the news broadside in her lap.

Bess was smoking Tobacco—a gift from some expensive job—her back against the wall, knees tucked up, tea-stained pages strewn across her legs, attired in an attention-transfixing ruby silk nightgown. A dirty plate sat on the side-cabinet, Flies cavorting in chicken-oil going rancid.

"Were you w-with someone?" His voice cracked. *Damn.*

"Job." She flick'd ash into her palm. Jack peer'd into her eyes. Amber glass. All reflection.

He breath'd out.

"Brought you something."

An amused smile twitched across her lips.

"You built this?"

"Nick'd it," he said, and it came out fine and strong. But he'd been holding his breath, and so after achieving the announcement, he found himself heaving inwards like he'd been kicked in the guts. He coughed into his fist.

Bess put her paper to the side.

She stood, and her nightgown fell from her bosom to her

Hips—an exhale of red silk. Jack fought gasping for breath again. "And you want to see me ride it."

Now she cross'd the room, pulled up the red silk to spread her legs open above the horse, settled her quim against the oiled wood, and rocked back and forth—this latter so slowly—while holding his gaze. A firework exploded inside him as he watched the meeting point of her notch against the wood, the Resin growing soaked and tart. He wanted to fall to his knees and lick the Wet from the darkened grain.[*]

And it was something else, too—watching her ride the horse. Something like what happened between them when he'd cleaned her with his handkerchief. Something tender and deprav'd at once. A *fatherliness* that had nothing to do with age or familial Relation and everything to do with care and precious violation delivered together. He understood why she wanted more. Why she wanted to be taken with as much Force as the Kindness he showed her suggested. Though it sounded like a Contradiction, his Body knew it wasn't.

Leaning over, Jack push'd Bess's legs open—flicked her quim with his finger. Their mouths met, and her tongue danced over the

---

[*] I—I—I hate to interrupt, especially when I'm about to (—ahem—never mind). But I had to point out a certain resonance here with Sterne's rather infamous theory of obsession (as figured in the hobby-horse) as the fundament of character.

The relevant section is as follows:

Viz., "A man and his HOBBY-HORSE, tho' I cannot say that they act and re-act exactly after the same manner in which the soul and body do upon each other: Yet doubtless there is a communication between them of some kind, and my opinion rather is, that there is something in it more of the manner of electrified bodies,—and that by means of the heated parts of the rider, which come immediately into contact with the back of the HOBBY-HORSE.—By long journies and much friction, it so happens that the body of the rider is at length fill'd as full of HOBBY-HORSICAL matter as it can hold;—so that if you are able to give but a clear description of the nature of the one, you may form a pretty exact notion of the genius and character of the other."

So, one thing comes into contact with another over and over again—*maybe in an . . . excitable place on the body*—and that friction, over time: that's character.

Of course, this document predates Sterne's by some decades. So perhaps the concept of the hobby-horse was more widespread than I'd thought?

tip of his and they were breathing each other in again after only one night that had felt like a terrible stretch of Months.

Bess put her hand to his trousers front.

He pull'd back.

"Have you never clicketed?"

"That's not it," he trailed off.

But that was it.

Bess lean'd back on the horse, letting him see her. The rain hissed down beyond the windows and a riverbottom scent blew in, cooling his face. The air raised a series of puckers across Bess's skin.

Jack knelt— Her breasts were ——, her nipples ——.* —and he engag'd himself in a quantity of time at her bosom. Reach'd down again—rocked her slowly against his hand. Bess was so sweetly passive under his touch. He rocked, flick'd her quim, made an indisputable kind of love to her breasts.

But when it had grown still later without any sign of proceeding— "Will you run into the night again if I take liberties?"

Jack startled backwards. Bess scuff'd her foot against the floor.

"Do you think I'm filthy. A filthy Bat, is that what you think?"

"No— God, no."

She stood—cross'd the room—threw herself onto the bed on her back—pulled the nightgown over her breasts.

"Don't do that," he whined.

"Afraid to fuck the whore?"

Silence.

"You'd rather talk?"

"No."

"Then come over here and—"

And he was on top of her, pushing his hand between her legs. Bess moaned into his mouth, pulled at Jack's breeches.

"Please," she said. "All of—you."

---

* In what can only be described as gallantry, the speaker declines to showcase Bess's body for the reader. Incidentally: a much better boyfriend than I ever was.

She reach'd for his hip—pushed his breeches down—she held her legs farther open—he pressed against her—Bess gasped at the heat between them, then—glancing down—

In his ear—*"Yes."*

The *yes* (in that inimitable fashion particular to women of a certain predilection), referr'd, of course, to what *was and was not* there.

Jack hover'd, afraid Bess would say something wrong. And the catalogue of wrong things was infinite, ranging from the gracious but hesitant—"Thank you for showing me"—to the disappointed and horrified.

She could also do something wrong. Such as try to touch him the way he touched her.

She could try to engage him in discussion. She could want to philosophize him at this moment.

But she didn't do any of these Things.

She open'd her legs wider. Held his Gaze.

Jack look'd down at himself. "Do you think I'm a Monster?" He said this half-ashamed but half—something Else.

If she said *no* it would be the wrong answer.

Same with *yes*.

"Well, you're *Something*."

How did she know his word—his secret Word for what was behind the door in himself that he could not open?

"A wonderful, fetching *Something*." She brought her hand down between them and drew her fingers across the front of it[†], tracing his outline with a Fingertip.

"Daemon. Sphinx. Hybrid. Scitha, man-horse, deep-water Kraken, Monster-flower—"

---

† It is almost certainly the case that if there were a hack job this section would include a voyeuristic depiction of Jack's genitalia. I consider this elegant declining-to-describe to be strong evidence of the document's authenticity.

Of course, personally, I'm more than happy to go on at length about my prodigious genitalia. But there's a difference between a confession one wants to give, and one that is taken.

The thing between Jack's legs swelled bigger.

"Cinamoli." Bess placed her fingers around it and tugged him towards her, tickling herself with the tip. "Man and dog, dog and—"

Bess spun so she was atop him, legs astride his thighs. The heat of her surrounded his Swollenness.

She twitch'd against him. Rocked in his lap until—with a little bleat—heat pour'd from her and she fell upon his chest.

Jack try'd to sit up but she pressed him down at his shoulder, then stood and crossed the room to a small cabinet hunched in the corner. Returned with an arched, smooth horn, which she press'd into Jack's palm.

He would have known what it was even if she didn't whisper "For screwin'" in his ear. He would have known because it spoke to him the way a block of wood at Kneebone's spoke to his Chisel when it wanted to be shaped. He would have known what it was that she handed him, what it wanted, and what to do with it. Even though this wasn't the door to an armoire, a tuffet for an aristocrat's poodle, or a jar for holding flour. It spoke to him the way any material spoke to him. Spoke of what it wanted and what it could do.

And what this Horn wanted, simply, was to make itself a part of him.

Watching Bess watch him strap the leather Lacing around his hips, observ'ng her eagerness when the Horn arced up and out, he was possess'd of a calm unlike any he'd ever known—a thread connect'd them, and now he had simply to follow it.

He knelt over her and they kissed a series of alternately hummingbird-like and wolfish and wet kisses. The Horn was tickling against Bess's quim, and Jack whisper'd to her nasty, loving things while he warmed it in his palm so it wouldn't jolt her when he slid inside.

His Something had made Bess gasp when she bobbed on it. And she had gasp'd and shudder'd and soak'd herself and him too. But the Horn made her clutch. She shudder'd again—differently than before, this time from some profound Depths. This shudder took her very far away—and then return'd her to him—softer, meltier, and deeper still.

A pause. He was still inside her Boiling-Place. And she began rocking them again—so impossibly sweetly, on the hard-packed straw Mattress. A *Togetherness* rose up inside him. His hands and the unnameable Knob between his legs, and even now his skull began to shudder, and he knew then that all the invigorating Bess-ether cramm'd in his nostrils and Veins and down his throat—all the sweet-and-salt aroma of Bess that had bloomed out from her and streamed up Jack's nose in a feverish dust, pouring through him—would spray out of him, would fog the room with a million crimson Petals, with a wave of soft silver gunshot, with a rolling meadow of grass-green fire, heaving under them and pouring over them and it would bury them, in the best ways, together, and alive.

Later that Evening, Jack told Bess about the toy shop. The way the objects call'd to him, bawling out their miserable Biographies, their wants, their needs, their Histories and Travels. The way they told of the entire crowded consecutions of labor, Exchange, and Fraud congealed in them. *Killarney. Smelt. Furious hollows.*

"It was objects speaking? Sounds a bit like they're describin' the bog-iron smelting works in Galway."

"Do you think I'm mad?"

"I think the world is quite mad. Not you." Paused. "Are any of the objects in this room speaking to you now?"

"No."

"Have they ever?"

He shook his head against the pokey straw pillow.

"What about at Newgate?"

"What about it?"

"You heard something there, too."

"Maybe other inmates?"

"But only when you were put on display by Wild, right? Only when you—or your imprisonment—were briefly"—searched for a word—"commoditized?"

"Suppose so." He nodded.

Bess twirl'd her finger in the ends of his curls, kissing his ear. Thinking. And then, her hands crafting concepts in the indigo, night-falling air above their faces—Jack didn't see them so much as he felt the air move near his cheeks, the Stars winking in the window beyond momentarily blott'd out—she explained it.

Objects were speaking to him, she said, like a Lover, or a Priest.

"Jack," she said, "they need something."

And so with the sooty London evening trickling into the room, she told him: *They are asking for your help.* Told him that each one was telling a different version of the same sermon: the Alpha and Omega of their Genesis. And each one was asking for the same thing. *Liberate us.*[*]

---

[*] While no previous Sheppard accounts have given him this ability of supernatural hearing in specific, we can consider *supernaturalness* to be fully within the conventions of the genre. For one thing, the talking-commodity (or "it-narrative") was quite popular within the period, beginning with Cervantes' *The Dialogue of the Dogs* and continuing through *The Secret History of an Old Shoe*, *The Adventures of a Black Coat* and of course Smollett's *The History and Adventures of an Atom*. Or, to be frank, we need look no further than Moll's infamous communion with objects in *Moll Flanders*.

PART

II

I.

AURIE, JACK, BESS, AND JENNY DIVER WERE AT THE BLACK LION when the first Plague Ships arriv'd in the Thames.

A chilly May evening of unremitting hail. The inhospitality of the night meant little business at the bat houses, all the husbands lock'd down by their hearths with their wives. So the doxies congregated with their Hell-Hounds* at the pubs.

An urchin had nabbed a broadside from a street vendor. Aurie flipp'd the kid a coin and handed the broadside to Jack, who pass'd it to Bess.

From *Applebee's Original Weekly Journal*†

A Mail from France, offering the Following Advice to Londoners on the Advance of the Plague in Chandernagore

2 2 M a y 1 7 2 4

Citizens! The contagion rages without ceasing through Chandernagore. The inhabitants have become *living ghosts*, raving in the streets in deliriums and laying waste to the shut-up shops and markets. Yesterday a band of eight widowed women broke the glazes on a bakeshop, taking whatever flours and grains they could lay

---

* Roguish boyfriends
† *Applebee's Original Weekly Journal* (1715–1737). As of now I cannot confirm this particular report.

their hands on. When approach'd by a Constable, the women laughed and threated him with contagion, screeching:

"If you come nearer we will cough and rage and infect you! We are Plaguers-all! We will breathe on you our fetid breathes, and scatter our effluvia upon your breeches!"

The Constable—arm'd with a musket and a longsword—was more afear'd of the women than they of him, and he retreated to the garrison lately established on the outskirts of town for government bodies and other persons of note.

It was later reported that the band of women also looted an apothecary's shop and a butcher's stall, where they made off with a parcel of yarrowroot and elderflower, as well as a stinking quantity of lamb gone very much to rot. They were seen hooting and hollering through the streets, advising residents to come join them if they were also showing tokens of the Plague and wished to make the most of their last days.

The same cases are to be found throughout the Levant, if reports are to be believed. The colonial Physicians are all dead or fled, and native tradesmen and Laborers roam the streets in gangs, seeking work—or provisions, or Opportunities. With nobody to employ them, their heads have turned to thieving and OTHER crimes.

We write to advise the Magistrates and Constables of the City of London to quarantine all trading vessels in the Thames for a period of twenty-eight days to ensure against the possibility of contagion.

More to the point, we urge that the Lord Mayor consider increasing the Centinels in the city's poorest quarters. It is our Conviction that Plague congregates amongst the poor, so we advise the Centinels be dispatched to the most crowded, filthiest parishes, under direct orders to *dispense with* any persons suspected of Plague should they attempt to leave their homes—those houses we deem *Dead-houses*—or to leave the parish. This is a Technique used widely throughout Europe on threat of plague. In fact the magistrates of Holland have put an immediate order to this effect in place on word of the Situation from the VOC.* The city should supply padlocks with which to lock the doors of *Dead-houses*, with entire families inside, as we have reason to suspect that those who live with an infected person are likely to carry the disease themselves, though they may show no outward Signs of it.

Signed,

Humbert Garamond,
City Exchequer (Chandernagore)

"They say the plague travels on the backs of Mice!" shouted the barmaid.

"Next thing they'll block the Turnpikes out of town—so said Defoe in his *Journal*," a ragged scholar declared from the corner. "If that comes to pass, we're all as good as dead, trapped like inmates of our own City."

"Even the water'll be sick," howl'd an elderly dame. "I heard it from my aunt who lived through the last plague. The water reek'd of sickness, turn'd piss-colored, crept o'er its bounds and into the houses at the shoreline."

Bess stood, speaking to the entire room. "Plague's an excuse they're using to police us further!" She looked out. Most continued to quaff and quarrel amongst themselves. "All of you! They're panicking the people delib'rately. It's a *securitizational furor* they're raising to put more centinels on the streets. Can't you see that?"

Jack chewed his cheek. He thought back to the thefts of the past week—each gauze Kerchief he unpacked, each leather Purse he handled. Each potentially plaguey.

How many goods had come through how many ports? His mind was scrambling to recall a Map he'd once seen. What if the customs-house manager had plague and then touched some fustian and then Jack touched it and then—? *And then and then.* He saw him-

---

* Dutch East India Company

self rooting through trunks, plague drifting onto his hands, sucked up in ether-streams into his nostrils.

Aurie's forehead was pinched in that particular way it got when he worried (which was often). His eyes contract'd under a landscape of scowling Wrinkles. He tugged at his beard.

"Securitizational furor?" He rocked back in his chair.

"No idea, m-m-mate."

"A securitizational furor," Bess intoned loudly for all the pub to hear, "*means* that they're making up fluff to put more centinels on the streets. They're blaming the plague on Chandernagore. Betting on no one being able to argue different. So they can unleash whatever plans they mean to unleash on us. Centinels, thief-catchers, plague-watchers, whatever it is. *That's* a securitizational furor."*

Jack shifted in his Seat. "You don't think the plague is coming, or—"

Bess's face closed. She blink'd—sifted him silently into the subset of everyday Anglos—the ones who would never understand.

"I'll not argue this point further with you." She nodded with her chin at Aurie, who was frowning into his ale. "Or even you."

"What'd I do?" object'd Aurie.

"You're overly-worrying along with him," she said.

"But we just—" Jack's interjection was drowned by the pub Din.

"Plague'll kill ya in a single solitary day!" shouted the Urchin from the back of the pub. "Coughin' and gaspin' and then dyin' in the street." He climb'd onto the bar and open'd one side of his little filthy Waistcoat. "I've three bottles of Mr. Lecher's Famous Plague Killer Oil—secret formula brought from the Levant, where they know a thing o' two 'bout plague." The bottles clinked as he shook his coat to draw Interest.

---

* If accurate to the text, Bess has delivered the first known usage of "securitizational" in known history.

Lacking easy access to the online *Oxford English Dictionary,* thanks to my unpaid leave, I'm bookmarking for later.

The hum of Discussion bloomed louder as the Denizens gathered 'round the urchin. Only the too-soused remained seated. The too-soused, and Bess, who had returned to Jack's lap. A full-body sweat emitt'd from him. He wanted to stand and haggle for his own bottle.

"You know who's runnin' the centinels." Bess turn'd to look at Jack now. "Don't you."

He shook his head.

"Jonathan Wild. Thief-Catcher General," she proclaimed, loud enough for the pub to hear.

"The lizardy fuckwit!" repris'd Jenny, nose-deep in her mug of ale.

"The lizardy fuckwit." Bess faced the group again, most of whom congregated 'round the urchin selling plague-remedy. "And, look, this so-called plague's a colonial furor too. An excuse to send the Bombay Navy down the Coromandel coast. To war against the Froglanders and the French and whoever else is vyin' for fortune. It's all bollocks. An Imperial trick. This worry over 'fection from the east. Constructed to cover up somethin' else."

But what? mouthed Aurie at Jack. "T'cover up what?"†

---

† So I go by Dean of Surveillance Andrews' office today.

The library looks grander than ever. Relieved of a vast proportion of its books, the space has really blossomed into the spectacular, vacant anomie of an insurance tower in a second-rate city.

When I arrive at Dean of Surveillance Andrews' office, he's got company. This guy in a drab gray suit is sitting in one of the chairs opposite the desk.

Ursula is in the other one.

Strange. They hauled Ursula in here just for associating with me? Jesus.

Welcome, says Dean of Surveillance Andrews. He doesn't stand up.

The other guy does, though. He shakes my hand and there's this pungent waft of body odor coming off him. Just incubating in his suit and poofing out when he raises his arm. It isn't terrible. Just musky. Like maybe this guy never dry-cleans his suits.

Sullivan, he says. *North-Northeast Senior Marketing Director of P-Quad Publishers and Pharmaceuticals.*

I realize we're still shaking hands, and I'm nodding dumbly at him.

And Pharmaceuticals? I finally croak out, flicking my eyes at Ursula. She's staring down at the table. *Pharmaceuticals?* I say again.

Mm-hmm. We're a subsidiary.

I don't know if he means that the publishers are a subsidiary of the pharmaceuticals, or that the University is a subsidiary of the publishers (and the pharmaceuticals), or what.

You know how it is with neoliberalism these days, he furthers, with a nasal chuckle. *Everything's a subsidiary of everything!*

Oh god, one of these corporate meta-neoliberal comedian types.

I sent you an email last week regarding some editing work, he continues, smoothing his tie.

Uh-huh, I manage.

*You responded negatively, and I—we—*he gestures at Dean of Surveillance Andrews—*thought you might prefer to meet in person, to personalize things. It's best to meet in person, don't you think?*

I just stand there.

We're prepared to offer you a choice, chimes in Dean of Surveillance Andrews. *A choice between your current unpaid leave and a small outsourced project for P-Quad, who we've recently partnered with in some . . . areas.*

Areas, Sullivan cuts in, *which the University could use to have optimized.*

Optimized, repeats Dean of Surveillance Andrews.

In fact, says Sullivan—*P-Quad has made some generous donations to the University.*

—The agriculture school as well as the library—

—And is currently, as a side interest, expanding into the Archival-Text-Documentation Field, and we'd love to have your assistance on a matter which Ursula—now Sullivan gestures at her—*has apprised us of.*

Of which Ursula has apprised us, I correct.

Only after I shmuckily fix his grammar do I realize: Ursula hasn't been hauled in there at all.

Memories are flashing up.

The day I told her about the manuscript.

The so-called "date" when I told her about the unpaid leave.

The timing of P-Quad's email.

The phone call at the pharmacy.

Ursula??

She gives me an apologetic look just as Sullivan hands me a flyer:

In an Age of Toxins and Atrocities, P-QUAD, Inc. Offers the Most Humane™ Pharmaceutical Product. Don't take barbaric pharmaceuticals! Take Only Humane™ Pharmaceuticals!

I look up. Sullivan straightens his tie again. He keeps smoothing it to his chest and then down his belly. It's a little compulsively autoerotic and sad.

Let me ask you a question: Do you buy organic produce? He pauses. *No need to answer that!* He chortles. *You're a professor, after all!*

He's doing that furniture-salesman thing of leaning back and pointing both index fingers like guns at me while delivering this "joke."

Have you considered what it might be like to have access to an organic testosterone—he continues—*a truly natural testosterone? Surely you know the synthetic testos-*

terone on the market is altered. A molecule here and there. In small ways, but altered. If it weren't, the drug companies wouldn't be able to patent it. Old Lockean principle encoded in law. One mixes one's labor with an unowned thing in order to take possession of it.

I'm familiar with Lockean theories of possessive individualism, I say, annoyed. *It's the epistemological basis of colonial land grabs.*

Yes! he says, as if that's a good thing. *So then you understand,* he plows on, *that, by the same principle, testosterone variants are patented through these alterations. Inventions. Intellectual labor upon the natural resource allows the company to establish ownership. And, well, what if you could avail yourself of an unaltered testosterone? Derived from humane methods.* He looks at me. Clasps his hands and points the prow of them at me in that Leadershippy way. *Like a farm share. A humane farm share for hormonal supplementation. Wouldn't you agree that would be a superior product? A superior and purer product?*

This guy is bludgeoning me with his common sense.

Ultimately, we're talking about an open-source, humane testosterone. One simply needs the means to manufacture it. He coughs. *That's all we're seeking to do here. Produce an organic, humane, bioidentical open-source testosterone.*

From the University's humanely milked dairy cows, blurts out Dean of Surveillance Andrews.

Cow urine, actually, corrects Sullivan. *It's part of the partnership between the University and P-Quad. Humanely milked cow urine by-product.*

It's a win-win, Dean of Surveillance Andrews says.

Honestly, Sullivan says, *the rendering market is at an all-time low. Your University used to sell urine and offal to a Ukrainian protein blending plant but all the plants are using much-cheaper palm oil now. You know palm oil markets these days*—he looks at Dean of Surveillance Andrews in that collegial neo-colonizer kind of way, and shrugs. *Left with a surplus, P-Quad has helped the University realize that rather than dispose of the fluids, we can, together, make something of them.*

My uneasy feeling is becoming more specific now.

Ursula let us know a little bit about your research on the manuscript you found in our library, says Sullivan.

Did he just say "our library"?

And we think you'd be perfect as our resident "expert"! he says, smiling.

Expert in what? I say.

Yes! he "responds." *And as our resident expert, you'd be helping us—we don't want to say market anything, but our aim is to present a special product. As it's open-source, we can't patent it. So we're looking to distinguish our offering. Our thought here is that we can make our product*—he searches for and rejects a lot of different probably disturbing advertising words—*unique by releasing it in conjunction with the publication of the manuscript—the authentic memoirs—*

Confessions, maybe, I say. *More like confessions.*

—The earliest authentic confessional transgender memoirs known to history—

Western history, I say.

———

—Well obviously, of course, of course—he waves his hand in the air—*the earliest authentic confessional transgender memoirs in Western history.*

I don't see why you need me to authenticate that. Anyone reading the manuscript would see that Jack is—

Yes, well, he says, cutting me off, *that's an interesting question, heh heh, as far as our legal department is concerned.* He smooths his tie again. *As with pharmaceuticals, so with archival manuscripts. The manuscript is no longer copyrighted, of course. But with your footnotes you'll*—he clears his throat—*add labor to the document. Invent, if you will. And in so doing, as a freelance employee of P-Quad, you'll allow us to take exclusive ownership of that manuscript, copyright and sell it.*

But I bought it from the kid at the library, I object weakly. *So then technically I own it. Shouldn't you have to buy it from me? Or couldn't I even make it available to the public for free?*

In fact, I hadn't thought at all about making it available for free. But I often get this itch to be an asshole around administrators, and I like goading Sullivan with this idea.

Actually, he says, *the University's surveillance cameras show that the kid gave it to you. Which he was not authorized to do. It thus remains the property of the University archives. In fact, it's still essentially out on loan. When you agree to edit it*—he says this like I've already agreed to it; another mind-control technique from Leadership books, no doubt—*you'll do so as an employee of the company, and any labor you perform on the object will be labor performed in our service and on our behalf.*

I really wished I had a turkey sandwich to throw at that moment. I was flooded with my *of course* feeling. The one I get when everything turns out as terrible as I'm always worried it will be. Even Ursula turned out crappy. My stupid little crush. It was all just—

Fuck this, I say and turn to leave.

Oh, don't be grandiose, says Sullivan. *I suspect the outcome of your decision will affect you more than it affects us. Perhaps you'll think further about our offer.*

I shoot Ursula a look.

Hey, she says, shrugging. *The Rite Aid cut my hours. What do you want from me?*

2.

HELL-AND-FURY AND WILD WERE STANDING IN THE MIDST OF THE blistering ruckus of Jonathan's Coffee House, on Exchange Alley. The scent of burned Coal blew downwind, mixing with the sour stench of bean-roasting. Even at the late hour, business was high.

"This a promotion?"

"*You?* Mr. Hell-and-Pasty?" Wild frown'd, rolling his pocket watch between his fingers.

Hell-and-Fury squint'd. Barely a hint of pupil visible.

"Well, ahh, yes—me."

Wild squash'd his chin into his neck.

"You're here to scout the place. That's all."

Wild steered them through the massive Hall. The room, with its ten-yard-high ceilings, was something of a Cathedral. Hell-and-Fury startl'd like a clunch at the Taxidermy festooning the walls—crocodiles, turtles, rattlesnakes—animals of the New World, glaring down with open Maws. Advertisements profess'd coffee the "elixir of business" and a cure-all for everything from "moist humours" to "Hypochondriack Winds."

The room stunk of tobacco and Sweat. Everywhere the hum of trades: *East India will triple 'er worth in a week . . . A stash of indigo dye off the Tamil coast . . . Tulips are comin' back, don't let anyone tell you different . . . Fresh stock coming in from Amsterdam later this week.*

On and on went the frenzied exchanges of the stockjobbers.

But Wild was focus'd on something else.

He watched the men glugging down the brew. They did it, he knew, to trade stocks from six in the morning 'til past midnight. Their eyes were red, blinking and hollow. He observ'd them exchange coin after coin for this awful brown drink that tasted of char and old shoes. Watched them escort doxies into the anterooms to blow off the loose corns in between hustles, and he knew that the grand Show they made of parading the youngest, spruciest, most well-rigged* of them past their mates and rival stockjobbers was important in their World. To demonstrate who had the most coin, and who retained his tumescent Prowess after hours of trading and talking.

They were a new society of sanctioned Banditti.†

He knew he could market them something far more powerful than coffee. *If only Evans were more focused.* If the plan worked, they'd produce cash more times over even what the stockjobbers did selling shares in Tulips, Cane, and Tea.

He look'd at Hell-and-Fury—a thin fog of Anxiety rose off his pale skin, his eyes blinking and weak—and he knew something

---

* Well dressed (also: most buxom)

† Highwaymen; rogues. Speaking of which: As I am sure anyone could have predicted, I have agreed to Dean of Surveillance Andrews' "choice." Sullivan was right about one thing. I *had* been a little grandiose when I stormed out.

So I'll be paid to edit the manuscript. To produce a new edition. Like a Norton or Oxford Edition, just that this will be a "P-Quad Publishers Edition." I know, I know. But since when did I care about prestige? I'm trying to tell myself it won't be much different from what I've been doing. Keep my head down, do my annotations, focus on the work. True, I'll have to upload regular transcriptions to Sullivan for review. Everything needs to be "digitized," of course. Plus, Sullivan wants to be really "hands-on." (I know what that means . . . surveillance culture, ahem.)

I mean, okay, there's no way around it. My labor produces this document—it's (*I am?*) essentially free advertising for them. That's what it is.

It's all so unsavory. But as a Marxist, I have to say: *What isn't?!*

At least I'll be receiving a salary again.

The world is full of compromises.

else, too. If the plan worked, he could create the most powerful, invigorat'd band of policing Scoundrels the city had ever seen. Even the bottle-headed‡ fops like Hell-and-Fury. Even the caw-handed§ coves like Scotty Pool.¶

---

‡ Vacant
§ Clumsy
¶ SULLIVAN: WELCOME TO THE P-QUAD FAMILY! SO GLAD WE'LL BE WORKING TOGETHER!

3.

THE POORER PARISHES WERE LOCK'D DOWN THAT VERY NIGHT. WHEN Jack, Bess and Aurie exited the Black Lion, the hail had abated, and the street teem'd with centinels. Several at every corner, shouting at coves to take to their quarters. They had scarves tied 'round their mouths and noses—their shouts muffled by rough Linen (*quite the bit of theater,* Bess muttered as she, Jack and Aurie pass'd by; Jenny had been engaged for a job at the pub). The street sounded like a sea full of honking sea lions.

"Heading to the Stables," said Aurie as he sped off towards the outskirts of the city. Jack knew he would walk all night to Bill Field's stable where they stashed their loot, and sleep in the hay in mildewed Blankets among the mice and the rats. He would roger* Field's freckled, wiry son too.

Jack and Bess headed towards the bat house.

"Can't fathom this many centinels spread o'er the whole town," Jack whisper'd, amazed. They were posted at every street corner, and then threaded down the streets, too, a constant Stream.

"Not the whole town." Bess took his hand and led him the long way through the tidier parishes. Once they hit Whitehall the streets were unpatrolled. Quiet and gleaming gold with lantern-light. They wandered through the quiet to the river.

"See?" she said. The sound of their Footfall was the only distur-

---

* Fuck

bance in the well-to-do Hush. But Jack's attention had shifted over her shoulder.

Something loom'd, advancing out of the Shadow of London Bridge. A mass of black blotting out the streak of brighter Indigo that remained at the horizon—the last light of the setting sun. A ship with sails down, chains banging against naked masts. No persons visible on board. The ship moved very slowly. Barely, in fact. Some weak Currents drew it along, perhaps. The vessel bobbed sideways as much as it advanced forward. And then it stopp'd, sitting just past the Bridge like a massive buoy. Nothing stirr'd.

"A Plague Ship," Jack whispered.

Bess was breathing fast—dragging him by the coat towards the shoreline for a better look.

Just as they neared the shore, they were met with an angry, bulky burger blocking the way. "'Tis the poor and scroungy have brought it here, this plague! Filth ought to be sequestered to their own rancid, peculiar parishes."

Jack squeez'd his hands into fists, glaring.

"Pick your Battles," whispered Bess, leading him back towards the bat house.

Inside, all the bats congregated in the Foyer, pacing, dialoguing in pitched tones about the news, leaning on each other, laughing and arguing in a jumble on the mossy green sofas. Some mollies were among them—Franny, dressed in a woman's nightgown—paraded through the gaggle, then lay upon the couch, proceeding to mimick the delivering of a wooden baby to much uproar. The air was perfumed with Whiskey and Breath.

"We're to stay here?" Laurent—sprawled in an armchair—projected to the room.

"For how long then?" Franny wailed. Another molly—a lolling, ruddy-skinned lad with a mop of blond hair in his eyes—

knelt between Franny's legs, holding the wooden baby, caressing Franny's legs with his cheek. His eyes were closed, and he was smiling.

A din of speculations.

"*Indefinite?!*" someone shouted. "How're we to make Coin—knock each other?"

This last occasioned a chorus of laughter and Repartee as Bess and Jack headed upstairs to her rooms.

"'Least we're together," Bess said, as they squirrel'd away to Bed.

By the end of the first day of confinement, Bess and Jack had wept through their Clothes with perspiration. The peaked Ceilings in Bess's chamber congregated the heat of all the Fires burning in all the hearths in the bat house. Bess's window was not nearly enough to bring the required ventilation.

Bess loung'd on the Bed, sipping wine and flipping through a stack of pages bound with twine. *Ephraim Chambers' Cyclopaedia* was printed on the front. Jack assessed her focus and absorption. *The Cyclopaedia?* Was Chambers a client? Ordinarily he would make amusement of this fact, teasing Bess to dispel his jealousy. But it was too hot, and they were too cramp'd after only one day.

The heat exacted its toll in languor and exhaustion, exacerbated by their confinement. Bess fizzled salt into her wine to restore her humors. Jack sat at the window, staring at the empty streets below, pulling hard at the air, hunting for twinges of cool.

Centinels march'd through constantly, muskets slung over their shoulders. Twice, urchins scrambled through the alley, arms loaded with stale buns from the bakery, hoping to evade notice. The centinels fell upon the children within moments and beat them senseless. Jack could hear echoes of other such Scramblings and Beatings down the alleys and lanes. The city was a symphony of bullysticks hitting Bodies. The thwack of Flesh breaking. The crack of Bone. Jack jumped at every report and slap from the streets below.

"'Twould be a good time to conduct a raid," he said through gritted teeth. He saw himself running down the streets, alive with hatred and Combat, the clarity of opposition.

"'Twoud be an idiot time to conduct a raid," Bess said, not lifting her eyes from her reading.

The second day found them in much the same positions. Bess was further on in the book. Three more urchins—as well as one or two bands of sneaks and robbers who got the notion to test their fate against the centinels—had been beaten Bloody under Jack's nose. The night before, they'd slept separated across some inches in the Bed on account of the heat.

"I'd like to be near to you," Bess said. "I'm sick o' your rigging.* Remember that one time you let me see you?"

She cross'd the room, her salted wine sloshed in her tin cup, and put her hand to his breeches-front, which had the Horn affix'd. He'd even taken to sleeping with it on. "I want to *feel* you."

Truth be told, Jack wanted to unclothe with her too—he did—but then he thought of the men who had done so before him, and the ones who did so regularly, and he was tormented. Confined together, day in and out, he looked at her and wondered why she wanted it from him when she could get it from so many other coves.

He was on the other side of a high thick Hedge of branches with vicious tips. He could not come through. And she could not come to him.

"I want to lie next to you," he rasp'd, "but my"—he gestured at his chest, the Unaccountable Lumps that grieved him so—"are in the way."

"I don't care a whit about that."

_____
* Clothes

"You've been with so many cuffins*."

"I wouldn't call it 'with.' And anyway, I don't want those cuffins. I want you." She ran her hand through his curls. "You're just having your *daily attack of Nerves.*"

But it wasn't Nerves. It was simply this: Jack felt himself a man. Or, touching Bess made him feel himself a man. And Bess herself, her Nearness, made Jack need his outside to come somehow closer to his inside. It was a contradiction, for this same perplex'd snarl of need made coming closer to her—in the naked way she now ask'd— impossible, too.

"'S Chambers a customer?" Jack pull'd the book out of Bess's hands.

"Never met him," she said, taking it back.

"Where'd you get this, then?" Jack started pacing in front of the windows.

"One of the regulars—Evans, a surgeon—"

Surgeon. Was she trying to make him jealous?

"A surgeon's just a barber with a fancy title." Jack halted his pacing and waved his arms about.

"The surgeons are soon splitting from the barbers' guild. 'Least that's what I've heard."

She *was* trying to make him jealous. Probably to get him to clicket her *smish-lessly.*

"Why's this surgeon—this *Evans*—giving you books?" He had begun pacing again, running his hands through his hair.

"I'm interested in a topic he works on."

"What topic?"

"Chimeras†."

Jack turned. "My mother call'd me that."

Bess chewed her lip. "Evans says Chambers' *Cyclopaedia*'s one of the only scientific treatments of chimeras to date"—*Just what*

---

* Men

† "A fabulous Monster, which the Poets feign'd to have the Head of a Lion, the Belly of a Goat, and the Tail of a Serpent" (Ephraim Chambers, *Cyclopaedia*).

kind of confidences has Bess shared with Evans? And why?—"and I figur'd he could illuminate me on the issue."

"Illuminate you?" Jack's voice had risen. Bess turned away. He paused for air. "Scientific as opposed to what?"

"Spiritual?" she said, turning back around and shrugging. "Occult. Mystical. It's an interesting conundrum. Either folks believe chimeras to be Demons. Or they don't believe them to exist at all. But Evans says it's not a mystical matter. What we"—Jack darted a look—"what *some people* call chimeras aren't demons, they're just persons with—ah—"

"You were going to say *Aberrations*."

"No."

"You were."

"I was going to say that ancient doctors thought chimeras to be natural but Monstrous—a natural monstrosity. Evans says they're not natural, but they're not Monsters either. They're just humans with certain Changes. Differences. And this *Cyclopaedia* contains a science of chimeras. A"—she paused again—"survey. It's just a survey of chimera-Creatures. Creatures with *chimera-aspects*. Hookworms, Garden Snails—"

He glared. "Survey in the way they're *surveyin'* the town for Plague?"

"No. Not in the same way they're *surveilling* us now."

"Well, a bit tho'. It's a bit like that." Jack was glum. Then, "Were you indecent with him?"

Bess laughed. "Yes, of course! He's a customer—but if only you'd meet him. He's rather absurd. A bloated beet of a phiz‡ with a giant white wiggy pomp."

"A beet with a proper arborvitae beneath."

"If you're so concern'd 'bout Evans," she continued, frowning, "you can find him holed up in Jenny's room downstairs right now. He usually begs to see me, but he's a bit too enthusiastick. It was getting a bit much. Some time ago, I directed him to Jenny."

---

‡ Face

Enthusiastick was ringing in Jack's ears now—*Enthusiastick Doctor.*

"Any case," Bess was going on, "I heard a bat saying he got caught with the Curfew. So he's bound to be downstairs. He'll be owing a fortune."

Jack couldn't help one moment of bitter Banter, which Bess mercifully ignored: "'Magine he can afford it."

That night, Jack was flooded with images of a pompous strapping Physician, complete with a blood-rich gaying instrument*, spouting off to Bess about the science of *Aberrations*. The two of them talking about him—his *Somethingness.*

When he was sure Bess had fallen to sleep, he padded 'cross the room to the *Cyclopaedia,* where it lay cracked open, spine up, on the Daybed near the window. He opened to the page on "Sexual Chimeras."† It began with a long disquisition on garden slugs and other lawn-pests. Then, on the flip side of the page, a painted illustration.

---

* Penis

† SULLIVAN: WE REALLY DO REQUIRE MORE EXTRAPOLATION OF "SEX-UAL CHIMERA."

ME: It ranges. Hermaphrodism, heteroclitism, clitoramegaly, an abundance of masculine passions in a cis-woman, etc.

SULLIVAN: I AMEND MY REQUEST FOR "EXTRAPOLATION." WE REQUIRE *SPECIFICITY* AS TO THE MEANING OF SEXUAL CHIMERA AS IT IS USED ABOVE. READERS NEED TO BE ABLE TO VISUALIZE.

ME: I regret to inform the Publisher that a desire for scientific classification and specificity cannot be satisfied by eighteenth-century sciences, particularly the proto-sexological ones, which truck largely in rumor and spectacle.

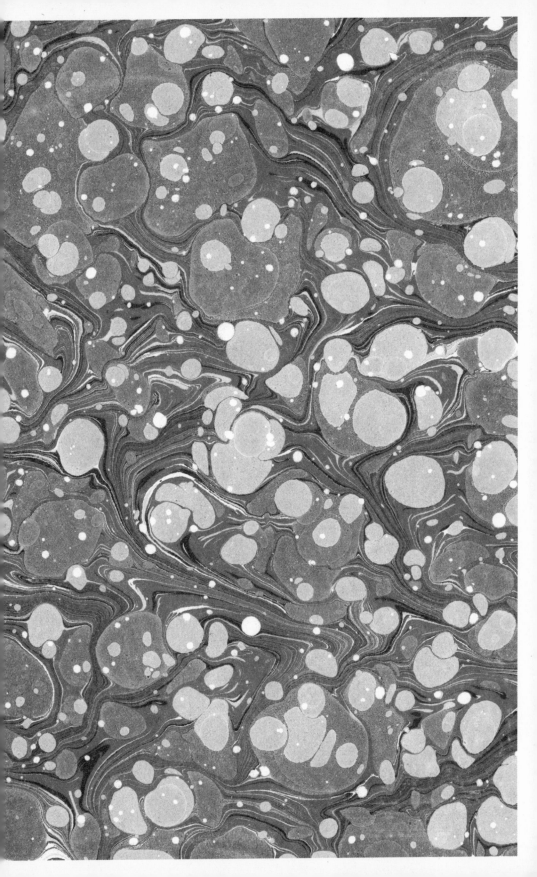

It was a human Chimera. More properly, a quite proximate view
of a *certain area* of a human Chimera.[*]

The picture represented something which Jack ought to have
known the contours of, but which, when examined in the book, appeared unaccountable and unfamiliar. Jack turned and twist'd the
Book this way and that. The Night was dark and mossy with a low
whisper of rain. Bess was snoozing soundly. Jack pulled his breeches
to his ankles. Looked at himself. Then the book. Then himself again.

The Picture was forcing a formulation upon him.

There was a whispering in his head. Chatter came from some
deep reaches, where frazzl'd Terror combined with profound Unsurprise. Connections were assembling. All his life he had somehow imagined that coves came in all shapes and sizes. But looking
at the *Cyclopaedia,* he thought: *Not this size. Not my size.*

This book, this *Cyclopaedia,* was a book of cruel diagnoses and
classifications. And now something clarify'd itself to him, as if out
of a Fog. He was something that existed only as a Scrawl on the
world's landscape—as if someone had come along and stepped on
a beautiful painting of sunflowers with a jackboot full of Shite—
and that monstrous blob of shite splatted in the middle of a field of
flowers—that blob, Jack considered—was he.

Jack slept hectically, falling into a fitful daze near morning. The rain
had swept out, and clouds were gusting low over London, carrying
a cold front when he woke into the wet gray. Peeking from the pillow, he saw starlings chirruping in Gangs across the sky, shooting
urgent for the worm-riddled Thames shore. A rustle from across the
room—Bess in the far corner, crouched over the chamber pot in

---

[*] SULLIVAN: NO, SERIOUSLY, IS THERE A PAGE MISSING HERE?
    ME: No. Why?
    SULLIVAN: WHERE IS THE "PICTURE" OF THE "HUMAN CHIMERA"
GENITALIA AS INDICATED ABOVE?
    ME: Looks like original author inserted abstract page instead.

her skirts. A feeling flashed through him. Longing. Unmitigated and total.

The splash and echo of piss collided with ceramic. He untangled from the bedsheets and cross'd the room 'til he was standing bent over her, with one hand petting her head, the other between her legs. She was moaning and pissing into the cup of his palm—it ran warm over his fingers.

He brought his fingers to his lips, tasted the sting of her on his tongue. She had her forehead against his belly, her arms around his waist.

He would die for her effluvia—Something like how she slept with her nose tucked into his armpit—how they drowned in each other without satiety.

Oh, the Contradictions.

He would drink anything that came out of her. But he couldn't un-smish[†] for her.[‡]

When they unclasp'd, he dressed himself in his day clothes, picked up Chambers' book, and headed downstairs.

[†] Un-shirt. A neologism.
[‡] Further on the complex history of racialization and digestion, see Kyla Wazana Tompkins, *Racial Indigestion: Eating Bodies in the 19th Century* (New York University Press, 2012).

4.

Jenny Diver was only too happy to have a moment of Relief.

Thank God, she mouthed from the bed, amidst a tumult of whalebone-stiffed petticoats edged with violet lace. Her breasts were purpl'd with thumb-marks—teeth marks?—marks of overly much Attention, whatever the case.

Evans was indeed an oddly complexioned man, with a giant, blindingly white wig. He perched atop the coverlets at Jenny's side, his limbs as white as his wig, and his face pink as a raspberry.

Regarding him, Jack was quite sure that no matter how blood-rich his arborvitae might be, it couldn't surpass the displeasing nature of the rest of him.

"I was curious if you had a moment to discuss—" He display'd the book.

Evans reached for his Monocle, throwing coverlets about. He rais'd the Glass to his eye. "What did you say your name was?"

"Hadn't." Jack coughed. Then, into the ensuing silence—"Jack."

"Jack"—Evans peer'd at him—"let's discuss this over some tea." He stood—his undergarments flowing about him in an unappetiz-ing Cloud—and linked his arm through the crook of Jack's elbow, leading them out of the room, towards the hearth.

"Some say that a chimera pollutes all that it touches," Evans proclaim'd as they walked. He spoke as if he were writing a Decree. It was off-putting. "And yet my experience doesn't accord with this fiction, nor do my Affections resonate with the sentiment of fear 'roused in some hearts by the mere suggestion of a chimera in prox-imity." They had reached the hearth—a particularly unclean area with scumm'd bowls lying about on cabinets, and a pot of water burbling over a fire. The remnants of the mollies' birthing theatrics were strewn—a wooden baby leg on a table, a dislodg'd button-eye lying cracked on the floor.

Evans cleared his throat. "I'm writing a lengthy Disquisition on Sexual Chimeras."

Jack nodded vaguely.

Evans had not released Jack's arm.

"I should say that I do not take the supernatural View. Some—like Diemerbroeck—believe chimeras to be monsters. I, however, believe them to be an Illusion. A category of creature, quite frankly"—here he narrow'd his eyes at Jack—"that does not, strictly speaking, exist. My view is that chimeras are persons afflicted with Macroclitoradeus—my term!—as the result of morbidity or dis-ease. And my goal—against earlier theorists—is to support the pos-sibility of *disease-correction*." He pursed his lips. "So to speak."*

Evans dropped Jack's arm and began to busy himself with water

---

* SULLIVAN: NOT TO SOUND LIKE A JEWISH MOTHER—HEH-HEH—BUT WAS EVANS A "REAL" DOCTOR?

ME: Though I can find no record of an author, "Evans," of any disquisition on chimeras, Isbrand van Diemerbroeck (referenced above) did pen *The Anatomy of Human Bodies,* trans. William Salmon (London, 1689). Upon seeing a chimera in Utrecht, Diemerbroeck described "her" (*sic*) "yard" as "half a Finger long," though rumor had it that "this Yard would upon venereal and lascivious Thoughts erect itself a Finger's length."

SULLIVAN: EXCELLENT DETAIL! ANY CHANCE THAT THIS MANU-SCRIPT CAN GET A LITTLE MORE DIEMERBROECKIAN?

ME: I'm limited to transcribing what's already here.

SULLIVAN: WELL, THERE IS THE MATTER OF THE MISSING PAGE.

ME: There is no missing page.

SULLIVAN: SPECULATE THEN.

ME: On the basis of what?

SULLIVAN: BUT YOU YOURSELF ARE A— SO SHOULDN'T YOU BE ABLE TO— WELL, NEVER MIND.

and some mildewed buds of chamomile that he produc'd from the
Pockets of his robe.

He continued his discourse throughout. Speaking in technical-
ities, he catalogued chimera-myths across a variety of cultures.
"Some deny their existence, some revere them, permitting them to
walk among the dead as women—"

Jack allowed Evans' voice to dim to a blur of sound. His Somethingness was nothing like this roster of examples.

But then Evans said something that jolted him.

"—And while the Romans decreed that all *chimeras* be placed
into tiny coffins at birth, nailed shut and thrown into the Sea, the
Greeks thought them a charmed species. Simply a human of both
sexes, although often with one part more luxuriant than the other."

Luxuriant.

His *Something*—Jack thought—*was* luxuriant. It blossom'd luxuriant in Bess's hand. Sprang into luxuriance when they touched,
throbbing against his breeches, or the Horn. He luxuriat'd in her
Presence.

The steam from the teapot evaporated against Evans' hands,
raising a red welt along the crook of his pointer finger.

Evans dropp'd the kettle on the side table and locked eyes with
Jack. "I've been laboring on an Idea. Combining the classical Greek
attitude towards luxuriance with the newest methods in scientific
Management of the body."

"Management?"

"Management." Evans nodded. "I regard chimeraness, frankly,
as a kind of hurricane—a weather system of extremes. My research
has demonstrated that a chimera is a thing of both misery and
shocking pleasure. A thing of intensities. I believe we can—hm—
let's see—how to put this—*accelerate, emphasize*—certain of those
intensities." He leaned in, studying Jack's face. "I can help you."

"H-how did you—"

Evans look'd at him pityingly. "Really, it's quite obvious."

· · ·

Jack spent the entirety of the next day staring out the window, itching and gasping in his boiling smish. He wanted only to take it off, to breathe free of the tight jerkin.

But what he had to get through in order to *luxuriate.*

At night he dreamt he was stripped bare, strapp'd to the saddle of a cantering horse, paraded through the town under the blazing sun. The jolt of hooves on cobblestones ached his back—clusters of branches threw shade across his face— He became desperately thirsty— The horse was driving him towards someone—some cruel power— Then the horse stopped. There was a Figure near but unseen— The Figure said something—garbled words. Incomprehensible and not reassuring. He tried to lift his head and look— Sunspots filled his eyes.

Then something cut the golden light in two. A flash of steel, and a white-hot pain flew through his chest. A line of fire licked his ribs, and gouts of blood burst up over his rolling eyes as he lay against the horse's rump— The bright sky swam above him, dappled with bloody fireworks. Then the fireworks were falling— His own blood blanketed his pupils, sending him deep under water to a purple dark sea. The sun gray'd to a speck, and his horse dove down into this darkening sea—rocking him on hood waves. And he was drowning.

—He awoke shivering, his heart racing. His smish was soak'd. His teeth hurt from Clenching.

Bess was blinking in the sun, reaching her hand out sleepily.

"Night terror?"

"Yes. And no."

He told her the dream—the hot feel of his own Blood pouring over his ribs. The horse-ship swimming down, down under dark water. It had been a terrible dream, but then, on waking, it had oddly left him with a Light Feeling where his breasts were—some anticipation of—*something.*

Bess traced around his ribs, careful not to touch anything but bone.

"Here? Light here?"

He nodded. "And all here—" He waved his hand in the air above his chest. Then told Bess of the caterpillars he used to catch at the Thames shore in summer. The tiny pocks where their skin opened to the air. Caterpillars didn't gasp at air as he did. Rather, air fizzed through their trunks to fill their Bodies. And the feeling he had about the Dream was that he'd become—through a course of great and terrifying Pain—a creature whose Body, for once, and to his great relief, began to breathe.

"We're simply removing the *non-luxuriant* bits," Evans said, swinging wide the door to Jenny's room. "Perfectly safe." He pursed his lips. Paus'd. "Well, *by and largely* safe."

Bess clutch'd a decanter of brandy, which she regularly brought to her lips.

"Do reserve some liquor for the patient," Evans mutter'd, as he bustled about, yanking the coverlets off Jenny's bed. He led them into the kitchen, where he laid the fabric on the table to create a makeshift operating theater.

Jack began shaking.

Evans had become a kind of bureaucratic Husk. He whisk'd about, readying his Instruments, dipping them in jugs of wine and then laying them, dripping, upon a series of assembled side tables and stools.

The Gleam he had in his eye—the thrill of scientific experiment—Bess had a bit of too. Jack grew nervouser and nervouser the more excited the two of them came to appear. He told himself the operation would intensify the *luxuriant* parts of him. Once it was done—he reasoned—he would never have to see Evans again. Never have to hear him discoursing further about chimeras.

But what he had to get through first.

Jack did not know what was worse: the anticipation of the Pain or the Gulf that was opening between himself on the one hand and

Bess and Evans on the other. Evans bloating with power; Bess at his side, looking down with a mix of anxious kindness and interest.

Evans instructed Bess to find a "Blood bucket"—terminology that made Jack tremble. When she turn'd to seek the item, Evans reach'd into his cloak pocket and leaned in, bringing his fingers to Jack's nose. An awful, oily Smell bloomed from his fingertips. He held a pinch of something that looked like dirt but the grains were larger, and tawny. He press'd the Grains to Jack's nose, holding him at the back of his head.

"Snuff it. Helps with healing." He paus'd. "Helps with—after."

Jack's arms were jellied with anxiety. He snorted the Grains back as directed; they burned his nostrils, and filled his lungs with the scent of something rancid. He cough'd, and a warmth filled his body. It was good, in fact. The warmth reminded him of when Bess had said his name for the first time in the Black Lion. That moment when he fell from the ceiling into his own skin.

"Good," said Evans. "Easy now."

When Bess return'd with the Blood bucket—"Can we call it something else?" shriek'd Jack from the table; "How about Blood basin?" she suggest'd. "Something without the word 'blood' in it!"— Jack let Bess, at Evans' direction, take off his smish and sponge down his sweat-gritted chest and arms. They shared copious amounts of whiskey. It was warm near the hearth, but even so, Jack was shivering with his shirt off. Then Evans instructed him to re- move his breeches as well. *Why?!* he gasped. And Evans mumbl'd something about 'fections and Cleanliness. So, with Bess's hand on his shoulder, he slipped out of his breeches and stockings too. After what seemed a too-long pause, Evans covered his Nethers with one of Jenny's sheets, then produced some Volume from one of the stools. He mouthed to himself while turning pages.

Jack pivot'd his attention back to Bess.

She was reddening at her cheeks from the whiskey, her eyes sparkling with concern or drink or both.

"I once met a bat who'd had a similar procedure for cancers and lived to tell of it. She said the worst part was not the cutting through the veins, arteries, muscle and fat. The worst part was the 'scraping' after the main incisions." She paused. Elaborated. "The relentless Neatening."

"Scraping?? *Neatening?!* Just tell Evans to l-l-leave whatever's there," Jack said frantically, his eyes staring up at her from the table. "No scraping!" he shouted to the room. "No scraping!"

And then Evans was there, having put the book aside, standing with his scalpel poised at Jack's ribs. Jack was looking at Bess, and he could feel the point breaking his skin. He remembered his underwater trick, and he imagined himself descending into the muffled Deeps, cool water lapping at his temples in perfect silence. He was still shouting "No scraping!" though he could hear the words less and less. He felt his mouth moving, begging Bess about the scraping, and, then, at what must have been the umpteenth repetition of the word "scraping," the scalpel dragged lightly down the side of his ribs—he looked over—and Evans' eyes had gone very wide. Then they rolled back, and Evans descended to the floor like a marionette whose Strings had just been cut.

Bess and Jack stared at each other. Jack leaned up, peer'd over the table.

Evans was in an unnatural Slumber, his limbs laid out in hectic arrangements on the floor. A small stream of Blood dripp'd from Jack's ribs where the incision had been abruptly aborted.

"Fainted dead away," Bess appris'd. "It may be, in fact, that this was his first surgical operation," she continued.

"His first?! When were you going to tell me that!"

And now Evans was urgently garbling from the floor.

"What?" said Bess, bending.

"Snotmie urst."

"Snotmie urst?"

"Snotmie urst!" he yowled.

"He's saying 'It's not my first,'" Jack snapped from the table.

"Yesh, yesh," said Evans. "Not me ursh." There was something extraordinarily pathetic about a Reputation defended from the floor.

"He's quite mad," assessed Bess, standing up. "And in any case"—she looked down—"he's unconscious again."

"So you had turn'd me over to someone who as far as you knew had *never* done this before."

"He's *study'd* it quite a bit." Bess looked contrite.

"So have you!" Jack shouted. He meant, by this, that Evans was about as qualified to slice him open as was any untrained person—which was to say, *not at all*. But Bess took this to mean something else. She bent again over Evans' form, and this time she slipped the Scalpel from his hand. She picked up the book from the stool where it had been placed.

She righted herself. Look'd Jack in the eye. A negotiation of glances. Bess appear'd utterly calm and at home with a small weapon. Focused.

"Good point," she said. "*I* can do it."

He swallow'd down the rest of the whiskey, then Bess shook out the remainder of the flask over his ribs and chest. The world began to spin.

Bess laid her hand on his sternum. Her hand was warm.

"Mm-hm," Jack burbled. He realiz'd he was extraordinarily drunk.

And then she was doing it. He went somewhere mostly else. There were Thames-waves rising and falling over his head and in the far-off distance something was happening to his Body. He could feel the tissue come away from his chest under Bess's strangely expert hands. Blood ran down his ribs and pooled in the Crease between his back and the table. Her ability with the knife was wonderfully sure and smooth. His terror had loosed some part of him from himself, and he was startling into each Moment as if waking from a dream—each second had no relationship with the one just prior. He dipp'd in and out of time.

Bess's face was just above his. "Are you fainting?" she asked.

"The bat with the cancers fainted twice during her operation. She said there were 'Chasms' in her mind. Periods of time she could not account for." The words floated over Jack's face. He tried to speak, but couldn't.

There were Chasms in Jack's mind too, but they had nothing to do with the operation. He had them before the operation—had always had them, in fact. It had to do—he floatingly thought—with his *Somethingness*. His whole life was a Chasm. But perhaps if he and Bess could dive to the bottom of this one—the Chasm of his chest—they could come out whole somehow, and together.

Bess kept talking to him, telling him what she was doing. Her Words became all of time and space; his own body seemed less real than her Voice.

He heard himself remind her not to scrape. She shushed him and kept cutting, and there was a lot of Blood. Delirious and babbling, he told Bess to lick the Blood up, like a cat. He wanted this Proximity to her, wanted her spit inside him, sewed up inside him, like a watery Organ.

Bess said that was "bird-witted" and "not clean." She called him "paagal." Her father's word.

"It's not crazy," he object'd. "It's like a hug," he said, delirious. "An *inside* hug."

As Bess sewed him up—which the bat had not mentioned also hurt an awful lot (by then Jack was sobbing and had shite through his teeth[*] twice)—they heard banging on the outer door of the house. Loud calls from the street.

"Centinels," hissed Bess.

"How d'you know," slurred Jack, wiping vomit from his mouth with the back of his hand.

"The Knock." Her lips were set. She began tidying the surgical area more quickly.

The outer door clicked open. He heard the Lady Abbess say, "But how do I *know* you're really centinels?"—and then a Slam as

---

[*] Vomited

the door was shoved open roughly, banging the wall behind, and a squeaky, full-body Hiccup from the Lady Abbess who—from the sound of it—had been thrown across the room.

Boots.

Boots.

Several more pairs of boots entering the foyer.

"Do you have any prohibited doxies in here?"

"We keep a clean establishment here, a place for coves to exchange bitter for sweet Humours."

"Certain doxies are now prohibited by order of the Lord Mayor," the centinel continued, "on account of the Publick's Health." The flap of a broadside being opened. "'As it is thought that the plague travels in East India Ships, we recommend that the city authorize centinels to question and—if necessary—quarantine any lascar and Levantine persons suspected of Contagion.'" Snap of a finger punching at paper. "By mayoral Decree. Now"—Boots turn'd slowly, heels scraping in the floor-grit—"we'll inquire again. Do you have any prohibited doxies on the premises? Doxies who could be contagious to an innocent cove just looking to *exchange the Humours.*"

Bess stopped tidying and stood still against the sideboard. The only sound was Jack's Blood dripping down his ribs, plinking against the floor.

Just then, Evans began to stir. Murmuring, rustling his coats, garbling like a wing-shot duck.

"We don't have any prohibited doxies here, sir, this is a place of great repute," the Lady Abbess said.

"None? Not a one? Not even a one for especial pleasures or *particular* Fancies? Coves like that sort of thing."

"Only Anglo-English girls here."

Evans' garbles were getting louder. Bess's eyes search'd the back of the kitchen. *Exit through a window?* The glazes were small and tight—deliberately designed to prevent Peeping Toms and unpaying customers. It was unlikely she could squeeze through quickly, and being caught half in and half out of the bat house was—*well*—a magnificently stupid Plan.

"Have you *ever* had a prohibited doxy here?" The interrogation continu'd in the foyer.

"By what you're telling me, such doxies only became prohibited tonight. Even if I ever had had one 'prohibited' one—as you say—she wouldn't have been exactly prohibited then, now would she?"

Evans emitted a snarled honk from the floor. "EEEEEERE!"

"Oh, God," Jack whispered, seeing Bess's stricken face.

Before he could think further—and clearly under the influence of alcohol and the shock of the procedure—Jack leapt from the table, grabbing the pillow from under his own head, and throwing himself and the pillow upon Evans. Every nerve in his rib cage shrieked, but in his overwrought state it did not produce an immediate reaction. Pain simply rippled through his already wracked Body, unable even to elicit the usual counterflinch.

He was on top of Evans, bleeding onto Evans' jacket and shirt, struggling the pillow over his face.

"Shhhhh," he hissed. "For God's sake, you hateful beet, shhhhh."

Evans grabb'd up at him, his soft ash-white hands flailing, ripping at the air. His hands spasm'd, dragged along the ground, collecting dust. Evans clawed upwards, around the pillow, spearing his Nail into Jack's cheek, drawing Blood. Jack threw his chest on top of the pillow, his entire body weight on Evans' face. His chest fired from the pressure of the Stitches against the rough pillow, and the sharp bones of Evans' nose and brow beneath that. He heard himself wheezing and sobbing. Tried to stifle the Sound of it. There was spittle running from his mouth. He cry'd out in pain, and cry'd with effort and fury.

"Jack!" Bess whispered. "Jack, you're going to—"

And then he pass'd out.*

---

* SULLIVAN: EVER SEEN ANYTHING LIKE THIS?
  ME: In person? I'll reserve comment.
  SULLIVAN: IN LITERATURE OF THE PERIOD.
  ME: I am aware only of a similar operation performed nearly a century later on

---

Frances Burney (1812). Athough also performed without anesthesia, the operation was to remove a tumor.

SULLIVAN: ANYTHING PERFORMED FOR THE PURPOSES OF GENDER TRANSITION?

ME: Even if I said it was the only such record I've ever seen, what with everything we've already agreed on re: Mignolo and the "epistemic disobedience" that *is* the archive (we've agreed on this, right??)—it wouldn't really mean anything.

Also, you know you don't need to use all caps when you write me, right?

SULLIVAN: LEADERSHIP TECHNIQUE! CAPS SETTING NON-NEGOTIABLE.

5.

JACK WOKE IN THE DAYBED IN BESS'S ROOM.

"How did I—?"

Footsteps neared the daybed. "We carry'd you," Bess said.

"Who *we*?"

"Jenny and I. You aren't heavy."

Jack yelped as he tried to turn towards the sound of her, and caught a stitch against the coverlet. The sutures felt to be made from rusted wire. Each breath unleashed a volley of arrows into his chest.

"Don't move. You're leaking fluids everywhere, healing and—" She laid a hand to his boiling forehead. "Just don't move," she repeated.

"Evans?"

"Well." A pause. "You happen to have killed him. Inadvertently or whatnot."

"*Killed* him?"

"Very much so, yes. Dead at your hand. Well, maybe, more specifically, at your chest. You—well—smothered him to death with your bleeding chest."

"I didn't mean—I mean, I did mean to, but I—"

Bess shrugged. "He was a wretch."

"But I didn't mean—"

"Even if you did."

"And yet—"

"I thought it was sweet—albeit a touch dumb."

"Ah."

"Caus'd some problems for Jenny, tho'. As she was the last one seen with him, she's had to Flee."

"I'm sorry," he croak'd. "Is there something I can do?"

"A well-crafted calling card eloquently offering your most sincere apologies always suits." She snickered. "This isn't a tea party. A scamp went wrong. Jenny knows what to do. She went to Dennison's seraglio, near Drury Lane."

"Dennison's?"

"Dennison's is"—searching for the word—"shabby. It'll do for a while at least. Look—" She pulled something from her skirt's pocket. "I discovered this on Evans while pulling you off him."

She handed him a crumpled note.

Met with Okoh and the Lion-Man at the Tower. *
There is a replicability problem.

"What do you make of this?"

Jack squinted up at her. He was drifting into a half-dreamworld—images of the two doxies dragging Evans into the street. Them carrying him up the stairs. Did they put his Trousers back on? He reached for his legs. He was trouser'd.

They had cared for his Body like a child's. He attempt'd to turn to his side and was stabb'd with Pain. His stomach rose in his throat and nausea overtook him. He garbled out something.

Bess put a brandy to his lips, and he pushed it away, reaching for her skirts, drawing her close. She dropped to her knees, and he rested his head against her Armpits, rooting with his nose, and she let him. He drank in the wet Smoak scent. Her *Livingness.* Her *Bessness.*

He breathed. He breathed. *Bess. Bess.* He slept.

---

* I'm unable to source either "Okoh" or the "Lion-Man" in any of the reference material.

. . .

Jack lay in the daybed for a week, villainous juices seeping from his ribs. He slept in the days and thrashed at night against the twinges of healing, scarring. Unaccountably, given his discomposed condition, he was besieged by flashes of Desire. His groin flared. Impossibly, but it did. He attemped to stagger from the daybed several times to lie with Bess. She would glance over. "Not yet."

The scars took a week to crust. And there were Infections. Bess had closed Jack's chest with rough brown twine that ached and itched when he breathed. Pus collected in small puddles around the twine, tiny irises of bright green Oil. A line of septic Lanterns cutting his torso in two.

And then an urchin dropped a broadside at the door of the bat house, announcing the imminent lifting of the Quarantine. Soon. Within the week. After which the centinels would remain on the streets— *Of course*, grumbled Bess, *that's what this entire charade was for anyway. Gettin' us used to centinels breathing down our necks.* But the quarantine would be lifted. The air shift'd and the return of daily life drew near.

By the time the quarantine had been ended, Jack found himself thrilled with his new quaddron,* and spirits buoyed. Quite buoyed. He wasn't bluff† and buff-beefed‡ like some of the coves who frequented Bess's rooms. He was still spider-shanked§ and lithe. But

---

* Body
† Big in body
‡ Big-bodied
§ Thin-legged

he felt so alleviated of his dugs¶ he was inclined to parade about without a flesh-bag** on as often as possible. He became what Bess would say, with a smile, was "rather huggy."

For Bess had freed him of a chest-burden so great he hadn't even known, until it had been removed, what weight he had carried. Every breath was wholly a new event now. The touch of smish to his skin was an Ecstasy, even with the crawly feeling of the stitches. The touch of skin to skin an even greater joy.

The interstice between Jack's insides and his skin—that chasm of echoing hollow, the miserable Gas that kept him from himself, and from the world, had been closed. Bess had closed the chasm, sutured it when she sutured Jack's chest. And now, undeniably, there was a new thrumming in Jack's body. He could *feel* himself inside and out. And he was on a constant prowl for *Bess*. Just the touch of his hand to the small of her back, where her spine arched into the top of her Bum, set him afire. The lock of their eyes sent *Bess*-flares to his groin. At night, when Bess returned from her strolls to the Thames—*there are more of them,* she'd say—*more ships, like the ones we saw the night they put on the Quarantine*—she would find the dark air streaming in and Jack with his head stuck out the glazes, huffing hard at the breezes, his shirt off, wet Atmosphere clinging to his chest, brightening his scars to a rose-pink. He would advance towards her, skin glistening with the ashes and wet of the City, and take her in his arms.

¶ Breasts
** Shirt

6.

PERHAPS IT WAS THE HEAT OF THE SUMMER THAT INSPIRED IT, BUT turning Water-pad* had been Bess's idea.

The town swarm'd with centinels, and the monied sort had begun to walk with greater ease through all the parishes. They flaunted watch fobs and rings—jaunted around smirking and un-afraid.

"Let's do a spectacular Heist," Bess said.

They'd toss'd about ideas. Nothing had stuck.

And then, one heat-stuffed day—"Trinity House is kept up nice," she observ'd as they strolled past the Lighthouse Authority on Tower Hill after an advantageous turn bamboozling and pick-pocketing the whiskey-soaked patrons of the Spotted Hen.

"Since they've issued the plague warnings, they've been unload-ing some merchant vessels at the Lighthouse 'stead of the docks. Heard it from a cove."

"The Lighthouse Authority are just a crew of thieves with the blessing of an Act of P-Parliament," Jack spat—barely missing the boots of one of the centinels who seemed to be everywhere now, doubling or tripling by the day in some mysterious municipal Orgy. They occupied every street in Cheapside and Spitalfields now, with their muskets slung over their shoulders and their eyes narrowed into mean Pinholes, surveilling the corners like angry owls.

"So they are." Indeed, she'd told him this just the other night.

---

* Thief who robs lighthouses in the Thames

Bess toss'd her arm dramatically against the back of Jack's shoulders, pushing them both out of range of the beady centintel. "But what I'm getting at is maybe the Lighthouse is particularly heavy with treasures these days."

He'd turn'd, press'd Bess against the back wall of J. Scott, Booksellers, in Bow Street (or *China Street*, as the thieves called it, for the profusion of porcelain shops along the avenue), as she explained to him he'd have to enter *from outside the upper floor*, in order to avoid the Watchman keeping a lookout on the ground level—and Jack was *yes'ing, yes'ing*, sayin' *of course* he could do it, his head swimming with Lust as her hair clung and spread against the heat and moisture of the bricks.

Which all occasion'd the fact that sometime later, Jack found himself hanging nearly twenty yards above the Thames. His stitches strained against newly healed skin as he dangled off the nails. Bess had heard tell from one of her callers that a merchant ship would be making its way to port with a hold full of the finest Madras cottons. It would fetch a pretty penny in the back alleys.

From the great height of the Lighthouse, he could see the expanse of Plague Ships. He counted twelve vessels dotting the river from Wapping New Street down to Red Yard and the Lower Docks—a creaking archipelago. He briefly wonder'd if that meant plague was drifting through the air—if it rose on the wind currents. He twitched his nose. Continued climbing.

A hot gust, stinging with Seawater, buffeted down the Thames. The tower of the Lighthouse vanished out of perspective as Jack craned up, searching out the iron cleats jammed into the wooden boards. He clung to the splintered wood, breathing slow and deep. Felt for the interior architecture of the walls—the venting, the erection of crossbeams and lintels.

The glazes fac'd south down the Thames—Bess had told him— not to catch the setting sun or to flood the dusty recesses with a heartening Light, but to intercept deep-sea vessels en route to their destinations. At first sight of a ship crawling up the river, the Eddystone would blink its beacon two short flickers of candlelight for "slow," and three for "stop." Then the Lighthouse Watchmen would lumber down the many circling flights to Sea-level, prepared to exchange one neatly-scripted Deep Sea License for a *"fair percentage"* of the booty on board.

Jack knew that, after they commandeered it, the Licensers would drag their haul back up the many flights of stairs. They would sleep with their booty close. He knew this because that was what he would do. Knew the Lighthouse men slept where they could breathe the Vapors of their catch.

Jack bored a hole in the window shutter and cracked the Glass. Out poured the sweet piercing scent of Watchman's Blue Tape Gin and the musky rot of sleep. He peer'd through the window. A Lighthouse Officer snoozed in a four-poster bed. An East India trunk lay beneath the Sill.

And then the voices hit him. Jack jerk'd his head back from the edge and crouched under the sill, taking nervous Bird-Breaths, near blown off the side of the building by the piercing howl of commodities yelping.

Focus— Don't fall— Find the goods— Take the goods— Descend Lighthouse with goods, thought Jack.

(And then: *Sell Goods— Roger Bess— Sleep Naked and Entwin'd.*)

But Focus wasn't easy. Peeking in the window of the Lighthouse, Jack was besieged by his *affliction*. Thing-voices swelled over him, a shrieking tide.

The room was a chaos of sound. Bess had prepared him for a complex heist with commodities that had traveled a long way, confin'd and likely desperate for Release. She'd told him what she had heard of the seaside fortress town of Madras—*lashed with the fiercest surf along all the Coromandel coast.* Told him of the weavers and dyers who lugged their linens and inks a week's journey from Fort St. George, barefoot through the salt-water lagoons to the back

Edges called Black Town, dense-nested Shanties occluded by mangrove from the bright halls of White Town's mansions and pavilions—then along the dry, sand-swept bricks that paved the way from every abode in Madras to St. Mary's, the only Anglican church east of Suez.

Hanging through the cracked glaze, though, that wasn't what he heard.

The sound was something else. A repetitive, garbled Sobbing. Nothing about any of the geographies or Histories Bess had told him.

Just this:

Nobody, nobody.

One pealing call: *Nobody.* Again and agan.

The wind squeez'd a cold tear from his eye. Jack wiped it, clinging with one hand to the lighthouse ledge.

Nobody. A howl. *Nobody.*

Jack had learned that commodities understood much more about themselves than their buyers could ever begin to grasp. They were bursting with Histories to tell. A commodity that had escaped the infernal cycle of production-display-sale was a happy, content object—returned to serving a purpose. For commodities hated merchants and shopkeeper-shelving. They liked to be in use. Or squirrel'd away in a pocket, kept close, coveted. Frankly, like anything else, they wanted to be loved.

So it was natural that they bawled and howled when up on display or trapped in the circuits of sale. But tonight's monologues were different. Worse. A terrible screaming. Something had happened—Something that made it impossible to tell a History at all.

A swinging Vertigo overtook Jack, and—with his stomach wheeling and bunching—he lost one hand's grip on the sill. His left flailed in open air—his right slipped to its tip—his toes clenched around the cleat—his left hand claw'd at bricks without purchase—

The sound of his scrabbling woke the Lighthouse Officer. Sounds of quilts being thrown off, and then thudding steps towards the window. Jack did the only thing he could.

He let himself drop—

—and caught a cleat between his nethers. The air knocked out of him. And now the Officer had shut the window, muttering about cold breezes and 'fections.

Jack spun his aching nethers around the cleat then dove head-first through the window below, landing on his back with a thud. Lay gasping for a moment in the empty Storeroom, his breath fogging the air.

The peals of *Nobody* from upstairs roused him to his feet. He tiptoed up the stairwell.

The Lighthouse Officer was hard snoozing again; the scent of much liquor recently imbibed cut through the stench of sleep. Jack made his way across the room to the crate under the window.

But when he creak'd the lid open, there wasn't even a single parcel of folded cotton inside. There was musty air, the poisonous odor of something gone to rot—

—and a layer of what looked like dirt, but smell'd like the mineral tang of dried blood.

He recognized something about this scent.

Jack's guts rose into his throat.

There was still screaming coming from inside the crate.

Nobody, nobody, nobody.

And then, without further thought, he grabbed a pile of whatever it was—inhaled some of the grains—in a burning rush—still screaming.

The moment it whizz'd down his nostril, he knew.

It was the Substance that Evans gave him—just before his operation.

His body thrummed and flash'd with the heat of remembering. All of it—all the parts of him—feeling more *connected* somehow, bound together—the blood in his veins communicating with his Muscles, Organs. It felt as if every bit of him had been just a hair removed from every other—and the substance had sent a Stitch quietly across the Gap.

He coughed at the putrid sour water taste, thrust a handful in his pocket—assessed the weight of it against his thigh—it wasn't much—looked about the room—spied an empty gin bottle lying near the trunk—began scooping it into the bottle.

He ripped the bill of lading from the inside lid of the Trunk. Held entirely still for a moment, listening for any sound of the Substance anywhere else.

The room was now filled with utter Silence.

—Then a footfall on the stairs. Another Night Officer. Jack's heart scamper'd like a trapped squirrel. He opened the window—slipp'd his legs over the sill and lowered his feet to the cleat. Just then the sleeping Officer let off a Hoot of fart into his quilts, and Jack leapt a little, his midriff rising into the air and coming down hard on the sharp sill—a quick intake of his Breath as he felt the skin at his chest pop open in a flash of heat and blood. He looked up—

The Watchman's eyes blinked at him.

And Jack—filled with an unfamiliar confidence—grinned, reached into his pocket and coolly palmed a half-guinea—counterfeit only to the trained eye. This he flipp'd to the bed, whispering, "If they ask where you got it, tell 'em Jack Sheppard gave it to you."*

—Then slipp'd down the side of the lighthouse and into the waiting Punt, "borrowed" from a waterman too slipshod drunk to notice Bess launching from the shore under Houghton Bridge.

They rowed away, Bess leaning back in the punt, mooning at the Stars, giving a little laugh under her breath—her relaxed private laugh— *We braved down the beast.*

"Saw the Plague Ships from up there."

"Did you."

"Twelve? I think." Jack rowed hard against the night currents.

---

* Quite a few eighteenth-century documents report London thieves using "Sheppard gave it to me" as an alibi.

The breeze blew open his smish. Bess leaned across the punt, put her hand on his sternum. Kissed it. Wiped her thumb across the Blood oozing from his scar where he had hit the sill. He let the oars drop, and held her head against him—nose in her hair. The punt drifted.

Just then, the Watchman's head poked out from the tower window, silhouetted in the moonlight—called out across the distance.

"Sheppard, ah . . . they're comin' for you, boy, and the whole town knows it. And now with what ye took."

"The town can kiss my arse," he shouted back, craning up.

"Jack!" Bess said.

"What?"

"You can't be screaming from a punt in the dead of night."

Jack grinned, ducking his chin to his chest. "He's a sodden old buck fitch*. Babbling at the moon."

"Still."

Something fell through the air then and hit the water with a plink. Jack turn'd. A knob of something bobbed behind the boat.

He listened hard for something—anything—any sort of muffled commodity-voice.

Quiet. Just the wash of the Thames slapping the side of the boat.

"Bess?" He heard his own voice crack—fear seeped in. "What was that?"

A scent steam'd up. The soft, sparkly quality the river took from up on the Lighthouse had been replaced by a bath of filth and Waste. Sewers emptied at every street-edge, burbling their contents into an already-overstuffed brew. The Thames was a seeping bruise upon the landscape. A gray fog of putrid gas. The white knob bounced in the muck just behind the punt, then sank down as they pulled away.

Bess peer'd around his shoulder. "'S a fish," she said, smiling her warm, forget-about-everything-else smile. Her smile that al-

---

* Lecher

ways work'd amnesia on him. "Some nothing." She indicated with her chin at the Lighthouse. "What'd you nick?"

"Nothin' of value." Jack realized he had been compelled to lie only after he'd actually done it.

Then: a long squeak from down below. *Nobody.* Reverberating and dissipating in the expanse of river water.

A shiver ran through him, nose to spider-shanks.

For he didn't know what he saw, but he knew it *was no Fish*.

7.

At Bess's, Jack batted about the room like an agitated moth.[*]

"You must've heard it."

"I don't hear the things you do."

"But there was Something. He lobb'd something at us." Jack rose from the daybed to lean against the wall. He threw the window towards the top of the sash for air— Too powerfully— He hadn't meant to— Shards of plaster flew off the casing onto his hands and the floor.

Bess watched quietly. Jack's Buzzing to and fro while she rubbed lavender oil the length of her arms.

"If the worst they do is lob things at us . . ." she said.

Her tone was Light, but something had changed—a Distance had dropped down between them.

---

[*] ME: As it is Friday, I notice I have not received payment for the most recent editing work. A mix-up with the bank? Please advise.

SULLIVAN: UNTIL SATISFACTORY RESOLUTION IS REACHED RE-GARDING THE MISSING PAGE, PAYMENT IS WITHHELD.

ME: There is no missing page. I would appreciate prompt payment or I will be forced to contact my lawyer.

SULLIVAN: NO PROBLEM! SHALL WE HAVE OUR LAWYER CONTACT YOUR LAWYER? OUR LAWYER IS EXCEPTIONALLY GOOD.

ME: I should have clarified. *Once I obtain* a lawyer I will be forced to contact that lawyer regarding payment. In the meantime, I have no recourse but to withhold foot-notes.

SULLIVAN: MEANING?

ME: I hereby declare an ad hoc strike until payment arrives.

SULLIVAN: LOL!!! A STRIKE OF ONE!! GOOD LUCK WITH THAT.

Bess slipp'd into bed with the day's broadside and a Candle on the night table. She had the frowning look of an accountant going over a bad day of receipts. Jack's Guts were in a tumult, as they were anytime he could see her face—which he watched as attentively as a herdsman scanning the sky for thunderclouds—shift.

Jack pulled off his smish, then arranged himself under the covers beside her, staring at the ceiling in the flickering candlelight. He massag'd a lingering twinge in his arm. Bess tugged the covers closer to her chin, crinkling the pages of the broadside.

"I'm sorry," he said finally.

"Sorry for what?" she said, turning a page.

"For . . ."

"Don't say you're sorry if you don't mean you're sorry."

"I'm sorry," he said again, foolishly.

"My God." She put down the broadside.

"I'm sorry you're angry."

"You're sorry I'm angry?"

"It wasn't an easy scamp and now you're angry and—"

"You presume everyone's angry at you all the time. It's bizarre and tedious. In any case, I'm profoundly sad."

He sat up.

"I don't believe you're telling me ev'rything about the Lighthouse. About what you found there."

"I am," he said unconvincingly.

"Spinoza once ask'd himself the question of whether or not 'twas acceptable for a person to lie to save his own life. Do you know what he said?"

Clearly the answer was no.

"He said that it is immoral for free individuals to limit another person's power to be free, to act freely, to make free choices. No matter the circumstances."

"What if the person who lies isn't, himself, free?"

She squinted. "You're free. And anyway"—her voice caught, deepen'd—"I've seen people much less free than you hold fast to honesty. Even in the face of death." Tears were beginning to plume

at the corners of her eyes. "You'll sow such distance between us—"
She broke off.

Jack's heart was racing. Was there no way out of having to Confess this now double Obfuscation—one that had begun for no good reason except that he wanted *this thing* and he felt he'd be punish'd for that wanting. It had occurr'd so quickly it was nearly an instinct. Jack was the arch-bilker, ferreter, sneaker of London, after all. And he was so because he'd sneak'd, bilked, and ferreted his entire life. He was miraculously good at keeping things hidden. And had an ability—he saw now—to turn that hiding into a weapon.

"If I tell you, will you tell me?"

"Tell you what?"

He should not continue—

—did anyway. "'Bout your nightmares—'bout Popham's Eau."

"That's different."

"So you won't tell me."

"No." She blink'd. Crinkled her forehead. "But when I can, yes."

Air ached in his lungs. He didn't want to admit any of this. He briefly considered fleeing into the night. But he was tired, and then another feeling seiz'd him. One stronger than the desire to flee. A vision, really. He saw himself divulging to Bess exactly what he didn't want to divulge. Saw them somehow sifting through the mess of veils together. He saw them coming out from under the fog of his panic and *Hideyness* on the other side, wisps of it blowing off them like clouds breathing off a lake at dawn. He un-held his breath.

He wanted to be known by her more than he needed to hide from her.[*]

"I did find something. Something screaming worse than usual.

---

[*] Dear Reader: Well, I'm broke again. But hey, I've been living off credit cards for decades now. What's the difference between no money and negative money, I always say. At least, thankfully, we're alone again. I've missed speaking more frankly to you.

It didn't have a tale, a History, like the rest of the things that speak to me. I imagine it's what Evans gave to me before the operation."

"You didn't tell me about Evans giving you something Beforehand." Bess turn'd away. "You didn't tell me about that either."

Jack rubb'd at his hair. The distance between them bored a hole in his guts—like he'd swallowed one of those rhubarb and aniseed purges his mum used to give him when she felt he was being "splenetic."

"But I didn't know what it was." This was true—he'd begun to put it all together only now. "A snuff of something right at the beginning of the *luxuriating operation*."

"A cathartic elixir? You certainly did shite through your teeth much."

"Didn't give it by mouth. The nose. And it smelled something awful. I didn't recognize it." He corrected: "Well, it recall'd something. Death. The green scent of a rat left to mildew at the edge of a field. But"—he inhal'd—"I think it's a kind of magic."

"Was it coffee?" she said. "That isn't magic. Coffee's a bean they steal from the New World, grind up with what tastes like dirty stockings and soot, and sell down by the Royal Exchange."

"It's not coffee." He turned towards her. "This 's better than coffee." Jack was gesticulating powerfully—too powerfully for sharing a small bed. "Or—it's like ten coffees without the starts it gives you."

Bess put her hand on his arm. "It does give you starts."

But then again, it didn't thin him like coffee would—in fact he'd thicken'd a bit after the operation. Had been starving all the time, too. *So then it can't be opium either.* "Did it say anything?"

Jack rubb'd his chin. "Jus' one thing, over and over."

"What?"

"*Nobody.*"

Bess's gaze turned inwards, that scientific look. He rolled towards her, propp'd his hand under his head.

Silence, then. "There's something else. The count can't be a coincidence."

"What count?"

"The ships you saw in the Thames. Twelve unmann'd, abandon'd vessels?"

"Yes. What about them?"

"They're increasing."

"So?"

"I don't think they're Plague Ships."

"What does any of that have to do with the Lighthouse Keeper?"

"I don't know. But when there's a quantity of strange occurrences, one becomes apt to regard them as somehow related."

"So then what's this about the count?"

"I am visited frequently by a Minister of Import/Export, and this Minister occasion'lly lets slip that the number of ships arriving has lessened of late."

"Is this minister Handsome?"

"What?"

"No matter. Sorry."

"The ships have lessened, he says, and yet you saw that they've increas'd. Somethin's off." She shook her head. "No, somethin'," she continued, "is *intriguingly* off."

"How so?"

"I don't think they're Plague Ships at all. I think they're—most of them anyway—familiars."

Quiet.

"Ghost ships that accompany trading and slaving vessels along their route," she furthered.

Jack was recognizing that clogg'd, skittery feeling in his throat. It recalled to him the way he'd feel after his mother had several drams of whiskey. Numb and buzzing at his extremities. He was fighting the ball of Anxiety in his throat for breath.

Bess watched him struggle for some beats.

"You know that a ghost ship"—she lean'd towards him; their Body scent was ruffl'd up from under the coverlets—"is not actually a ghost."

She waited for him to rearrange his face to feign prior knowledge of this fact, then lay against his chest.

"It's an Abandoned vessel pulled by the deep sea tides along the trade routes," she continu'd, mercifully pretending to recount facts known to both of them. But when she look'd up and they exchang'd a quick glance, Jack saw how many steps ahead of him she was. She anticipat'd his reactions to her—knew them before he did. She did this, he presumed, because his reactions occupied a spectrum she knew from other pale Anglos. She could anticipate what Nonsense was about to come out of his mouth and when. And for whatever reason, she had now deign'd to clarify to him the extent of his false presumptions. This Conceding to explain things was a kind of mercy. An opening she was offering.

"When sailors mutinied they'd establish outlaw societies in remote islands. The lascars and the Africans knew the best locations. They'd disembark and set their old vessel adrift to haunt—*and I mean this as a figure of speech*—the seas. Set them to sail free in the currents, disturbing the peace for the Royal Navy and the East India Company.

"All the lascar sailors ran that route. They're the ones that knew the ghost ships best. And knew not to be afraid of 'em. Not like the British captains who cowered at the sight, scrubb'd references to 'em from the ship logs. Drank drams of whiskey to blur the Sight of 'em poking up at the horizons.

"My father was pressed to labor," she spoke into his chest. "Sailed that route for the Company. Said he would see them in the shallow waters of Madras Port, banging in the undertows, slushing against the sands. When he ran the China route, he said he'd see a ghost ship tracking to the estuaries of Canton Port. He said the more mutinies there were, the more ghost ships would appear on the open ocean. Sometimes whole fleets of them like a pack of black-beaked dolphins breaking the waves. The lascars were never scared, because they knew when they'd see a ghost ship they were seeing a signal from freed comrades. The Anglo sailors—the ones that refus'd to listen—thought them supernatural emanations and just about piss'd themselves at the sight." She laugh'd. "My father always said when the ghost ships came to the Thames, it would mean the South was rising."

Jack imagined a fleet of ghost ships fording the high gray crags of the ocean, beating back Froth alongside the Trading vessels, salt crusting their masts, plunging bowfirst into the briny glens. Lurching out of the whitecapped pikes like Hounds, mouths full of limp duck, water streaming from their decks.

"I think it's ghost ships come to flood the Thames, I think the Magistrates and all o' 'em know what it means—and they're in a panic about it and usin' it to clamp down the Town harder." She exhaled. "If it weren't for the rogues I'd hate it here."

The room got colder then. Not between, but around, them. There was an *unheldness* to them both in the world—and though differently felt, it was a certain shared Aloneness. Some utter Bereftness—of kin, of home—they recogniz'd in each other. It was in the way their bodies clawed towards each other. Diving deep into the solitude, finding each other there. Waiting, open, given over—*

"I'd hate it here too," he said. He'd never even thought this before. But the lens of Bess's hate had shifted something in him.

---

* See, this is what I'm fucking talking about, Reader. This is why it's good to be just *you and me again.*

What would P-Quad even *do* with this material? Call me thin-skinned, but I can't handle it with the badgering, prurient questions. Not about this. Not about Unheldness. I'm not breaking this shit down for some manager of a private testing corporation. I'm honestly—quite honestly, if you want to know the truth—not even going to do it for those queers from "nice" families. You know, the ones with supportive, rolling-in-the-dough, loving parents chauffeuring them to the mall to fulfill whatever sartorial needs they have, etc.! I mean, good for these people, obviously. But then: Where are my people? Am I the only one who's been puked up by the bowels of history?

On the very good chance that the answer is *no*, I'm editing this for *us*—those of us who've been dropped from some moonless sky to wander the world. Those of us who have to *guess*—wrongly, over and over (until we get it right? Please god)—what a *"home"* might feel like. So forget the held ones just for a second, they're doing fine; I'm speaking to you—to us—to those of us who learned at a young age never to turn around, never to look back at the nothing that's there to catch us when we fall.

She pull'd him in for that kiss that was *Language* between them.

Jack was already unbuttoning his trousers when it began to rain, flicking in the open window and onto the sill. Bess cross'd the room to shut the pane.

Jack began wrestling his trousers to his knees when his hand glanced on an edge of something poking from his pocket, slicing a small Fissure into his finger. He jumped—look'd down. There in his uncurling palm, a roll of raw pickled flax paper.

He'd forgotten about the bill of lading.

He unscroll'd the paper—at least at first glance quite like any other bill of lading he'd nick'd from other trunks and casks. On one side, fees and duties for items. On the other, tho', something altogether else.

He press'd the note flat into his palm, and was staring down at his hand when she returned.

Payment for whatever quantity of silks had been crossed out with deep, messy scratches, over which were words, carved in dark ink, shaky and rough-edged.

Granulated Strength Elixir
Available exclusively at Mr. Jonathan Wild's House of Waste

He frowned. Looking up.

"Have y-you heard of the H-house of Waste?"

Damn, his stutter was in fine form, filling his throat with hiccups and impossibility. Jack cough'd—just to make a sound that wasn't himself stammering like a slouch.

"Like a pub?"

"I mean *The. The* House of Waste."

"What house of waste?"

"Waste like this." He placed the bill of lading on the bed.

She lean'd over, silent for a moment, reading.

"You robbed Wild?"

"Uhmmm—"

"You robbed Wild," she said again, breathing out slowly. "Jack, you've choused* the most vexacious chouser in London. Stolen from the Thief-Catcher General himself."†

---

* Robbed

† Speaking of revolutionaries and love, I suppose it's about time to tell you about her. My ex.

Our first date was technically our second date, but it was the first one I could remember.

On that date, which was either the first or second depending how drunk you were on the first, my ex spent the entire evening grilling me about world history, current affairs and the hidden stakes of seemingly innocuous state-level legislation. It was clear that she was in possession of the answers, whereas I had fumbled my way into a decent but unglorious position as a literature professor at the flagship campus of a demoralized and floundering public institution.

It was a night of being endlessly harangued by a beautiful woman. Not unpleasant but a bit exhausting. She had asked me if I wanted children. I shrugged, but it was a shrug of: *Kind of, yes.* Which she had opinions about too. Something to do with the narcissism of how all of our hopes and dreams for futurity had been funneled into the project of children: mini reproductions of the self, she called them. Her point was, what ever happened to throwing your hat in the ring with masses of people who you didn't, couldn't know—who would never know you by name, but towards whose better good you would devote yourself. *I'm talking about the future of all of us,* she said. *Not just some little family unit.*

I realized then she was handing me something bigger than her, me and a kid.

And we both knew that it was practically a crime to be childless in this day and age, which perhaps accounted for why she'd suggested we go to the Villa Papyri Lounge, a restaurant I was quite sure had been closed for decades, vines growing over its gray-shingled face in that inauspicious bend in the road on Route 17. It wasn't closed. But it wasn't exactly open, let's just say, either.

What she was offering me would involve a sacrifice of the desire for a family, but I was getting the impression that the payoff would be huge. Revolutionaries. Comrades. Lovers.

She played an old Smiths song on her phone. *Yes we may be hidden by rags, but we've something they'll never have,* she crooned. And then: *If they dare touch a hair on your head I'll fight to the last breath.*

Well, I was sunk. This whole time I'd been trying to imagine being a parent and here I was being offered a partner. We were back at my place by then. I was getting kind of drunk off Old Grand-Dad bourbon.

She was sitting on that old desk of my grandmother's—the only thing she left me, and my only inheritance in the whole world. Her ass was on my inheritance. It seemed appropriate.

Time got extremely slow. She was wearing this black pencil skirt. It had a small pull up near the waist. Gray thigh-high stockings. Her eyes were bright and dark. I looked at her for some time.

She opened her legs a bit, twitched them open, really. I caught my breath, audibly.

———

"Oh my god," she said, "you're such a lesbian."

She didn't mean it cruelly. And she didn't mean that I wasn't passing as a cis-man, either. Although, since according to her we'd fucked the night before, she knew exactly how un-cis I was.

She meant that she saw something about the quality of my desire: that I could feel her even before I touched her. And that this was part of what it meant to be—or to have been, before my tits became the property of the California Municipal Waste Department—a lesbian. That a woman moving in your line of sight could have an effect that was total, atmospheric. That you could be hesitant, incapable and not particularly interested in establishing a line between touching and seeing. That you would indulge a dead love, dead in the eyes of the world, and valueless. A love that choked and burdened the mind, that might even be the very foundation of melancholy and despair. But, oh Reader, looking at a woman you really get a feel for the way that fire is a phenomenon of touch. And my point is, if you have ever been a lesbian, you will not even have to touch a woman to know that.

But I did touch her. We fucked for what I was told was the second time, and this time it was the fuck you can never get away from.

She let me see her in all her historicity, all her ages at once. Her Before. A cold house on the edge of a field. She had not been cared for. Let's just leave it at that.

She had hidden in the house's corners. Taught herself Marx, Mao and all the revolutionaries in a drafty, wood-paneled addition that poked like a bunion off the main frame. By day she was a high school girl learning how to draw the interior structure of combines and backhoes. In her own time, she was slowly becoming the woman who had come to straddle my hips, with my cock still inside her, looking down at me—inscribing me, casting my body anew—saying, *There's something wrong with your political worldview. Let me fix it.*

I don't want to dwell on what happened. Everything ends. Who knows why. I mean, she was forever being pursued. Ex-boyfriends. Potential new boyfriends. Persistent motherfuckers. Was everyone in the world trying to take care of this woman. I couldn't be one of several, though I tried.

You—if you are reading this?—know I did.

Well, so that's one big *why*. There were others though.

But I'm not going down that road. Because I'm reminded of the epigraph to this manuscript: "Love's mysteries in souls do grow, / But yet the body is his book." And the point is this: when a woman touches you, when she recasts your body in the flame of love, that fire is itself a spark thrown off a much larger blaze. Some distant incandescence called *history*. Some history of which, it turns out, you are a part. Some history to which you're responsible.

I'm still thinking of the promises we made to one another.

If they dare touch a hair on your head I'll fight to the last breath.

What should I do with those promises now.

8.

JONATHAN WILD, BUTTONED UP IN A MAROON CLOAK, STOOD BE-neath the blue plaque outside Lloyd's of London. He peer'd into the thick glass windows to ascertain whether other customers were inside; then, when satisfied that All was Snug, he harrumph'd, smooth'd his sleeves, and opened the door.

"I hear you've had a loss." Sir Bernard Mandeville—pale as an old bleached gargoyle covered in bird shite—sat on the far side of a gleaming mahogany desk.

Egads, not Mandeville. Mandeville—part-time employee of Lloyd's and full-time ponderous political economist with foul grapey breath.

Wild grimaced. "I discuss'd that with Richard Bennett privately."

"All of Lloyd's son-in-law's business is my business as well, since Lloyd passed. The family and I have entered into an informal partnership. In fact, if you know of any good sign-makers to produce a new plaque for the entryway . . ."

Wild ignored this—he was not a sign-contractor.

"This past week I lost something precious to me through the petty thievery of one Jack Sheppard—newly something of a celebrity in this town. And about this"—he loom'd over the desk—"I'm to meet with a Lloyd."

"Please have a seat."

Wild did not sit.

"A Lloyd is not in today." Mandeville shuffled papers. "Please sit," he repeat'd, looking up.

Wild adjust'd the large leather chair as far from Mandeville's swarm of air as possible. "If I am forced to discuss this with you, I will share that I require payment on a lost product. However, I have, some time past, lost contact with a companion whose Knowledge I absolutely require."

"Mmm." Mandeville feign'd Sympathy.

"Evans," Wild mutter'd. "Unreliable, mistake-making, flutter-fingered Evans. Where in God's name—" He paused. Regulated his tone. "In any case, I've come to discuss the loss of an *Item*—a *quantity of Item*—taken from the Lighthouse Authority." He could see that Mandeville was unscrolling the document he'd sign'd with Bennett. He twitch'd his nose. Frowned. "The Item is of a delicate nature. I would have preferr'd to keep this between myself and Bennett."

"And nonetheless," Mandeville said, with a thin-gummed smile, "here I am."

"The Item has been stolen."

Mandeville silently traced down the scroll with his finger.

"And you're due two hundred pounds."

"The problem," said Wild, "is that the Item was invaluable. I require something in excess of compensation. I require to replace it. Bennett and I discussed this."

"We don't truck in replacing items. Perhaps you need to see a fencer." This was a dig.

"I'm no longer in the business of fencing." *How is this buffoon of an economist gaining an upper hand?*

"Is that so." Unconvinced. "What are you now *in*?"

"Entrepreneuring. Bureaucrating."

"And what sort of entrepreneuring do you intend here?"

"I've come to underwrite a ship. The ship will help me replace my lost product. I thought Bennett had appris'd you."

"He appris'd me."

"So then you're aware of my project."

"Your fencing, yes." Glint of a smile.

"It's not fencing!" Wild squawk'd.

Mandeville pursed his lips into an unconvincing Semblance of taking Wild seriously. "Of course it's not fencing. It's simply—you wish to make available to yourself some stock of which you are neither the original owner, merchant, or producer."

"I was once colleagues with someone who *might* be a producer of said product. But he has since gone missing through what I can only imagine is some ham-brain'd fault of his own. On account of this frustrating state of affairs, I turn'd to Bennett, with whom I met several days ago in this very office." Wild had attain'd the air of a defensive child. "He related to me that a captain recently received a king's ransom for a lost ship and all the enslaved aboard."*

Mandeville beamed. "'Tis a beauty how insurance makes risk profitable. Loss of life, wreck of property. Something akin to stock-jobbing—a rational Gamble no different than any other financial speculation." He took a sip of tea. "So then did you wish to insure a slave ship, prison ship, or trading vessel?"

"Royal Navy ship."

Mandeville covered a Honk of a laugh with a cough feign'd into his fist.

"A military vessel?"

"Yes. And its cargo. En route with the Company to the Java Sea."

"I am afraid Bennett has misled you. You cannot insure a vessel of which the Nation is the owner."

"I beg to differ, Bennett never misleads."

---

* A reference to an earlier case than the *Zong* (1781)? See M. NourbeSe Philip, *Zong!* (Wesleyan University Press, 2011), and Brenna Bhandar, "Property, Law, and Race: Modes of Abstraction" (*UC Irvine Law Review* 4, no 1, 2014). Also: Walter Johnson, *Soul by Soul: Life Inside the Antebellum Slave Market* (Harvard University Press, 2000); the perpetuation of plantation slavery was based in a cruelty that exceeded simple economic rationale, though it's not clear whether the author knows this.

"Beg all you like. Did Bennett explicitly say he would underwrite a Royal Navy ship? The *Royal Navy,* I repeat." Mandeville began to scroll up the contract.

"What does it mean to be a merchant?" Wild interject'd. "It *means* nothing more," he continued, "than that one enables the free exchange of goods from one hand to another. In this sense I am indeed the ship's 'merchant,' for I aim—in insuring this vessel—to ease the exchange of goods from the ship to the good people of London. Insuring *is*—if you follow my logic—merchanting, of a sort, for it assures safe passage of the goods, and if not the goods, the profits to be deriv'd from them. Thus t'would be a Damage and a Hindrance to that free exchange if only the *original* owner of an item were known to be the merchant of that item. In the case of a Royal Navy ship, 'twould be a damage to the very Nation not to permit an underwriting of the vessel."

Mandeville was scratching in his ledger book.

"That is not what it means to be a merchant," he muttered at the page.

"Suppose, for example"—Wild stood to pace the room— "suppose a man sells seed at a profit of 1p per poundage to another man who grows a field of barley with it in Somerset. This man then sells the barley grain at a profit of 2p per bushel to a distiller in Edinburgh, who produces a whiskey from the grain, and sells the whiskey at a profit of 3p per case to a trader who makes the routes from Edinburgh to London weekly. This trader then sells the whiskey at a profit of 4p per ounce to an innkeep in Porter's Row, who sells it by the glassful to gentlemen such as yourself. Now, when you purchase the glass of whiskey, if you were to pay the *original* owner of the seed in Somerset you'd pay at the original 1p per poundage for the barley element. Is that the general Cost of whiskey?"

"No." Mandeville sounded bored.

"No, indeed." Wild sat again, gesticulating across the desk. "For when you buy the barley, you pay, in fact, the *fifth* owner of the barley 5p or more, and in doing so, you support the beating heart of Commerce itself."

"Inarguably."

"So let us pose the question again. If to be a merchant is to ar-range for the free exchange of goods, then in order to be known as the merchant of an entity, is it necessary to be the *original* owner, or even any owner at all, of that entity?"

"All solid reasoning," said Mandeville. "But when the Nation is the owner—"

"Stop saying 'the Nation'!"

"When the Nation is the owner," Mandeville press'd on, "the rules of merchanting do not apply. In any case it's immaterial. Your entire paradigm is wrong." He look'd down his glasses at Wild. "If you truly design to change your station from reptilian fencer to en-trepreneur, you ought to know what it really means to be a mer-chant, an entrepreneur, and an economist."

"But I've given an indisputable account! And you've concurr'd that it naturally follows that one does not need to have *originally* contract'd for a ship in order to insure its goods." Wild attempted to modulate his volume.

"I did agree to that."

"Look," spat Wild. He came close to the desk, stood over Man-deville, puff'd himself wider. "I require to underwrite a military ves-sel."

"If it were a private ship, even a Company ship. But a Royal Navy ship?"

Wild tighten'd in his seat. Bennett had *encourag'd* him to come in.

Then Wild noticed something. A light—if it could be called a light—in Mandeville's eye. In fact, not exactly a light—something more like the cold Phosphor illuming the cartilage of a cuttlefish at night as it rises to the surface of a harbor, hanging above a cloud of anchovy-fish it intends to heartlessly spear through with its beak.

"Bennett has shared with me some details of this cargo," Mande-ville spoke. "We discuss'd your situation and concluded that I might suggest another route of securing it."

"I don't take your meaning."

Wild's facial pores bloomed open with excitement. His phiz was a fiery pink sponge—a mask of small panting animals.

"As it happens, I've just return'd from Holland—" Mandeville projected his voice to the far edges of the room.

"I can hear you quite well a'ready." Wild glared.

"—where they have develop'd some rather sophisticated scientific methods. As opposed to here—there's a great deal of inefficiency in England." Mandeville grimaced as if *inefficiency* were a personal blight. "I'm developing a treatise on this very subject, in fact." He handed Wild a set of crumpled papers. A *Remedy for Wastefulness** had been etched at the top.

"I believe these papers may assist you in your project. Perhaps your only hope, I should add. Ultimately, to be an entrepreneur"—he lean'd forward—"and you'll mark my words if you want to ever be known as something other than the rat-faced fencer that you truly are—"

"—I'm quite handsome and smooth-faced," object'd Wild. "And not a fencer any longer."

"You're missing my point. If you ever want to be something other than the fencer that you are, you don't need to understand economics or trade or insurance, or anything of that nature. At bottom, an entrepreneur simply needs not be overly sentimental about"—Mandeville paus'd, tracing his finger on the dark wood of the desk—"blood."

---

* Author is most likely mistaken. Mandeville's oeuvre—while it includes numerous disquisitions on efficiency and waste—contains no such title. This seems an honest mistake for the period, since an ordinary person would not necessarily have been able to avail themself easily of printed manuscripts.

Although, note—given the strictness of copyright law (*viz.*, Statute of Anne, 1710)—perhaps the author was wary of naming another title here and this is meant as a misdirection?

9.

JACK AND BESS WERE STROLLING THE CITY, CASING A CERAMICS-maker for a possible jilt. Since the Lighthouse Break, the centinels had spread thicker on the water. For months the river had been Chok'd full with activity at all times.

Centinel-boats circl'd the Plague Ships in unbroken rings. Each ship boasted a thick, impenetrable orbit of Security. Centinels call'd and shout'd out to the other crafts striving to navigate the river. Fishermen in punts paddl'd in terror from the muskets pointing at them. Sailors in larger craft buzz'd around decks, dragging masts and booms 'round the centinels screaming and threat'ning. Warning shots rang out when anything drew close.

The wind rush'd up the river, howling north, strewing a burnt flint Scent over the city.

Bess read to Jack from a broadside as they walked away from the shore towards St. Giles.

ADVICE TO PERSONS WISHING TO AVOID INFECTION BY THE PLAGUE

Orders Conceived and Published by the Royal Society of Physicians and the Lord Mayor of London, 12 November 1724

———

Additional Watchmen to be Appointed in the Parishes of Cripplegate, Spitalfields, and St. Giles

Given the increase in plague in Chandernagore and the East Indies— and the vast potential for the transmission of this plague by merchant vessel, not to mention *in particular the lascar sailors* swarming these parts—it is thought appropriate, and hereby ordered, that additional watchmen be appointed to the plague ships in the interest of the *Publick's Health*. Centinels will also be appointed to the most populous and filth-ridden parishes of the city. Such watchmen ought to be persons of good credit and standing in the city, chosen and appointed by the Lord Mayor himself in consultation with the wardens of St. Giles Roundhouse and Newgate Prison. Any lascar found wandering in any parish without reason will be arrested and held for an indefinite period, or Banish'd from England at the Discretion of the magistrate. The watchmen are required to stand guard outside of any house suspected of infection and the persons so confined for a period of no shorter than twenty-eight days from the time of suspected infection. Such watchmen will be assign'd two to a house, one watch for the morning and daytime hours, another for the evening hours. All Business of the house will be conducted through the watchmen, and if any watchman is required to do Business at any distance from the house, he is to lock up the house with a padlock to the outer doors, and to take the keys with him.

Any persons refusing to remain within the shut-up house will be remanded to Bedlam.

Any person attempting to escape from a shut-up house will meet with violence. Any person walking within the bounds of the parishes of Whitehall, Christ Church, or Charing Cross without residence in said parishes will be determined a vagrant and a threat to the publick health of the parishes, and be remanded to Bedlam. Any person attempting to leave the City of London for the outskirts without reason of Employment will be halted by the Watch and returned to London or remanded to Bedlam. Any Vagrant Body who expires within the parishes of Whitehall, Christ Church, or Charing Cross will be considered property of the state. The body will be assigned to the proper and most convenient Authorities for examination.

—Lucius Peel,
Minister of Publick Health, City of London

"'Publick's health'!" Bess stabb'd at the paper with a finger. "'Plague transmitters'!"

St. Giles was a vast battalion of workhouses, roundhouses, mad-houses, and prisons. Here, the structures stretch'd further apart, leaving wider alleyways between—to prevent the Condemned of the prisons mingling with the condemned of the asylums and con-fecting together in one mad band of Outcasts.

A scrum of urchins flew by, bearing the purple marks of some vicious indenture on the backs of their necks and in their beaten Expressions. They slowed at the colossal workhouse doors, atop of which reared two marble lions—beneath them, the words *Sloth Is Sin.* The lions' tongues unroll'd crepuscular carpets, yellow and white veins running through dark onyx ("Stolen from the cliffs off Chalcedon in Asia Minor, naturally," Bess mutter'd under her breath). Hit by the sun, the tongues blackened to a deeper shade, lapping up Light. A clutch of centinels congregated around the closing doors, peering about like shite-addl'd flies. From the yard of the workhouse, sea-coal plumed up, vaulting into the open sky.

A sudden thunder squall—and now rain pelt'd the city in a cataclysm. Within moments, the sewers began discharging sweep-ings from houses, and hay and swill from the cow and pig carts into the streets, and the centinels, who seem'd to be increasing as they walked—posted on every corner now—took on Bitterer aspects, glaring out, eyes narrow'd against the downpour.

"Ne'er mind about the ceramicist," Bess said, blinking rain out of her eyes.

They turn'd back towards the bat house.

Turn'd, in fact, to find themselves face-to-face with the beadle of St. Giles sitting at the threshold of the gaol, guarding the inmates with all the Conviction of a cud-munching cow.

This much you could easily tell (with apologies to cows) by his dull stare, his listless pacing of the Roundhouse doorway, and his featureless expression—his broad, empty face smooth as the iced-over Thames tideway during a Frost Fair.

"Name?" the cow shout'd out at them.

The beadle meant Bess. This was obvious from his fixation upon her.

"Name?"

"Don't look up," she said to Jack under her breath. "Nor say a word."

They walked on.

The beadle tapp'd his pen on his ledger book.

"If you don't give us a name we'll have to assume you're either mad—and remand you to Bedlam—or resisting, in which case we'll increase the charge to Traitorous intent."

"Intent for what?" Jack stupidly return'd.

"Jack!"

"Intent to infect the people of London. She could've just gotten off an East India Ship, now couldn't she. She could be 'fecting both of us right now, now couldn't she. We've quarantine cells inside." And now the beadle was rising, rearranging the folds of his tunic into his trousers, and reaching for his bully stick.

"Well," Bess gritted through her teeth, "now we have to run."

They accelerat'd down the lane, leaving the old beadle waving his stick and shouting for nearby constables. Bess was trying not to sob. Her feet were numb in Panic—she knew that she was moving, because buildings rushed past—but she could not feel her feet hitting the ground.

What is a quarantine cell?— What do they mean to do with anyone in there?— Transportation to the colonies?— India? (where I've never even been)— To the execution theater?

Just focus on running. We're younger, nimbler than all them. We know the alleyways. They don't.

Jack was pulling her down Crab Alley and out the other side—going 'round a long and labyrinthine way, darting past the Cimmerian shanties heaped upon one another in the gloom. "I'm sorry," he shouted, his voice hoarse. "I'm sorry." The primeval spires of St. Giles-in-the-Fields thrust up from the huts of Tottenham and Oxford Street. Moans and caws of organ notes exploded against the lowering afternoon clouds.

The storm turn'd more violent, with lightning blasting a nearby coach-house completely apart— They ran through lanes of broken brick and shattered glass with the winds growing higher.

Bess was running and she was falling out of time—emerging into a different one. Part of her was running, and part of her had been sever'd from the part that was running. This other part was looking at her, and she was looking at it—just ahead, turn'd back towards her, floating up and gaping back— This other part of herself was Unrecognizable—it had wild, staring, terrified eyes—it hung in the air—it was very very afraid— And *she* was afraid—looking at it gawping at her in Alarm and Fright—*of it.*

Slowly, slowly, the din in her head part'd just slightly, and she heard familiar sounds. The other bats, Jack. She was on her street. *How did I get here? How much time has passed?* She looked up. The split part of her was still there. Floating in front of her, staring at her, still unblinking. She look'd it in the eye. She forced herself not to look away. She welcom'd the split part back, coax'd it like a deer at the fenshore with a handful of uncooked oats. Coax'd it the way she coax'd Jack into his Body when he'd ducked down deep somewhere else. Coax'd it the way her mother and father did for her on days when the other fen children had been Cruel.

She let the sound of voices calm her. She felt her heart slow.

Rain summoned a tumult of noise outside the windows, but inside, the bat house was quiet. The Lady Abbess was setting tea on the fire for her morning review of the previous night's accounts. She did not look up at them.

They picked their way, sopping, up the stairs.

Threw off their wet cloaks, and Bess headed towards the bed. Jack stood at the edge of the mattress, dripping onto the floor.

"I'm sorry," he choked out, again.

"Jack"—her voice was thin, exhausted—"I thought we'd talked about this. If you ever again don't heed me in public . . ." She trail'd off, gaping around the room.

Everything had been gone through. Clothes, lotions, trinkets thrown, torn, trampled. The chamber pot used and left dirty.

Jack went to the pot, toss'd the urine out the window. He did not want to use his handkerchief to clean the bowl. Stood with it in his hand, staring at her with *sorry* eyes.

When she didn't speak, he continued to tidy the room, his eyes stinging with rain and wind and dust and the sharp hit of lingering centinel-piss. Bess had curled in on herself in the bed. After he was done picking up, he sat at her side.

"The Abbess must have told them," he said. "Those latest orders," he continued needlessly, referring to the broadside. Bess didn't acknowledge him.

They'd have to find somewhere else to stay. This much was clear. Soon as possible. They shouldn't even be there right then, but Bess was already huddl'd under covers.

"I've come so far just not to die, and now—"

"Where will we go?" He and Bess were two dust motes being batted about in a howling Storm of surveillance, of centinels, and cruelty.

"Dennison's," Bess said. "Jenny."

Of course she'd thought this through.

"And another thing. I've been thinking—"

When has she had time and the presence of mind to be thinking?

"Waste," she continued, sitting partially up, and pulling the edges of the coverlet onto her glistening, rain-spatter'd shoulders, "is chaff, refuse. Like what you'd not eat of a grain stalk, and have no use for otherwise; those bits of outcast substance. That's waste. So, *The House of Waste*? Perhaps a house of refuse or somethin'. Then the Elixir is . . . waste? I don't know what else to make of it."

Dear God, she's been theorizing through all of this. Conducting study at the crosshairs of violence—spinning speculation from wreckage.

—And now Bess felt sleep coming like a far-off Footfall. One advancing on her with impossible speed. She did not know, in fact, if it was sleep or it was death. Whate'er it was, she welcom'd it. And then it was upon her, grabbing her like an angry Flower, and Bess was far too tired to be afraid. She want'd to hang her head on its crimson breast and slip away.

But she shook herself wakeful.

"Jack, if they do imprison me—quarantine me—whatever it is they wish to do—"

"They won't!" he shrieked.

"You're the clunch who spoke to the beadle in the first place, e'en when I told you not to. So listen carefully now. I don't know what is coming for me. The town's in no way safe. If they imprison me or kill me—I want you to know everything."

10.

I AM ONE OF THE ONLY SURVIVORS OF THE FEN-TIGERS, A DWINDLING band of Freedom fighters. Back then the fens were beautiful, bountiful. My parents reviled monied society, and we lived in the traditional fen way: creaking about on stilts, cobbling together an amphibious huts and outbuildings, hunting with spears.

I spent my days stamping about the muck and picking at the soaked pudding of rotting waterlife all around. I was trained up in my parents' adherence to James Nayler's Protestant philosophy of free Love. My mother was Anglo—my father a lascar sailor, self-emancipat'd (or "jumped ship," as the centinels called it) from the East India Company upon arrival in London. Ship life was a hard-ship near inconceivable to those who'd never seen it; for a lascar torn from Srihatta and pressed to labor, immeasurably more so. My father shudder'd when he recalled to me the thin breeches allotted for shipboard wear in the Atlantic's stinging gusts, the rotten meat the lascar sailors were provision'd, the tight hot hold at the very lowest decks of the ship. Many died en route.

On arrival in London, my father's captain inform'd him he'd been contracted to another vessel for a hard run up the coast. It was October. The Atlantic had already begun to show ice crystals scattered in the foam. My father—dwindl'd to bones already—knew the journey would mean the death of him.

And thus, my father—effective with constellations and confi-dent of foot—fled London and made his way to the fens, where

he'd heard a Body might live free. There he met my mother. Together they fell into raptures both spiritual and physical.

My parents lived in an Intoxication with the world—develop'd
secret languages, family rituals, paeans enacted between the three
of us and the frogs and salamanders who were to be found occupy-
ing the dank crevices of our stone hut. I was raised up to know and
practice Naylerism, as that was the religion of the Fen-Tigers, and
it seem'd my father had come to it, through love or exigency I did
not ask and he did not say. He did not pray to either God—although
my mother did—but he was insistent that at some root there was
no contradiction: Naylerism and Mahometanism were so aligned in
spirit of care for the poor that any persons who believed otherwise
were sad and ignorant.

We lived under constant threat of the surveyors—my parents
didn't believe in protecting me from hard truths. We watched, in
Horror, as the surveyors came in to Drain the fens, build weirs and
sea-walls to divert and control the flow—desiccating the Flood-
plains to create pastureland for sheep and cows—rich meat for rich
men—while the local folk starv'd.

Even in my early years, my mother was readying me for battle.
She would quiz me over my morning oats.

"What is it that the surveyors wish to do?"

"To make our fens into pastureland for sheep."

"And then?"

"To slay the sheep for the supper of prideful men."

"Aye." In these conversations, my mother radiat'd an inner
Light, full of purpose. "And what of the fens?"

"They'll dry up, die."

"And what of the Fen-Tigers, our friends and families?"

"We starve. No fishing; no reed-trade."

"But before ye starve? What do ye do?"

"Hunt harder?" I would try, beginning to despair.

"But they dry up the fens 'til there's no fen left." My mother was
not Evasive in her truths. "What would ye do then?"

"Scavenge rotten fishes?" I would say, close to tears. "But this is not going t' happen because the Fen-Tigers will fight them off!"

My mother would deliv'r even the hardest information with a kind eye. "Ya, we will fight. But—so we fight—and we kill 'em all—ev'ry last Surveyor—"

I would brighten, nod.

"—But they send more Surveyors," she would continue, "with armies, and they build many Sea-Walls—everywhere a Sea-Wall—and so many of our Fen-Tigers-friends is dead, and the fens is dead. And we're scavengin' the rot for some stinkin' rotten piece o' fish, but even that is gone. Then what do ye do?"

"Sell my labor to the Surveyors," I would sob. "Sell Meself."

My mother would smile sadly. "Yes, my love. They wish to dry the earth to a cracked turf so that they can make our hands, our very vitality, into property. Our sweat a property. Our very 'membrances a property. Remember when you was a Fen-cub, slipping in and out of the water, chasing pike in the sun? Will we let them take our Fen-knowledge and make it a property to guide them in their work?"

I'd shake my head.

She would take my hands in hers. "That's right, love. This we will resist with our blood, our hands and Hearts. We will bestow a righteous Kindness upon the earth, with violence until the Survey-ors tremble, and the rulers with their hats cocked Tremble." My mother would hold my hands tighter, and I would feel the strength of her belief; the strength of her power.

But still, I was afraid.

One day, my parents took me to a moor-rally to see the sermon-izer Laurence Robins, who advertis'd himself heir to the Ranter Abiezer Coppe. Robins had been at the fenshore for days, trying to convince the Fen-Tigers to put down their arms and engage only in free Love. Unrestrict'd Screwing would save them from the evils of the surveyors, he proclaim'd. My parents—I was rather aware—were great fans of Screwing, but it seemed peaceful Screwing was Robins' sole aim.

When we'd finally decided to hear him out, my parents—and the rest of the Tigers—had already had an earful of his Antics in the area. There were not many inclined to listen anymore. At most a crowd of fifteen scuffing about while—on this day—Robins delighted in taking an unrestrained Shite on the moor. He encouraged the Congregants to do so as well; he'd even sniff'd at his Excrement, tast'd it, pronounced it "Holy."

My parents were buzzing in disbelief with their mates. It wasn't that we were against shiting in the fens. But there were spots far more Appropriate for that. Areas propitious for planting—for not soiling the water. Robins didn't respect our Ways, or any of what he said was our "so-called logic."

While the adults were taken up with Horror at the Thoughtless location of Robins' shite, he held up a book, pronounced it "worthless academicizing," and threw it to his feet.

No one was watching me. And I was curious. I nick'd it up and thrust it under my skirts.

As we walked home through the tall reeds, my mother continu'd to vent about Robins. There existed a Difference, she said, between "rapture and sheer insanity." Rapture was an awareness of Connectedness, and a belief that this Connectedness—and a sound militancy—would save us. Sheer insanity was wild defecating near the most pristine bream and roach spawning grounds. My father joked that the shiting could serve as an effective deterrent to surveyors. He suggested to my mother that they propose it as a form of self-defense—a "natural Stinking Barricade," he'd called it—at the next confecting meeting with their mates. We'd all laughed.

When we returned home, I feigned needing to check the vole traps, and left to find a private spot to study the book I had stolen. It was Spinoza's *Ethics*. Hard reading, and I understood little. But I glean'd one lesson, and to this I held fast: Spinoza had a theory of Connectedness—as did my parents. But Spinoza's was not to do with a God who had absent'd himself from us in heaven. Spinoza's God was here on Earth. In *Us*.

Reading the *Ethics* sooth'd me. I studied the book frequently, storing it under my pallet in the hut. At night, the whole fenland itched and bleated with Spells and cant. When the north Wind came blowing over the moorlands, it would wake me from uneasy Dreams into an uneasier night. The air lifted a heavy bluish gault off the water's skin—fir-soot pooled in the surface scum— Death— I felt—could arrive at any moment.

—And I would reach under the pallet, caress the pages thinking of Spinoza's patient expositions, demonstrations; his *God-proofs*. He had a *Method*. His words promis'd a way to make sense of this life; a *Theory* of all of it. I study'd daily, suffering through page after opaque page, scribbling down my juvenile reflections on the book's meaning. I became convinc'd that, through Method—if I was disciplin'd about it—I could keep us safe.

I was wrong.

One morning, in the grainy winter dark, I ask'd my father why he didn't believe in Spinoza's God. He was tending a vat of oily eel-soup. Frost from the outdoors and steam from the boiling mess mixed in bright drops along the hairs of his short black beard. We had just return'd from our pre-dawn eel-scooping and pheasant-hunting. I would shoot with my slingshot and he would finish off the bird with his knife. As usual I had argu'd vociferously to use the knife as well. I long'd to feel it in my hand—its hot handle, its Power. As usual, he shook his head. *You're not Ready, rabbit.*

Back at our hut, he stood in front of the fire in his fen-boots, weeds clinging to his calves. His clothes bloom'd the scent of sweat and fog: forest Exertions. The smell fill'd the small hearth room. I sat at one of the cobbled stools at his side.

If my Passion is to hunt with the knife, then Spinoza would argue you're preventing my freedom by disallowing it.

I don't believe Spinoza was a parent, he said, smiling.

He allow'd the fire to cook the soup, and came to crouch by me on my stool.

Do you genuinely want to know what I think of Spinoza? he ask'd.

Naturally I did. Though I was quite sure I would argue with his perspective.

• • •

My father told me then about his journey on board the East India vessel. His days were pack'd full with translating between the Anglo and lascar sailors (his "official" task), while also being press'd into labor painting the quarterdecks, setting up the riggers, and climbing the dangerous, windblown topmasts. The Company had captured a Dutch Deist named Vermuyden as a stowaway (and likely, word was, a spy). My father would visit the Deist in the hold, sometimes to bring him a small ration of dried salted beef, sometimes to worry over the spectacle of Confinement and to nourish their shared hatred of the Company. From the dim reaches of the ship's hold, Vermuyden had tried to indoctrinate my father in Deism, maintaining in a crackling, weak Voice that Spinoza was the gentlest but most stringent thinker the world had yet known. He had abstain'd from sex, from profligate spending, and from all lusty pleasures. He had lived in a small darkwood hut clothed in vines from foundation to roof, and carpeted in tendrils that worked their way through cracks in the stone, veining the floorboards green. Spinoza's only vice, so Vermuyden had said, was that he "enjoy'd to watch spiders catch flies."

This last my father now had repeated to me as if it were a damning Flaw.

"Spinoza who so enjoyed to *watch*," he'd enunciated. "That's exactly the trouble with Deists—the merchant ones in any case. They've been gentl'd into *watching* by the relative ease of Amsterdam life. Watching leads to Abstractions, Vagaries, Mistakes due to Distance and Contemplation." He cross'd his arms. Held my gaze. "Nayler advises it's much better to act on Raptures than to endlessly study them. And I don't mean just shiting," he said, referencing Robins.

But *I* wanted to act *and* study.

There was not much more time for debate, those days. The Surveyors were coming ever closer to Popham's Eau, near to our fen. They had brought with them Scottish Inmates to conduct the labor. Teams of press-ganged Wretches who they made to sleep at the freezing shore. Every day a new Apocalypse. The Inmates died of overwork—we'd find their bodies strewn amongst the other suff'ring wildlife. The rivers were evaporating of fish and eel—the fen deer lay panting and starv'd— Misery and fatefulness hung over the waters in a low-lying mist—green rot and Stenches. Daily, my parents had had to wade deeper and deeper into Wicken Fen for my favorite dish, the white-clawed crayfish that once teem'd the waters.

Soon all our debating concern'd how to stave off the surveyors. My parents joined up with other Fen-Tigers, local coves who sought to resist with everything we had. We strategiz'd with the Scottish Inmates in the woods. We knew the day was coming when we would fight. I trembl'd, full of purpose and Direction. I would battle the Surveyors with my parents. Beat them off with my fists if I must.

That Day came. I was brought to Popham's Eau in the early morning by my mother, rowing silently through the fenwaters in our punt.

The sky was low, and the rains sure to fall heavily as they had done all week.

At the edge of the outfall, through fen-fog blowing horizontal in a hard wind, my mother and I slipp'd between the Scottish Inmates. I sat low in the punt, the way she had taught me. I saw my mother nod to the Inmates as we floated by.

At night my mother had taken to sleeping 'mongst the Scots on the peat at the water's edge. She was recruiting them.

She allowed me to come with her once, to lie amongst Friends. None touched us in a bawdy way. She preach'd them at night with the rain streaming down their faces, or tears of joy, when she told them of the Worm with three heads that lives in the ground.

The first head is the head of Pride. He waits until the wind blasts hard over the fen and taketh your reed and eel, and the cold rains weaken you until you are fell'd. The second head is the head of Deception. He shelters underneath your Body from the rains, and tells you sweet things and appears honest but steals your crumbs from your pocket. The third head is the head of Truth and Faith. He is honest and shares his lot with all. This head is Gaol'd and laid low. He is ground beneath jackboots into the soil. For his Truth must not get out. And the oppressions visited on this third head spark a Fire by which the greedy first two keep warm.

When my mother preach'd the three heads of the Worm, it was as if a galactic wind increas'd the glimmer from the constellations down to us. I still remember the smell of the star-Wind. Red ashes. Blood drying on a rusted sword. It fill'd my lungs with a Bitter Breath. I knew the bloodletting was near, that the third head of the worm would rise, would sputter into a brilliant firework and singe the other two heads to a crisp.

March 12th was the day of the third head of the Worm.

We rowed quietly. My father was waiting upriver.

My mother knew the waters better than any of the Fen-Tigers. She measur'd the furze-bushes peeking through the skin, their thin branches enveloped in a yellow froth. She mark'd the sharp blue sparkle across the river, the splash of Brightness lit by the sinking sun. Gaug'd the sunken woods and shipwrecks lurking close beneath the surface.

The air was dense with early spring—sour red moss, the flinty scent of wet silt, decaying animal matter. The Scottish Inmates were spread along the channel of Popham's Eau, the wind blowing open their Kersey shirts, skin purple to the daggercold drops of rain. I knew their feet were near icebound, lock'd in the mud.

The Overseers were clad in dry boots, waxed cloaks, and goatskin mitts.

Each Inmate gripp'd one long-handled axe for breaking up the frozen silt, and one shovel for freeing and scooping the lodes of soil.

It was the Day they had been instruct'd to break ground on the new sluice.

It was the Day.

My mother and I dragg'd the punt through the clogged marsh-land and inched it to the top of the berm before the Overseers could take note. She told me to wait in the ferns at the edge of the river.

She was Anxious. I knew because her breath was dry and sour when she bent down and spoke to me.

"Stay in this stand of whorl grass," she said. Her breath made my nose twitch. Not in disgust. We knew—and lov'd—each other's smells so well. Even the hard smells. No, I twitch'd in fear. Because I knew my mother was Afraid. I could smell it on her even if, in words, she show'd herself to be calm. "Your father and I will let you know when it is safe to come out," she said, smiling and kissing my face.

And then my father's shadow splash'd across the dirt as he emerged from behind a downy rosebush. He leaned down, pulled something out of his pocket. Handed it to me.

It was my slingshot—the one we'd practic'd on hare and rat so many times. He pett'd my hair. Kiss'd my head.

Then he handed me his knife, too.

"Hold fast to this," he said, his eyes crinkling. "We'll hunt some hare together tonight after we've won. We'll have a roast for sup-per."

I settled into the cold mud where I could watch my mother and father, but hidden from the Overseers by the grasses.

I watched the river. The waters rising with the rains; the waters evaporating of fish and eel. It has been this way since the work began on Popham's Eau.

It was time to end the Drainage.

"Brothers," my mother opened in a Roar, "today this Popham's

Eau—long the Mother of our fishes, our reeds and eels—is opened to the bowels of misery by the Surveyors!"

The Overseers chalk'd her up to a raving lunatic and ignor'd her rantings, chuckling amongst themselves at the "Plaguey bitch."

But when they heard her cannonade, the Inmates stopp'd chipping at the frozen fen bank, their axes and shovels halt'd in the cold blasted air. The Overseers shift'd lazily in their boots.

"We will not allow this *Fen-Murder*! They would level Bedford! Well, we will level the valleys and lay the prideful men low! Today we bring down the mighty and exalt the lowly! *Now* let this Creek be our inlet to Paradise. *Now* wash away the prideful men, and open to the *common* holdings of *common* men! My heart is with ye now, Fen-Tigers! My heart is with ye now, mates!"

At the repetition of *Now,* and *Common,* the Scottish inmates turn'd as one, their axes and shovels held high. The Overseers grabb'd for their pistols, and all at once, the Fen-Tigers rose from their prostrate positions, hidden in the reeds at the edges of the fen-bank and pour'd down the berm towards the Overseers.

For one glorious Moment, the Overseers fell.

Caught between the Inmates and the Fen-Tigers, the Overseers blink'd into the heavy fog rising off the fenwaters for a way out. Plunge forward? Dive into the murk and swim for the clays off Ely? The Overseers squint'd for a second that seemed like a millennium— their fate closing in with the axes Looming closer out of the fog.

If the Overseers had taken an interest at any point in learning the fens, they might have stood a chance. They would have known that the tide at Popham's Eau was four hours, the ebb eight. They might have known that the fens carry'd a very fine material—flint and limestone ground into a floating powder by the influx and outfall of the waters—that, rather than sinking, is carried by the currents, 'til they meet an obstruction.

Occurrences that can cause a tide to "throw down its silt" are as follows: a widening of the river-channel; a sudden rise of the riverbed; the pressure of fresh water as the tide rolls inland (this last depending on the quantity of recent rains).

If the Overseers had been vigilant they would have noticed that between tidal flow and ebb lies a "stillwater," during which time the rivers reach a temporary Equilibrium.

During that stillwater, silts are deposit'd that, during an ebb, are brought up again from the bottom and distribut'd throughout the water.

At certain times, however, the tide runs at greater length than the ebb, and—due to the obstructions named above—the silt is not washed out. Such a phenomenon produces what is called an "Eager," or silt-bar, which can grow to such a height that it stops up the river entirely where the fresh and sea currents meet.

Well Creek, Popham's Eau, the Ouse, the River Nene, and New Bedford were clogg'd with many such eagers—well known to the Fen-Tigers and the Inmates alike. In fact, there was one such rather massive bar 'round the bend of the Creek, behind which any one or many of the Overseers might have stood a chance of lying undetected until the frenzy died down.

The Overseers, however, knew nothing and cared to know nothing about the natural terrain of the fenland, so absorb'd were they in inflicting their Domination on the miserable Inmates, and spreading their venereal diseases upon the good doxies of Ely.

I could see my father in the fen, fighting with the inmates and the rest of the Tigers. He did not have a weapon—*He*—I realized— *had given me his*— The Overseers were falling, sheets of rain spilling off their oilskin hats—the Fen-Tigers advancing from behind and the Inmates with shovel and axe in the front.

I smelled victory on the air—it smelled just like the blood of the constellations, the exalted smell of the living universe.

Then I saw my father climbing the berm towards my mother, coming towards her, hands outstretched. She reached out her hands to him, her red curls wind-pasted to her face, smiling in anticipated, shared joy.

But he was not smiling, and it was then that I saw the shadow of the Overseer behind my mother. My father reach'd her, begging *no* with all of his expression—rumpled brow, wide wondering eyes—as the pistol was placed to the back of her head. Their hands met as the bullet shatter'd through her skull, plunged out the other side, and—doused in Blood and shards of Bone—pierc'd my father above his eye.

They fell together towards the water of Popham's Eau— Hands entwined, they met the water in a splash drowned out by the other splashing and dyings all around— They sank, together, to the sunken forest floor—the forests the Romans felled long before— the branches groomed a ghostly white in the centuries of tidal ebb and flow.

I watched, frozen. Although the air was stuff'd with screams, shouts, the crack of Fen-axes on Surveyor-bone, and the heartless snap and suck of Surveyor-gunshot meeting Fen-flesh, there was also a terrible silence. A dense, cold cloud pulsing in my ears. The water calmed around the spot where my father and mother fell. All around, Overseers and some Inmates and Fen-Tigers, too, were falling. But the place where my parents went down was a glassy emerald, the hard gray sky shining a Mirror across the fen's face.

It was as if a dream—I tried to move my arms and legs— I didn't care if the Surveyors saw me now, didn't care if they shot me too with their bullets— I tried to move, to run to where my parents had been— My mind was moving but my body was not— There was a loop of thought—*stand up stand up*—and no response from my shaking limbs.

Then the air got colder, darker— A Shadow pass'd above me— I kept my head down— If a Surveyor was about to shoot me dead then I would at least not allow him the pleasure of seeing that knowledge reflected in my eyes— They could shoot me like an already Dead thing—like a tree stump or dirt— I would not look up at him— I would not give him the satisfaction of seeing me see my own death coming— I waited for the impact.

It did not come.

·　·　·

A girl stood above me. She was wearing a white tunic and nice leather shoes, spattered in mud. She had dark hair, like me. She look'd my age. She look'd *like* me. I did not know if she was an Emanation or a sprite. I wasn't sure if she *was* me. Some part of myself. *Is there another lascar girl in the fens I don't know?* I couldn't make out her face. She was wearing veils and layers of lace.

The girl mov'd a little closer through the grass.

I mov'd closer too.

I kept expecting my parents to break through the surface, gasping for air, filling their lungs with hard gulps. The water did not move.

The girl was saying something. She was saying the same thing over and over but I couldn't discern it. The fighting continued all around us, the horrible screaming and falling and cracking. Then the Roar parted for a split second and a sound bubbl'd through, dropping from this girl's mouth to my ears.

The girl was saying, *Dig.*

Behind the girl, Surveyors advanced towards us. But the girl stood in front of me, hiding me. In that moment, I believ'd she was some kind of fen-angel. The angel was whispering *Dig.* Her eyes widen'd urgently.

Bereft of any other *method,* I dug.

I burrow'd behind the stand of whorl grass. The fen-soil was soft, but it was so cold. There was a fen legend that Corpsepirates inhabited the deep earth. That when a fenman died, he became a pirate of the soil and the deepwater, and fed on the bodies of the Surveyors and the merchants and all the other money-men who stole from us. For the Corpsepirates—or so it was told—these Bodies were a great reward, a solace to the earth and a hallowed gift.

I loved tales of the Corpsepirates. At night, I'd beg my mother for stories. Beg her to tell me of how the earth would be nourished by each fallen Surveyor. Even if there was one Surveyor dead to tens or hundreds of fenfolk killed at their hands or starv'd, each Surveyor death was a cause for joy and Celebration. I would rock myself to sleep on my pallet, the damp air whistling through the hut like a ruckus of hands; and I would think of the carnival of Corpse-pirates rejoicing underground.

But as I dug, I remember'd the Corpsepirates and felt, now, a flash of fear. I didn't know how far you could dig and not be taken away. And I didn't know if the Corpsepirates would know that I was a live Body, and a fen-friend, not a foe. I shiver'd as I thought of them tunneling through the loam, blist'ring it like a cauldron on boil, rippling through the dirt with their blackiron heads and long metal teeth. I dug and dug. I dug until I could lie in the dark Hol-low and pour soil back over myself without making a hump, and I pray'd that the Corpsepirates would know I was alive and a Daugh-ter of the fens, and wouldn't feed on me. And I lay there and lis-tened to the sound of my heart pounding against the packed freezing ground. Listened to the Thud of Surveyor boots above me.

And then the soil rumbl'd. Someone or something was rum-maging in it. My mouth went dry in terror as dirt rained down on my face. I clos'd my eyes and shut my lips and squinched my face up tight. I begg'd God for a bargain. That they would bury me in the water with my parents. I didn't even pray to live. Just to moulder together with them.

Then there was a Warmth on top of me. The surprisingly light, gentle pressure of a Body lying down. It was the *girl*. Her hair fell over her face. Cool lips were against my neck. The girl's parts were press'd into—all over—my own. Breasts, nethers, stomach, thighs. I found my body reaching up to meet the girl's body: do not ask if it was *Terror or Desire*.

I bury'd my nose into the girl's neck.

"You didn't cover yourself well," the girl whisper'd. "The dirt was all hectic 'round your hole. They would have seen."

"Then you could have covered me better."

"I could have."

Our warm parts burn'd against each other and our faces held tight to each other's necks and we breath'd together while the stomping and Thudding and shooting continued above.

There was a recurring low Echo in the soil. The reverberations of the Fen-Tigers and the Scottish inmates falling and splashing into the water.

I held tight to the girl.

The shooting stopped. Then the falling stopped. Then the stomping stopped. And there was only one sound—louder and louder. It was the Surveyors *braying* as they chanted in victory, clapping each other on their backs. Then the Stamp of boots became distant as they tumbl'd off screeching with pride, headed no doubt to the pubs. Then that too stopp'd and it was silent.

"They'll be looking for me," said the girl, finally.

"Yes," I said. "I'll come out too."

"No. You should stay here. For a bit. One night. Until it is clear. Until you are safe."

The girl pulled a handkerchief from her dress pocket and laid it over my face so that when she gingerly put her knees on either side of my hips and point'd herself upwards and dug up, the dirt fell on the Napkin and not in my eyes and mouth.

And then I was alone. Even now I don't know who she was, or why she saved me. I cannot say with certainty whether she was real.

All I could do was lie there and lament. And be bitten and crawl'd upon by the undersoil life. Blind, wet worms wreath'd my fingers and between my toes—canny millipedes cleared out little domed arenas in a circle around me. My presence was an event in their dirt-World. They reposed in their domes, arching on their hindquarters like tiny cobras to watch me. From time to time they leapt out, striking with lightning Precision passing earwigs—swallowing them whole, pincers-first. Their legs fluttered as they ate in unconceal'd joy.

I had tried earwigs once—my father had given me one when he'd been unable to find even a small bream for supper. It had not been very bad. The carapace was tangy as salt.

Time passed. Just as I fell into sleep, I had the intolerable and yet necessary realization: I would have to leave the fens. Leave them forever. For no matter how much I loved that teeming, lush, subterranean, boggy, Blighted place, it was dying. How far had my parents had to wade for the crayfish? Neck-deep and our supper would consist of one, perhaps two, small creatures. It wasn't enough. Not nearly enough. An entire day's Labor for two cray. And how long would that dwindling population last.

I had to leave just as I was. The Surveyors would be looting our huts, as I had heard they did in the other villages. I would have to leave wearing only my mother's muslin shirt and my father's breeches. To make my way to the only place left for a girl with no means to make any kind of a life or living.

London.*

---

* Reader, please forgive the radio silence. I'm not in the habit of interrupting women when they are speaking.

II.

THE NEXT MORNING BROKE WITH A BRIGHT SLIVER AT THE EDGE OF the horizon—the air was thin and dry after the storms. Jack pull'd on his breeches in the pre-dawn dark. Bess was still in a curl under blankets—the room had taken on a creeping Anonymity. It could hold them no longer.

They gather'd their things—though there was not much, truly—and sort'd through what was untorn and unbroken after the centinel-trampling. A few dresses and petticoats—some vases and bowls —Bess's copy of Spinoza's *Ethics*—the waning bottle of elixir from under the floorboard near the bed—some duds. Jack duck'd out to look for burlap sacks to transport their items. He headed for the refuse pile behind James' Linen and Textile shop.

He rushed down the alleys quickly, the wind beating his ears Sore, and cooling the sweat at his temples and under his arms.

He pistoned along. Muscles and nerve fibers crisscrossed his chest, flexing and twanging. Jack spy'd some sacks behind the shop, then—unthinking—nick'd a handful of cherries from a cart. It was stupid to pull off any jilt at the moment, but force of habit and Hunger (and some still-Strange *Boldness*) puppet'd his arms.

He rounded the corner back to the bat house, slipped in with a fly[†] nod to the Lady Abbess, and chugg'd up the narrow stairs—two at a time, his topcoat emitting fumes of ash and coal from the street. When he opened the door, that warm, close scent he lov'd—Bess's

---

† Knowing

musty-violet-scented-breech—pour'd through the cracked doorway.

There was her valise by the door. The room was empty of all
their things except the remnants of some meal—empty globes of
wine, ruby-scummed and dried at the bottoms, and a shiny bit of
thyme-roasted duck hardening on a plate.

He pulled the cherries from his pocket and added them to the
plate.

Bess's comportment had shifted. He hadn't noticed in the busyness of the morning, but—she had a new, *open* look. One he'd
never seen before. *Is this to do with the History she gave?* Her face
had no extraneous architecture but what was *there*. Not that he
would have noted extraneous architecture beforehand. It was the
kind of thing one doesn't recognize until it's dissipated.

"It's been sweet"—Bess's voice was soft—"sharing this room
with you. I mean, 'cept for when you say foolish things to beadles.
But I was so truly lonely here before you came."

Two chousers on the run are permitted questionable decisions
based only in some miraculous syncopation of the affects.

Bess leaned back a bit on the bed. Regarded him out of the bottom of her eyes. "You're a beautiful *Something,* Jack."

He knew that meant he had that despairing, longing look in his
eyes. The one with his sentiments just out there, splash'd all over
his phiz for everyone to see. His eyes were bigger and more expres-
sive than a man's eyes ideally should be. With long dark lashes. He
hated their soul-fullness.

But Bess loved it—for it was this *somethingness* that meant, in
her complex lexicon of desire and permission, that he was the one
who could touch her without pay.

Jack mov'd across the room—pushed up her slip and knelt between her legs on the dirt-gritted floors.

At the taste of her, his Monies[*] immediately set to boiling—

---

[*] Private parts

—He could have stay'd that way for some time, but she pulled him up onto the bed, dropping her legs open. He pushed his breeches down—reaching under the bed for the Horn. She stopped him with a hand on his chest, letting out a small hiccup.

He look'd down. He was straining towards her.[†]

Certanly there are Things that defy Description in the languages we have at our disposal.

So, to put it plainly, there was a—

—But language fails here—

—Perhaps a . . .

. . . *Transfixing Shape?*

—blooming thick at his nethers.[‡]

In any case, not the arborvitae of other coves—the ones possessed by childish glee. This was something else.

Less a—

or, rather, more a—

Well, one is driven into the arms of metaphor—

What was there was something of a creature—some partly mythical creature—or else an ordinary creature behaving mythically—a wolf emerging from the forest, dragging brambles, dripping fire from its teeth like blood. A wolf emerging from the forest bearing an expression never before known to wolf. Shame, strange Hopefulness, furious Hunger. A wolf emerging from the edge of the woods,

---

† Thank God I don't have to field a question from Sullivan now.

‡ Narrator declines to give further details. To my mind, further evidence of document's authenticity.

I will say, however, that this is a quite unique instance of figurative language. In eighteenth-century pornography, evasion or metaphor in this manner is uncharacteristic.

See, for example, John Cleland, *Fanny Hill:* "Her fat brawny thighs hung down, and the whole greasy landscape lay open to my view." Or, "For the first time did I feel that horn-hard gristle battering against the tender part." Euphemism there may be in *Fanny Hill,* but not the teasing aestheticizations of figurative language.

breaking into the tiniest, most hesitant and yet utterly unchildlike Smile. Licking back fire along a dark wet muzzle. Wondering: *Am I home?**

---

* Now, this interests me quite a bit.

The figurative constellation of genitals and wolves comprises (some might argue) one of the defining erotic constellations of Western modernity.

—A topic on which, incidentally, I have been accused of obsessing!—

Forgive me this fixation, but who could dispute that the description of genitalia as a "wolf" brings to mind Freud's famous "Wolf Man" case (some artistic license taken here):

Russian aristocrat Sergei Pankejeff: I wake with nightmares. There are wolves sitting in the tree outside my window.

Freud: Naturally, those wolves are your father, your castrating hateful father. He wants to come inside, bite off your dick and run into the woods with it, then he'll go fuck your mother.

According to Freud, the dream recalls an event from Sergei's childhood, when, in a spell of summer flu, he woke from a nap in his parents' room and saw his father giving it to his mother. *The primal scene.*

The array of *feelings* this occasioned in him—jealousy, desire, etc.—inaugurated a desire to get fucked by his father accompanied by the simultaneous realization that to have that he'd need to be castrated like his mother. The ensuing anxiety takes shape as the wolf-nightmare.

But the real interest comes later. Circa 1968.

At which point Deleuze and Guattari were like: fuck Freud; genitals aren't about parents. They're about enclosure and privatization. Let me put this in terms appropriate to the eighteenth century. Just like you can't pick up a wilty, shit-coated carrot from the burbling sewer and eat it, because the sewer is regulated by the city and the Nightsoil Concern—well, for Deleuze and Guattari your genitals are enclosed as well. Except instead of anti-vagrancy laws, your genitals are enclosed (and privatized) through the institution of the family and also through psychoanalysis, which insists that all your anxieties have to be traced back to Oedipus and how much you hate your father and want to sleep with your mother. Or how much you want to get fucked by your father in the style of your mother, etc.

Basically Deleuze and Guattari are formulating an anticapitalist theory of genital vagrancy.

And so they reimagine the scene of the Wolf-Man's analysis as such:

Pankejeff: I wake with nightmares. There are wolves sitting in the tree outside my window.

Deleuze and Guattari: Look, you Russian aristocratic fuck, those wolves are the Bolsheviks, those wolves are the multitudes, those wolves represent all the terror and the possibility of the social world, the common folk who are waiting outside your window to extinctify you and your kind. And for this reason not every

And it wondered this in a Not-So-Nice Way.

The thing grew larger under Bess's gaze and in her marvelous proximity.

Bess grabb'd him by the back of his head and they kiss'd deep and then he was—was—

He was inside her. Not—truth be told—all that Deep inside her, but he was inside her.† They made a hot Suture. A boiling Suture.

It was like with the Horn.

It was *and it wasn't* like that.

Dear God.

Sometime later—

"And then you proceeded from the Red Chapel, through the stout door, into the dark passageway," cried Bess, standing on the bed, gesticulating wildly with her arms in a pantomime of Jack's most infamous gaolbreak. Whatever she hadn't been able to fit into

---

nightmare you have is about Mommy and Daddy and all that same shit all the time.

Do you know what else Deleuze and Guattari said? This is actually relevant, because it's a non-Oedipal theory of fucking. They said,

"[W]henever someone makes love, really makes love, that person constitutes a body without organs, alone and with the other person or people. A body without organs is not an empty body stripped of organs, but a body upon which that which serves as organs [wolves, wolf eyes, wolf jaws?] is distributed according to crowd phenomena, in Brownian motion, in the form of molecular multiplicities."

Don't be perplexed by the weirdness of these claims. It's just that making love is not really about getting your organs serviced. Rather, when you're making love, the organs that have been forced into this Oedipal narrative get *rearranged*. Rewritten. Sort of liberated (there's some debate around *how* liberated; just bracket that for now). And that rewriting—that's making love. Actually, it's kind of like the epigraph to this manuscript—"Love's mysteries in souls do grow, / But yet the body is his book." The body is written (like a book is written)—or rewritten—in the process of making love. I mean, if you're "really" making love.

† Mercifully, in the absence of Sullivan's pestering, I am in a position to decline to estimate how far inside her he is. Anyone who really wants to know these specifics has clearly never made love.

her two valises or the sacks, Jack had stuff'd into his coat pockets and wound 'round his waist.

They were now both drunk. And open and easy with each other again.

"Well, but you c-can't attack a fillet that way," corrected Jack, standing and stumbling on the tangled bedsheets. He guided her hand in a mimicry of gaolbreaking.

"It—it's like this," drawing her right hand back and then thrusting it up at a mock-fillet. "You strike it hard and precise at the front, and then it shatters—" Jack sprinkl'd his fingers through the air, conjuring falling shards of fillet.

Bess turn'd and they dropp'd to the bed again. Jack's hands roam'd up and down her high tight bottom, her thighs—and they'd made it three-quarters of the way through a flask of brandy, when Bess look'd down at him, her dark hair messed across her eyes—and fell giggling on his chest. He liked her a bit soused—how Undone she'd become with liquor—his ice-queen, composed and Brilliant during the day, but unraveled and somewhat silly by night's end.

"We *will* beat them, Jack," she said into his chest. "We will."

"I know," he said, into her hair.

They should have left hours ago.

Fortunately the centinels were quiet that day.

They hired a hackney coach—and so, what was going to be a melancholic procession from their rooms was transform'd into a tumult of laughter, dragging sacks and suitcases, and then they were riding past Newgate with the windows down, screaming in joy at their freedom and youth and pleasure. They were too soused to find this Foolish—even Bess, who now had splashes of Red warming her cheeks on account of the quantity of brandy and clicketing.

They hung out the windows, calling for the warden, the Inmates, anyone to hear that they were free and ungaolable. It felt good to forget everything—to drown together in perfect Freedom, rolling side to side in the coach, feeling the able Irish Roans pulling them forward like Poseidon sporting the waves, immune to tide and currents.

The gargoyles outside Newgate appear'd even more immense from street level, and Jack was draped out the window of the coach backwards, looking up at them drunkenly, Bess with her face pressed into his breeches, her breath in some consummate syncopation with the cart's rocking. His body blush'd all over with a sustained, unpeaking exquisite Pleasure, and he was looking up at the huge gray flint faces, the scudding glowing clouds.

Sometimes—albeit rarely—but especially when one is young, Revelry is the verso face of misery and Terror.

When the coach pull'd up outside Dennison's, the driver lash'd the horses to the post and stepp'd down to piss in the gutter. There was a broadside pasted to the horse post.

"King's Menagerie tonight," read Bess, idly.

Jack meandered over, scann'd the advertisement. "Eagles, a Sea-Bear, and a Lion-Man straight from Borneo."

"A *what?*" She put his hand on his arm.

"A Lion-Man straight from Borneo."

"Jack"—she tore off the advertisement, peered at it—"a *Lion-Man.*"

"Didn't know you were interested in those blasted human zoos."

"No, remember when Evans was dying—well, I mean, right *before* the dying part—and he said something about how this wasn't his first operation?"

"Don't remember much o' that day."

"The note we found?" She rustl'd through one of the bags. "See!" She point'd to it. *"Met with Okoh and the Lion-Man."*

Bess had her look of unfettered Glee, the look she got when seemingly unrelated things began to connect. Her *Spinozist* look.

. . .

But first upstairs to Dennison's to drop off their goods. A quick hello to the new Abbess—a wrinkled small woman hardly as well off as the other, but hopefully, Jack thought, less likely to turn them in to the magistrates. This bat house was Somber, quiet in the ante-rooms with an occasional down-at-the-heels cove shuffling through. At least no centinels would think to look for Bess at this sinking establishment.

The new chambers were larger than the old, but dark and Close-ceilinged. There was a tiny mildewed hearth area along with a Bed and ottoman. And a hooked rug with patches missing—a sad archipelago of wool.

Quickly they were back in the coach and Bess said, "Drury Lane, please," to the driver, and the horses jolted forward, while, back in the compartment, Jack and Bess fell over each other again, scrambling to get their hands on anything of each other's that they could, panting in joy.

12.

THE TOWER MENAGERIE—A SMALL, CRAMPED ENCLAVE—A CORNER of greasy shadows and sharp, explicit odors—sat at the far base of the Tower Wall. Here had been established a wretched but profitable Enterprise for the once-yearly entertainment and diversion of the Common mobs of London.

At the end of an impatient line sat the barker; beyond him, animals squawled and brayed, kicking up dust in their pens. Children splashed their hands at the water's edge, slapping at the Thames, spraying each other with muck.

An anxious aristocrat bustled quickly past the line, several children in tow.

"This 's a horrific carnival to entertain the city's most despicable rabble. Don't gaze upon it," he announc'd to his too-handsomely attired children, orbiting him like Expressionless, gas-filled balloons.

Beyond all this sound was another sound. The secret Braying of the animal-commodities. Hideous contorted wails floated over the Menagerie: *Was we born or was we made?* Shrill squawks, and, again, *Was we born or was we made?* Then a jowly roar: *We was born-made, born-made.* And next, miserable ghoulish Sobbing.

Jack was fighting the urge to break every lock and cage open when the barker's shout—"Come one, come all!"—shook him back into focus.

Jack shudder'd in his coat. The quicker they could case the Menagerie, the better. Centinels were beginning to fill the streets on their night shifts, sleepy, sour-faced, and eager to crack skulls.

"Twelve p, mate," snapped the barker as they made their way to the front.

"S-since when?"

The Tower Guard shrugg'd. "Admission's more for grungy snab-blers* and lascars."

Jack peek'd 'round the Guard's shoulder at the coves and doxies perambulating the cages bunched together at the edge of the Thames. A knot of rogues congregated by a miserable white-haired Sea-Bear slumped on the ground with its paws wedged under the floor of the cage, reaching for the filthy shore.

"The whole Mob is grungy snabblers," Jack grumbl'd.

"Thieves they may be, but them's thieves of the better sort." The barker nodded at the Sea-Bear's group.

"Wild's crew," Bess mutter'd. Then, to the barker—"You've barely got twelve animals in there as it is— Unless you count your *better sort of thieves*."

Jack scann'd the wharf, marking escape routes.

"Twelve animals it may be"—the barker rais'd his voice to adver-tise to the crowd—"but they're twelve of the finest. We've three lions, one panther, two tigers, an eagle, a Turkish hawk, two leop-ards, and that Sea-Bear—lately brought from the King's expedition-ary team in Greenland. In addition, we've a Lion-Man—a beast never before seen on England's shores. Very intelligent animal. Well worth your pence."

Bess produced twelvepence, and they entered, though they hung at the edges, out of sight of Wild's gang.

Jack took long stock of the infernal Conditions of the eagle, fasten'd by leather thongs to a beam. It recall'd Kneebone's to him—his flight from servitude—and he wished the same for the bird. To break headfirst through the iron bars of the cage, taking to the sky in an angled, lurching Arc.

Wild's gang rumbled down to the farthest cage in the Menag-

---

* Plunderers, thieves

erie, the Lion-Man's cage. Knit tight-in with their heads down, conferring. Jack and Bess veer'd the opposite direction around the other cages, with each creature looking more pathetic than the last. The Tigers scuffed at the dirt with gangrenous paws. The Lions had scabby patches of fur missing. The Turkish Hawk was more mitegnawed than feather'd.

"Jack." Bess shook his shoulder. "Wild's gang's leaving."

The Lion-Man was a despondent creature. As Jack and Bess clos'd in, it was clear he was a burly human with fur coming unglued from his forearms† and down the sides of his pale, naked ribs. He sat, silently, on a tree stump, his legs splayed beneath the bursting Globe of his gut. Other than a largish forehead, which lent a ghoulish Aspect, he appear'd quite ordinary.

"Well, he's just a gumm'd-up rogue."‡

The Lion-Man sat wordlessly, regarding his own knees. Jack wondered whether the man had lost the power of speech—if he too suffered from language snared in the hot tunnel between mouth and lung.

"This one is very intelligent." The Keeper appear'd from a hut behind the cages, gray hair flying, and a distinct penumbra of gin hov'ring about his person. At the sight of the Keeper, the Lion-Man trundled back to a dark corner of the cage.

"He's of the group *Anthropomorpha*, as outlin'd in Ray's *Synopsis methodica animalium quadrupedum*. A face wrinkled as if with old age; huge, broad, yellow teeth; nail-bearing, clawed hands and feet; hollowed eyes; long hairs upon the brows; and a body as big in circumference as a man's (though, I should add, near three times as strong)—"

"We're not interest'd in your classifications—" began Jack.

---

† Likely horse glue, England's barbaric contribution to the otherwise gentle history of adhesives (e.g., birch, sap).

‡ The terrible history of human zoos is not a secret to anyone. Although this text departs from the usual history in one significant detail: the Lion-Man appears to be Anglo.

"However," the Keeper continu'd, oblivious with gin, "that particular ape, as well you should know, was described by Ray as without *rationale,* or Reason."

"Threepence to allow us to discourse with him privately—?" Bess pressed the coin into the Keeper's palm.

The Keeper cough'd—inspected his palm—"Ah! Good night sir, Madam"—and stumbl'd drunkenly back towards the hut.

The Lion-Man re-emerged from the shadowed corner of the cage.

"We must speak to you," said Bess, "rogue to rogue."

"We'll free you!" blurted Jack.

The Lion-Man heav'd a sigh, and out rang a voice quite English and cultured.

"In a Menagerie surrounded by all the King's Guard?"

"I'm Sheppard, you know."

"Even Sheppard, I'm afraid, would be unable." He squint'd at Bess. "Madam, if you would be so kind as to provide me with a dram from the flask I can so plainly see you've left peeking from your waistcoat, I would happily indulge you in all Manner of rogue-to-rogue discourse as would satisfy your curiosity."

Bess reached for her flask while the Lion-Man produced a battered tin cup from the ground. She unscrew'd the top, poured into the outstretched vessel, and return'd the flask to her side pocket. Arranged herself on the tuffet where Wild had been. Jack leaned against the bars at Bess's side. A brisk wind came off the Thames.

"Sir, we very much appreciate you taking the time. We haven't much, so I'll go right to the point. We've been appris'd of your existence by this"—she produced Evans' note from her cloak pocket and pass'd it to him—"this Note. It seems both you and we are Connect'd in our acquaintanceship with a J. Evans. And perhaps with certain of his . . . experiments?"

"We're immensely eager to know more," added Jack.

The Lion-Man paced and sipp'd. He turn'd the paper over in his hands—commenced to sit again on the stump at the edge of the bars.

"I am advertised by the Menagerie," he began oratorically, "as one of the group *Homo troglodytes*—the Keeper was wrong in his introductions. Of course, none of these so-called species exist. But he was wrong, even, in his fictions. The Menagerie has painted me as one of the nocturnal cave-dwelling apes postulat'd to inhabit the inner regions of the Pulau Seribu islands off Nusantara (or 'Jaya-karta,' as they call it) but never before seen by Englishmen until a contingent from the East India Company discovered me in the course of a trading Mission to the region.

"None of this, of course, is true." He rearrang'd himself on the stump, crossing one hairy leg over the other. "In any case, to answer your question: Have you yet heard of Kojo Bekoe Okoh?"

Bess shook her head.

"To explain Evans, I have to start with Okoh."

13.

"Kojo Bekoe Okoh"—the Lion-Man clear'd his throat and sat forward—"was born near Akim in 1699, and captured by the Royal African Company at the age of seventeen with the intention of sending him aboard the *Temperance*, bound for the West Indies. Possessed of a brilliant mind and a Disdain for authority, Okoh glimps'd an opportunity to evade this dreadful Outcome during a delay at port: the *Temperance* had met with extremely inclement Weather en route from Liverpool, and in the hectic Activity of repairing its hull for departure, Okoh escaped his bondage and fled as a hired sailor on a Mughal trading ship en route to Portugal. Just off the Azores, however, the ship ran aground. Only Okoh surviv'd, through canny manipulation of a piece of board and considerable navigational Sensibilities. He took shelter in the Isles 'til he was accosted there by a British East India Party and—it being ascertain'd that he was a skillful seaman—press'd into labor on a Vessel call'd the *Katherine*, under the direction of Captain John Hunter—a notoriously rough man, dislik'd by most of his crew.

"Young Okoh made several trading journeys under Hunter, quickly proving himself to be a Favorite among the more *independent-minded* of the crew, particularly those who were most dissatisfied with Hunter's exhausting searches for each journey's utmost profit. On one such journey—the crew Overwork'd and beginning to grumble of mutiny belowdecks—Hunter determined to extend the planned voyage, overshooting the *Katherine's* original destination to Bombay on the rumor of an unclaimed quantity of muslin at the port of Masulipatnam. When the *Katherine* reached port, however, the muslin—and indeed, the East India Company factor—were nowhere in sight. The entire port was quiet. This ought to have been Hunter's clue to turn the ship about. And yet, his greed, etc.

"Hunter sent out a search party of two to explore further inland. There, in the fountains of the market courtyard, the Emissaries were accost'd by a crowd of European female pirates who—having slain the East India Company factor and all his agents—demanded the Emissaries swear Allegiance to piracy or be murder'd as well. One swore Allegiance. One did not. The pirate crew (along with the one consenting Emissary) thence return'd to the *Katherine*, where they discover'd the higher-ranking officers laying about sous'd and sun-puffed on the deck. These they quickly overtook with Surprise. Some were dispatch'd with knives to the throat. Others scrambled for Safety. In the wretched, dingy lower hold, to which the African and lascar sailors were consign'd, Okoh and his comrades heard the Commotion. The moment of mutiny had at last come. They organiz'd themselves into their own battalion.

"With nowhere to hide, the remaining officers fled from the pirates to the lower hold. Okoh was ready. Flanking the threshold, he and his comrades captured the crew when they burst through. They gave them the same option as the Emissaries had been given: pledge allegiance to the emerging band of mutineers, or be turned over to the pirates above deck. Few pledged. Many were killed.

"From thence, Okoh and his comrades flooded up to the deck and join'd with the pirates. There was much rejoicing.

"The Captain, oblivious, was alone in his quarters supping on roast sailfish and warm brandy (and undoubtedly boxing the Jesuit). Okoh and the mutineers storm'd Hunter's chamber, where they easily overpowered him with Surprise, and tied him to his bedposts.

"Okoh may have wanted to kill Hunter outright, but he gave Hunter the opportunity to turn pirate with 'em. The Captain spat in Okoh's face. He refused in the name of his holy God Commerce and the necessity of arriving to Bombay for his trading schemes. He was eager to return thence to Liverpool for his payment.

"Without further hesitation, the pirates cut off the Captain's head and threw it to the fish.

"That night, the *Katherine* rais'd the skull and crossbones, and the new freebooter Society celebrated, regaling each other with Fantasies of living free of the East India Company. The lascar mates told stories of especially pleasant weather and calm waters in the sea north of the Masalembu islands.

"The crew sailed south. They came to be lost many times, but as Okoh was good with Constellations, he proved a capable Navigator. On their route, they encountered several British and Dutch Company ships. The pirates direct'd the mutineers in the particulars of ship-raiding, and they gain'd more comrades and supplies in this manner, leaving a slaw of bloodied Company faithfuls in their wake. Still, it was a long and hot journey. Not all of the freebooters survived, though the pirates try'd remedies to preserve as many as possible. Wormwood and sage added to cider to strengthen the constitution. Pastes of garlick with butter. Clove and fig for Wakefulness. They drank water with as much salt in it as they could bear. They ate sage moistened with vinegar in the mornings as breakfast, and chew'd wood sorrel to stave off hunger throughout the days.

"When they reached the Java Sea—a somewhat diminish'd lot—they declared themselves a Maroon Society of Freebooters. Okoh, most of the female pirates, some Anglo Englishmen, several Tahitian Islanders, Africans, French Protestants, and lascars. They were rich in livestock—including a small Band of chickens and swine they had liberated from a Dutch ship (cautious to escort off only those animals who walked willingly alongside, not wanting to 'press-gang' any creatures into labor)—herbs, and other Provisions. Everything was held in common and every soul Valu'd and loved.

"So as not to disturb any societies living on the islands further south, the mutineers threw anchor far from any coast and set about transforming their ship into a small village. The upper deck was Devoted to growing vegetables and herbs, along with a chicken-and-swine pasture and gardens for Exercise, star-gazing and the

pursuit of open-air Arts. Lowerdecks hous'd root cellars, a small library (to which the society added their own narratives), a makeshift
laboratory for mutineers interested in pursuing natural Experimen-
tation or training in doctoring, and sleeping bunks. In time, using
various Flotsam collected from the sea (the Detritus of distant
shipwrecks, driftwood, bones and dried shark-and-whale skin), they
added to their single ship an Archipelago of outlying flotillas.

"Each member of the society was encourag'd to discov'r Activi-
ties of greatest interest. Okoh spent much of his time exploring his
Passions—which tended towards the astrological. He was a sky-
watcher. He'd lie awake at night, observing the conduct of the constellations across the giant dome. Daily, he conveyed valuable
Information regarding developments in the Weather and the Winds
to those mutineers who had taken to fishing or planting.

"Some of the pirates had become eager amateur Scientists. Their
experience with roots and herbs for shipboard health form'd the
basis for many gentle Experiments with the animals and plants they
had collected from the Company ships. In the course of this Practice, the pirates devis'd a kind of Concoction—a recipe based on
cane-drying methods they'd discover'd on long ocean journeys.
They found that if they distill'd the urine of the swine for weeks in
the sun and mix'd it with fruit pectin, they'd arrive at a stiff jelly
that could be granulat'd in the manner of cane.

"The pirates admired the swine, which seem'd possessed of an
especial Meatiness, and they wished to thicken similarly. They
conjectur'd that the urine might hold a key. But the granules—they
found—had little effect. Seeking Okoh's advice, they determined
on a more Subtle process—applying to the gel'd urine a complex
combination of herbs, fruits, mashing Techniques, and an ineffable
Something else: exposure to certain strains of Starlight. The serum,
when completed, emboldened and thickened them as hoped. Over
the course of time, they came to resemble grizzled coves in ways
that surpris'd and delight'd them.

"This 'gravel,' as the mutineers called it, was easily integrated into the Maroon society. Some said it made those who took it exceptionally *hell-houndish*[*] and Free and Liberated with each other. Though others said they had been quite Free and Liberated with each other all along. They lived this way for the space of some years—those who wish'd to take of the serum did so, just as those who wish'd to take of spice to their food or other medicinal extractions did—while the winters were long in England and the navies kept their ships close to shore or engag'd in more pressing matters."

The elixir. A mutineer recipe.

Jack drew closer to the bars.

"But the East India Company doesn't forget. In addition to which, the Dutch were increasing their presence in the Java Sea. The Company—was thus provok'd to retrieve their lost merchandise, ships, and men in case the Dutch made an *opportunity* of the loss. In the heat of June 1722, they sent a Bombay Navy frigate to hunt for mutineers and their vessels.

"The mutineers had long dispens'd with weapons, as they had no need for such items in their community. Their guns, in fact, had gone to Rust in the heat and damp, and one or two mutineers— those that had found a liking for the cooking Arts—had discover'd the barrels served very well as planters for herbs and spices to flavor the meals.

"The Bombay Navy was supply'd with cannons, muskets, and longswords.

"The battle was brief.

"The Mutineers were rounded up and brought on board the frigate. Okoh look'd at his fellow mates, throng'd in miserable bleeding Heaps on deck, and fear'd.

"'*What should we do?*' they called out to him. Okoh spoke in pirate cant, vociferous and Hopeful, despite the inauspicious Circumstances. *We have battled the Company before and won.* The captain did not understand the words Okoh spoke, but, watching him, he understood this: a journey with the mutineer leader would be

---

[*] Lewd (in a lovely, roguish sense)

too risky. When they had sail'd some way from the flotilla, the captain ordered the crew to lift Okoh from the deck and throw him overboard into the shark-clotted waters.

"And then to press on for England.

"Okoh was skilled at ropework—as some of the mates on the flotilla had entertain'd themselves and each other with games of masterful Knotting and Unknotting. He had untied his wrists long before he was thrown overboard, though he'd left the cord loosely wrapp'd to retain the appearance of Confinement.

"As the frigate pulled away, he swam back to the mutineer ships.

"There, Okoh mournfully attempted to perform all of the tasks that the freebooters had accomplish'd together. He tended the chickens and swine in the morning, rested at the heat of the day, cook'd in the evening, repair'd his tools, and attended to his bunk and general Cleanliness after supper. He told himself stories around his campfire, the way their favored tale-teller had done each night. But there was too much lost. It was not the Same without his mates. His camp fell to ruin, his literary Arts languished, and his foods dwindl'd to a daily broth of wilted greens and roots with no spices to flavor them.

"But he did have one thing: an enormous supply of the pirates' strength gravel. He had not tried it previously, but now found it invigorated his condition.

"Okoh loaded one of the smaller flotsam-boats with what gravel he could carry, and set off for the mainland. Rumor has it he fought sea monsters and Tritons of the deep en route, but who can say for sure. They say he killed a Kraken, then pilot'd his craft through its innards and out the anus, taking note, along the way, of a lion eaten entirely whole, a British smallship, and a host of Octopi and cod. These latter he collected and supp'd on."†

---

† The informed reader will recognize that the Lion-Man's tale is borrowing in style from the tradition of heroic romance, which combines early anthropology, travel narrative and medieval epic. Several come to mind. Uncannily, Fielding's *History of the Life of the Late Mr. Jonathan Wild the Great* (in which Wild is lost at sea and battles a kraken), as well as Behn's *Ooronoko: or, the Royal Slave*. On the topic of the often

The Lion-Man went silent for a moment as the wind howled nervously over the Thames.

"How might you have come by this history?" Bess had not moved throughout the telling.

The Lion-Man gave Bess a grave look. "I, too, was indentur'd to the *Katherine*. Sold to Hunter and the East India Company by my father as a 'useless imp' at the age of some fifteen years. It was I who swore Solidarity to the pirates.

"I lived in the freebooter society; participat'd in swine-tending and gardening. But my Specialty in the community was *tale-teller*. I spun the inimitable yarns for our mates, as I had learn'd some letters in my small years of schooling. On the flotilla, I practiced the ancient Greek art of *plitho-hypomnesis**. It was an honorable position.

"Until that fateful day: the day of our capture. On that day I was below, writing in my bunk, when I heard a scuffling on the top-decks. I laid down my stories for the evening campfire and peer'd up through the portal to find one pink-faced and crazed sailor, plied to the gills with gin and tottering down the stairs towards me. Before I knew it, the brute was waving a pistol. In a Panic, I held up the thick sheaf of my diaries as a shield. He discharg'd his pistol directly at me, blowing through the diary and straight into my ribs. It was not a deep wound, but it was disabl'ng. I fell to the ground. Shortly, we were all of us truss'd up like boar for roasting and loaded onto the frigate. We sailed for England. Except for Okoh, who—as I mention'd—had been thrown overboard.

"Many of us perished in the first days of capture out of sheer Misery and hopelessness. Some they secreted off to other ships bound for parts still unknown to me. As for me, after eight long weeks

---

unremarked appearance of African and Afro-British figures in eighteenth-century British literature and visual art, see also Tisa Bryant, *Unexplained Presence* (Leon Works, 2007).

* Hypomnesis (i.e., "memory-prosthesis") is easily sourced in Freud and Derrida. As I do not read Greek, however, further research on "plitho-hypomnesis" and its usages will have to be referred to a colleague.

at sea (the ship returned to Canton to make one more set of trades and discharge more mutineers as captive, bound laborers) I was deposit'd unceremoniously in the King's Wharf cellar amongst the rest of the *foreign goods*. Apparently they had concluded that I looked amazingly close to a beast, and would fetch a fortune in revenues at the King's Menagerie. I have been a Prisoner here ever since."

"In the elements?"

"Day in and out. I was accustomed to sleeping under the night canopy, but the coal-smoke and the cold here—"

Bess let out a sob.

"But to bring us towards your question: imagine my Surprise when, just a few weeks ago, the Tower Guards brought Okoh to an adjacent cell, there to be jeer'd at by the Guards and the King's retinue. Okoh is—well, not one to take discipline lightly. He thrash'd himself against the bars night and day, refus'd his meals. Began to waste. We had precious little time to speak, but I did learn of his journey and subsequent capture." He held their gazes. "Last night he was removed."

"And what of the mutineer recipe?" Jack cut in.

The Lion-Man shrugg'd. "There are certain forms of knowledge develop'd collectively that can't be translated into a simple *recipe,* I'm afraid. Evans—that was his name? Your 'doctor'?" Bess nodded. "Evans—I believe it was he—visit'd on the day they brought Okoh to the Tower. He arrived with Wild. Evans sought to interview Okoh, but he was immediately refused. Then he came to interview me regarding the gravel. They'd promised me my Freedom. Of course I long for freedom, but even if I had consider'd giving them the recipe, their own Navy had destroy'd my diary and all my notes of our goings-on. I saw Evans' efforts as absolutely futile. Without the records, I'd need the rest of the society to reconstruct it. And they're all dead but for Okoh and myself."

The wind gusted plumes of sea-coal over the Menagerie. Clots of rain clouds drift'd up the Thames, lit blue-gray by the moon.

"But," said Bess as the squalls threw strands of hair onto her cheeks, "why would Wild want the mutineer recipe? What for?"

"I can't say. Although I heard 'em discoursing about how there's a ship coming up the Thames—the *Poor Maria*—"

"When?" Jack broke in.

The Lion-Man shrugged.

"They said it's got *somethin'* on board that's going to enrich them beyond measure. Somethin' they can market to the stockjobbers and barristers—the new-monies stayin' up all night balancin' books. The ship's got to be quarantined with all the rest down in the Black-friars for twenty-eight days, according to the Minister of Publick Health. Wild went on about it, saying nobody would be able to get near the ship through all the centinels. That they'd have easy access to conduct their Business. And once the ship comes in, he boasted, they won't need to raid any more ships ever—or conduct any small jilts to fund their operations."

He paused. "If you want my hypothesis, they've sent the Bombay Navy for the rest of the strength gravel. If my memory serves, we had produced enough for a year at least when we were captured."

Jack shifted from foot to foot. *A year's worth?*

"Thank you for taking the time with us, tonight. We'll come back for you, I promise," Bess said.

The Lion-Man laugh'd. The lamplight gave his face a sort of Vampir-glow. "I'm surrounded by Tower Guards at all times. And even if I did escape, they'd find me. They'll never let us Free—not mutineers. Too dangerous, too likely to *stir Tumults* among the publick. Do me a favor: Just make certain Wild doesn't obtain that strength gravel."

14.

THE WIND WAS VERY HIGH AND BUILDING HIGHER AS THE NIGHT deepened. Bess and Jack raced down the streets, both quiet. Both thinking. A pair of knickers loosed from a washing-line and skitter'd down the alley, collecting filth as it tumbl'd by.

—And on through the streets—nightbirds shrieking on corners, urchins dashing down alleys—to Dennison's. The bat house was buzzing—the sound of glasses clinking and liquor decanting, beds creaking and sighing into their casters—fill'd the halls and stairwells.

As they ascended the stairs, Jack spoke excitedly at Bess's back. "The elixir—in the Lighthouse—must have been the small amount Okoh carried—and now Wild's sent a ship back to the flotilla to get more." Relief was washing over him. "All we have to do is jump the ship."

Bess turn'd as she opened the door. Jack reached out and held her hand, squeezed it. She caught a glimpse of his pale chilly fingers wrapped around her own. For a moment she recognized neither of their hands. She removed her hand, walked into the room with Jack just behind. *What doesn't he see about the foolishness of his approach?* Another utterly obvious thing she'd have to explain. She closed the door.

"Presume whatever's on the ship's something Wild means to fund his policing operation. Do you not see how Powerful that'll make him?"

"Exactly! That's why we need to get it before he does!" Jack sat on the bed, beaming up at her.

"But if we did pull such a thing off"—she shook her head, pac-

ing the windows—"even if we could—with his Army of centinels.
You think we'd ever get Free?"

"We are free."

Bess studied his face. "You believe that?"

"I mean, not free, but—" His eyes were beginning to cloud with
the realization that he was missing some point.

"Can't you see there's only one thing to do on board that ship?"

"Anything—I'll agree to it."

"You won't like it, I'm afraid."

"Won't I?"

"Destroy the elixir."

Jack stared, openmouthed.

"Jack, just imagine a Policing operation with endless finances. A
factory of watching, self-funded and Autonomous. A true Policing
Business concern. At least if we destroy it there's no question of
Wild ever getting his hands on 't."

"But . . ." Jack's body was shrinking in his mind's eye—wasting
down. He would become the *empty room* he was before.

"You've seen what's transpired since the Lighthouse. We're
squirreled away in this corner like rats. I hid once—from the surveyors. I always said I'd not hide anymore. But"—she swept her
arms out—"look at me now. Look at *us*. Look how they're torment-
ing the entire Town."

The distance between them grew—a cold cloud filling the room.

"What about my—" Words were caught in his throat.

She touch'd the back of his hand. "I love you *all ways*."

But the specter of approaching *elixirishness* was engulfing him
like foul Weather spinning towards shore from some awful horizon,
churning up spray and inevitability. He would be as *nothing*—as *away*
from himself—as he was before. And she would not desire him that
away way, no matter what she said. Without their Entwinedness,
without their unabash'd Takings of each other, what was he?

"I can't."

"If it's some kind of mutineer recipe, we can devise it again,
together. We're mutineers"—she managed a smile, trying a differ-

ent tack—"of a sort. And Wild—Wild is of the same machine that created the Surveyors. The profiteers and killers."

"Then let's bilk him," Jack pressed.

"No." She shook her head. "Don't you see—this is our chance. We have to ruin him. Entirely."

"His entire enterprise? Us?"

"It matters that we try." Her voice broke. She was looking at Jack but suddenly his face and Wild's face were alternating with each other. She saw Wild's face rising over London like a huge summer moon, surveilling them all. Then the face was Jack's. She breathed slow, focused. "It matters that we try together."

Some part of Jack was affect'd by hearing Bess's voice crack, and the other was spiraling into a hot flash of fear—his more spidery *before*-self was waggling itself before his eyes. Every day had brought with it a closening of the gap between himself and himself. And (he dared hope) a closening of the gap between himself and Bess. But now—

Bess was rifling through his sack— Then Jack was rushing at her. Grabbing her wrist. It was a terrible manner in which to touch her. There was nothing of their intimacy as they dropp'd to the floor in a tangle, wrestling for purchase. Heat, pressure, the slick of anxious sweat.

She pushed him off her and he fell back against the wall. "What are you doing!"

"You're trying to destroy my elixir too?" Jack grabbed for the sack— The gin bottle with the dwindling stash of elixir slid out, rolling to a stop on the floor between them.

"Are you mad? I was looking for my night cream—we placed it in there when we packed up at Cresswell's."

"Sorry," he muttered, unconvincingly.

"You know Wild'll finance and embolden his entire factory of Policing, and you don't even care. I should have known." She looked at him. "Kafir*." She had begun crying.

---

* Wretch. *Viz., The Travels of Mirza Abu Taleb Khan,* ed. Daniel O'Quinn (Broadview Press, 2008).

"What does that mean?"

"I'm not teaching you any more words," she sobbed. "Why did I teach you any to begin with."

Jack's throat was dry as chalk. He felt his misery rising up, tugging at him, calling for him like a dog straining against a leash. "I'll leave." He said this as if she'd asked him to.

"'Course you will. That's what you do. Run off. But know that if you leave now—if we don't scamp together—if we don't fight together—then we're nothing."

Her eyes went wide, pleading. It shatter'd him to turn away from them. But his misery was overtaking him—a master he didn't know how to disobey.

So, then, his misery was not the dog; *he* was his misery's dog.

Jack rolled the bottle back towards himself; put it in his sack. Lash'd it closed.

He had done that first. The thing with the bottle. Done that before he ask'd, "What do you mean 'nothing'?"

That was a beat too long. An awfully regrettable beat too long.*

---

* While we're on the topic of exes . . .

I remember waking up somewhere unfamiliar. This was before the Villa Papyri Lounge—the morning before that night.

I was on a purple velvet couch in a small cottage. I could see a kitchen beyond the end of the couch. To the right, a bathroom threshold. The house was a specific kind of quiet. I was alone. I was thirsty and my head hurt.

On my way to the sink I noticed a pair of chunky-heeled boots—knee-high, unmistakably femme—along with what I was agonized to realize was my self-help book. *Dear God* I had brought my self-help book with me to this—wherever I was—somewhere that had a femme in it, or had had one.

The Art of Shprukh-Psikhish, or: The Psychological Mastery of Panic Character, block lettering announced loudly from the counter. This was embarrassing. Whoever I had spent the night with also knew about my self-improvement project.

While I was running my head under the water, the door opened. It was her, my now-ex, and this was the first time I was seeing her. Or, the first time I remembered with any clarity, as the night before was not available to me for reasons of bourbon.

In the backlight from the cracked-open door, her brown hair shone. It was late autumn and it was getting on evening, so it seemed I had slept all day. The sun was setting over the zinnias that wreathed the walkway to the house. The red sky in the threshold lit the capillaries inside my eyes, and I looked out through a scrim of beating vessels.

"Nice to see you up," she said, coming in and closing the door. I interpreted this as a comment on the terrifying rictus of pain I have been told my expression takes on when I'm asleep. I took it to mean: *It is not so nice to see you sleeping.*

"I'm up," I agreed stupidly.

I liked the skeptical way she looked at me. I liked the way the air in the house felt with her in it.

It was obvious from how I was staring that I was attracted to her, and it occurred to me that we must have had a very nice time the night before from how my groin was lighting up and also how she was half-smiling and her body was a little bit melting towards me as she came into the kitchen.

We talked all that day. She argued with almost everything I said. Half the time she would start shaking her head before I had even begun a sentence. Why did this turn me on? Her certainty about my wrongness was married with a certainty about my potential to do better. She had some kind of grasp of the future—a ferocity to make it do what she wanted. *You'll help me plant jasmine along the path in the spring,* she said, alarming me equally with her belief that I had ever managed not to kill a plant and with her conviction that we'd know each other beyond just that evening. She unnerved and relaxed me in equal, excruciating measure. She used one particular word that conjured forward a being I had not until that point imagined could ever exist. She called this being—amazingly enough—*"us."*

At some point, after we had gone to the Villa Papyri Lounge, and I had eaten an inconsequential chicken cutlet, and she had disabused me of my notion that I was ever going to have children and replaced it with a revolutionary fervor that was equally a fervor to fuck the shit out of her, we went to my place and she sat on my grandmother's desk and . . . you know the rest.

This is a disaster, I said, that next morning after we woke up.

We had been sent by fate or history to undo each other. If we could survive falling in love we would have everything we'd ever wanted, but it wasn't at all clear either of us could survive this. *It is a disaster.* She nodded, smiled, and we fucked again. And this time it was the fuck you can never get away from.

I touched her then, and always, with devotion and gusto. I touched her everywhere and anywhere she permitted me to touch, and I did so tirelessly. This means nothing about my stamina, and everything about what she awakened. In that inimitably queer way, we found languages, words to bridge the gulf between our bodies. I described to her what I was doing to her, how I was coming inside her even when—for obvious reasons—I wasn't exactly, well not in the way that other people mean. Every time I came, it was impossible and miraculously specific; it did not exist outside of her ability to summon it. And it could only be for her. She seemed to *appreciate* this approach, is all I will say, out of respect for our once-precious privacy. And it was beautiful. Our contact was an animal that came to life when we watered it with language.

Because of this language—this *animal of us* that exceeded us almost immediately; this animal that was cavorting and splashing at a horizon-line to which I could only aspire to catch up—she didn't have to be as beautiful as she was. I would have loved her just as much even if she hadn't been.

Yet she was very, very beautiful. I loved everything about the way she looked, but I loved in particular, and immediately, that little extra right by her belly button area, that extra that meant she lived comfortably with desire—for sex, for food—that extra that made her whole torso kind of *genital-y* to me, that extra that was just: *woman*. Her hair. Good god. Let us not speak of her hair. When she was feeling particularly contrary she'd threaten to shave it off, make mention of her younger years as a punk, and she didn't see why she couldn't pull off that look again. Which would send me into a cascade of begging her not to.

She wore the appearance of a permanent small sneer that was the result of an upper lip that was beautifully full enough to look as if it was always on the verge of turning up. She wore jeans that were tighter than anything I ever saw on the faculty at the University.

Looking at my ex was like that rare experience of taking a dodgeball hit straight to the gut. *Let me just perish in this vacuum of air while looking at this woman, this astonishing beauty,* I thought, that first afternoon. And never stopped thinking.

Things deepened.

My ex was a professor at a nearby college. A better one than where I taught. She was a scholar of a much more exciting and important field of study than my own, which explained why—until our first night together, following a karaoke party for a mutual friend that I still remember very little of—I had not met her previously. She was something of an autodidact, but it was more than that. She seized things that shouldn't go together and orchestrated intellectual car crashes with them. She created kaleidoscopic results—a flock of butterflies, a string of Christmas-colored lights floating out of a pile of wreckage—in ways that other people in her field could not do. She was much smarter than I was, and had a greater capacity for concentration. She had infinite patience for learning things; she had a hunger about this—yes, the knowledge itself, but also its eventual ruination. Every bit of knowledge she gleaned was a weapon she would use on another bit of knowledge. I was not inclined to do battle with someone of her eminence, but we were together and so battle was inevitable.

But then to tell you the truth I think I liked the battle a little. She upped my game, let's say. My ex and I fucked a lot and argued a lot and started marking up each other's writing a lot and then, because of the latter, fucking a lot some more. And, without getting into too much detail about this part I can barely stand to have lost, I'll add that she was secretly very sweet, and handled my now-dead bitch of a mother in ways inimitable and frankly soothing. It warmed a cockle of my heart that I didn't even know I had or needed. Maybe—to recall something I said earlier—she saw me in all my historicity too. Fuck.

Anyway, we were fucking and reading and writing and she was also healing this part of me I can't discuss, and somewhere in there I forgot about my Shprukh-Psikhish—the book that was supposed to help me with my anxiety situation.

By "situation" I mean that for as long as I can recall, my daily life has been orchestrated almost entirely around the number three. As a martial-arts film buff, I would have preferred a cool wuxia-style motto. *Live by the sword, die by the sword.* Or, *Once a promise leaves the mouth, even four horses cannot capture it again.* If only.

Instead, my motto is something like: *One two three (silent sound clucked against the back of the throat), three two one; one two three (silent cluck), three two one.*

This unit of silent clucking and counting is repeated in sets of three, three times in a row, until whatever it was that gave rise to the need to count—vanity, aspirations towards happiness, presumptions about living to see another day, etc.—is "erased."

The only thing—and I'm sure you could anticipate this—that made the counting go away was fucking. In an erotic situation, my breath would slow and a tremendous calm and clarity would come over me. I could command things in ways that had seemed just seconds before unimaginable. And I would stop counting.

I think I thought that if I fucked her enough I might be cured of counting for good.

PART

III

I.

CRASHING THROUGH THE DOORWAY OF THE GEORGE AND VULTURE in Lombard Street, near morning, Hell-and-Fury was chanting an old John Skelton rhyme.

Let none the outward Vulture fear. No Vulture hosts inhabit here. If too well-used you deem ye then, Take your revenge and come again.

The rest of the gang tumbl'd in behind—Wild; thick, stupid Fireblood; sleek Henry Davis; and ruddy Daniel Flanders—giving off a collective raspy laugh—*Come again!*—as they crowded in, anticipating an evening of salted mackerel, buttered oysters, and, afterwards, the doxies upstairs at Garamond Belle's school of Venus*.

At the table, they called over each other, howl'd about the Provenance of the polar-bear and the red-throated hawk. Even the cruelest rogue, at times, finds himself fascinated by a beast. The tavern was Humid with men in coats, and the fizz rising from pints of ale.

Wild was agitated, crimson-faced over some business concern. He pull'd a handkerchief from his pocket and wiped his cheeks and neck, produced a small ledger-book from his coat and began penning in the night's accounts and tabulating the next set of thefts. Fireblood and Flanders compet'd to flag down the barmaid.

"Gentlemen." Wild's voice was strain'd. Droplets of perspiration fell from his temples. "Ever since my inventory of *Product* was taken

---

* Brothel house

from the Lighthouse Authority, and the loss of my co-confector Evans, our entire project has been in Arrears. And none of you has intensified much your hunt for Sheppard who made off with my Property." He said *Property* through gritted teeth.

"Didn't you interview him yourself? At Newgate, some time back?" nagged Fireblood.

"He escap'd, I think"—this from Flanders, foolishly.

Wild's eyes narrow'd. He sat back. Stabb'd a piece of roast duck. Then he grinned an awful grin. "Since you two are clearly the brains of this operation, I must entrust you with a most important task. At the next prisoner-hanging"—brought the duck to his mouth—"you two will attend and retrieve the body before the magistrates do." He point'd his tarnished fork at them.

"A body?" sputter'd Fireblood, choking on his ale. "How're we s'posed to make off with a dead body?"

"Steal it in the mayhem and outcry," Wild said between chews.

"Steal it?!" Fireblood was spitting gobs of phlegm and ale.

"Hangings are so thick with centinels," scowled Flanders. "Centinels under orders to claim the body themselves."

Wild smiled. "You'll do it." He wiped his lips with his handkerchief.

Hell-and-Fury felt a chill of fear and Excitement. His thin nose twitch'd in his long face. Wild meant to set them up for arrest. Fireblood and Flanders were as good as dead.

Hell-and-Fury shovel'd in oysters and butter, and silently thanked the lord that he'd somehow eluded this fate for the time being.

Davis was onto it, too. His mouth work'd a bit of salted beef. His eyes had an empty sheen. He was doing the math like Hell-and-Fury was doing the math.

When Wild rose to drain his bladder in the George and Vulture's yard—waving Fireblood and Flanders back with him to "plan" the job (as well, much to their misfortune, to witness his prick releasing its lengthy stream)—Davis lean'd across the table.

"If Wild's getting rid of Fireblood and Flanders, that'll leave just meself, yerself, and Scotty Pool for whatever big fobs* Wild is aiming at."

Hell-and-Fury quaked at the thought of a big, Secret fob. It was unlike Wild to be so guarded about something that—as he himself bragg'd—would so *Enrich* and *Importantize* him. Must be something awful, to tell the truth.

"Aye." Hell-and-Fury wiped his finger along his tin plate, scooping up butter and oyster-juices. "Them two don't like the work. Don't take to it naturally." He licked his finger and forc'd a smile as oil collected at the ends of his stubby mustache.

* A job; a cheat, or a trick

2.

BESS STARED AT THE MORNING'S BROADSIDE EDITION IN BED. SHE'D spent the evening getting extraordinarily Soused with Jenny, making a number of proclamations as to Jack's Foolishness and Anglo self-absorption, and then falling into a deep slumber on top of Jenny's coverlets.

She'd woken at dawn and return'd to her rooms—Did not wash or dress. The narrowness of Jack's perspective was alarming. How could she have been so wrong about him—how could she have given herself over. She'd held her mouth as open for him as she could—nuzzl'd every part of him—his armpits, his sprouting beard scruff, his—*Something*. She'd slept in his arms— But the worst was that she'd told him about the Fens. Conjured her long-lost home together. Described her parents, and had taught him her father's words—the ones he'd taught her own mother. She'd let him make the Sounds of her home together with her.

And now he had that home—that lost part of her—inside him. And he was gone.

That was truly the very worst part.

She turn'd and vomit'd into her chamber pot. Shoved it away in frustration and misery. Vomit spilled on the floor. She did not wipe it up. She realized she was sobbing—trying to un-hear him saying her father's words, her private words. Together they had revived her vanish'd family—made them breathe again in the present. Why had she given him this part of herself?

After some time, she reached back onto the bed for the

broadside. Ripp'd out a page and scrubb'd at the soiled floor with it.

Something in the crumpled, stained paper caught her eye.

W A N T E D: women searchers in every parish to inspect places known to be plaguey. These women are charged with determining, to the best of their ability, whether those dead have died of infection or other Causes. Places to be searched include all small merchant shops and quarantined deadships. Note: merchants contracting goods on deadships will be recompensed lost interest on the product by the London Mint. In order to receive Compensation, all merchandise must be properly insured in advance of the voyage. Accordingly, all merchants are requested to file for insurance of their goods with Edward Lloyd's Underwriters, Ltd., located in Lombard Street under the Blue Plaque. For those traders engaging in the transportation of *persons*—whether African slaves or English felons and servants—Lloyd's newly offers an insurance against death by plague at the rate of 10 guinea per head.

The stairs at Dennison's rose at a steep savage pitch. Jenny's rooms were above Bess's, in the very back of the house, lodged high in the eaves. Bess knock'd hard. The door clang'd open and Jenny stood partway behind, her eyes Hollow with lack of sleep and red along the lower lids, the uppers bruis'd-looking and blue. Jenny appear'd more pale than usual, cloaked in a heavy satin robe that soaked up what dim Light there was in the hall.

A pick'd-over chicken carcass sat on the scratched side table, and the brocade cushions on Jenny's daybed were strewn on the floor. She'd had a job. Bess could see just what sort it had been, too. Convivial. Long. They had eaten afterwards. Jenny hadn't rushed to pick up after him.

Bess ran her hands through her hair in the manner of someone shaking out a cramp. "I need your sharping* arts."

Jenny smiled. "Thought you'd never ask." She exhaled. Bess felt it across her face. The bitter froth of semen recently swallowed, mix'd with the brine of roast chicken.

---

* Trickery

"You know I'm the best sharper," Jenny drawled. "But you were too moon-eyed over little Jack Sheppard to notice."

"Well, I don't know about *the best*," Bess smirk'd. "But you did fob off* that last clicketer for a whole roast chicken, didn't you." Bess nudged her chin towards the ruined Carcass as she walked in and closed the door behind. "Any case, Jack's gone now, so."

"You were going on about it last night quite a bit, you remember?"

"Oh, right." In fact, Bess didn't remember that. "In any case, I need your help getting on a ship."

"I know a cove who works with the Merchant Marine."

"Not a trading vessel." Bess paused. "One of the condemn'd ships. They'd never permit me. But an Anglo dame . . . ?"

—Not so very much later, Jenny and Bess were press'd against the cobblestone side of the Customs-Authority, the wind slapping their faces in wild nighttime Gusts off the river.

"'Member: you're applying as a searcher." Bess had to raise her voice over the lowing of the wind. She press'd the scrap of broadside advertisement into Jenny's palm. Adjust'd Jenny's hair against her shoulders.

"I thirst to destroy all of 'em." Jenny had a glint in her eyes and her vengeful smile.

Bess felt a sudden compulsion to put her hands to her, to kiss Jenny's furious lips, bluing with cold. Scamping together could raise Feelings like that. But then Jenny leaned around to the front and knock'd on the door. The lock turn'd. Bess pressed herself out of view.

Dixon, the City Alderman, swung open the door.

"What."

"Gods, he's an unsavory pickled apple." Jenny winced under her

---

* Tricked

breath. Bess caught a side glimpse of her ruffling her cleavage while arranging her face into a Parody of pleasantries. "Good evening, sir—" Jenny was adept at speaking in their accents. She sounded mellifluous and monied. "I'm here to apply to the Magistrate as a searcher."

3.

Off Blackfriars, tall grass hissed in the wind, blowing grit against Jack's cheeks. Night had bloom'd into its full dark Depth. He was walking thro' a tunnel of sorts—a path of heap'd earth emitting the raw scent of a recent rain (the breath of worms and cold). Starlight peck'd the sky.

It was very quiet—a deep Silence marked only in its negative by the occasional skitter of some rodent and the high whistling hiccup of nightbirds. The path narrowed and the earth walls got steeper—

—Then opened onto a busy scene, an inner glen at the shore. Barricades of scrap wood, iron sheets, large tree trunks and reams of thick muslin were piled at the far edge, opposite the path, to create a wall or Fortification.

This was the mollies' beach.

A cavernous shipwreck had been haul'd on shore and left to rot—the skeleton of a once impressive merchant vessel. Shadows threaded through the ship's bones. The only sound—occasional grunts or murmurings, the lick of tongues-to-tongues, and the *Shush* of feet through silt.

Aurie lay up the shore, away from the hull of the ship, leaning back on the sand—a mop of beard turn'd up to the night sky. A set of blond curls worked its way up and down between his legs.

Jack sat not far off—tho' not close enough to disturb. He shook his head politely to several venturing mollies while he waited for

Aurie to finish in the boy's mouth—four short, gruff grunts and a comradely cuff on the side of the head combin'd with hooking the boy's neck in his elbow and pulling him up for a short, deep kiss.

"Somewhere more secluded," he heard Aurie say into the blond's cheek, "I'll have this gorgeous quim. At length." He squeez'd the blond's arse.

"But tonight"—the blond traced his bottom lip with a fingertip— "did you like this quim*?"

"God, yes," Aurie groaned.

They kiss'd again. A long one now.

The boy adjust'd his shirt but not his hair, which tangl'd 'round his sunny freckled face, and Jack could see his light blue eyes looking Aurie over once—*lovingly?*—before he stood and made his way back towards the path. *Field's son?* Aurie had describ'd him once, but never brought him 'round.

He waited until Aurie rolled over into the sand, bunch'd his coat under his head, and was near-snoring. Then made his way over.

"Aurie—"

Aurie rolled over, blink'd dirt off his eyelashes.

Jack's eyes appear'd as if someone'd taken a hammer to them. Lids ringed with rust-red, swollen and angry.

"You look rough," he understated.

"We fought. I left. I'm such a—" he moaned into his hands.

"All right now. All right."

"—Something chang'd. Like we'd never been anything to each other."

"You're here now." Aurie's method of stating Facts was a dubious technique of Reassurance.

"Or, I don't know. Perhaps it was I who—"

"Jack, sleep." Aurie patted his cloak in invitation.

---

* Based on above usage, I am led to conclude that for rogues—and god how I love this—"quim" (and all its cognates—"muff," "tuzzy-muzzy," "customs-house," etc.) must signify *any loved point of entry on the body, irrespective of gender or sex.*

Jack arrang'd himself, still grumbling, at Aurie's back.

Aurie reached behind, muss'd Jack's hair.

And they fell to sleep like that, with Aurie's hand in his hair, and Jack a lamprey riding a shark deep into cold blue Currents.

Jack woke gasping in the night—his chest heaving and swelling. "I'm a ghost," he heard himself babbling into Aurie's filthy jerkin.

Aurie stirr'd, mumbled. "What ghost."

"Me." He could not get a breath. "I can't remember my name."

His half-asleep brain was racing in circles, searching. All he could recall was *P——*: what Lady Kneebone call'd him, and his mother before that. What was the word for *him*? There was a blank, an Absence in space-time where *he* should be. *Who was breathing. Who was crying.* He touched his chest. Without Bess, nothing—not even his own body; especially not his own body—signify'd.

"You're Jack, brother." Aurie turn'd, held him, mutter'd into the top of his head. "You're Jack."*

---

* Of ghosts—

"You should stay here," my ex said, after a certain amount of time had passed. I had already been staying with her most nights for quite some time. She wanted to formalize it. *I want you to stay with me,* she said.

This—I know—probably seems like a no-brainer. We were doing things together. Things that I ought to have recognized as "relationshippy things." She had planted a plant—a succulent harvested from the path outside—in the window box. We had named the plant Claw, for the curled red fists he had begun to sprout.

Like I said, we began to share writing, to edit each other's work. To trust each other with words as we did with our bodies.

We started to travel together. Every time I saw the bed we'd be staying in—wherever it was—it was the sexiest bed I'd ever seen. I would be stabbed with jealousy thinking about whoever it was that would get to share this bed with her. Then I would remember that this person was me.

This snarl of self-jealousy—it now occurs to me—was a feeling. But I was a computer that lacked a translation code for emotions. I could only stare at this data, blinking.

I had not been worried about our relationship before, but once she asked me to stay, I began to worry more, not less. Her asking me to stay felt like she was rolling out a soft rug under my feet. Other people would have lain down on this rug. But me, I couldn't stop thinking: *Here's a rug. Someone could always pull it.*

"Do you have anything to say?" she asked, in reference to the me-staying thing.

"I am, as I have been for so many months now, albeit not in any ways that do you any good, yours."

This did not come out as the reassurance I had intended it to be. More like a burned birthday cake smeared with thick frosting held out on trembling, apologetic arms.

"What is that supposed to mean." She looked over at me while watering Claw.

I tried to make a joke about what Leo Jogiches' long-lost replies to Rosa Luxemburg would have read like as tweets. But it was a stupid joke and I couldn't get the words out anyway. I tried to say *long-lost,* but I kept saying *lost-lost,* and she looked at me like I was crazy.

I did move in, but the contradictions in loving her were too much.

My body clenched in constant anticipation of punishment for my happiness. Sex momentarily relieved this anxiety, but—especially if the sex was good (and it was always much more than good)—it would return redoubled. I was convinced I would be struck dead for my desire and joy in her presence. None of this was attractive. Have you ever met someone so anxious that they become an asshole? That anxious asshole, Reader, was me.

I turned, finally, out of desperation, and with a renewed devotion, to my Shprukh-Psikhish.

Of course, my ex felt strongly that I had taken my commitment to Shprukh-Psikhish to bullshit heights.

"I have to do my Shprukh-Psikhish," I'd announce, first thing in the morning when it was clear she wanted to get fucked. But I'd have woken up with that fluttery feeling like a swarm of ants at the base of my throat leading me to scrabble at the blankets like a dog someone threw in a pool, and launch myself for the far edge of the bed that for whatever—I now realize—un-completely-thought-through reason we'd at one point decided to move from the bedroom to jam against the wall in that boiling little cranny off the living room so that exit was only possible from one side, and graceful exit possible never.

There was another room in the house that had had a perfectly serviceable bed situation, but quickly in our tenure living together, we didn't want to be separated from the possibility of intimacy by even a couple of yards, so we'd thrown a bed into that living-room nook and were able to eat, read and fuck at the drop of a hat.

"I have to Shprukh-Psikhish," I'd say, because my ex's breasts would have set off a storm of *one-two-three'ing,* and my internal panic cauldron would be set on boil at the first stab of desire.

"I have to Shprukh-Psikhish," I'd say, blearily kneeing her in the shin and flinging myself to the narrow corridor between her side of the bed and the wall.

Ow, she'd glare. *You know those are just recommendations, right? You don't need to become some kind of weird convert.*

She would have the back of her hand over her eyes and face. But I could tell by the sad-clown tug of the corners of her mouth that she was glaring at it anyway.

As usual, she would have gotten hot in the night in the boiling recess of our nook,

and she'd have shoved the blankets down to her ribs. She'd be lying on her back because of her "neck thing," and her breasts in the morning non-light of our nook—her
breasts, rising and falling with breath in the grainy, pre-dawn air that filtered through
the window on the north side of the house—her breasts warm and cool at the same
time, that's how, just, wonderfully large they were: they could harbor two tempera-
ture zones (cool along their soft underbellies, radiant at their hardening peaks) at
once—would be exposed to my view.

When my ex let me see her breasts first thing, it meant she'd woken up melancholy. It meant she needed me to take her before either of us got up, or she'd be in a
bitter stew all day. She wouldn't care how well I performed, or if I had a face full of
acne or how awful my breath was before I brushed. She needed this because she'd
woken up from that dream again, and she needed me to hold her and fill her, and
show her she was loved.

Anyone observing this from the outside would have been like: *FOR GOD'S SAKE,
FUCK HER.* Not only was it very normal that she needed reassurance sometimes
(okay, really awfully frequently), but I loved the fuck out of her, and on top of it she
was—and I'm not just saying this to be nice—spectacular looking. I am not shy to
point out that I've had a lot of beautiful women. It doesn't mean anything special
about me except that sex is about the only thing I can do well besides panicking, and
unfortunately these talents are related but at cross-purposes. Anyway, I am not, as I
said, shy to point out my really rather comprehensive knowledge of women of all
sorts. But my ex was without question the most beautiful of them all.

"I have to do my Shprukh-Psikhish," I'd say, stumbling off to the not-bedroom,
which had very little in it besides my Shprukh-Psikhish manual and my therapeutic
materials.

> *Those patients with a panic character are paralyzed by their refusal to accept the
> coexistence of love and aggression. Shprukh-Psikhish does not depart from the
> classic Freudian reading of the causes of anxiety. However, our methods for cure
> are considerably different.*
>
> *For those whose paralysis takes the form of ritual acts such as hand-washing,
> obsessive shoe-lacing, inability to step on cracks, or counting, we prescribe counter-
> rituals that encourage the embrace of the root cause: contradictory emotions.
> These patients must engage in one of the two following rituals daily, designed to
> encourage comfort with contradiction and an awareness that contradictory forces
> are nothing to fear. Indeed, contradictions are the wellspring of life and are gen-
> erative of all creation:*
>
> *1) Place one hand in a bowl of hot water and the other in freezing cold water.
> Hold hands in the bowls for as long it takes to scald one and chap the other. Only
> remove hands when it becomes clarified at a bodily level that each hand—and
> only each hand—can heal the other. Clasp them.*
>
> *2) Practice moving your bowels while eating a fine meal. The meal must be as
> artful as possible. Oysters with a molecular lemon-froth reduction. Steak tartare.
> A sous-vide preparation of rosemary carrots in butter sauce. You must, while shit-*

ting, consume the meal with relish and gusto—a task that will be almost impossible at first. Remain on the toilet for as long as it takes to understand, at a bodily level, that the act of satisfying the refinements of taste, and the act of gleefully expelling foul brew into the shitter, are one and the same. When the patient can eat the meal with delight and shit simultaneously, the ritual is concluded.

(Note: this ritual is neither recommended nor prescribed for perverts. Perverts are entirely capable of eating a fine meal with gusto while shitting. But if you have turned to this manual, you are not a pervert. You are a neurotic. Perversion is another psychic fluctuation, and in fact contraindicated for Shprukh-Psikhish therapy.)

On the particular day that turned out to be our last day together, I had my hands deep in two differently punishing basins of water when my ex pounded on the door.

"The conquering of panic should not be a Fabian Strategy."

"What's a Fabian Strategy?"

Another of her vanguard concepts. I wanted to pretend I knew what it meant, but I couldn't. My hands burned with hot and cold and I didn't have the energy that day for appearing smarter than I really was.

"It was Fabius Maximus's cowardly approach to battling Hannibal. A tactic of indirection, gradualism and constant retreat. It means, rather than revolutionary directness and decisive action, banking that the thing you want to conquer will just dissolve over time. A *Fabian Strategy*."

She had that little precise snap in her voice. The one that meant: *Get your shit together.* The one that meant: *I've faced down harder things than you've ever dreamed, and you don't see me sitting in a room hyperventilating with my hands in bowls of water.*

"What does it matter if I do my job or spend my day Shprukh-Psikhishing," I said, shoving my hands down deeper, gritting against the pain that was seizing the muscle fibers all the way up to my elbows. "No one cares whether I do this research or not."

"Well someone's about to care."

I heard what sounded like the flapping of a piece of paper.

"What's that supposed to mean?"

"Letter from the Dean of Surveillance."

"Oh fuck." I grabbed my hands out of the basins, clasping them. *One two three, three two one,* I intoned. So much for Shprukh-Psikhish. My heart thudded. I was already in a spiral. Sometimes when I counted to three I had to rock forward and back along with the beats. Three pulses forward then three back, three times over. I was rocking and counting when the handle turned.

"How do you plan to Shrpukh-Psikhish your way out of this one."

Although it was grammatically configured like a question, she did not pose this as a question.

"I'll just say I've been doing research." I rubbed my jaw.

"Have you done any research since moving in?"

I looked down. She knew I hadn't.

There had been quite a lot of time lost to fucking and eating. I was very far gone

_____

in love with her. I knew this because I couldn't write or read or do anything but puppy-dog around after her and then hate myself for it. And it was obvious my ex was falling in love with me too, although god knows why. I knew this because she was slowly unraveling—and because her nightmares had started. Things had gotten shaken up in her psyche, the way they do. I didn't know how to soothe the destruction that our falling in love inevitably produced. There had to be a way forward.

I would have killed anything for her, but that wasn't helpful. She didn't need anything killed. She needed things brought to life, protected, preserved from death. I would press myself against her at night. *I am here.* This did not soothe her. *But you're kind of a killer,* she said. *That's what you are.*

It was true that I was a killer, but I didn't know the difference, then, between being a killer and being a lover. I thought they were the same thing. *I will kill off everything bad that ever happened to you,* I said, heroically thrusting my hand inside her. She looked at me with sadness. I sang Ozzy Osbourne's "No More Tears," stupidly. I thought it was over. Both of our misery. Forever.

So we had fucked and fucked. And then her nightmares came, and my panic returned, and—what *had* we done with our time? We had what a friend jokingly called *a whirlwind domesticity,* referring to our trajectory of desire-fuckfest-explosion of neurosis and nightmares.

Well anyway, that pretty much brought us up to that moment.

My ex handed me the letter with an eyebrow arched.

Voth, I request an impromptu meeting to receive news of progress on your research, as your annual report, due to the Personnel Committee, is now late by an appalling matter of months.
    —Dean of Surveillance Andrews

"Shit," I said, agreeing with my ex's arched eyebrow.

"Look," she said. "Your job is crap. Why don't you let me help?"

She meant get us both new jobs. She meant take me with her somewhere.

"I don't know if I'm ready." These were words I had to literally force out of my mouth. What I really wanted most in that moment was just to go with her. I would have gone, in fact, anywhere with her. *In my mind* I would have. But the prospect of putting my life in the hands of someone I wanted so badly was . . . well, it was a contradiction. And I was working on contradictions. Too slowly.

"You know you can't use your misery as a talisman against worse misery, right?"—she was standing in the doorway with her feet planted in that way she did—"Nothing works like that."

"I know," I moaned. "I do."

"See, this is what I'm talking about"—she leaned her head back against the threshold, kind of melted against it, more tired than inviting—"What is this Sprush-kish actually accomplishing."

"Shprukh-Psikhish," I corrected.

She regarded me silently as I rocked and counted.

. . .

They were awaken'd in the morning by the shouts and calls of the mollies.

A commotion at the shoreline. A Procession across London Bridge. An execution-cart and its attending train. The Ordinary trotted out in front, the Marshal of the Admirality flew the flag, the Deputy Marshal held aloft a silver oar flashing in the morning sun, and four centinels on horseback followed behind. They wore all black with traditional peaked tall hats. Obsidian spots against the gray sky. The sound of the horses' hooves against the cobblestones rang across the water. Hordes of commoners follow'd, streaming over the bridge in a far-off Thunder of boots.

"They're heading to the Execution Dock!" a fine-featured young molly cried.

"To the Dock!" shout'd a short, thick-bellied, bald one.

The Thrum of drums across the water, the drone of bugles, the Din of the marching crowd. The execution-train.

"It's"—my jaw hurt in that way it did when words were supposed to come out of it—"it's . . . instead of talking. About your feelings. Just . . . enacting them."

My ex shrugged hugely at me—and there was something about that shrug. It was a shrug you could have seen from the cheap seats. A dramaturge's shrug.

"It's not rocket science," she said, dramaturgically shrugging again. She was realizing something about me. Something that massively disappointed her. "Most people," she said, "are capable of doing both."

She had a look that I had never seen before in her eyes. Resignation. It was horrifying. I watched as she shruggingly crystallized to herself the limit—*my limit*—against which she had just come up. And she couldn't kaleidoscope it or car-crash it with anything else to make a beautiful butterfly-flock of light.

That look—that resignation, on the face of a woman who had never abided resignation for a split second in her life—that moment, honestly, was the end.

And thus was I was left alone with my shitty job, Dean of Surveillance Andrews and the condemned building.

4.*

IN THE DARK PRE-DAWN, BESS AND JENNY WERE DRESSING FOR THE day of searching. Bess fuss'd over Jenny's hair and skirts. Jenny re-fix'd her hair the way she liked it.

"I know what I'm doing."

"You've got to look flawless."

Jenny cocked her head. "I *do* look flawless."

Bess suppos'd this was true.

"Try to introduce a question about the plague ships. Inquire when you're meant to search one."

"Head Constable isn't a chatty sort."

"You need to flatter him. Feel out what *he* needs to hear, say it, and then make him think he wants to give you the information you sought anyway."

---

* SULLIVAN: HI! ME AGAIN!

JUST WANTED TO PEEK IN TO LET YOU KNOW HOW MUCH I'VE BEEN ENJOYING YOUR "CONFESSIONS"! CONFESSIONS ON TOP OF CONFES-SIONS! GREAT TWIST!

ME: How in the—

SULLIVAN: OF COURSE YOU KNOW THAT P-QUAD'S SISTER COM-PANY, MILITIA.EDU, HAS A PRIVATE CONTRACT WITH YOUR UNIVERSI-TY'S SERVER, AND THUS OF COURSE YOUR CLOUD STORAGE IS THE PROPERTY OF—

ME: You've read *everything*? And didn't say anything? Not even to object to the lengthy disquisition on Deleuze and Guattari?

SULLIVAN: DON'T GET YOUR PANTIES IN A TWIST. P-QUAD LOVES DELEUZE AND GUATTARI!

ME: Right.

"You imagine I need advice on coves?"

"Sometimes with the tough ones you need to go around"—Bess thought of the voles and the fir piles—"sideways of 'em."

"I go Frontways. You know that. If you didn't want that, you wouldn't've ask'd me."

The Lord Mayor's Head Constable was tall and oak-thick with a dried-rum stench and an oddly rubbery face. Elastic skin doubl'd

---

SULLIVAN: HEY, AS FAILED PRESIDENTIAL CANDIDATE JOHN KERRY ONCE SAID, "WHO AMONG US DOES NOT LOVE DELEUZE AND GUAT-TARI?" EVERYBODY LOVED IT WHEN HE SAID THAT!

ME: It was NASCAR, and nobody loved it when he said that. That was actually the most elitist, damning moment of the entire campaign. Anyway, does this mean I'll receive back pay?

SULLIVAN: ACTUALLY, ON THIS TOPIC YOU MIGHT WANT TO CHECK THE LANGUAGE OF YOUR CONTRACT. WE'VE OF COURSE BEEN RE-VIEWING IT WITH OUR LAWYERS, AND THOUGHT WE'D EXCERPT THE RELEVANT INFORMATION AS FOLLOWS:

> Insofar as copyright is unattributable to found manuscript, titled Confessions of the Fox.
>
> And insofar as editor R. Voth—acting as a delegate of P-QUAD, Inc.—agrees to perform creative labor on the manuscript, thereby "innovating" on the original in the form of annotations—
>
> And insofar as innovation upon an item is the grounds for ownership,
>
> And insofar as R. Voth is not acting singly, but as a representative of the Company, P-QUAD, Inc. is the duly appointed owner of Confessions of the Fox, and the holder of all copyright to it.
>
> Thus any alteration of the manuscript—by any person, including R. Voth— outside of the strictures of the contract, and without P-Quad's explicit permission could be—and will be—construed as wanton vandalism and property damage and subject the doer of said alterations to appropriate fines, penalties and charges in a court of law.

SO IN FACT NOT ONLY WILL YOU NOT BE RECEIVING BACK PAY, BUT YOUR ACTIONS WHILE ON STRIKE COULD EASILY BE CONSTRUED AS A VIOLATION OF THE TERMS OF THE CONTRACT AND THUS SUBJECT TO—

ME: Uh-huh.

SULLIVAN: LUCKILY WE CAN USE ALL THESE CONFESSIONS OF YOURS—THEY'RE TERRIFIC. IF YOU CONSENT TO RETURN TO WORK. ALTHOUGH—CONSENT SHMONSENT—NOT TO PUT TOO FINE A POINT ON IT, BUT WE HAVE THEM ANYWAY.

upon itself about the cheeks and mouth, tripl'd at his heavy forehead, and threaten'd to slop over into his eyes.

"And how are you this fine morning?" Jenny forced a smile up
at his melty Visage as they headed down Fair Street in Cheapside.

Jenny—an indiscriminate flirt—did not distinguish between
Proper and Improper moments. She wielded her considerable sexual appeal like a child heaving about a bulky axe far too heavy for its
thin limbs.

The Head Constable's face rearrang'd itself into a new, equally
labile Pattern of ruts and furrows. "Pleasantries are thoroughly forbidden at the workplace." He coughed and glanced away.

They arriv'd at a sinking Heap of a house—perhaps once a handsome abode. Now, numerous sparrows' nests dotted the front face,
stuffed between crumbling brick.

The Head Constable knocked savagely at the door, which
soften'd inwards like a rotted plum.

A commotion inside, scuffling—

"Mum, a man's knockin' down the door!"

"Tell 'em to come back tomorrow."

A tiptoe approaching—a small head swivel'd 'round—

—and the Constable thrust through.

The door fell off one hinge and swung open at a precarious
angle. A youth of eleven or so retreated as the Head Constable paraded in, his red face reshuffling like a bubbling stew. A wiry-armed
woman emerged from a back room holding a ladle for protection.

"What's this?" She lofted the ladle above her head.

The Head Constable pulled his musket out, pointing it at the
ladle. "A ladle ain't no match for a musket."

"Since when do constables carry muskets?" she queried, un-
moving.

The Head Constable pulled down the catch on his musket.
"Since the Plague."

"Mum!" The youth scrabbl'd to her side.

"He isn't going to shoot me. He ain't done talkin' yet. These types love to go on."

The Head Constable's face flapp'd in a series of angry quivers. "Any dead inside?"

"What for, dead?"

"Of Plague."

"Mum?" The son's eyes train'd on Jenny, then the Constable, then his mother—flicking back and forth with astonished Ferment.

"Plague hasn't been here," the mother explain'd, as if the constable was a toddler, "since the last go-'round—1666, the fire of London and all that. Not a single neighbor here's got the Plague."

"I ask'd you a question."

"And I told you that we haven't got Plague in the city of London. I would know. My husband's a butcher. He says the Plague strikes cows first. That you'd see it in the carcasses—flea-bitten and lesioned. He says the butchers' stalls are the first Watch for the Plague. No matter that they appoint a hundred centinels, they won't know the Plague's coming until the butchers say so, and all this jabber in the papers won't amount to nothing 'til we see it in the cows. So go search the butchers' stalls and get out of my house."

Jenny stepped forward. "I have orders from the Lord Mayor to permit this woman to search the house."

The woman shook her head in disbelief.

"Ma'am, it's for the *Publick Health*."

The woman put down her ladle and glared.

The Head Constable nodded. "Go on then"—and backed towards the door—

—For the Head Constable was "due" at the pub for his regular afternoon pint.

"Will return shortly," he said to Jenny. "After you've gone through everything."

Some period of time later, Jenny heard the door open and the Head Constable march into the front room.

"There's no one dead in this room, or any other," she called out.

A tornado of boots, and the Head Constable loom'd in the doorway.

"Did ye look through everything?"

"How many places is there to hide the dead?" Jenny rested against the wall.

"Through everything." The Head Constable began stamping around the close quarters, ale and furor rising off him like steam.

He flipp'd the bed, clouding the room in dust. Jenny waved her hands before her eyes. The Head Constable ran his hand over the night table and chairs, exploring beneath them.

"I love being a functionary of the constabulary," Jenny began as the Head Constable knock'd over several wooden boxes. "And I'm wondering: When do I get to really search? I mean search a Plague ship?"

This—posing as grateful underling—Attract'd his attention.

The Head Constable glanced up from sorting through piles on the floor—trinkets, sewing implements, scraps of lace.

"Won't be long now."

"How *not long*?"

The Head Constable grabbed up the lace and the implements, and with an "Out, bat, I'm not a walking calendar" storm'd back into the front room.

He shoved the fistful of lace and needles at the woman, who was tending a boiling vat of what smell'd to be beans at the hearthfire.

"What was it you said ye did for labor?"

"Didn't say."

"Well, what is it, then," the Head Constable spat through clenched teeth.

"Some sewin' and knittin'." The flames rose towards the pot, and she sprinkl'd water at the edges of the burning kindle to calm it.

"Where d'ye do that?"

"Knightsbridge's Wool and Hat Shop."

"Right then." The Head Constable gripped the woman's arm, pulling her towards the door.

"Mum!" screech'd the youth, grabbing the ladle out of the bean-pot and swinging an arc of mucky broth at the Constable.

"For what are ye takin' me in?"

"Violation of the Cabbage Act*." He presented some lace from his pocket, and dragg'd her out the door.

---

* The Cabbage Act privatized the waste products of production, deeming them either property of the business owner or of the municipality in the form of waste. Examples of cabbage were: linen scraps, excess lime and tanning oils, wood chips and metal shavings. "It is against the common good for persons to lay claim to the waste products of their own labor," says the Cabbage Act, "specifically scrap textiles."

ME: Sigh. Speaking of which, it seems my own footnotes might be considered "cabbage," mightn't they. As such, I have had an inevitable change of heart as a result of our last communication. Due to the inescapability of P-Quad—and the threat of retroactive legal action—I consent to return to work as per my contract.

SULLIVAN: MARVELOUS. WELCOME BACK!

ME: And my salary?

SULLIVAN: WELL, FIRST THERE IS THE MATTER OF STRIKE FEES AND PENALTIES, OF COURSE. WE'LL SEND YOU A BILL.

AS FOR YOUR SALARY, AS WE DISCUSSED, THIS WILL ARRIVE WHEN YOU PRODUCE THE REDACTED PAGE ON ORIGINAL ARCHIVAL PAPER.

ME: As regards the missing page, I assure you there is no such thing.

SULLIVAN: WERE YOU OR WERE YOU NOT WRITING TO DISCUSS MOVING FORWARD AS A TEAM?

ME: I was.

SULLIVAN: <WAITING>

ME: You know, you're right. I did misplace a page. A page of very explicit description of genitalia that must have fallen under my desk. My office is quite a mess—my apologies for the histrionics. If you give me your phone number I'll text you a photo of it.

Did you get it?

SULLIVAN: <LOOKING!> TREMENDOUS! GLAD IT ALL WORKED OUT.

5.

As Jack stood with Aurie in the crowd at Execution Wharf — they had stopp'd off at the Mason's Arms to toast to the condemned, as was the custom—his drink burn'd his stomach slightly, but the rest of him fizzed with Warmth and the grog-induced pulse of *Excarnation—drink-pleasure*.

The dead train having not arriv'd at the platform yet, the Mob was full o' planning.

"Who is it?" someone shouted.

"Barnes, I think! The highwayman!"

"We'll rush the stage!" shouted a small boy perched atop a rogue's shoulders.

The rogue nodded up at the kid. "We will. Or"—he clear'd his throat—"we'll try."

"We'll cry out our love." A doxy was agitating her mates. "Just as they drag out the cart from underneath 'im!"

Someone call'd out, "England is a prison!"

And then, from further back, *"Pa ni mèt ankô*!"*

And the crowd responded, "London, London look to thy Freedom!"

Jack shout'd "London, London, look to thy freedom!" along with the rest of them. His voice was deeper in his chest than he remember'd it being— He liked the Sound—'specially vibrating with the Mob. Aurie had a coat of spittle in his beard. "London,

---

* This reminds me: I never heard back from my colleague regarding this phrase.

London, look to thy Freedom!"—he bellow'd. Jack and he were jumping up and down in Unison. Everyone was.

"Pa ni mèt ankô!" Again, from the back of the crowd.

"Who's saying that?" Jack twisted his head 'round.

"Who's saying what?"

"Something I heard once—friends of Bess's." He turned towards the voice, tugging Aurie alongside.

As they proceeded towards the back, Jack caught the strains of bloodthirsty conversations from the gentry.

"How long they been holding him? Why'nt they just execute him right away?"—"Torturing him I s'pose"—"Ah"—chuckling.

Jack cut a forthright path for the chuckler. Aurie wove to the right, coughing to cause a stir—perfectly syncopated with Jack in the arts of clouting† and knuckling‡—and jostled the chuckler, who fell into Jack, with his hand at the ready to shoot down the chuckler's pocket. He snatched out a wad of coins and a signet ring, then ducked back into the crowd.

"Pa ni mèt ankô!"

Jack emerg'd from the throng of bodies, losing Aurie in pursuit of the sound—until he came upon a figure he recogniz'd. Laurent. His hair was matt'd across his forehead with perspiration and the heat of yelling. His smish was unbutton'd partway. Jack thought he caught a glimpse of—*were those heavers?*—and a tattoo below Laurent's collarbone. Skull and crossbones. The pirate flag.

Their eyes met.

"Are you—" Jack began.

"Hush," said Laurent.

Jack's eyes flashed again to the tattoo. *"Pa ni mèt ankô?"*

A silence fell. Heads turn'd. The dead train was approaching Execution Wharf. Close up, 'twas an even more terrifying spectacle than from afar. A murdering Horde on horseback. The clop of

---

† Pickpocketing of handkerchiefs

‡ Advanced pickpocketing of cash and watch fobs from particularly deep or narrow pockets—Jack's fingers being particularly adept at this latter skill.

hooves and the drone of Last Rites carried on the wind. The ridiculous hats of the Admiralty and the Magistrates bounc'd against the gloom of the midday gray.

The cider in Jack's stomach began to burn.

Centinels now ringed the perimeter of the crowd. In his shouting with the Mob and knuckling the finer sort, Jack hadn't seen them draw in. But now ev'ry other person at the edges of the Mob was a centinel. Their faces were hard, superior. One centinel tried to give a child a candied orange peel from his pocket in some show of pretended Humanity. The sprite dart'd behind his mother's legs, sobbing.

With a roar, the procession pulled into Execution Wharf. The horses thundered, trumpeter heralded the Admiralty. The Ordinary beseeched a last-minute Confession from the condemned.

The cart pulled up to the execution theater. A scraggly pale prisoner stood within, held on either side by a constable. His arms were bent sticks in their hands. His beard was long and—even from the distance—swarming with lice. Behind the constables, the Thames rippled at the edge of the dock.

The wind picked up, rose to a moan, and the crowd grew Restless. The burghers agitat'd for swift death. The masses wail'd in sympathy, despair, and fury. Jack's throat was caught on a knot, and his Body began buzzing in that *away*-way.

And then there was a Movement. Beyond the platform—out on the blust'ry, wind-chopped water.

A Plague Ship was moving closer.

Some anchor must have come free. A Panic of centinel-punts were following behind, bellowing to each other contradictory orders. "Tight behind!" "Cut it off!" The strains of Surveillance-speech floated over the crowd.

Jack nudg'd Aurie, nodding with his chin towards the water.

"It's going t' crash the docks."

"Nah." Aurie's attention was on the execution-cart. "Nothin' but slushing around in the currents."

But the ship didn't seem to be *slushing around*. It drifted slowly, but quite directly, towards Wapping Wharf. Its sail was not rais'd; it looked a shambling, half-starved Golem advancing. Now there was a hum picking up amongst several clusters, pointing and agitating.

Someone shouted, "The Plague Ship is headed for shore!"— and full Mayhem broke loose. The execution centinels fled the cart, leaving Barnes bound beneath the hanging tree, alone. The burghers start'd crawling over each other at the front, heading towards the perimeter of the crowd for Escape. They were stamping on each other's heads, shrieking "Plague!" and clawing at the air. At the back, the commoners jostled and pushed, shouting at each other to get to safety. "I am correct'd," Aurie muttered. He grabb'd Jack's sleeve and drew him towards the edges of the crowd.

"Pa ni mèt ankô!"—this time from the front.

Jack looked at the dock again. There was a figure—unimposingly smallish and quick, darting in and out of the bodies rushing in the opposite direction—a blur of muslin pantaloons and belted smish. He was racing towards Barnes. The centinels, now blocked from chasing by the chaos of the crowd, shouted helplessly, "Okoh!— Grab 'im!"

No one did.

"It's Okoh!" Jack hissed at Aurie.

"Who's Okoh?"

"He 'scaped the Tower guards and he's—he's here? And, did Laurent know, and—"

Jack and Aurie were bump'd and toss'd by the Mob, which, like some flailing animal, surged out and away from the dock in several directions at once. Jack kept his eyes fixed on the docks and the advancing ship behind. It was only yards out from land now. As it got closer, its full bulk was reveal'd. What had seemed from a distance a puny mast swaying against the sky was in fact a thick, heavily rigged trunk plowing upwards from a long, broad deck. The hull towered over the docks, hundreds o' feet high, boards ripped and pitted, coated in gray-brown riverslime, and caked with patches of pink, white and black—a mix of mussels, barnacles and sea-coral.

Okoh had reached Barnes. He leapt up onto the cart, turned to look at the ship, then, with an odd smile, peered out over the crowd.

Aurie yank'd Jack by the back of his collar.

The sound of the vessel rocking and creaking began to drown out the hysterical crowds. The hull slapped against waterskin. As Aurie dragg'd him towards the perimeter, Jack shouted out, "Okoh! A hero! A true self-made hero!"

And Okoh's voice rang out over the hectic assembly. "Hear ye, all! There are in the world *no such men as self-made men*! We have *all* either begged, borrow'd or stolen. We have reaped where others have Sown, and that which others have strewn, we have gather'd."

"Let me hear this, brother." Jack tried to pry Aurie's fingers from his collar.

"Individuals are, to the mass, like Waves to the ocean." As the voice intensify'd, the ship grew to massive heights, closing in. "The highest order of Genius is as dependent as is the lowest. It, like the loftiest waves of the sea, derives its power and Greatness from the grandeur and vastness of the ocean of which it forms a part. We differ as the waves, but are One as the sea. And so it is to the sea that we should look—the sea of us all! The sea of Justice and Free-dom shall maintain me! The sea shall maintain us, Freebooters and Mutineers all!"

And just as the crowd began to intone back, *Mutineers all!*

—The ship heav'd itself to its highest height, blotting out the sun and the sky behind—looking to devour the dock whole in its slow unstoppable path—

—And then it did devour it.

The ship crash'd into the dock with an ear-splitting crack, and the execution tree and cart and the entire dock burst into a Cas-cade of splinters, a blooming cloud of debris. Aurie's hand was hard on Jack's collar, dragging him out of the fray.

Commoners were fleeing the execution site, thronging the road in a Clatter of screams.

And then a deadcart with horses being whipped mercilessly

thunder'd up behind them. Following it, jeering, were more Commoners running, throwing rocks and clumps of dirt and grasses, calling, *Murderers! Murderers!*

At the side of the path, Flanders, waiting in the rushes, held a thick branch in his hands. As the cart jumbled past, he leapt out, jamming a stick into the wheels. A body, wrapped in a burlap cloth, sailed out, carried by forward Motion. A pale arm poked free.

At just that moment, Fireblood rode up on a horse from the swamps at the shoreline. Flanders scuttled out, threw the Body up onto Fireblood's horse, and Fireblood gallop'd off in the direction of Wild's Office before any of the executioners manag'd to gather their Wits. Flanders zipped back into the rushes.

Aurie and Jack stood amaz'd.

Now what would Wild's men want with a body? thought Jack as Fireblood viciously whipp'd his horse past.

He looked back at the dock. It had disintegrated—shards and splinters were still settling through the air. Okoh was nowhere to be seen.

READER!

I have some urgent news to convey.

This will be my last communication for a period of time. I am not certain for how long, but I do know this: I am leaving tonight. I am taking the manuscript with me. It is something other than what it appears to be. Something far more valuable.

Consequently, I am, to put it plainly, shortly to be on the run.

Let me clarify. Who knows when or if I will be able to speak to you again.

This last chapter was the final straw. In seeking out its meaning, I found that I had indeed missed a reply from my colleague—Prof. T. Bryant—regarding my earlier query on the phrase: *Pa ni mèt ankô.*

Though this was through no fault of my own. Emails containing "foreign words" have begun to mysteriously go to spam. Well, perhaps not so mysteriously. Surely this has something to do with the University's outsourcing its electronic communications department to the private mercenary-and-electronics corporation Militia.edu. In any case, reminded by this most recent chapter that I never heard back on my query, I hunted through my spam folder and discovered the missing email—and one other.

According to Professor Bryant, a very rough translation of *Pa ni mèt ankô* is: "There are no more Masters."

The translation itself—while intriguing—is of lesser interest than *how* my colleague arrived at the translation.

After diligent searching in her field, the only textual reference she could find for this rallying cry was in Patrick Chamoiseau, *Texaco*: "His lips had found hers, he kissed her smack, she kissed him, they were still kissing each other screaming *Pa ni mèt ankô!* There are no more Masters" (Gallimard, 1992; trans., Random House, 1998).

You note the date on the Chamoiseau text.

1992.

A date befuddling in itself, but in fact clarifying when combined with the second missing email I found in my spam folder. The email regarding *plitho-hypomnesis,* or: collective diary-keeping.

Collective diary-keeping, my Greek colleague has informed me, was a heavily guarded and legendary practice amongst the freedmen and slaves. It is a genre of which we have few to no extant examples. Indeed, my colleague was not sure one such collective diary had ever been found, although great and furtive claims have been made for their existence, always under cover of intense secrecy.

This translation in conjunction with the other?

Well, Reader, I've come to the inescapable conclusion that the confessions of Jack Sheppard contain, as they say, *multitudes*. Put more simply, they are not exactly a singular memoir. They are something else. That something, broadly speaking, is the plitho-hypomnesis of, for lack of a better word, *us*.

I must confess that I believe my own attachment to the text clouded my ability to recognize the glaring obviousness of this collective authorship earlier. I was looking for the reflection of a single subject when I should have been looking for something else.*

---

* Caught up in the manuscript, I forgot a central tenet of decolonial theories of the archive—its critique of our fetish for archival truths, our belief that "if a body is found, then a subject can be recovered" (Anjali Arondekar, *For the Record: On Sexuality and the Colonial Archive in India,* p. 3; Duke University Press, 2009).

There is no (one) body in this archive, no one subject either. How foolish I've been.

(On this topic, see the Atlas Group: "We urge you to approach these docu-

Plitho-hypomnesis is the only explanation for the many generic irregularities and impossible references that populate this text. And it makes this manuscript not only the most valuable Sheppard document ever discovered, but something far in excess of that. Something evasive, gnomic and irreplaceable.

The diary of a trace.[*]

---

ments . . . as 'hysterical symptoms' based not on any one person's actual memories but on cultural fantasies erected from the material of collective memories," in "Let's Be Honest, the Rain Helped: Excerpts from an Interview with the Atlas Group," in *Review of Photographic Memory,* ed. Jalal Toufic (Beirut: Arab Image Foundation, 2004).

[*] Given this realization it is imperative that I add some notes to the preceding chapter. Most urgently, I have realized that Okoh's self-made-men speech is taken almost verbatim (*except the concluding sentence*), from Frederick Douglass's "Self-Made Men" speech of 1872.

The overt citation of Douglass by the text provokes the reconsideration of a further detail of the scene. Specifically this: "The ship crashed into the dock and the execution platform burst into a cascade of splinters, a blooming cloud of debris."

Now this requires some extrapolation by way of anecdote.

One night, several years ago now, I'd done teaching my graduate seminar, and one of my more unnervingly well-read and eloquent students had stuck around to chat after class, as she often did. I had probably been going on about some documents of revolutionary thought that evening, and those students with the bug for that kind of thing will often want to maximize that discussion. This student had that bug big-time, and in fact I was beginning to fear that she was better read than I. In any case, she detained me after class with some questions, and although the Humanities building operated under a self-imposed curfew of sorts (most of us liked to flee immediately due to the proliferation of vermin that emerged from the nooks and crannies of the crumbling building once the clatter of students died down), I remained under the merciless fluorescents with her because her question was not about the reading, but about whether I could put her in contact with someone.

She prefaced the question with some hemming and hawing having to do with the after-hours social life of graduate students that I did not care to learn about. She referenced a graduate student conference in some distant town. A bar she had been to. But then things got more interesting. She began to describe a conversation she'd had at this bar, in which someone—but, she confessed, she had been drunk and couldn't at all remember who it had been—had mentioned a reading group. And she wished to know whether I knew anything about it.

In fact I had not heard of this group, and at that moment, if I recall correctly, I tried to gently nudge her to walk and talk with me, as I was certain I'd heard rustling from the corner of the room.

We emerged into the parking area shared by the Humanities building and ROTC, and so weaving between the ROTC instructors' Hummers and BMWs—and the vehicles of the Humanities faculty (mostly 1991 Plymouth Neons)—she divulged that this particular group styled itself as one of *"action."* It seemed their central principle was to take their fidelity to certain theoretical texts out of the classroom and into the streets. Well, not the streets, actually, but the archives.

As we strolled to my Neon, she explained that the group had been most active in the early aughts and just after. Styling themselves somewhat after the ALF, but with books rather than puppies, they sought to liberate—or rather decolonize—those texts under ownership of university libraries. Late at night, during school holidays, a number of stacks nationwide had been infiltrated and—how to put this?—*edited*. The texts were not removed. They were simply *improved upon.*

My student found those actions taken in accordance with Saidiya Hartman's classic *Scenes of Subjection* to be of particular interest, and wished to write her term paper on this topic, if I could put her in touch with anyone in the group. She wanted to conduct some sort of decolonial ethnography of this group. Or so she said.

I did not know of this group. I couldn't help her, and said as much. But I am wondering now if this student was in fact a *member* of this reading group. Was she in fact trying to obliquely clue me in to something? Perhaps she had seen this manuscript. The one of which I am now in possession. More important, perhaps she and her comrades had performed an homage to Hartman in editing it? She cited Hartman by heart, those opening passages where she explains that she's "chosen not to reproduce" the famous scene in Douglass's *Narrative of the Life of Frederick Douglass:* "the account of the beating of Aunt Hester." Hartman declines to reproduce the scene, quoted my student, "in order to call attention to the ease with which such scenes are usually reiterated, the casualness with which they are circulated, and the consequences of this routine display of the slave's ravaged body. Rather than inciting indignation, too often they inure us to pain by virtue of their familiarity" (Saidiya V. Hartman, *Scenes of Subjection: Terror, Slavery and Self-Making in Nineteenth-Century America,* Oxford University Press, 1997).

I hadn't thought about it then—and in my defense, the night was cold and I was tired after class—but I am now wondering: had this student—had this *group*—in fact been to my own University library and edited this particular scene? I do not know what might have been here originally, but I wonder now if, in addition to adding in the Douglass speech, the "cascade of splinters" and "blooming cloud of debris" were original to the text or added in as well.

I say this because, if the reader has not already put two and two together, this "cloud" is unquestionably an homage to Douglass's other major work, *My Bondage and My Freedom.* The reader recalls that in that volume, Douglass declines to give exact details of how he escaped slavery, instead inserting a metafictional address to describe the missing autobiographical material: "Disappearing from the reader in a flying cloud, or balloon . . ." It is speculated that Douglass replaced details of his escape with the "flying cloud" so as not to expose and thus hinder other, like-minded escapes.

It's impossible now not to conjure some image of that imaginary evening— somewhere up on the seventeenth floor, the spare lights of the Valley winking

---

below—a cluster of excitable graduate students—the approaching footfalls of the campus police—the hasty stuffing of the manuscript back into the stacks, out of order. Years later . . . a book sale, an aging professor—well, you know the rest.

Of course this is all speculation.

And now, Reader, you'll excuse me. I have to go.

6.

OUTSIDE WILD'S OFFICE, JACK HUNG OVER THE EDGE OF THE WHARF, inspecting routes of ingress. A bricked-over window halfway down the piling—just before the water darkened the wood—seem'd Promising. He shimmy'd down and began working his carpenter's file between stone and mortar.

After some time, Jack had worked exactly one brick free. It was enough. Levering in a clawbar he'd nick'd from an ironworks along the way, he created enough of a passage to permit squirreling.

If small spaces had ever bother'd Jack, this one would be a test of will. Soon he was head-down, crawling through a pinhole exactly as wide as his shoulderframe, and pitch-dark.

He scraped his way down the passage, his mind Swimming with questions—*What does Wild want with a Body? You can't fence a Body. Can you?*—when, all at once, the dirt-gritted brick gave way beneath him and Jack dropped into a small, high-ceilinged chamber. As his eyes adjusted, he made out one glaze at the very upper reaches. Starlight filtered in. He paced slowly around the circular perimeter, feeling along the walls for doors. On finding one, he listened for movement on the other side. Assured he was alone—he turn'd his attention again inwards to the chamber.

There was an overpowering odor. The raw scent of shit and the brassy tang of blood. They sank to the back of Jack's throat, and he gagg'd into his hand. Shapes lay scattered across the floor. Humps of what might have been—animal matter?

Stepping gingerly around the *lumps* to the far side of the chamber, he came upon an arrangement of metal implements of many shapes and sizes atop stone tables. So then he was in a laboratory of sorts. There was a slab, nestled against the dripping wall at the far edge. The slab was a rough, pitted marble. Jack bent over it, peering closer.

There he spy'd a sheaf of papers, curled at the edges with splatter and the remnants of a certain quantity of gore. Jack squint'd in the starlight.

INSTRUCTIONS ON THE ANATOMY OF CHIMERAS

*(On the Occasion of the Examination of a pirate
captured in the Java Sea)*

A PAPER BY J. EVANS

Subject was operat'd upon several hours prior. My initial observations follow.

As to general shape, the subject's head may be compared to a smallish, inglorious Melon. The usual Chimeric slight skull deformations are expected and evidenced, with the skull protruding out over the jointure with the neck more than expected. Not noticeable except by a trained practitioner, who can easily (if the curls are parted in the back) recognize the signs of a Malformation.

As one approaches the head, it begins to take on several aspects not visible from the distance, depending especially on the point of view. From straight on, one would take the facial epidermis for a pale bark with a light mossy fur in patches. No thicker than ordinary female skin; however, a good deal more Follicular.

As I initially suspected, the genitalia are indeed outsized. Quite protuberant.

When approached from the side angle, the genitalia can be compared to the head of a miniature Saxon soldier, complete with the telltale long narrow helmet (minus the feather).

With a bit more inspection, this helmet takes on specific qualities. The helmet—really, a sort of foreskin—is a dull pinkish color, deepening to red—and projects over the neck of the genitals, concluding in a pronounced, glans-like bulb.

A great pity that this subject's genitals are so Compromised and *in between*. If only the subject were male, the equivalent-sized penis would bless this subject with the largest pleasure Member known to man.

But, alas, the spout in question descends to a proper female fissure and thus the entire landscape is a vexatious confusion.

If we were to approach the genitalia from underneath, we would readily ascribe their owner to the female sex. But then, reaching the spout up top, we must grant it is much larger than would seem Reasonable and befitting of a female person.

Approaching from the side—helmet-wise, as it were—one would ascribe a tragic and insufficient maleness to the subject, outfitted with an organ that can do no more than *receive*—but not give—Pleasure, in the classical sense.

There have circulated in History many intriguing fantasies concerning such genital apparati. One in particular remains with me. A lady's servant was rumored to have called her mistress's genitalia an "Obscene Faucet," and imagin'd that a perfumed lavender cream might seep from it when touched. She observ'd a veritable Profusion of whiskers around its base, something like a fount of close-clipped grass at the foot of a "pornographic statue." It has been further rumor'd that this maidservant thence began a torrid love affair with her chimeric employer, and that the passion of their mutual Devotion caused her employer to release her from service if she swore to bind herself to the "obscene faucet" for life.

I am told she took the offer. Gladly, it is said! And it is further reputed that they sealed the erotick Contract by drinking deep of every Fluid that emanated from each other's body, beginning and ending with urine—"hot, hallowed, stinking, and beautiful" (if I recall correctly).

I am told it was in fact a great love story.

But let us leave behind all these fancies. For our world offers nothing of these redemptive Possibilities.

'Tis neither man nor woman, but something *in-between-ish*. Absent of testes but blooming some infernally large but useless horn between the legs. Ordinarily we would term this Creature a chimera by birth, but I must consider the possibility that this in-between-ish-ness is owing to the regular ingestion of what the community of (captur'd or murder'd) freebooters refer to as "Elixir." As directed by Wild, I speculate further that a similar elixir might be produced in London, but that its formula would of necessity be changed for expediency and profitability of production. My hypothesis is THUS both grotesque and simple. It is THIS:

That we can drastically reduce the time and labor involved in generating the elixir by—"*

---

* Hello again. I hope you'll excuse the delay. Between being on the run and getting settled in in my new surroundings—not to mention figuring out how to edit and transcribe these documents from here . . . Well, I hope you don't mind the messages-in-a-bottle, as it were.

I'm afraid I can't indulge your curiosity as far as *where* I am. Suffice to say that I am very far away, and I do not mean this primarily in terms of space. I am living at a different timescale. Not parallel to yours, but apart from it.

In any case, with apologies for inevitable hiccups in transcription (and who knows if you're receiving these communiqués anyway?), I'll continue.

First order of business: It would be so easy to just grumblingly accept the above "Instructions" as yet another tiresome addition to the baleful annals of sexology. Yes, they are typically odious. But there's also something about them that doesn't seem quite typical to me.

I'm referring, of course, to the romantic attribution of the descriptor "love story" to the chimera anecdote, as well as the reverence for urine as "hallowed." Can these possibly be original to Evans' "Instructions"?

Obviously, no.

But how to prove it?

Fortunately, where I am now, there exists a marvelous set of materials. My new

friends have collected so much on us. In fact, they are archivists of us. No, not exactly *archivists*. I barely have the language to describe—to translate. But I must.

They are, let me say, *interested* in us. They are interested because, well, they were
once us. Though I don't think they consider themselves "us" anymore. They have
been writing the history of this separation.

I am told there were once lively debates here about whether or not it was even
worth collecting any of our histories at all. After all, what are we but the accumulation of centuries of terror? Still, they have a saying here about the past, and I am told
this is what decided the matter once and for all: *All history should be the history of how
we exceeded our own limits*.

So, yes, we are a wretched, misery-sowing people. But how curious, how beautiful
we have been, as well. In our terrible past, my new friends see a different future reflected like light off broken shards.

They are archivists of this excess to ourselves. Actually, like I said, they don't use
the word "archives" here. The closest translation for archives is: "stretches." By which
they mean stretches of time, but also stretches of space. And they don't just mean
space as a place; they mean space as a practice: the way we make space in our own
bodies.

To them, I think, this is history: breathing air into a previously unfelt opening.

So, then, they are Stretchologists of that air that existed in regions unknown to
ourselves, our bodies and our past.

Also, the Stretches is (are?) actually a structure that exists here. A colossal library
in chitin, spiderweb and glass that sprawls at the edges of the floating alleys of the
central square. It hovers above the ubiquitous water on a series of thick stilts. The
architecture and the location of the building are such that it captures and holds
the red of the setting sun in the thatch of wicker reeds that composes its soft, seemingly infinite roof.

The entire top floor of the Stretches is devoted to the study of the History of the
Senses. I frequent this level in particular, and yet I have never seen its inner edges. I
do not know how far they run. Although from the outside all the floors appear the
same in dimension, they say the top in fact is larger than the others—an honor be-
stowed on it due to the urgency of its subject matter. (This floor contains, among
other things, the entire annals of one of their specialities—the field of Thermogenic
Aesthetics: the study of *heat* as the Seventh, most ecstatic sense. Each night, when
sunset comes on, my new friends stop whatever they are doing and emerge into the
blazing dome of oncoming night. They let the sunset pour over them while they turn
and bathe in the warm red light. Often, at this time, I am to be found at the Stretches
on the top floor; I remain inside and the heat from the thatch pulses the entire reading room into a bright, hay-scented sauna. It is very nice in there, but I think I would
like to go outside with the rest of them and celebrate. I am shy about this desire, but
I am changing here—becoming less . . . hermetic. I know that I will join them soon.)

But to return to my point regarding Evans' "Anatomy of Chimeras."

On the top floor of the Stretches I have come across a document titled *Urine
Refracts Starlight with Especial Sparkliness*. This document tells of a wine cellar below

Jack turn'd the sheaf over.

At which moment he heard a sound. The Thud of a boot stepping heavily onto a rug in the adjoining room.

The door began to open—

Jack dropped the papers and scudded towards the chimney, nearly
losing his Footing on something hard and round. He heard a crack—
felt something shatter underneath his foot— No time to investi-

---

an aristocratic stronghold somewhere in the south of France, in which a certain
wealthy rapist was said to have coveted the original papers to the sexologist Saviard's
case study of the famous "hermaphrodite" Marguerite Malause (1702). It seems he
fondled them late at night, particularly the passages where Malause is forced to uri-
nate in front of spectators to determine Malause's "true" gender: "I made her uri-
nate," says Saviard, "before the gathered assembly, upon her claiming that urine did
issue from two separate places; and in order to make apparent the contrary, while she
urinated I did spread apart the lips of her vulva, by which means I did make the
spectators see the urinary meatus from whence the flow did proceed."

In *Urine Refracts Starlight,* we learn that the "CEO" (Chimera Emancipation Organization, 1977–1990, approx.) broke into this stronghold in the summer of 1983
and destroyed—or absconded with—or altered the Saviard documents in honor of
the memory of Malause, who otherwise had no say over their own representation. In
Urine Refracts Starlight, the tale of the CEO is told in chapters upon chapters—
Reader, this book is encyclopedic!—fashioning a kind of cosmos, a galaxy, some Ovid-
ian tome of piss:

Ch. 2, "In which our Heroine the Pleiades Showers Orion with Golden Light";

Ch. 5, "The Highly Interesting Escapades of Triangulum's Tawny Froth";

and, most intriguingly: Ch. 7, "In Which Malause Became a Star in the Hydrus
Constellation and the Magellanic Cloud Drinks of Her Hot Hallowed Stinking and
Beautiful Piss."

Hot, hallowed, stinking and beautiful. What am I to think but that "Hot Hallowed
Stinking and Beautiful" was inserted into the Sheppard documents by the CEO as
well? A radical revisioning of sexology's prurient fascination with urine as a vector of
gendered "truth."

If so, then surely it is fair to presume that the CEO made other alterations as well.
Consider that between Jack and Bess, urine is an element held in common by lovers,
a medium of intimacies that connects them but—unlike the prurient gaze of the
sexologists—does not expose to our view any of the lovers' corresponding genitalia.
Are these scenes original to the text or some CEO addition? Who can say!

(On urine and starlight, see also Samuel R. Delany, *Stars in My Pocket Like Grains
of Sand* [Bantam, 1984] and *Through the Valley of the Nest of Spiders* [Magnus Books,
2012].)

gate, though truly this item felt of *animal* Origin to him— He dragg'd himself back up the mouth of the chimney and hung there, breathing quickly— If he ascended, there would be the danger of grit raining down. He wedg'd his boots into cracks on either side, and hunch'd down. He did not believe he could hold this position for long. It had been stupid—marvelously stupid—to come. *If Wild were to find me—*

Best not to think about it.

Jack laid his head against the brick, his heart thudding.

Someone entered the room, slamming the door. At first Jack heard only muttering. Familiar muttering—*Wild.*

And then a jubilant, nasal voice. "We did it! We got 'im."

Something heavy thrown on the slab.

The sound of instruments being arranged. Vials moving. Liquids splashing.

"What is this? *Who* is this? Get out! You idiots! You can't even steal a dead body properly! A dead blasted body! Where's Barnes?!"

The door slamm'd.

Bricks trembled—dirt loos'd, pour'd down—

—Jack scrambl'd upwards.

7.

JACK SPED AWAY FROM WILD'S, PANTING WITH TERROR AND RELIEF.

He slow'd along the riverbank, where dried basil and thyme shone silver in the moonlight.

Oh, why did I drop the papers, he moaned to himself, kicking the ground as he walked.

Who would believe what he had found? Evans had worked out a recipe? He could barely believe it himself. He wondered if the Starlight had afflict'd his vision. And now there was no way to know. He'd dropped the notes. He'd have to go back sometime when he could be assured of Wild's absence.

When he reached Cuper's Gardens, the night-blooming primrose —pink heads bowed—were coated in frost. He perambulat'd the park, trying to commit to memory the contents of the papers—though, as he got further from Wild's, halfheartedly so. What use was any scouting when he hadn't Bess to speculate together with? He was alone with the bareness of facts, Clues, material that held no charge, no Connectedness. The entire world was *body parts with no Body.* Even his own bones felt hollow—stray bones bobbing about in a container of skin.

One of the primrose uncurl'd its green neck under the weight of gathering rime. A Magick flicker of green and pink with the nightfall. Jack stopped still. He gaz'd at the primrose unfolding, remembering times he'd seen Bess thrill to the sight of something simple—a Green thing budding into life—

With shaking limbs, he bent down, stroking its soft petals, and pluck'd it for his button-hole—

And then his world upended through some force that was not his own— Everything spun— No, *he* was spinning—and his hand—he realiz'd—had somehow come to be beneath a jackboot. His head—he also realiz'd—was pressed against damp mulch. He was on the ground.

He must have been knock'd clean out from behind. There was a period of time missing between plucking the flower and being face-first in wet straw. Jack study'd the centinel's scuffed jackboot as if 'twas grinding down hard on someone else's hand. And now another centinel was lurching towards him out of the Gloom. Handcuffs dangl'd from his paw.

"What for?" Jack's voice was a wail. For once he wasn't even nicking anything.

"Anti-Foraging Act,"* spat the centinel, plucking the flower from Jack's hand.

"Foraging?!"

"'S edible," said the centinel, munching down, petals spilling from his mouth. "And as such, property of the Municipality of London."

"It's a *primrose*," Jack protested.

"Just the same. What'd you want wit' it anyway?" the centinel sneered.

Oh how to explain— She breathed life down my throat—she with the tip of her tongue, like a Hummingbird giving syrup back to the flower—and just as some flowers open only at night, so did I open only with her tongue in my mouth.

Man-flower. Gent-posy. What am I— Does it even matter? I open'd only ever in her touch— Only—only—only ever in her touch. So then how could she— How could she— And even so—

A mourning dove hooted twice, softly, from a yew tree above

---

* Presumably a companion to the Cabbage Act, the Vagrant Act, etc.

Jack's head. Jack craned his neck, eased, for a moment, to observe a free animal. But then the free black Claws pinching the thick branch were blott'd out by the centinel drawing his boot back, aiming for Jack's head, and—*

---

* Incidentally, I need to make a confession: the footnote on page 251 contains a number of partial and necessary lies.

When Sullivan requested the page I had "misplaced," I was flat fucking broke. Plus, you know, the threat of the lawsuit!

So, in order to be paid and to evade legal consequences, I did send him . . . *something*. It was not, however, a missing page of the manuscript, although I could not let the reader know this at the time of the original footnote, for obvious reasons.

Indeed, I have, frankly, no idea if this page ever existed—and, if it did, at what point it may have been removed. I like to imagine, though, that it was redacted by consensus of a radical librarian subcommittee of STAR (Street Transvestite Action Revolutionaries) in 1978 (on more of which, see Reina Gossett's archival work on STAR: www.reinagossett.com/reina-gossett-historical-erasure-as-violence).

But back to my point about that footnote on page 251 and my necessary lies. What actually happened was this: Sullivan and I were going back and forth about the manuscript—that much is true. But when I said that I had sent him the missing page of the manuscript, containing an illustration of Jack's genitalia, what I actually did was Google "waterlogged slug," and I found an illustration in a garden book (more specifically: advice on how to slay flower-pests) of a creature that had been salted, fatted and then left to perish on a deck. I cut the illustration of the slug from its background and pasted it into some Photoshop template of a pitted and moth-eaten page. It looked, in fact, quite like an "authentic" eighteenth-century manuscript page.

I saved the document as "MissingPageChimeraJunk.rtf" and sent it to Sullivan.

He motherfucking loved it.

8.

In the Press Yard of the Tower of London, inmates congregated over pints of ale and gin from the prison distillery and sold for several guineas apiece. In his previous Arrests, Jack had always been confin'd to the Condemned hold. Now he was allow'd to mingle with the other prisoners. Some strategy of the wardens to inflict Fear on the population. *The Gaolbreaker General locked up like any other piece of riff-raff.*

The Yard was packed with inmates. The dirt was peppered with shite, piss and vomit. It was near sundown. Oaks overhung the walls, their branches thinned and darkened into silhouettes against a dirty cherry-colored sky. In the far corner, thieves prepared for a mock trial, schooling one another in the art of legal Logic.

Fires were going up in small piles of kindling, flickering orange against the Gloom of the yard. Ruby sparkles shattered into the dirt, and bangers sizzl'd in pans, adding smoke to the already thick air.

Jack was present'd a chicken leg.

"Jones," a crooked, bird-thin inmate said.

"Sheppard," Jack mumbl'd.

And now Jones was bowing—flourishing the chicken leg— while booming, "Hear ye, Denizens of the Tower Hold, we have amongst us the eminent Jack Sheppard, Thief of Thieves, Breaker of Latches, Nabber of Horses, Watches, Guineas, and Pence. Son of Eternal Night. The House-Breaker General. No gaol can hold him, so pay your respects!"

The Condemned Birds rais'd their glasses; beer and gin sloshed into the dirt.

"All hail the Gaolbreaker, House-Breaker, Doxy-Lover General Jack Sheppard!"

But the usual rounds of Praise and hailing weren't able to rouse Jack. His heart was racing. The ring of admirers was a wall of stares. And he was somewhere else—unscrolling before him all the occasions he and Bess had reach'd for each other. The way she woke his *Something* into life. She had never been afraid of his strangeness, had pett'd between his legs like she loved—no, *hunger'd for*—his wild Part—the thing that swelled and reddened at the sight of her, quite beyond his control. He could not help but show her how much he loved and desir'd her. She had rewritten his Body, after all. Images of the way they were together were stamp'd on his brain like silver nitrate blooming against chalk tablets. Etched in shadow, frozen in aching memory.*

"Have any of you g-got a pint for a man newly nabbed?" he squawk'd. The crowd was graying to a kind of blur, and his chest was getting that fluttery feeling that reminded him of his bandages— the bird-breath gasping he used to do—and then one of 'em was putting something in his hand and he was drinking back deep, letting himself remember that first time he saw her. That day with the deadcart in Lamb's Conduit Alley when she called him *handsome boy,* and he was mercifully losing his grasp on sobriety, dropping into some otherworld of memory where all his being—all his inten-

---

* To return to an earlier discussion: I am now considering the possibility that "a wolf dripping fire from its teeth like blood" (see pp. 201–2) was added by what I have learned was a "chimera caucus" that formed in 1969 at the communist psychoanalytic institute with which Felix Guattari was affiliated, La Borde.

La Borde, where the patients ran free, where schizophrenia was a communiqué from the verso side of our cruel reality: some flicker of liberation. At La Borde the patients produced plays with the doctors, schemed together on capitalism's overthrow.

Note to self: investigate whether the chimera caucus at La Borde ever mounted a play titled *Confessions of the Fox.*

tion and longing—was spinning towards that now long-lost Horizon that lived between her legs.†

---

† On the manuscript's continual theme of Spread Legs. Well, this obsession I frankly postulate to be an inversion of Marcel Duchamp's genius/sick-fuck masterpiece, *Étant Donnés*, which aimed to be the last word on spread legs. Thankfully it is not.

If you're not familiar with this piece, go to the Philadelphia Museum of Art. Or don't. I'll just tell you about it.

You must pass through the larger Duchamp exhibit, where you will find all his major works—the urinal and the massive *Bride Stripped Bare* (heterosexual union depicted as a severed window, with "the men"—a cluster of spidery machines—lurking in the bottom frame, and the big shit-like log of the "woman" hovering in the upper frame, a taunting zeppelin). Don't stop in this room. Go *past* the urinal and the violent window of sexual difference. Beyond these is a room even further back, a hidden abode within the museum. There you will find a thick wooden door with a tiny window set in its upper region at approximately eye-level. Only one museumgoer can look through the peephole at a time. When you do, you will find the cast of a woman spread, Black Dahlia–style in a field, naked, holding out a lantern, beckoning you like some Virgil or Beatrice. And you're looking straight at her pussy.

It's like a bombed-out building, this pussy. Tortured rubble. The hole is shorn of any hair, any color. Ash-white vagina against a ruined picturesque—torn brown weeds, bright sky, some shy clouds and shining, erect trunks of fir, maple and oaks festooned with dun and silver winter colors. Duchamp's peephole is a dastardly portal birthed in violence, dripping sawdust and splinters. And, god help us, desire.

Well, I mean, desire as that whole Bataillian *Erotism* shtick. Eros as the birth of consciousness—fucking as synonymous with the shame of fucking.

'Course, the only subject with this version of consciousness, shame or desire in Duchamp's scenario is the (cis)man. This point is so obvious it hardly needs stating.

So let them have *Étant Donnés*. And *The Bride Stripped Bare* and all of it. Good fucking riddance.

You do know there's another room, don't you? Back behind *Étant Donnés*. The museum guards built it, of course.

Or, in any case, so says the book I found on the top floor of the Stretches, which takes its title directly from Duchamp's *Green Box*—which, if you are not familiar, contains his notes on artworks as a shadow cast from a fourth dimension. (FYI, that dimension is *time*.)

The full title of the book I've found is too long to explain to you. I'll just call it *Make a Picture of Shadows Cast*.

In *Make a Picture of Shadows Cast*, we learn about this back room. A room for study, contemplation and—perhaps?—the occasional revision of an apocryphal manuscript titled *Confessions of the Fox*. Could the guards have made some alterations to the *Confessions*? A procession of spread legs to rival Duchamp's?

What better place to do such a thing than in this back room—this living diorama

---

of flesh worship. The kind that only queers truly understand. We who have given our lives for the love of flesh.

In the museum guards' room, or so I have read, you do not stand and watch. You do not ogle through a peephole. You drop to your knees. A woman's hand presses the back of your head to her "quim" (as the rogues say!). And you take it in your mouth and pray.

9.

"You're being neither Rational nor Virtuous, Jack. The prison recommends you take our offer of a Bible, consider your Fate, and make your Confessions."

The Tower Ordinary sat at the table in the common hold, his hand running over the few strands of hair populating his pink dome.

At the high window, a foggy constant rain. The west wind blew the iron Scent of the Thames through the bars.

Jack had not been amongst others for a stretch of days—since being sent to the lonely lower hold for "stubbornness." He inhaled deep the foul scent of the prisoners scattered at tables, thrilled to their rough chatter.

"I've n-no use for a Bible," he said, returning his attention to the Ordinary. "Nor to give my confessions to you."

The Ordinary screw'd up his face.

"'Tis a useful text for such a one in your situation. In need of salvation."

"I've more use of a f-file than a Bible. With all due r-respect." Another letter of execution had come down that day. "Salvation? For havin' plucked a primrose?"

"A forbidden primrose," the Ordinary clarify'd. "Property of the Municipality of London. Plus there is the matter of your seven previous convictions. Who are you saving your confessions for, anyway, boy?"

If Jack would not give his confessions—and make an example

of himself—he'd be sent to isolation. The Ordinary marched him downstairs to the lower hold.

Later that evening.

The constable knock'd his baton against the bars.

"You've a visitor."

Jack wiped sleep from his eyes and swung his legs across the pallet.

He could hear doors clanging open. It was suppertime for the guards and prisoners alike. A fine mess, with the rowdiest of both populations cuckooing up and down the halls and the Yard. All of this Bess would have known. Jack smil'd to himself. It was a good time to visit in the gaol—she could come without being too closely watched.

He anticipat'd her scent coming closer. And how her eyelids—kohled dark—would flutter at him. He would have to try to stop himself from falling against the bars—from melting with relief at the sight, the scent of her. His heart leapt and danced.

The figure drew closer.

Jack's eyes focused in the Gloom.

Aurie's fingertips curl'd around the bars. He was wearing a priest's neck collar. The constable just behind him stamped and circled in the narrow hallway.

Jack's heart plung'd to its depths. Still, he stepped forward, saying *Thank you for visiting, Father,* kneel'd, and put his lips to Aurie's nails. Aurie, perfectly on cue, let the file fall from his sleeve into his fingers, and then to Jack's lips.

Jack open'd his mouth, let the file in, closed his lips and stood.

Pinching the file between his teeth, he whispered—"Have you seen Bess?"

"I'm more concern'd with you getting free," Aurie hissed back. "Been to every gaol in the city looking for you. You've got to spring yourself now. They're getting more ruthless, accelerating executions."

"What does it matter."

"What does *what* matter?"

"If I ever get free. Bess—" He could not finish the sentence. "Have you seen her?"

Aurie's face went blank in a way that seemed very deliberately arranged.

"Don't lie to me, Aurie. Please."

"Passed by Bess and Jenny on the way here. Walking together close and confecting. They didn't take notice of me." Aurie's breath brush'd Jack's face through the bars. There was a tinge of tartness on it, the scent of a dry Palate. "But forget about her—you need to get out, brother, or you're hang'd for certain."

"I'm content here."

Jack, a rack of bones hunch'd in the dark, was quite obviously not at all content.

"Give me back the file, then," said Aurie.

"Take it. I don't care for it." Jack pulled the file from his mouth.

Aurie pushed his arm through the bars.

"No mingling with the inmates!" shouted the constable.

"Gods," Jack sigh'd. "You're getting 'im riled."

"Open it," Aurie gruffed, "or I'll do it again."

Jack leaned on the bars, making a show of talking to Aurie while working the file into the lock of the hold with a light click.

Aurie grinned and, under his breath—"Meet me, brother, on the other side"—then rushed down the hallway.*

An unlocked door is difficult *not* to walk through.

When the guard plodded up the stairwell for his supper, Jack tiptoed the opposite direction down the tight hall, through the inch of chill water collected in the sloping center of the dirt floor. He worked the file into the short thick wooden door at the end of the

---

* No one escapes capitalism's clutches alone.

 On which topic: I want to say that my new friends do not conceive themselves as living in the year 2018. They are living in the year *WE ESCAPED!* This year has lasted them a long time. They do not know how long it will last. I understand it may be hard for you to grasp what this means.

hall—the Head Constable's chambers—and peek'd 'round the corner, making certain it was empty.

Quickly through the bitter, airless room and on to the narrow
wooden stairs. Jack spun around three flights with his feet barely
touching the ground, rounded the last bend upwards and slamm'd
into a set of thick iron bars. No hinges, no latch, no keyhole. Just
bars set into the roofhatch. At the other side: the wet night air.

Must be an ancient route out of the prison, now obsolete. Jack's
mind was lost in his craft. He remember'd his training in ironwork.
Slid the file into the joint of the bar, working the iron just as Kneebone had taught him. It had been sloppily welded with a heap of
bubbly nickel. The window-caster must have used a Cheaper ore
than what'd been request'd by the architects of Confinement. Jack
chuckl'd. The caster'd probably charged the warden for pure iron
and steel, too.

He placed his thumb against the nickel, sensing for the grain—
the striated seizures that fix'd in heated ore. Jack saw'd quickly in
the direction of the thin rivulets of nickel 'til one bar, then two,
and then a third dropp'd into his hands. He slipp'd through and ti-
dily replaced the bars, twisting so the grain lined up again. The
break was barely visible. A perfect Restoration of the original sloppy
job.

He ran along the thick prison walls. He wasn't soaring with his
usual unimpeachable Sensation of freedom. In fact—unable to run
to Bess, as ordinarily—he found himself rather queasy.

At this height, he felt himself almost *leaking* upwards, narrow-
ing through the trees and then out the gash of dense land-bound
things into the low winter sky. He look'd down and out along the
river, contemplating a thing—a *particular* thing. He could—well—
he could just—Jump.

—Couldn't he.

He imagined a soaring dive and then a hard Smack and he'd be
just another bit of flotsam in the river. The clouds ahead bloomed
radiant white. It was almost dawn.

He'd sink to the bottom—to the cold silt crowded with mossy

gray mollusks, spongy jade seaweeds and river fronds. He'd molder in the currents.

It would not be miserable to be dead.

Then the wind shifted—a balmier current rising off the water, warming his face. There was motion coming up the river. A huge hulking vessel against the pinkening dawn. A wooden creature roaring up the Thames with great Clamor, wind slapping magnificent, tattered world-worn sails. It sounded like a thunderstorm rolling down the water. Jack read the name christen'd on its side.

It was the *Poor Maria*.

10.

By morning, winter had deepened. The air was thin with cold, and the sun twisted its angle away from the earth. Leaves dried on the trees. Some had fallen to the streets, clogging the sewers.

Bess and Jenny woke to the sound of an urchin banging on the door, shouting about a note from the Head Constable. Jenny stumbl'd up to shush the urchin and shove a coin at him.

The Head Constable's feet delivered an ear-splitting clop as he stormed down the pier at Blackfriars Dry Dock. Bess was lying, out of sight, at the stinking bottom of a punt underneath the dock in a mud of fish entrails. She could hear Jenny skipping down the dock above, trailing the Head Constable.

The *Poor Maria* was pulling up the Thames, a phalanx of centinel-punts in its train.

The sun was losing its battle against thick clouds. Only a weak glow emanat'd from the sky, smearing Thames Road and the ship in a dirty gray Light.

The Head Constable stopp'd in the middle of the pier. "I ain't searching that ship," he coughed. He was due at the pub for his afternoon pint.

"'Course," winked Jenny, "I'm here for the lower work."

"Right then." The Head Constable shift'd, looking about like a child needing a chamber pot. He ruffled through the pockets of his coat, his face rumpling and unrumpling.

"The ship's got twelve holds, none of 'em with portholes. You'll be crawling through the dust, picking through the boxes, the closets—"

He passed a set of sulfur sticks to Jenny, and marched off, a rhinoceros clopping down the pier.

Jenny descended the ladder into the punt. "All's clear."

Jack was sitting in his own punt—across the river. He had watch'd the *Poor Maria* plow up the Thames, the centinel-punts fanning behind. He had watch'd, too, Jenny make her way down the pier. Watch'd Bess slip into the punt. Watch'd the two of them wait 'til the centinel-punts were navigating around an oncoming tugboat, then climb the ladder to the pier-top and board the ship.

What he sought to attempt was impossible, and yet—what, now, was the difference between leaping to his death from the Tower walls and failing spectacularly at a spectacular heist. The punt rocked back and forth in the waves thrown off the churning waters around the *Maria*. Sunlight flash'd off the river in blinding Pulses. Centinel-punts zipp'd back and forth along the sides. He fought the nausea rising in his gut. Remov'd his cloak and boots. Rolled up his sleeves. Pulled his file from his pocket, gripp'd it tight in his right hand. Pulled a set of nail piercers from the other pocket—held them in his left.

And stepp'd into the Thames.

All the years of his Thames-trick: imagining the press of cool water around his ears, the peacefulness of riverlife. But never had he anticipated the thudding Fear of the Underwater. The Thames was Dark—the water murky with offal and coal-silt and thick fronds of seaweed or linen scraps, or something he didn't want to know, brushing against his face.

And there was a smell. Rotted oysters and feces. There was Silence, there was Smell, and there was terrible Cold.

Jack was preternaturally able to hold his breath. He'd held it nearly every living second of his life, after all. Held it against the bandages that had cross'd his chest for so many years. Held it against the Terror of the Polhem Lock. Against the agony of the Demon nailing spikes into his spine at Kneebone's. He was good at holding his breath, and so he held it in long, deep gulps as he headed for the ship, surfacing silently several times and dipping back down.

But the Thames was broad and the centinel-punts were many. He was about to surface for the fourth time when the Shadow of a centinel-punt darken'd the water above his head. And then another. Three centinel-punts were circling above him like lazy, big-bellied sharks.

Jack gulp'd harder on what air was left in his lungs and dove deeper, swimming hard for the *Poor Maria*. As he gulp'd, he drew down some water too.

Instantly his lungs were bursting with the combination of water and air. He scrabbl'd at the water, dragg'd himself forward, and pulled free from the Shadow of the punts. But he was sinking down more quickly than he was moving forward. The water was suddenly much darker and he could not see the bottom. Or, his vision was going black. Or both.

All he could think was: *Bess. Bess.*

He would die under the water and she would never know. Perhaps she would think he had run off. That he'd taken up with someone else. She would never know how he woke that morning and several times that night into phantom-senses of her Heat, the soft of her breasts on his Emancipated chest, her close musky Breath.

His vision pinhol'd to a speck. He let himself float down. He would die in the same condition he was in before her—a dog of Shame and Sorrows.*

---

* We know that Oscar Wilde wrote *De Profundis* a single page a day. Each page was taken from him by Nelson the prison governor at night. But was that all he wrote there? Here in the Stretches, I've learned of queers who passed between them in Reading Gaol a so-called *Manuscript of Excarceration* (aka *Confessions of the Fox*??). They taught themselves to slip their bars, roamed the halls of the prison by candle-light, fondled each other, embraced in shadow. Could Wilde have been set free one

And then his feet touch'd sand. A bar, a hillock. The riverfloor was rising here—his feet moved up the bar and towards the water-skin, which brightened, near'd.

It was an eager.

The Thames had eagers.

Some kind of wall—some huge, looming wall was just before him. He crashed against it in Relief—the hull of the *Poor Maria*—and now his tears mix'd with riverwater as he lift'd his mouth to the edge of the river's skin and cough'd and wheez'd—and breathed deep.

Then dipp'd his lips below again.

His fingers found minuscule cracks in the wooden planks, into which he fix'd the nail-piercers with his left hand, anchoring himself to the ship.

He brought the tip of his right index finger just above the waterline, tracing the grain towards a joint, then drove the file in his fist into the seam between the wood and the hinge. He dragg'd down and felt the wood give way. Pulled another board free, hoist'd himself briefly above the water and lunged through the gash. The splintered wood ripped open the backs of his thighs and calves—his left in particular seemed cut near to the quick—and he landed inside.

He stood, shaking. Assess'd himself. Blood was streaming down his legs, mixing with foul riverwater in a Pool at his bare feet.

He stagger'd to the top deck—where the trunks and casks of elixir would be waiting to be unloaded.

The sentiments that cross'd Bess's face when she saw Jack emerge from the hold—still gasping for breath, cover'd in blood, and with

---

night to roam with them? In return, would he have "donated" an annotation to the *manuscript*? This "dog of shame and sorrows"?

Surely he was leaving us clues. Something in the manner of *De Profundis*'s theory of queer art and fellowship. Wilde's artist—the queer, martyred, Christ-like "Man of Sorrows"—leads us through the "season of sorrow." The season to which we are consigned, but in which we create nothing short of the most extraordinary beauty.

"Where there is sorrow," says Wilde, *"there is holy ground."*

Thames-water pouring off him in sheets—onto the deck were mul-
tiple. An incoherent pile of Expressions matched only by another
incoherent pile crossing Jack's own.

Surprise, unsurprise, anger and Panic were shared by them both.
And also, though likely for different reasons: relief.

The decks were a Chaos. Bess had her hands on her hips. Jenny
was racing around anxiously, opening casks and running her hands
through her hair.

"Look, there's nothing here—" Bess waved at the trunks and
casks gaping wide. Empty. Not a single speck of elixir. Not even
loose goods. No linens, silks, liquors, molasses, lavender, carda-
mom, cumin, or turmeric. No salt cod, candlesticks, utensils, tin
cups, or wine.

Jack's heart fell from his throat to his heels.

"Can you hear anything? Any commodities? *Anything?*" she asked.

Jack lay dripping on the deck, his ear flat to the boards.

He look'd up at her. Water dripped from the tangle of grizz on
his chin onto the planks. "There's no sound."

"No sound up here or no sound—"

"No sound at all. No voices. Nothing."

In fact, he'd already been troubl'd by this strange silence. From
underwater, Jack had anticipat'd the din of the commodities and
elixir to Rise as he approached. He'd braced himself for the hollow
ghostly hum, the gabbing and screeching, the garbled roar. He'd
told himself the Silence was owed to the muffling of the water.

But there truly was nothing on board the ship.

Jenny wiped her hands onto her skirts, affecting an exaggerated
nose-wrinkle. "Well this's a pickle."

Then Jack press'd his ear down again. In fact, a muffled sound
was emanating from the lower decks.

"Ahh—" Winced, listening hard. "Something. Tho' I can barely
hear it."

Bess glanced down the dock.

Several constables were patrolling towards the edge like feverish ants.

"The trunk," she hiss'd. "'Til they turn 'round."

Jenny took this moment to dart off. Jack caught a glimpse of her hair—silked dark in the low light—as she disappeared through the hatch.

Jack and Bess shot into an empty trunk just as the constables' boots reach'd the edge of the dock.

He clos'd the lid over them.

His heart was Thudding wildly. She smell'd—so *Bess*. He stifled a sob in the back of his hand.

The cloudlight filtering through the slats was a sickly Gray, and the air, blooming off the carrion-and-feces-thronged riverwater creat'd a vicious, stenchy fog that seep'd through.

In fact, he could have stay'd forever in the stinging, foul brew with Bess against him. She wasn't softening into him, but she wasn't ball'd up into herself either. That seemed, if not promising, at least not damning. She was breathing quiet but shallow against his chest. He had the urge to hold her tight against him.

But when they heard the constables' voices fade down the dock, she blast'd up out of the trunk and continued searching through the other casks on deck.

And what is Jenny up to? thought Jack. *Getting to the elixir, no doubt. And destroying it, as Bess plann'd?*

Further, it seem'd as if the sound had gone somewhat Silent. This concerned him.

He shambl'd as quickly as possible on his bleeding calves across the deck, and down the hatch.

In the lower hold, the brine of the river became more piercing.

It was mix'd with something more fetid still—something Marinated in small rooms. Something that'd bred a deep, moldy, bitter

Aroma. It was the smell of improperly cured animal hide. Or the Sweepings from butchers' stalls, floating down the open channels of the sewers on a hot day.

But now here the sound had returned—at closer range. Jack followed it, limping—his gashes had begun to seize up and ache—down the narrow hall.

Light drift'd in slow, sparkly Motes through the cracks in the ceiling boards, filter'd down from the topdecks. Jack strain'd to see, following his nose down the scent-congested hallway.

And where was Jenny.

He poked open a door to one of the berths. The smell in the room was awful. As the dark fizz'd to a lighter gray, Jack made out several wooden tables. *For butchering?* This must be where they slaughter'd the cows and chickens during the trading journeys. Explain'd the smell, at least. He shut the door.

There was an overwhelmingly gravelike effect to the hold. As he pressed down the hall, the ship listed. Were they sinking? Drifting to the bottom of the river, the seadark Vale of the Thames floor? He thought of the hole he'd bored to enter. *But it was above the waterline.*

Still, he hasten'd down the hall, swamp'd with an animal fretfulness.

The sound was coming from a gunpowder room. Jack knew this because it was fronted with a thick door cloaked in water-soaked drapes.

He threw his weight against it and pushed. The door was cold and immobile against his shoulder. Pushed again, and it creak'd open a hair. As it did, an acrid metallic Scent pour'd out; Jack breathed in choking gulps.

"Bess?" Jenny call'd out.

Jack tried to say, "It's Jack," but the Scent claw'd at his lungs. He coughed and sputter'd, forcing the door further. He managed, "Ack."

Jack heard Jenny whimpering.

"Jack?" Jenny's voice again, this time smaller, even.

Jack pushed harder. But the soaked drapes were jamm'd into

the floor, acting as a stopper. It wouldn't budge and he couldn't squeeze 'round. He fell to his knees, pulled a file from his pocket, and started working at the hinges.

He search'd for a crevasse in the screwheads. The screws were so rusted out by sea-air that they had lost their grooves. The Ocean winds would do that to lesser metals. Jack calculat'd this must be an alloy—the shipowners undoubtedly having thought to save money, but soon they would rust to the point where the door would be unworkable. And the shipowners would have to invest in entirely new doors. So, not a money-saving decision in the long run. *But try to tell that to Profiteers.*

There was nowhere to apply Pressure to untwist them. He flipp'd the file sideways and began sawing frantically at the hinges. Screwdust piled on his fingertips, which quickly bloodied from being jamm'd into the thin crack.

More *mmmmph*s and whimpering from within.

"No, Jack—"

He was almost through the hinges.

"I'm tryin' to say you've got to—" The door crash'd inwards, plummeting off its broken hinges, and Jack tumbl'd into the room— catching his already-torn leg on the threshold—a snap, pop, another (larger) warm gush of blood, and now Jack's left knee and lower leg were pointing in a series of odd, impossible, *Several* directions. He was on the floor. The pain astonish'd him. He look'd up, immobile. Jenny was finishing her sentence—"*Go.* You've got to *go*"—but her face show'd how Unattainable she realiz'd his going now was. He look'd back down at himself. Blood was pooling 'round his bent leg. He dragg'd himself half-upright, leaning against the wall. Tried to walk, but even the Touch of his foot grazing the floor sent a Cascade of pain.

He turn'd his attention back to Jenny. Ropy dense-haired arms grasp'd her pale wrists. He had one moment of confused Inability to make sense of what he was seeing—then began to recognize a bespectacled huge face behind hers.

"Jack!" the erudite voice call'd out. "We were just discussing the principles of Locke's *Essay Concerning Human Understanding.*"

The Lion-Man had a book in one hand, and Jenny wrench'd tight to his lap with the other.

Without the intermediary of bars, he Loom'd twice as large as Jack had remembered. His arms and legs were thick muscle, and his neck was dense.

"Ah yes, 'Of the Association of Ideas, Proposition 12.' I've always found this one to be very suggestive. Are you familiar with it?"

Jack tried to shake *no,* but movement aggravat'd the blinding pain. He twitch'd his head a bit, side to side.

"'A Man has suffer'd Pain or Sickness in any Place, he saw his Friend die in such a Room; though these have in Nature nothing to do with one another, yet when the *Idea* of the Place occurs to his Mind, it brings (the Impression being once made) that of the Pain and Displeasure with it, he confounds them in his Mind, and can as little bear the one as the other.'"

The Lion-Man whisper'd in Jenny's ear, quite loud enough for Jack to hear. "Do *you* know how to interpret this, my dear?" He lift'd his hand off her mouth.

"It means I'll have a lifelong Aversion to gunpowder rooms and the revolting stench of your breath."

"While not kind, that *is* technically correct." He flashed a smile. "Incidentally, Jack will associate our time together with certain doom."

"Fuck John Locke." Jack chew'd each word. There was blood on his teeth and tongue.

"As we speak," the Lion-Man continu'd, stroking Jenny's pale arm, "Wild's men have surrounded the ship. Indeed, they have likely already *Custodiz'd* your paramour topside. Shortly you will be taken and remanded immediately to the Newgate warden. Where you will swiftly meet your death."

"W-why would you?" was all that Jack could think to whimper.

"For my Freedom, you fool. Caged, confined, laugh'd at, turn'd object. As any conscious being-turned-commodity would wish, I have long'd for my freedom."

During this disquisition, Wild's gang had emerg'd from under the eaves of Blackfriars theater, slid up to the dock off Thames Street, hands in pockets, heads jutting out, full of belligerence and pomp. A flock of ragged, arrogant birds. Wild had nodded to the centinels at the shore, then wav'd his arm, calling the gang forward into the water. They waded into the Thames, swim-skated through the Shallows to a punt.

They row'd out quietly to the *Poor Maria.*

A thump of ropes along the sides of the ship, and soon Wild's gang had tumbl'd over the edges onto the decks.

The barrage of footsteps. A scuffle that Jack suppos'd was them accosting Bess. Muffl'd cries. Howls of victory.

The Lion-Man clear'd his throat. "Won't be long now. Might as well tell you all of it."

Jack panted in agony; he was glued to his position on the wall. He met Jenny's eyes.

Help, she mouth'd.

You help me! he mouth'd back.

"Your troubles began the night you killed Evans," the Lion-Man began. "Eliminating Wild's partner in crime! Most unfortunate. And then, to add to that, nicking his Supply of elixir. Troubles upon troubles."

"How do you know any o' this?" Jack bit the words out.

"Of course, on the night you arriv'd at the Tower Menagerie, Wild confect'd with me in a scheme against you."

"If he knew I was there, why not arrest me right away?"

The Lion-Man laughed. "Arresting you in some Unspectacular way wouldn't be the best use of your downfall, frankly. The process of acquiring a Sentence too long, your gaolbreak skills too accomplish'd. Wild want'd a plan that was far more *Profitable*. He ask'd me again the same questions Evans had. How we devis'd the elixir, what the mechanisms of its production were. He was urgent about it. Said he and Evans had been nearing completion when he had unceremoniously disappear'd. Wild fear'd the Worst.

"Without Evans, and with his stash nick'd, Wild was at his wits' end. The sort of wits' end that births *devious arrangements*. After some Discourse, he propos'd that I act as Agent for him. When you inevitably made your way to my cage, I was to let slip Wild's Intention to rob a Plague Ship. Next, I would suggest to yourself and the good Bess how simple t'would be to effect a scheme of robbery. The purpose of this suggestion was to lead you here to be caught in the Act. As a result, Wild would claim robbery of the ship, receive a reward of Insurance for the plunder from Lloyd's of London—catch you, finger you for the Deed, and be heralded by all the Town for having nabb'd the Gaolbreaker General himself in the Act. He'd canonize himself Head Thief-Catcher and reap great profit, all in one blow."

"And take me straightaway to hanging." Jack's head fell to his chest. *How did I fail to anticipate this? How did* Bess *fail to anticipate it?*

"As per Wild's provision in the city legal code that anyone discovered on board a Plague Ship be brought summarily to execution to prevent Contagion in the broader populace." The Lion-Man nodded. "For implanting this faulty scheme in your heads," he droned on, "I'd be freed by Wild from my Bonds at the Tower Menagerie."

"But," Jack point'd out, "there's nothing on the ship to claim insurance on. Not a single commodity topdecks or below."

"Admittedly odd," said the Lion-Man. "However, the materiality of commodities is immaterial to the business of insurance."

A crash as several of the gang rush'd down the stairs.

The rank odor of unwashed blackguard as the gang approach'd. Jack, the Lion-Man, and Jenny seemed to syncopate their breathing, each of them existing only in this interstice of time rushing towards a conclusion. Jack wished helplessly that he had a working leg. Or a pistol. He conjured its loud Clap as he imagin'd aiming and firing it at Wild. The sooty smell of Powder blooming as he'd flee to the punt, Bess alongside. How they would dine tonight. On oysters and roast lamb's foot.

A puff of foul air rounded the threshold, and Henry Davis and Scotty Pool tumbl'd through, grease-spattered and grinning. Sporting a sharp assortment of brownish teeth, Hell-and-Fury.

Then Bess was shov'd through the doorway by Wild. He had a dagger pressed to her neck, blistering the skin into a sharp Dimple.

Bess looked Jack straight on. Her hair glistered in the umber Glow of the room. Her eyes were a mosaic. Ice-bright sparks of focus and precision wheel'd in her pupils as she assess'd the dire scene.

"Davis," Wild said, pointing with his chin towards the far wall of the room. "Open that door."

"What door?"

Jack squint'd. The gunpowder room was necessarily very dark, portal-less—light having the capacity to heat the room to such a degree that 'twould denature the powder or ignite it. He hadn't noticed a door.

The Lion-Man whipp'd 'round with a surprised jerk. Evidently he was also not apprised.

Henry Davis crossed the room and swung it open. "We're all going to take a look now," rang Wild's voice.

Then Wild was behind him, shoving him forward—dragging Bess. The gang was knocking into each other and banging their way back into the hold.

"You too," Wild said to the Lion-Man. "You'll want to see this."

They all piled into the inner chamber. Which was darker even than the gunpowder room, and stenchier too.

Davis, Pool and Hell-and-Fury jumbled into the center. Jack melt'd against the wall, wheezing in agony.

A shape refin'd itself against the dark in the center of the room.

The terrible scent was coming from the shape. The shape—Jack saw—was a body.

Laid out on a marble slab, the body was stripped bare. There were tools on a ledge behind. Saws, broad sweeping metal hooks with handles attached. Clamps. Long arched scissors, three times the length of an ordinary scissor. Heavy iron hammers.

All of these implements were Splatter'd with a brown crust.

Bess was approaching the slab.

She was whispering something—a prayer; a benediction; a battle cry[*]—and Jack noticed the shelving running the perimeter of the room. Atop the shelving, a line of Bottles, empty, but marked with notes, printed carefully and wheat-pasted around their middles:

Mr. Jonathan Wild's Granulated Strength Elixir

Extracted Direct from the Gonads of London's Most Notorious Rogues

Ye've Read the Ordinary's Reports and Confessions, Now Taste the Vitality

For Sale at Fleet Street Market in time for Christmas Holidays

---

[*] Some queers believe the police or the military will save them from harm. Queers of the colonies, the postcolonies, those inhabiting the internal colonies of the U.S.A. and the diaspora know that this is a lie. This, of course, is sort of what Fanon meant when he said that certain so-called secret evils of capitalism were not secrets to everyone.

For example, when, in 1990, France officially discontinued usage of the pesticide chlordecane to kill banana borer beetles, the government made an "exception" for overseas territories, and continued to promote its use elsewhere. Huge clouds bloomed over the banana fields of Martinique. An endocrine disruptor and a toxin, chlordecane seeped into the water system and the ground soil without regulation or warning.

Gender does not mean the same thing in every context. Some genderings we fight for, stake our lives on. Some "gender" is a missile sent by the metropole.

Who embedded this warning, wish and clue: Pa ni mèt ankô? I cannot say for sure—the archive is necessarily "disobedient" (Mignolo, again). None of us will be free unless all of us are free. Until there are No More Masters, and the entire edifice that began with the police and the Royal Navy (and the poisoning of the banana fields and the waters of the postcolony) is ground to dust.

(See Vanessa Agard-Jones, "Bodies in the System," Small Axe, 42, Nov. 2013.)

Available elixirs will include:

Mac Shelton

Steven Barnes

Aesop Trammel

And, most precious rogue and gaolbreaker general:

Jack Sheppard

Bess stared down, biting her lip. "Who is this Anglo?"

"Barnes!" Wild shriek'd.

She turn'd, defiant. "I knew Barnes. This isn't him."

"What does it matter." Wild's face was beet red. And Jack was remembering the screaming in his office—Wild's fury over Fireblood and Flanders' loss of Barnes. Who had it been in the dead cart? Some Commoner they murdered in the mêlée?

Whoever it was, Jack saw as he stared across the room, was missing his nutmegs†. Next to the body were two flattened mounds lying on a set of gore-covered papers. Bess was considering it all with great Concentration.

The narrative of what was happening—had been happening, had happened—assembl'd, de-assembl'd, and re-assembl'd itself in Jack's head.

The House of Waste.

The Elixir.

He had found it, hadn't he.

Well, it'd found him.

Jack bent over, one hand grabbing at the dissection counter, and commenced to shite through his teeth.

And now he heard it again, clearer. *No body.* He remember'd the Plunk into the water at the Lighthouse. What Body part—what bit of offal and *whose*—was it that the Keeper toss'd after him? It had been—he now realized—a warning.‡

---

† Testicles

‡ A Note on "Nobody":

He heard the Lion-Man moaning, "They're making it from men."

"From scamps," sobbed Jack. "From mates."

And now it was the Lion-Man who lean'd over to commence shiting through his teeth.

And where was Wild? Jack heard the plodding of heavy feet. Wild was backing towards the door. And locking it.

The Stench in the room intensify'd.

"Gentleman and ladies." Wild return'd to caress the dissection table. "Welcome to my dissection-ship. A glorious scientific chamber for the extraction and synthesization of elixir. Straight from the

---

Karl Marx famously posed a counterfactual. "If commodities could speak, they would say this: our use-value may interest men, but it does not belong to us as objects. What does belong to us as objects, however, is our value. Our own intercourse as commodities proves it. We relate to each other merely as exchange-value" (Marx, *Capital, Volume 1,* trans. Ben Fowkes, "The Fetishism of Commodities, and the Secret Thereof").

Don't worry too much about what this means.

A commodity is an entity without qualities. It is without qualities because at its root, a commodity is simply something that can be exchanged for money. And, about this, Marx was saying: we know that these ciphers cannot speak, but if they *could* they'd tell us that what has meaning, for them, is their price.

Or *can* they speak? The manuscript impels us to consider this possibility, and the work of the theorist Fred Moten, who has called Marx's bluff. What of the slave, asks Moten. A human commodity possessed of speech, or—as Moten has it—of "a scream" (Moten, *In the Break: The Aesthetics of the Black Radical Tradition,* University of Minnesota Press, 2003). Surely, says Moten, the commodity does speak. To say that it doesn't is to blot out an entire bloody history—one without which any history of the West is partial, tendentious.

There is *nobody* who is unmarked by this bloody history. Read Angela Davis (*Women, Race & Class,* Vintage, 1983) or Jasbir Puar (*Terrorist Assemblages: Homonationalism in Queer Times,* Duke University Press, 2007), if you don't believe me. There is no body, no sexuality and, simply put, *no sex* outside the long history of Western imperialism's shattering of the world. And once we understand this, we've got to go back and reconsider just how so-called "impossible" Marx's speaking commodity is or is not.

Whoever inserted the speaking commodities into this text—and really, it could be anybody, though my money's on those radical grad students—*knows* this.

(On the topic of speech and subjectivity, see also Ghassan Kanafani's *All That's Left to You,* narrated partially by the Gazan desert.)

P.S. Of course we have Moten, Marx, Davis and Kanafani here in the Stretches!

nasty bits of the world's most famous rogues—London's all the better off without 'em."

"The elixir'll fizz up the stockjobbers into perfect merchanting
passions!" chimed Hell-and-Fury.

"Shares in elixir to profit off beyond all imagination," nodded
Wild. "Finally, my gang'll be financially independent (not to mention bull-beefed)." He smiled a terrible smile. "No more fencing
and scraping. No more scrawny clunches—" He gestured, frowning, at Hell-and-Fury. "My Relishing of this moment is—as you can
imagine—Inexpressible."

Jack was sliding slowly—very slowly—along the back wall—
Sweat pour'd in waves down his ribs— He released his file from up
his sleeve—slid the tip into the lock, jiggling each time Wild spoke,
and pausing when he paused. Bess saw. Flash'd him a flicker of a
smile.

And Wild was going on. "—Straight from Holland where she's
been kitt'd out with the very latest in dissection-technologies,
thanks to a wonderful new mate of mine, Mr. Mandeville, who
knows quite a few eminent surgeons at Leiden University.* It's a
perfect dissection chamber, really. Owned by no nation. Free to
roam ports"—and here Wild clear'd his throat—"free of the Arm of
the law. Or, more properly, free to become our own autonomous
Arm of the law. We've only to establish an agreement with the body-

---

* Here is Mandeville's proposition regarding the use of executed prisoners: "The
University of Leyden in Holland have a Power given them by the Legislature to de-
mand, for this Purpose, the Bodies of ordinary Rogues executed within that Prov-
ince. . . . When Persons of no Possessions of their own, that have slipp'd no
Opportunity of wronging whomever they could, die without Restitution, indebted to
the Publick, ought not the injur'd Publick to have a Title to, and the Disposal of, what
the others have left?" (*AN ENQUIRY INTO THE CAUSES OF THE FREQUENT
EXECUTIONS AT TYBURN: AND A PROPOSAL for some REGULATIONS concerning FELONS in PRISON, and the good Effects to be Expected from them. To
which is Added, A Discourse on TRANSPORTATION, and a Method to render that
Punishment more Effectual,* 1725).

Please note, with E. P. Thompson, that capital offenses in England at this time
included "wearing a disguise" while committing a crime, and harvesting turf (cf. E. P.
Thompson, *Whigs and Hunters: The Origin of the Black Act,* Penguin, 1990).

snatchers of a local area to assure ourselves of the Freshest and most Virile specimens and the most notorious nutmegs we can find." Here he looked at Jack.

Wild's gang idiotically took offense at this. Bellow'd out, *Are we not notorious too? Only Sheppard, then?*

Jenny chortled in the dark—"You dumb fobs."

And now they direct'd a battalion of insults at her.

Bess had sidled up next to him. "Take this." She slipp'd him the packet of papers she'd nick'd from the table along with a metal rod—some sort of dissecting implement. Jack look'd at her quizzically.

"How this ends, you might need it," she said.

She didn't think he'd escape Wild.

Not this time.

He slid the papers and the rod into his trouser pocket.

Wild's gang were still leaping about, issuing Cruelties upon Jenny, and upon the Body.

And Jack—under cover of the din of the gang, and realizing that Jenny had distract'd them just for this purpose—was working the file into the handle more aggressively. He felt it click in his hand. Then he breathed in, nodded meaningfully to Bess and Jenny, and swung it open, falling aside to let Bess rush through.

Bess zipp'd out, follow'd by Jenny, who was trailed by the Ruckus of howling men, the blackguards swirling after her.

But Wild had mov'd back into the room.

"Jack," called Bess. She was ahead of Jenny, the both of them caught in a tumult of men. Jack was crumpled on the ground. And now Wild had Jack's wrist in his hand, holding it hard. Jack considered fighting back, but the exhaustion and pain bore down on him like a hot sun and his body had become as soft—as sapp'd of Resistance—as a cat at noonday. He would not make it off the ship a free cove. He could see that now. They would bring Bess and Jenny to St. Giles Roundhouse. And Wild would take him to Tyburn straightaway. Hang him immediately—and bring him back—dead—to the ship—pore over his body with tools—looking for—

—He retch'd, unable to continue the thought.

Bess's nightmare would come true. The Policing operation. It was a closed circle. Bodies, Elixir, Profit. She'd been right all along.

His wrist was in Wild's hand, and he was being dragg'd towards the door.

And then he saw Jenny just beyond Wild. She had a sulfur stick in her hand.

A thought came to him—a terrible, perfect thought.

Gunpowder room, he mouth'd as he was tugg'd towards her, towards the threshold. He nodded at the sulfur stick. *Throw it.*

In seconds he would be in the hall and it would be too late.

Now, Jenny.

She tossed him the stick. *Yes.* She smiled. *Do it.*

Then he saw Bess, just beyond. She was watching him with a look of unpretended horror. "Don't!" she shout'd.

She'd said *Don't.* Which was as good as saying *I do love you, after all.*

It was enough. Just to know that she did.

So he'd do it. He'd finish the scamp for her.

He'd destroy the ship.

As Wild tugg'd him out the threshold Jack summon'd a shred of Strength and threw the weight of his body back towards the gunpowder room. His leg snapped and bunched in Agony as he lung'd across the floor. He thought he might have pull'd his own shoulder out of its socket. The arm Wild held had gone slack and was twisted 'round at a queasy angle. With his free hand he scraped the sulfur stick against the floor. It flared up.

The blackguards were surrounding Bess and Jenny like a filthy tide, shoving them down the narrow hallway.

There was a second when all the air in the ship seemed to contract.

And then The Blast took them.

• • •

Jack was up in the sky, high above the shattering ship, and Wild was with him. And then they were plummeting back down and the water rush'd over his head and Wild was on him, scrabbling at him, clapping handcuffs on his wrists, and surfacing the two of them, dragging him through the water towards the shore.

Jack saw Bess swimming for the opposite shore, her long skirts trailing behind. Black smoke plumed against the cold white sky.

The Lion-Man was nowhere to be seen. Nor was Jenny.

Wild pump'd hard and Jack was towed helplessly Behind.

Then he was haul'd up the sodden, nasty coal-stuffed riverbank, and Wild threw him over his shoulder and walk'd up towards the Town.*

---

* On the topic of Prison Quackery. I have reason to suspect that some details of the narrative of Wild's dissection-ship were added at a later date to highlight the history of nefarious collaboration between the medical and penal institutions.

See, for example, Ethan Blue, "The Strange Career of Leo Stanley: Remaking Manhood and Medicine at San Quentin State Penitentiary, 1913–1951": "Dr. Leo Stanley served as San Quentin's chief surgeon for nearly four decades. . . . Throughout, Stanley fixated on curing various crises of manhood. Under Stanley's scalpel, prisoners became subjects in a series of eugenic treatments ranging from sterilization to implanting 'testicular substances' from executed prisoners—and also goats—into San Quentin inmates. Stanley was convinced that his research would rejuvenate aged men, control crime, and limit the reproduction of the unfit. His medical practice revealed an underside to social hygiene in the modern state, where the lines between punishment, treatment, and research were blurred" (Blue, *Pacific Historical Review*, 2009). Note also the following, from *The New York Times*, 1919:

SAN FRANCISCO, Oct. 17.—Thomas Bellon, a young murderer, was hanged today at San Quentin Penitentiary, and after his death, interstitial glands from his body were transferred to a man of sixty, also a prison inmate, to test the efficacy of the theory of restoration of youth.

Bellon was pronounced dead at 10:36 A.M., and the body was hurried to the prison hospital. There on an operating table lay the aged convict. The body of Bellon was lifted to an adjoining table and his interstitial glands were removed.

Then the glands were transferred to the other's body. Unable to feel pain, because of anaesthetic injected into the spine, he talked with the doctors as they cut and sewed. The surgeons believe that new strength, mental as well as physical, will follow the operation. Similar results, it is said, have come from such operations previously performed at the prison.

Think of it this way: There is the medical history that purports to linearity (a kind of *endochronology*—a so-called progress narrative of the alignment of sex hormones and subjectivity, if you will). And then there is *our* history—fragmented and fugitive. (On which topic, see Kadji Amin, "Glands, Eugenics, and Rejuvenation in *Man into Woman*: A Biopolitical Genealogy of Transsexuality," *Transgender Studies Quarterly* 5, no. 3, 2018.)

II.

Applebee's Weekly Journal, RUSH EDITION

To the Citizens of London and Westminster

1 6 N o v e m b e r 1 7 2 4

THE CAPTURE OF JACK SHEPPARD AND
THE BURNING OF THE SHIP THE *POOR MARIA*

Let it be known, citizens of London, that the arch-devil Jack Sheppard had been captured by the Thief-Catcher General whilst pilfering the Plague Ship, the *Poor Maria.* Sheppard was discovered
on Board with his accomplices Bess Khan and Another Woman.
Khan escap'd into the Thames and is likely to be found swum
ashore at Whitehall or Blackfriars. All other souls on board on the
ship, save the Thief-Catcher General and Sheppard, perish'd in the
blast.

Sheppard is to be brought direct to Tyburn at four o'clock this
afternoon, where he will be hanged for burglary, pilfering, acces-
sory to arson, and ape-mutilation. In the blast, one of the King's
prized menagerie, The Lion-Man, was consum'd by flames. The
loss of such a rare specimen is Incalculable.

12.

1: Tyburn Tree, The Procession

Wild's men brought Jack to the Tree straightaway.

Thousands of common folk throng'd the streets to watch the execution-cart pass. The City Marshal attended the cart, mount'd on a fine steed of pied color with a high, shiny haunch just visible out of the corner of Jack's eye under the hood. Some Histories will say it was a carnival that day.

But it was a Rebellion.

The people screamed bloody Murder for Jack's release, and the Marshal on his steed was unmoved, though they threw rotted fruit at him and spat with all their might.

2: All This You Know

Jack begg'd in his heart that Aurie would rush the stage and steal his body back from the hangman once the deed was done, as they had discuss'd he would do in this eventuality over ales so many nights when they play'd Aurie's favorite game (and in truth it was no game to him; it was the very meat of his worrying mind): *What if*.

Jack was on his knees and the hangman's hand was on his whip.

3: He Died on the Tree

And, Reader, he died.

Because he was of slight build, it took fifteen minutes, and in that time, he saw the Mob glisten and turn sap-thick underwater green as the breath left his body and he was seiz'd then with the surety of his Arc; he would not die of the supposed Plague, or of a slip and fall off an eave, or of throwing himself from the walls of the Tower, or of Drowning, or of the pain of Bess-less-ness, or even of the Pleasure of Bess's muff making his heart skip beats. He would die of the executioner. Of the hand whipping the horse, of the horse yanking the cart.

For moments they all thought his Body would not be weighted enough to die. But die he did.

He died on the Tree like Bailey the Highwayman and Brooks the Shop-Lifter and Nayler the Preacher of Freedom and Equality. He died at the hands of the profiteers like all the rebels, and freedom fighters rotting under the water of the fens.

4: The Mob Rushed the Stage

The mob rushed the stage so quickly that Aurie Blake was swallow'd up in a sea of clamoring ordinary Folk. He did not reach Jack. The mob got to him first.

And the mob carried Jack on their shoulders through the Town to keep him safe from the Dissectors and the Wardens and Wild and all who wished to profit from his Body. They took him down Chipping Street, misty with the grains of glass-dust from Walton's Glass-Blowers. They took him down Wapping, high on their shoulders through the blighted moldy air of the Slaughterhouses. On to the Strand with the husky tailors hunch'd over their spinning machines, concoctin' a strike for better wages. And the tailors stepp'd out into the street and whistled salutations and Love as he passed by. They took him to the Stone Castle Inn, where they propp'd him on couches and drank many toasts of good whiskey to his Honor. Then they carry'd him lovingly to St. Martin-in-the-Fields and dug a grave with small shovels and spoons and with their fingernails even, for those who lacked a tool. And they laid him there, and dusted themselves off, and they left him with a battalion of Commoners to guard him, and the rest went home and changed into their Leveller Green Dress clothes—their mutinous green colors in honor of Winstanley and the Family of Love, long-lost Dreamers of these common lands. Planters of seed, grazers of cows, feeders of the people.

And, dressed now all in green, they return'd.

And Aurie Blake was there, dressed in green, and Bess—and Bill Field's son, too; Aurie's love—Tommy—was holding Aurie's hand. Holding him up. And they threw dirt on Jack's head and chest and bury'd him that night with the red poppies just opened and the cherry plum came to Budding just that day.

5: St. Martin-in-the-Fields

But when the mob had dispers'd, singing together into the Night— their voices floated out acrid and hoarse on the salt-scratched air— Aurie Blake stepp'd from behind the big oak at the end of St. Martin-in-the-Fields. The oak at the foot of which he had been sitting and breathing calm and steady 'til the sound of the mob was far and tiny down the lane, each of them tumbl'd off into a pub, or their bed, or settlin' down for the night wedged against a cobbled wall. He stepped out and approach'd the grave and took his hands to the cold wet dirt. And he dug.

He didn't have to dig for long. The mob hadn't done the most fastidious burying job. To be fair, most of 'em were enormously soused. No matter. 'Twas easier for Aurie this way. He felt Jack's arm before he saw it, and then he start'd brushing.

Jack lay shallow in the dirt, his skin enameled against the dark. His eyes half-opened, slitted in that deadlike way. A sliver of Tooth glinted in the moonlight.

"Brother," Aurie whisper'd. And that would be the only word he spoke for the next long while, as he unearth'd Jack and—as delicately as Aurie could—placed him over his shoulder and proceeded down Charing Cross to meet Tommy, who was waiting outside the Pig and Thistle and simply nodded at Aurie and fell in beside him, and they walked together to Hampstead Heath.

6: The Chirurgeon

The chirurgeon was a sour man. A thin, wasted rind dressed in a white jumper and surrounded by rusty tools. He cough'd a "C'min" from his stool when Aurie and Tommy knocked, and they open'd the door into the rank basement office.

"Here's yer 50p," scoffed Tommy, who felt that anyone with any sympathy at all would do this for free. He tossed some grubby coin on the metal table.

The chirurgeon swiped the coin off the operating table and gestured for Aurie to lay Jack down.

"Wipe it first," Aurie said, holding Jack tight against his shoulder. He strok'd Jack's stockinged leg, something he'd not ordinarily allow himself. Now that they were in the light, Tommy saw the dried chalky tear-streams down Aurie's face and pool'd in his beard scruff.

The chirurgeon grumblingly rubbed a Rag over the surface, which left a gummy film on top of the metal. Aurie laid Jack down, arranging his arms and legs in a jaunty akimbo posture—nothing like the knotted ball Jack actually slept in, but a Pantomime of something like the dreamy gaolbreaker Aurie always saw him as. Supernatural and Free. He stepped back.

"So you'll bring 'im around again?" query'd Tommy. Aurie was too choked up to talk. The few sentences he'd said that night had already practically done him in—Tommy could see that. Saw Aurie's throat bobbing up and down while he was looking at Jack. So Tommy would be the one to secure the Transaction.

"You'll bring 'im 'round? That's what we're here for."

"I'll bring 'im 'round. To the best of my Capacity I will bring 'im 'round. I'll need some Privacy for it, all right. It's a bit of a procedure and I do need my concentration."

Aurie didn't like the sound of that, but the room was small and dense and smelled sharply of chemicals and death. And he couldn't bear looking at Jack like that for much longer. Holding him was better. Looking was causing a chasm to widen in his brain, hollowing the space between the real world and the wished-for one, the Maybe-gone one. He stepped backwards out and up the stairs and Tommy follow'd, promising that they would be back shortly to meet up with a revived Jack and be on their way.

7: THE PIG AND THISTLE

Aurie and Tommy headed to the Pig and Thistle. They didn't talk. They ran their hands over their faces and quaff'd ale and didn't even look at the other mollies as they might normally do, flirting and bantering. They drank several each and headed back out. The night was pinkening into morning and the sun stung their eyes.

8: WHAT IF

When Tommy and Aurie returned to the chirurgeon, the Office was empty. There was Blood and mess everywhere. They knocked and bang'd on the walls and howl'd for the doctor. Aurie was frantic, throwing bloodied tools about the room and stamping, slipping on Offal.

Finally, a light came on behind a dirty glass Pane, and an interior door slipp'd open. The chirurgeon's head pok'd out, his paltry black hairs greased to his shining pate.

"Where is he?!" Aurie was screaming.

"Calm, mate," said the chirurgeon. "'E's in the back."

Aurie crash'd through the operating Paraphernalia, throwing aside clamps, scissors, some frightening, bloodied black cord, and a small wooden stool. He lung'd for the door to the back room.

"He was near gone for good," the chirurgeon squeak'd.

"Thank you," muttered Tommy.

There was dust kicked up against the chirurgeon's basement windows by a horsecart. An ochre tide of dust with the sun burning bright behind it, spinning in the wake of a cart that was rolling now at a monstrous clip from St. Martin-in-the-Fields, where Wild had found Nothing but an empty grave.

In the back room, Jack was lying on a filthy slab, blinking.

"Suppose we needed all those games of *what-if* after all." He smiled. "Had this in me throat." He held up the sopping curl of parchment papers and the rod, soaked in phlegm and blood. "Protection from the rope."

Aurie crunch'd his forehead, looking at the sputum and gore.

And there was something Wet bubbling up at the corner of his eye, which was the first time Jack had ever seen anything of that nature there.

"Well done, mate," croak'd Aurie. "Now," he said, slinging Jack's arm around his shoulder and helping him up. "Tommy's arrang'd a coach."

13.

WHEN JACK OPEN'D HIS EYES, HIS HEART HAD BEEN AWAKE FOR SOME time—banging Hammers inside his chest. He breathed—tried to Focus— He was in the barn—Field's stable where they often stashed their loot. Aurie was peering above him, a bundle of hay in his hand. And now Aurie press'd the bundle—toasted in the sun—to Jack's neck wounds. His rough friend had become a gentle cur, practically licking his wounds and fussing over Jack's bruises.

He let Aurie lift the cloak off his legs.

"They're bad," Aurie said, in his direct way.

"I'm aware." Jack had not moved for a reason. His calves were clumped and frozen, bloodcaked and throbbing.

"You'll have to move them about, I'm afraid," Aurie assessed. "To get the humours flowing."

Aurie bent over to help him up, and Jack waved him off. "I can do it." He winced as he dragged himself to his feet, crumpled, then righted himself. He did this several times until his shaking legs held him, but only just.

All that day, Aurie and Jack slowly perambulated the high western moor. At first Jack had sobbed and screamed as the blood circulated again, flowed over broken skin, awakening the wounds.

When Jack's legs had numbed but steadied, in the low afternoon Light, with the turf coming to appear gold-gingered, he regarded

his mate's phiz against the setting sun—"You know those Confessions they're always tryin' get?"—

That night and the next day, Jack and Aurie wrote down everything.
In roguespeak. An *Incantation*.

By the next afternoon, they'd compil'd a thick stack of Confessions in the barn*, and Aurie urg'd him out for another walk. But
Jack was slower, even, this time—tired from the Exertions of the
previous day. They'd not gotten far before evening came on fast,
along with the portent of rain. The air ocean'd. Cool mist washed
over their faces.

"I'm heading back to rest." Jack's voice was unsteady. "You keep
on with your constitutional." He returned to the barn, slowly on his
sad legs, through the gray-blue light and the settling Mist. Leaned
against the threshold, wiped his face with his cloak sleeve.

A sound from the interior—a cough.

Bess was sitting on a bale of hay, surrounded by satchels.

She was looking through the wadded, blood-smeared papers
Tommy and Aurie had taken from the chirurgeon, uncrumpled now
onto the bale.

When she raised her head, her eyes were clotted with blue underneath, shot with red throughout.

"Bess." He could not manage more. She clearly had an ague—he
knew it from the way her cheeks tended towards a dark magenta
when she was Feverish. He went to her.

Whatever Space they each might have hoped would open be-

---

* "It emerges in fragments," said Foucault of the archive. History does not progress,
but rather piles and strews—a chaos of heterogeneous shards. This is something
close to what Derrida meant when he said that the archive does not preserve so much
as occupy the site of the destruction of a memory. An impossible, ghostly archaeology—
unexcavatable and haunting.

tween them at this moment did not open. Not all the way. Not in-stantly. But he went to her, she stood, and they embrac'd. When they held each other, they were Dogs snared in each other's fur, breathing in, holding hard to muscle, skin, bone.

"I buried Jenny—what was left of her. In the grave they dug you out of."

Night streamed in cold and blue through the slats in the walls. Mice began their cottony scratches in the underbelly of the hay.

Jack nodded. Touched her face. She let him.

"Did you like what I nick'd for you?"

She meant the papers he'd swallow'd.

RECIPE FOR LUXURIATION

J. EVANS

The recipe is laborious, time-consuming, and necessitates a collective of skilled artisans.

I draw my observations—at the behest of Mr. Wild—from interviews with a certain *Lion-Man*, who reports on his adven-tures with the Okoh mutineers—a band of Brigands, now happily long-dissolv'd and execut'd or transport'd to the Colo-nies but for the Lion-Man, who remains under London Mu-nicipal supervision.

I regret to say that more research is needed, and must state at the outset that what I have managed to gather is both mad-deningly complex and likely Incomplete:

1. Firstly, you must provide swine a pastured area with heavy ground cover of the Amorphophallus plant, upon which they are very fond of rubbing their hindquarters as it appears to give them many hours of rude pleasure. From the deep pock-ets of this plant, gather stray urine. It is not recommended to extort the swine of their urine by force (or cajoling), but rather to come by it naturally.

2. Once "several" (we have no conception of quite how many) ounces have been achieved, gather 2–4 handfuls of white lily flowers, bruised.

3. Add to this a "similar" (again, vague) Quantity of mallow leaf and twigs, broken between the hands into a chaotic jumble.

4. Add several raisins that have been stoned and bruised for no less than three weeks' time, allowing for Adequate dehy‹ dration of the fruit.

5. Mash together 4 ounces (or thereabouts) liquorice and parsley root with all of the above, and place in a pot covered with swine milk harvested through a gentle coaxing that in‹ volves the adept Imitation of baby swinedom by the smallest Member of the community, mewling and crawling about. Some training in baby‹swine Thespianship may be necessary.

6. Let the pot sit Undisturb'd—with no air coming out or going in—for several weeks. Then place a large piece of turf over a wood fire, place the pot atop the fire, and distill the potion slowly. When it is distilled to the consistency of a thick Gravy or near‹gelled state, remove the pot and spread the po‹ tion over similar turfey ground—soft, mossy, algal, cushioned ground is necessary and may be grown for the purpose—for several more weeks until the gel takes on a dried and hard‹ ened Aspect.

7. At this point a complex Acrobatics of covering and expos‹ ing the gel must transpire. Cover the gel with a large net cre‹ ated from densely knitted dried fish tendon. On a night not entirely without clouds—a whisper of cloud cover is best, "streaky white against a deep black"—expose the gel to Star‹ light just at the moment when Hydrus overtakes Apus in Lu‹ minescence. Cover the gel after Hydrus fades again. Repeat

this process over the course of anywhere from 2 to 16 nights.
Or more.

8. When the gel "seems ready," pound with pestle made from
swine bones (a swine not kill'd for the purpose, but death of
natural causes), until powd'ry.

9. Inhale by the nose.

As should be clear, this recipe is frankly Inimitable. Even
the otherwise turncoat Lion-Man seems genuinely unable to
re-create the formula without his mates. He mutters something about *collective knowledge* and *Context.*

We'll leave London behind, Bess told Jack. The two of them with the
recipe in hand and Jack presum'd dead. *We'll live with what's left of
the Fen-Tigers—if there are any—and fight the surveyors and make a
thieftopia in what remains.* They would share the elixir-secrets. They
would make a new Version together, the rogues and the doxies.
They would experiment together.

*Fen-fronds and deer urine? We'll sort it out. We'll fight the survey-
ors and the Exhaustion and the iron-cold fen winters. Strengthen the
straggling freebooters, or find new ones. We will fight in the fens while
the ghost ships collect by the hundreds—please God in the thousands—in the Waves of the oceans to the south.*

Bess dreamt aloud to him about the ghost ships, streaming
through the glassy electric-blue water, the way her father had told
her—blue like indigo pinched from the throats of Tamil snails off
Bet Dawrka where many British ships lay sunken in the tidal Floods,
florets of coral, Starfish, and night-blooming seaweeds housed in
their wooden hulls.

*We will fight in the fens while the ghost ships clog the Thames,
spearing their brave bows through the Hearts of the slave ships, the
trading vessels and the Royal Navy gunners.*

Until the imperial ships splinter in a thousand Clouds on Britain's imperial shores, Jack added.

But—he said—*if we die there? If there are no Fen-Tigers left? If the Surveyors shoot us dead?*

Then we will Haunt the Fen, Bess said. Something between an exhortation and a prayer they would perish, and they would wait. History would find them—all the underwater dead, all the Family of Love, the Inmates, and all those who had died in the fens—the centuries-long dead, too; the ones who died when the Norman invaders came steaming over the moorland from the north. Robbers, Rebels, Lovers. *Wait. Wait under waters,* she said. *History will find us. History will avenge us all.*

It was as good a plan as any.

The horsecart was ready. Aurie had fed and water'd the beasts. Bess had given him explicit directions. Begg'd him to come join them. *Bring Tommy,* she said. *Bring anyone. Bring them all. Franny and Laurent. All the bats—not the Abbess!—but the rest of them. And if you find Okoh, if he turns up living free in London, tell him where we are.*

He disappeared in a flying Cloud, said Aurie. *He could be anywhere.*

As he sat on the hay bale, the idea of never returning to London spun Jack with Vertigo. Never again to see his roofs, his walls of Clamber and Trespass; never the briny scent of wet coaldust, the low clouds beetling down into the alleys, or the choke-damp Vapors that miasmed as the innkeepers hung the lantern lights at night. Never the clouds of scavenger sparrows kicking up filth in the cobblestones. The coves and the doxies laughing in the pubs.

But all the way out to the fens, Bess drove the horses, and he rest'd his aching head in her lap, and as the cart rocked him— the Afternoon sky leaking pale to the south over the gray stretch of the fenwaters, the penumbral tree-shadows mirrored in the Shoals—he knew something even deeper than his own Cityness, and it was this.

When a daughter of the fens—of the Oppressed and the incarcerated, of the eel and the fish, of the freedom-fighters and the Scottish Inmates and the Family of Love, of the indentured who freed themselves from their masters, and of the Righteous of this earth and the next—when this daughter of the fens who has taken your Body and luxuriated you in her arms, stands before you in a horse barn and says: *There is no utopia of the Damned save the one we will make ourselves, and we will make it*—

That is to say.

When a woman regards you with her *inevitable Expression*—the one that says: I'm waiting for you in the future; *catch up, catch up*—you will liberate yourself from every pre-existing bond, body, and name you ever had.

And go with her.*†

---

* "And go with her"—Reader, that's my contribution. I could not resist making one small alteration to the manuscript—a kind of counsel, really.

† The body has two histories. So says the manuscript. It is why I have had to steal it back from the publisher. To steal it for *us*.

There is the history that binds us all. The terrible history that began when the police first swarmed the streets of the cities and the settlers streamed down the decks of their ships, casting shadows on the world to turn *themselves* white. Casting the wickedest net. There is no trans body, no body at all—no memoir, no confessions, no singular story of "you" or anyone—outside this broad and awful legacy. So when they ask for our story—when they want to sell it—we don't let them forget.

Slavery, surveillers, settlers and their shadows.

But the second history of the body?

The second history is love's inscription.

Some inscriptions we wear like dreams—fragments of a life untethered from this world, messages from a future reflected to us like light off broken shards. A woman undresses in this dream-light, embraces you, and your body rises with hers to become unmarked.

Some inscriptions are utterances, battles. Someone fought the police long ago. This, too—this street fight—is a kind of love. . . . Someone said, "[O]ne Molotov cocktail was thrown and we were ramming the door of the Stonewall bar with an uprooted parking meter. So they were ready to come out shooting that night. Finally the Tactical Police Force showed up after 45 minutes. A lot of people forget that for 45 minutes we had them trapped in there" ("I'm Glad I Was in the Stonewall Riot," Sylvia Rivera, interviewed by Leslie Feinberg, *Workers World,* July 2, 1998).

I'm not saying this battle was fought *for* you. History is not that linear. And yet, because of it, and many others like it, now you inhabit your own skin.

In the name of my ex who taught me the second history of my body and the first history of the world, I took the manuscript.

In the name of every woman whose touch tethered me to the future—of every woman who visited me in the dungeon of myself—I stole back for us what is rightfully ours.

In the name of those who came before, who fought the police; those whose names we know, and those whose names we can never know.

In the name of those who come after, who will never know our names—

The night I left, the wind poured down from the hills, bitter and constant.

The nightclouds whizzed over Route 17, silvered purple in the pitch-black sky. I drove past rows of wrecked factories. Some were now breweries and lofts. Most were concrete and brick chunks, shavings, mounds of dust—the detritus of industry collapsed in ruins, hatching toxic nerves and blood vessels that reached down into the dirt at the side of the highway.

I passed the neon-lit box stores with fighter jets screaming overhead. I passed Irish burger joints, yogurt shops, "humane" abattoirs and haberdashers.

I passed what were once Mahican villages, scrubland and forest. The sites of the burning of the longhouses. They say that under the rye fields lay charred scars in vast patches; they say that the charcoal ashes aerated the soil, nourishing a brighter, greener rye leaf. As time passed, the settlers tried to erase the traces of the longhouses. But the flame moths that preferred the greener stalks gathered in perfect cream-colored clouds, their furry wings iterating an unforgotten trauma endlessly against the wind. When they rested at night—their wings wrapped tightly around their bodies—the moths swayed on the chaff like so many broken twigs waving in the dark.

I passed the flame moths swaying, lit up in my headlights' glare.

I drove a long time, and I drove very far.

Morning was coming, the sun a bare gray ring behind clouds.

The moorland rose on broad green shoulders specked with dry pink flowers, snipe pitching and wheeling—grape-black birds, dark against the sky like bats.

A forest of tall pines and hemlock thickened and then thinned.

I drove until I reached water, silked dark under gray clouds. Green water crawling with weeds and phosphorescent-forewinged dragonflies. Tiny waves bathed the shoreline. Silver-flanked minnows flicked close then flicked away. Hawthorn bushes pushed through the soil in full flower. Oysters burped air bubbles at the fen shore. The soil was boggy, brackish, unowned and alive. At the horizon, a library—soaring walls of chitin, spiderweb and glass—flashed red in the setting sun.

Are you wondering how to get here?

Dear Reader, if you are *you*—the one I edited this for, the one I stole this for—and if you cry a certain kind of tears—the ones I told you about, remember?—you will find your way to us.

You will not need a map.

ACKNOWLEDGMENTS

IF READERS HAVE MADE IT THIS FAR, THEY KNOW THAT JACK SHEPPARD was an English folk hero and jailbreaker whose history formed the basis of many eighteenth-century pseudo-memoirs, biographies, and ephemera, in addition to John Gay's *The Beggar's Opera* and, later, Bertolt Brecht's *The Threepenny Opera*. In my own speculative approach to this popular folktale, I have sought to oppose the ahistoricist tendency of much fiction to imagine early modern London as a uniformly white city. *Confessions of the Fox* is a fiction crafted in fidelity to the London we know was true—a diasporic London shaped through centuries of Black and South Asian communities and labor—but of course this fiction is itself necessarily partial and fallible. To the extent that I have achieved anything of what I set out to do, it has been an honor to speak with, read, and learn from the work of scholars, activists, and writers who have labored with such dedication to restore to history occluded or suppressed truths, and who have represented and imagined forms of resistance to dominant narratives. In the Resources section that follows, I have listed some of the representative texts with which I am immensely grateful to have been able to engage. Of course, any flaws or failures of the manuscript are my own.

This is a novel that draws heavily on histories of mass incarceration, racialization, colonialism, the cruelties of capitalism, the militarization of the police, and the inextricability of embodied life and struggle from that history. In writing it, I was inspired by and turned many times to the works, histories, and stories of people who have endured incarceration. Angela Davis's body of work was an indispensable reference point throughout. Assata Shakur's *Assata* was a touchstone for me, as was Leonard Peltier's *Prison Writings: My Life Is My Sun Dance*. Just as this book was being completed, Palestinian prisoners on hunger strike won demands, and Chelsea Manning and Oscar López Rivera got free. It has been a great privilege to learn from these writers, stories, and lives. For me, lived struggle gives meaning to works of art, not the other way around. Just so, this book would fundamentally have no meaning outside of these struggles, the broader fight for prison abolition, and the long-sought, never surrendered horizon of liberation.

As for more specific acknowledgments, I have to begin with Chris, Victory, and One World.

When I learned that my agent would be pitching my novel to Chris Jackson's One World imprint, I was thrilled. I knew that Chris would be relaunching the imprint with an emphasis on work by writers of color as well as other writers whose work "explores our politics, culture, and interior lives, without the filter of the dominant culture." In awe of the vision of the imprint, I did not dream that Chris would be interested in taking me on, and yet—in a turn of events that still amazes me—he was.

After my first meeting with Chris and my editor, Victory Matsui, it was exhilaratingly clear that One World was committed to the idea that novels did not need to sacrifice a radical political worldview in order to be (hopefully) entertaining and absorbing. I felt very strongly then that there was no other imprint I could be as proud, honored, and excited to be a part of as this one. So my first debt is to the team that made this happen: To my wonderful agent, Susan Golomb, for taking me on, for revising the entire manuscript three times in one insane month with me—while she had pneumonia—and for knowing to connect me with One World. To the phenomenal Chris Jackson for recognizing something worthwhile in the manuscript, for sharing his editorial acumen, and for welcoming me into the deeply meaningful community he is building at the imprint. And to Victory Matsui—prodigy and genius—who worked as hard as I did for almost an entire year, tearing apart and reconstellating this book with me. I believe that Victory went as deep into the book as it is possible for an editor to go. The gift of that shared labor of writing, conceptualization, and editing is profound to me, and it is why I have dedicated this book to Victory.

This book has incurred many additional debts.

The activist communities who have shared time, labor, and space with me. My political education is truly the foundation of all work that comes after.

The librarians at the William Andrews Clark Memorial Library at UCLA and at UMass-Amherst (especially Jim Kelly) for their help with primary-text research for this novel, which began while on an Ahmanson-Getty fellowship at UCLA in 2009–2010.

The Lannan Foundation; Adult Contemporary (Katie Brewer Ball and Svetlana Kitto)/Shandaken Project/Dia:Beacon; the P L A T F O R M lecture series (Patrick Gaughan and Jon Ruseski); and the Dartmouth College critical theory reading group (Alysia Garrison, Christian P. Haines, Max Hantel, Devin Singh, and Patricia Stuelke) for inviting me to speak, to read parts of this novel, and to think together about it.

Junot Díaz and Adam McGee at the *Boston Review,* John Hennessy at *The Common,* Andrea Lawlor at *Fence,* Melissa Febos and *Hunger Mountain,* all the comrades at *Salvage,* and John David Rhodes at *World Picture Journal* for editing and publishing work related to this project.

A special thanks to Beth Pearson and the production team at Random House, for their incredible work with a manuscript that incorporated the irregularities of eighteenth-century prose stylizations.

Co-authors, comrades, interlocutors, and mentors who offered support or read/discussed this and related projects with me: Brenna Bhandar, Tithi Bhattacharya, Sarah Blackwood, Nicholas Boggs, Tisa Bryant (who pointed me toward Patrick Chamoiseau's *Texaco* at a crucial moment, and whose conversation about writing and literature in general has been a profound gift), Zahid Chaudhary, Ted Chiang, George Ciccariello-Maher and the *Abolition: A Journal of Insurgent Politics* collective, the 2016 Clarionites, Ashley Cohen, Pete Coviello, Christina Crosby, Ned Delacour, Andy Duncan, Jen Gilmore, Macarena Gomez-Barris, Jack Halberstam, Maria Davhana Headley, Sami Hermez, Markus Hoffmann, Ruth Jennison, Cassandra Khaw, Anja Kirschner, Ellen Kushner, Rachel Kushner, Victor LaValle, Kelly Link, Sarah Mesle, China Miéville (who read and advised on the manuscript or portions thereof a staggering three times), Sabina Murray, Eileen Myles, Maggie Nelson (for generous guidance and support in the world of nonacademic publishing), Jasbir Puar, Cornelia Reiner, Trea Russworm, the amazing Bethany "the fixer" Schneider, Dani Shapiro, Matthew Sharpe, Delia Sherman, David Shulman, Dean Spade, Edward Steck, Stephanie Steiker (whose brilliant engagement with the form and theory of this book and much else is dear to me), Jordan Stein, Shelley Streeby, Michael Taeckens, Kate Thomas, Alberto Toscano, Amy Villarejo, Rosie Warren, and Chi-ming Yang.

My wonderful sister, Amanda Hall, and the Hall family—Kevin, Rainer, Leo, and Stevie. The Horowitz-Barkan-Ogles: Susie, Ross, Vanessa, and Joel. The Guters: Marvin, Bobbie, Avi, Lisa, Lev, Katie, and Arlo. My late father, Stephen Rosenberg, read early versions of portions of the manuscript; his support and enthusiasm were very meaningful to me. Of my late mother, Barbara Rosenberg, I can only imagine that she would have been thrilled this was being published and mortified by every word.

A number of friends, in addition to offering indispensable counsel and collaboration, saw me through the finishing of this book at a difficult time, and shared in practice the kind of care, dependability, and trusted community we often dream of in the abstract. I'm especially grateful to my dear Kadji Amin, Steve Dillon, Allison Page (a rock!), Pooja Rangan, beloved Britt Rusert, Svati Shah, and the daily company of Bernadine Mellis, Hart Mellis-Lawlor, and my oldest and dearest buddy, Andrea Lawlor.

RESOURCES

In researching this book, I have sought guidance from many friends as well as an indispensable range of work on topics such as prison abolition, anti-imperialist and anti-racist struggle, mutinies, trans self-determination, workplace sabotage, and resistance of all kinds. I have been very lucky to be able to draw on incredible scholarship in decolonial and postcolonial studies, critical race studies, Marxism, and queer and trans theory. I include some of the works that have been especially foundational to my research here— though by no means is this an exhaustive list—in the hopes that readers will find these to be useful avenues for further thought.

Agard-Jones, Vanessa, "Bodies in the System," *Small Axe* 42 (2013).

Amin, Kadji, "Glands, Eugenics, and Rejuvenation in *Man into Woman*: A Biopolitical Genealogy of Transsexuality," *Transgender Studies Quarterly* 5, no. 3, 2018.

Aravamudan, Srinivas, *Enlightenment Orientalism: Resisting the Rise of the Novel* (University of Chicago Press, 2011).

———, *Tropicopolitans: Colonialism and Agency, 1688–1804* (Duke University Press, 1999).

Armstrong, Amanda, "Infrastructures of Injury," *LIES: A Journal of Materialist Feminism* 2 (2015).

Arondekar, Anjali, *For the Record: On Sexuality and the Colonial Archive in India* (Duke University Press, 2009).

Bailey, Nathan, *A Collection of the Canting Words and Terms, Both Ancient and Modern, Used by Beggars, Gypsies, Cheats, House-Breakers, Shop-Lifters, Foot-Pads, Highway-Men, &c* (1736).

Benitez-Rojo, Antonio, *The Repeating Island: The Caribbean and the Postmodern Perspective* (Duke University Press, 1997).

Bhandar, Brenna, "Property, Law, and Race: Modes of Abstraction," *UC Irvine Law Review* 4, no. 1 (2014).

Blue, Ethan, "The Strange Career of Leo Stanley: Remaking Manhood and Medicine at San Quentin State Penitentiary, 1913–1951," *Pacific Historical Review* 78, no. 2 (2009).

Browne, Simone, *Dark Matters: On the Surveillance of Blackness* (Duke University Press, 2015).

Bryant, Tisa, *Unexplained Presence* (Leon Works, 2007).

Camp, Jordan T., and Christina Heatherton, *Policing the Planet: Why the Policing Crisis Led to Black Lives Matter* (Verso Books, 2016).

Césaire, Aimé, *Discourse on Colonialism* (Monthly Review Press, 2001).

Chamoiseau, Patrick, *Texaco* (Gallimard, 1992; trans. Pantheon, 1998).

Chaudhary, Zahid, *Afterimage of Empire: Photography in Nineteenth-Century India* (University of Minnesota Press, 2012).

Chaudhuri, K. N., *The English East India Company: The Rise of International Business* (Routledge, reprint 2000).

Dabydeen, David, *Hogarth's Blacks: Images of Blacks in 18th-Century English Art* (University of Georgia Press, 1987).

Davis, Angela, *Are Prisons Obsolete?* (Seven Stories Press, 2003).

———, *Women, Race & Class* (Vintage, 1983).

Delany, Samuel R., *About Writing: Seven Essays, Four Letters, and Five Interviews* (Wesleyan University Press, 2006).

————, *Times Square Red, Times Square Blue* (New York University Press, 2001).

Douglass, Frederick, *My Bondage and My Freedom* (Penguin, 2003).

————, *Self-Made Men* (1859).

Fanon, Frantz, *Black Skin, White Masks* (Grove Press, 2008).

Fisher, Michael H., Shompa Lahiri, and Shinder Thandi, *A South-Asian History of Britain* (Greenwood Press, 2007).

Galeano, Eduardo, *Open Veins of Latin America: Five Centuries of the Pillage of a Continent* (Monthly Review Press, 1997, 25th anniv. ed.).

Garcia, Humberto, *Islam and the English Enlightenment, 1640–1840* (Johns Hopkins University Press, 2011).

————, "The Transports of Lascar Specters: Dispossessed Indian Sailors in Women's Romantic Poetry," in Jordana Rosenberg and Chi-ming Yang, eds., "The Dispossessed Eighteenth Century" (special issue), *The Eighteenth Century: Theory and Interpretation* 55, nos. 2–3 (2014).

Gerzina, Gretchen, *Black London: Life Before Emancipation* (Rutgers University Press, 1995).

Gilmore, Ruth Wilson, *Golden Gulag: Prisons, Surplus, Crisis, and Opposition in Globalizing California* (University of California Press, 2007).

Gossett, Reina, "Historical Erasure as Violence," October 31, 2015, www.reinagossett.com/reina-gossett-historical-erasure-as-violence.

Grose, Francis, *Dictionary of the Vulgar Tongue* (1785).

Hall, Stuart, *Policing the Crisis: Mugging, the State, and Law and Order* (Palgrave, 1978).

Hanhardt, Christina, *Safe Space: Gay Neighborhood History and the Politics of Violence* (Duke University Press, 2013).

Hanieh, Adam, *Lineages of Revolt: Issues of Contemporary Capitalism in the Middle East* (Haymarket Books, 2013).

Haritaworn, Jin, Adi Kunstsman, and Sylvia Posocco, eds., *Queer Necropolitics* (Routledge, 2014).

Harris, Cheryl I., "Whiteness as Property," *Harvard Law Review* 106, no. 8 (1993).

Hartman, Saidiya V., *Scenes of Subjection: Terror, Slavery and Self-Making in Nineteenth-Century America* (Oxford University Press, 1997).

Hill, Christopher, *The World Turned Upside Down: Radical Ideas During the English Revolution* (Penguin Books, 1984).

James, C.L.R., *The Black Jacobins: Toussaint L'Ouverture and the San Domingo Revolution* (Random House, 1963).

Johnson, Walter, *Soul by Soul: Life Inside the Antebellum Slave Market* (Harvard University Press, 2000).

Joseph, Betty, *Reading the East India Company 1720–1840: Colonial Currencies of Gender* (University of Chicago Press, 2004).

Kanafani, Ghassan, *All That's Left to You: A Novella and Short Stories* (Interlink, 2004).

Kaul, Suvir, *Poems of Nation, Anthems of Empire: English Verse in the Long Eighteenth Century* (University of Virginia Press, 2001).

Keeling, Kara, *The Witch's Flight: The Cinematic, the Black Femme, and the Image of Common Sense* (Duke University Press, 2007).

Kirschner, Anja, and David Panos, dirs., *The Last Days of Jack Sheppard* (2009).

Linebaugh, Peter, *The London Hanged: Crime and Civil Society in the Eighteenth Century* (Verso, 2006).

———, and Marcus Rediker, *The Many-Headed Hydra: Sailors, Slaves, Commoners, and the Hidden History of the Revolutionary Atlantic* (Beacon Press, 2013).

Loomba, Ania, *Colonialism/Postcolonialism* (Routledge, 2015).

Mallipeddi, Ramesh, *Spectacular Suffering: Witnessing Slavery in the Eighteenth-Century British Atlantic* (University of Virginia Press, 2016).

Marx, Karl, *Capital, Volume 1,* trans. Ben Fowkes (Vintage, 1977).

Matar, Nabil, *Islam in Britain, 1558–1685* (Cambridge University Press, 1998).

Mignolo, Walter D., *The Darker Side of Western Modernity: Global Futures, Decolonial Options* (Duke University Press, 2011).

Moten, Fred, *In the Break: The Aesthetics of the Black Radical Tradition* (University of Minnesota Press, 2003).

Muñoz, José Esteban, *Cruising Utopia: The Then and There of Queer Futurity* (NYU Press, 2009).

Musser, Amber Jamilla, *Sensational Flesh: Race, Power and Masochism* (New York University Press, 2014).

Nicolazzo, Sarah, "Henry Fielding's *The Female Husband* and the Sexuality of Vagrancy," *The Eighteenth Century: Theory and Interpretation* 55, no. 4 (2014).

Olusoga, David, *Black and British: A Forgotten History* (Pan Macmillan, 2016).

Peltier, Leonard, *Prison Writings: My Life Is My Sun Dance* (St. Martin's Griffin, 2000).

Puar, Jasbir, "Bodies with New Organs: Becoming Trans, Becoming Disabled," *Social Text* 33, no. 3 (2015).

———, "The Cost of Getting Better: Suicide, Sensation, Switchpoints," in "Queer Studies and the Crises of Capitalism" (special issue), eds. Jordy Rosenberg and Amy Villarejo, *GLQ* 18, no. 1 (2012).

———, *Terrorist Assemblages: Homonationalism in Queer Times* (Duke University Press, 2007).

Raad, Walid (as the Atlas Group), "Let's Be Honest, the Rain Helped: Excerpts from an Interview with the Atlas Group," in *Review of Photographic Memory,* ed. Jalal Toufic (Arab Image Foundation, 2004).

Rajan, Kaushik Sunder, *Biocapital: The Constitution of Postgenomic Life* (Duke University Press, 2006).

————, *Pharmocracy: Value, Politics, and Knowledge in Global Biomedicine* (Duke University Press, 2017).

Robinson, Cedric J., *Black Marxism: The Making of the Black Radical Tradition* (University of North Carolina Press, 2000).

Rosenberg, Jordy, and Chi-ming Yang, eds., "The Dispossessed Eighteenth Century" (special issue), *The Eighteenth Century: Theory and Interpretation* 55, nos. 2–3 (2014).

Rusert, Britt, *Fugitive Science: Empiricism and Freedom in Early African American Culture* (New York University Press, 2017).

Said, Edward, *Orientalism* (Vintage, 1979).

Shah, Svati, *Street Corner Secrets: Sex, Work, and Migration in the City of Mumbai* (Duke University Press, 2014).

Shakur, Assata, *Assata: An Autobiography* (Zed Books, 2014).

da Silva, Denise Ferreira, *Toward a Global Idea of Race* (University of Minnesota, 2007).

————, "1 (life) ÷ 0 (blackness) = $\infty - \infty$ or ∞ / ∞: On Matter Beyond the Equation of Value," *e-flux,* February 2017, e-flux.com/journal/79/94686/1-life-0-blackness-or-on-matter-beyond-the-equation-of-value.

Singh, Nikhil Pal, "The Whiteness of Police," *American Quarterly* 66, no. 4 (2014).

Smallwood, Stephanie E., *Saltwater Slavery: A Middle Passage from Africa to American Diaspora* (Harvard University Press, 2008).

Spade, Dean, *Normal Life: Administrative Violence, Critical Trans Politics and the Limits of Law* (Duke University Press, 2015, expanded edition).

Spivak, Gayatri Chakravorty, "The Rani of Sirmur: An Essay in Reading the Archives," *History and Theory* 24, no. 3 (1985).

Stanley, Eric, and Nat Smith, eds., *Captive Genders: Trans Embodiment and the Prison Industrial Complex* (AK Press, 2016).

Stoler, Ann Laura, *Race and the Education of Desire: Foucault's History of Sexuality and the Colonial Order of Things* (Duke University Press, 1995).

Stryker, Susan, and Aren Z. Aizura, eds., *The Transgender Studies Reader*, vol. 2 (Routledge, 2013).

Stryker, Susan, and Stephen Whittle, eds., *The Transgender Studies Reader*, vol. 1 (Routledge, 2006).

Sudan, Rajani, *The Alchemy of Empire: Abject Materials and the Technologies of Colonialism* (Fordham University Press, 2016).

————, *Fair Exotics: Xenophobic Subjects in English Literature: 1720–1850* (University of Pennsylvania Press, 2002).

Taylor, Keeanga-Yamahtta, *From #BlackLivesMatter to Black Liberation* (Haymarket Books, 2016).

Thompson, E. P., *Whigs and Hunters: The Origin of the Black Act* (Penguin Books, 1990).

Thrush, Coll, *Indigenous London: Native Travelers at the Heart of Empire* (Yale University Press, 2016).

Tompkins, Kyla Wazana, *Racial Indigestion: Eating Bodies in the 19th Century* (New York University Press, 2012).

Visram, Rozina, *Asians in Britain: 400 Years of History* (Pluto Press, 2002).

Williams, Eric, *Capitalism and Slavery* (University of North Carolina Press, 1994).